Troubled Waters

Also in this series ....

Winner of the 2016 Indie Excellence Award for Crime Fiction!

When terrorists apparently strike one of Boston's MBTA transit stations during the famed St. Patrick's Day parade, the onslaught of federal and state officials turn the city into a chaotic police state. Only a veteran transit cop, jaded by his memories of growing up in the shadows of Boston's forced busing and desegregation, knows the truth: The enemy is not some international terrorist cell but the politics and hubris that continually pit the haves and have-nots against each other in one of the country's oldest and most-congested cities. *Code Black* delves into the many contradictions that shape Boston: wealth and poverty, liberal and conservative, academia and working-class, and even black and white. *Code Black* is an historical fiction thriller that will keep you guessing until the very end.

Troubled Waters

By
Bill Fleming and Joe Peters

The following is a work of fiction. While it contains references to well-known and real events, places, and public figures, they are used only as descriptive context, and no assurances are given by the authors or publisher as to their accuracy.

All other characters, incidents, and locations are fictitious and bear no intended resemblance to any actual people, events, and places.

Opinions and language attributed to the characters are used purely as a literary device and are not intended to portray the beliefs of the authors, publisher or any real-world entity.

Cover design by Elizabeth Fleming

Chapter illustrations based on images courtesy of Boston Archives.

Printed in the United States of America
Second Edition (September 2018)
Print ISBN 978-1-387-81943-0
Ebook ISBN 978-1-387-98899-0

Eire Associates
PO Box 2117
Woburn MA 01888-0011
www.eireassociates.us

Prologue

"I didn't see nothing! I swear," she screamed.

The man in the nice suit said nothing. Something about him was familiar, but every day the woman saw familiar faces even though none of them saw her. When she was younger, they all stopped and stared. Even though her mind had long since been poisoned by a lifetime of heroin, she could remember how it made her feel.

At the time, she thought their glances were admiration, and they filled her with a false comfort. Over time, she learned the truth – that such looks were just the leering of wolves at a piece of meat.

"Let me go!" she screamed. "I gotta close the door. Momma will beat me if the meat spoils!"

"What the fuck?" said one of the men holding her.

"She's a whack job. Probably high on something right now," said the other.

She couldn't wait to get free of these men, but what had she just said? Her brain and her body refused to cooperate with each other. It all started many years ago after the man with the long arms tormented her one night. She grimaced. "I'll kill that fucker!"

"Jesus!" said one of the men.

"Nail you to a fuckin' cross!" she screamed.

The man in the suit shook his head, and as he did so, the woman's brain found a connection. Yes, she knew him, long ago, back when she was beautiful, back when her voice sounded sweet. Not like it was now, hoarse from yelling and cigarettes and degraded by having to move through rotted teeth.

She started to sob. Why her? Why did life shit upon her? Even right now, she was here because she happened to have looked left when the big man had hit the skinny man with a bat.

"Homerun!" she shouted. "Deep drive center field. Skinny man's head goes over the wall."

She clenched her teeth, but it was too late. Her mouth hated her, just like everyone else.

The man in the suit shook his head again and looked over to the shadows. "Shoot her up," he said toward someone she couldn't see. "Make sure she doesn't feel anything. This is all getting fucked up in a hurry."

"No problem," said the voice in the shadows. "Grab her arm."

The woman fought, but her skin and bones were no match for those holding her, especially the big man. "I know people!" she shouted. "I know cops! They'll fuckin' bury you. You'll see."

The voice spoke again. "You don't know shit," it said. "No one is going to fuckin' miss you."

While her body continued to struggle, her mind froze. She knew that voice. It couldn't be. Life had always been too cruel to her. "No!" she screamed as she felt the needle pinch her arm between several of the old marks. "Not you! No!"

She started to cry but felt her heart pump a wave of heroin through her upper body. Half a second later, the next pump pushed the drug farther, and she could feel her brain begin to sleep. She imagined a white rabbit, running and leaping over green covered hills.

Her body went limp, but she never felt it hit the ground. Instead, it was as though she had dropped into a pool. Her mind flashed on memories of swimming in the Quincy quarries. It was summer again. Everyone loved her, and she was beautiful.

Chapter 1

Morris Fitzgerald stood on the sidewalk, staring down the stairs that led to the subway below. Even in the poor light of overcast morning skies, he could tell they were slick from the overnight rain, but it wasn't the condition of the treads that halted him.

He had been down these stairs many times since the incident eighteen months ago that nearly killed him and catapulted Boston into momentary chaos, but something about them caught him today.

Morris was a cop who grew up fatherless in South Boston. He wasn't used to his mind saying one thing and his body doing another. It's not that he had never experienced panic or fear, but he had learned from a young age to be always moving. Now, here he was standing still.

"What the fuck?" Morris heard from behind as someone bumped his shoulder going around him. He looked to see a kid, maybe five feet tall, with a blue hooded sweatshirt, snarl at him. Then a twenty-something Asian-looking woman walked right into him. Her straight black hair was pulled back behind her ears, which featured a pair of earphones connected to her smartphone, which still held her gaze despite the collision.

"Oh sorry, sir," she said, finally looking up. Her expression changed as she eyed Morris more closely. "Oh, I am so sorry," she repeated with more emphasis. "Do you need help getting down the stairs?"

Morris felt confused by her concern. He was in his late 50s, but he didn't feel that old and broken. "No, no thanks," he said, and the woman gave him a smile as she returned to her phone and scampered down the long flight of stairs.

His hesitation left him, and he realized that the commuting public would push him down the stairs if he didn't get going on his own. With that first step, he felt the familiar pain in his right knee. Before he left his triple-decker on the corner of G and 8th streets this morning, he grabbed a walking stick to help him negotiate his travels. While he wasn't dutiful about visiting his wife's grave at Cedar Grove Cemetery, he did try to visit at least once a month. In a world gone mad, she was still his rock.

Today was November 1st, and while Morris had a selective recall of his Irish Catholic upbringing, this was a holy day he could remember.

All Saints Day celebrated those souls who had surely entered Heaven. It was now nearly five years since his wife Mary Ellen had passed away, her body ravaged first by cancer and then by the corrosive drugs intended to kill the disease.

The real test of his faith wasn't that God failed to hear his prayers. He couldn't blame God for ignoring a sinner like himself. No, the real divine nonsense was how such a good person like his wife suffered the curse of not just being taken too soon from this earth, but to have it done in such an excruciating and drawn-out out way.

As he looked at those stairs, part of him wanted to turn around and go home. His head hurt, still suffering from the migraines that came as part of the cost of foiling a pair of terrorist incidents eighteen months ago.

As much as he wanted to turn around and go back to bed, he took his first step down the stairs. Mary Ellen never stopped fighting.

Certainly, if there was a saint he had met in his life, it was her. Damn his faith, he couldn't turn around today. As he lurched toward the next step, and the dark-red migraine-therapy sunglasses shifted on his head, the reaction of the woman who bumped into him became more clear. "Shit, I'm not blind," he said to himself.

He picked up his pace despite feeling the hurt in his knee and a headache starting to swell behind his eyes. Morris' body was showing the signs of the mileage he had put on it. Still, a year and a half of limited duty didn't satisfy his persona or his pension, which he had to borrow against to make tuition for his two college-age daughters.

He needed to get back to work as a detective sergeant with the Mass Bay Transit Authority police. Of course, no one called the transit system that. In the most formal of settings, it might go by its acronym of MBTA, but everyone in Boston and the 175 surrounding communities it served called it, simply, the T. And as a member of the police force, Morris was better known as a T-cop.

As he neared the subway platform for the Red Line, he spied the escalator and had a flashback to the St. Patrick's Day gassing at this very station that nearly killed him. But the city had recovered from the attack. The evidence of which may have been a female patron on the platform to his right.

Apparently, one of the transit workers had noticed her son stepping close to the edge of the platform, and he tried to warn her, in his broken English, that her son was in danger.

"Mind your own business, you third-world shit talkah!" the mother bellowed as saliva flew from her mouth. "You say another word, and I'll call the cops, tell them you tried to molest my kid."

Yes, Boston was back to its normal all right. As the woman meandered down the platform, her nose stuck to her cellphone, and oblivious to her son dancing inches from 600 volts of certain death, Morris made his way toward the worker.

"Hey buddy," he said, handing him his business card. "You did the right thing. If anything ever comes of this, give me call."

The man hesitated to take Morris' card, but he seemed to reconsider when he saw the MBTA logo on it.

Still, Morris must have looked like an odd Samaritan. It was at this very station that a year and a half ago, Morris intervened during a gas attack at the annual St. Patrick's Day parade. Then, a few days later, the madman behind the incident decided to blow up a bus full of politicians. Plenty of tears were shed, but the city quickly moved on. Morris' recovery, however, had been far less rapid. The combination of the fentanyl gas followed by a severe concussion from the explosion left Morris' brain and body in an uncooperative state. Some days were better than others, but today didn't feel like it was going to be one of them.

Still, while much of the city mourned the loss of its political class, Morris thought it may have been the best thing to happen to Boston since the Sox won the Series in 2004.

But into the vacuum of power flowed the replacements – half of them just as corrupt as their predecessors, and the other half so naive that they became easy accomplices.

Physically, Morris was nothing remarkable. Slightly below six feet, with thinning gray hair, his preferred attire was a hooded sweatshirt and jeans when not on duty. If he had one physical gift, it was his vision, first recognized as a boy learning to box down at the L Street gym. As much as he was often undersized when he went up against his peers, he could see and react quicker than most.

As a transit cop, that vision remained his best asset. Most of the patrons on the platform didn't notice, for example, the slightly disheveled man to Morris' right, but Morris' peripheral vision saw him, slightly over six feet, maybe 180 pounds, an unkempt beard, and a tattoo of a pitbull on his right hand. But it was the slight bump at the bottom of the man's left pant leg that really deserved attention.

Someone else might have thought it was a rolled down sock, but Morris knew it was a GPS device attached to the ankle.

There were only two possibilities of seeing someone with an ankle bracelet on the T. One class may have been a lowly white-collar criminal, awaiting trial on house arrest. Having been caught defrauding investors or partaking in some other scheme, these suited pariahs must turn to public transit, having been stripped of their corporate parking spaces.

The other class of individual making such a fashion statement would be registered sex offenders, who represented the conservative-liberal paradox of the criminal justice system. They had served their court-assessed time, but they were still judged to be such a danger to society that they had to be monitored around the clock.

This guy certainly wasn't wearing a suit.

For the leftists, such policy indulged their bleeding hearts. For those on the right, asking Big Brother to keep track of sex offenders satiated their need for social, moral, and economic detachment from such convicts.

The T, with its sudden stops and lurching movements, was a pervert's dream, bumping into unsuspecting patrons, enjoying every glancing rub or grind. Morris kept an eye on him as the train pulled into the station.

He stepped into the subway car, joining the punks, pickpockets, perverts and patrons riding outbound to the Andrew Square Station. Their blank stares as they looked out the windows covered in scratchitti spoke volumes as the train headed south in the moving asylum known as the T. It was well known among the T-cops that one person's peaceful commute was another's journey to the gaping maw of hell. The motorman was like the maestro at the Boston Pops, in charge of a moving train, dutifully hurrying passengers off and on at designated intervals.

Morris chuckled at the sight of an electronically immersed commuter, oblivious to all around him, lost in his playlists as he slipped on a puddle of urine. If Rosa Parks had lived in Boston, she would still be standing; the seats of the T were so filthy. The other passengers had their iPads and iPhones out except for two male passengers reading *The Poor Man's James Bond* and the *Anarchist Cookbook*. Morris braced himself against a pole as the Red Line train swayed, rattled, and creaked its way toward Andrew station.

But once at the station, they were delayed for some reason. As he limped toward the front, he saw a pair of fellow T-cops, George Salado and Stevie Piacenza, step into the train. They didn't notice Morris but instead went ahead, rousting a drunken patron who had soiled himself.

"Oh, here, take this seat."

Morris turned right and saw a woman, who couldn't have been much younger than him, offering up her seat. He just shook his head, his damaged ego keeping him from saying anything more.

Morris moved closer to the two T-cops, who now had the patron on his feet but stumbling toward the door.

"Hey, fellas," Morris let out.

Stevie Piacenza turned quickly, right-hand on his holster, left hand raised. "Sir, back up."

"Stevie!" Morris responded.

Piacenza had a confused expression and then softened.

"Jesus Christ, Morris," he said. "What the fuck happened to you?"

At that, Salado spun around but kept his arm on the drunk. "Holy crap, Morris. You look like the love child of Archie Bunker and Stevie Wonder."

At that, the drunk began to sing "*I just called to say I love you,*" and Salado gave him a subtle poke in the gut.

The two officers were better known as Axe and Smash among T-cops, and it was an accurate portrayal of their policing style. The pair got their nicknames years ago when they were asked to serve a warrant on a former T bus driver who had skipped his arraignment for stealing coins from the old fare boxes. When Piacenza and Salado showed up at the guy's door, he took a swing at them with a baseball bat. As could be expected, the two cops didn't take kindly to having their heads mistaken for a piñata. As such, the two tried to make a point to the thief once they disarmed him, smashing his apartment to pieces.

Axe and Smash got suspended. The thief not only had the charges dropped but ended up getting a six-figure settlement out of the MBTA.

"Hey," Salado said to Morris. "Did you sign the petition?"

"What petition?" Morris asked.

"You didn't hear about the body cameras?" Piacenza interjected.

Morris stayed silent.

"Yeah, they want us to start wearing body cameras," said Salado.

Morris had a cynical smirk. "It's a good thing we didn't have them in the old days, or you two would be getting out of prison right around now."

Axe and Smash laughed, but Morris was only half kidding. In policing, you had to have priorities, and the top priority was always making sure you made it home that night. It's easy for a lawyer, judge, or newscaster to pass judgment because all they do is move from the comfy seat in which they sit to their luxury car to their luxury home. Meanwhile, folks like T-cops are chasing the deranged and drugged-out down alleys and into tunnels, never knowing what is lurking behind or around them.

Morris leaned forward and said quietly, "Be careful guys, and let me give you some advice. The days of the asphalt cowboys are over. Try treating him with kindness."

Salado laughed, and Morris smiled. He had hoped the two might take his counsel. It's not that he abstained from handing out subway justice from time to time. Among some of the T's more despicable clientele, Morris was known as simply "The Fist." Growing up boxing, he learned how to throw a punch much better than average, and over the years, he hadn't been afraid to demonstrate his expertise if suitably provoked.

Still, Morris always had a soft spot for those on the lowest rung of society's ladder. They were like an abandoned dog — someone who been dealt only bad luck in life. More often than not, it wasn't their fault. Still, abandoned dogs can be rabid and violent. At the end of the day, it was always better to be judged by twelve than carried by six.

"Good luck, guys," Morris said as the two took the drunk off the train, and the doors started to close. "Hopefully, I will be seeing you around more."

The train continued on, rumbling its steel wheels, and the shrieks and creaks from the car's undercarriage began to amplify in the reverberant Red Line tunnels.

Upon leaving Andrew Square, the train ventured into daylight, running above ground toward the JFK station. To his left, Morris spotted the brick wall adjacent to the Old Colony Housing Project, covered in graffiti. His mind flashed on a quote from Hunter S. Thompson, "Graffiti is beautiful: like a brick in the face of a cop."

As a 50-something, white, male cop, Morris fell into the only demographic that had no entitlement to umbrage. Elitists like Thompson taught college kids and others to hate the police. Those folks should spend less time reading Saul Alinsky's *Rules for Radicals* and more time on the subway helping the homeless and the walking dead, thought Morris.

Next stop, JFK, and as he looked out the cracked, grime-covered window of the train, he was initially puzzled to see a group of high-schoolers gathered on the platform during the mid-morning. Then it struck him. Boston College High School was out today since it was a holy day.

"Oh fuck," he muttered, looking at the gathered group. Nothing was worse than a bunch of rich suburban kids wanting to play city punk for the day and who viewed the MBTA as an urban amusement park. As the number of young riders increased arithmetically, the problem for the police expanded geometrically. Today was no different as this rowdy pack of kids, who apparently considered themselves untouchables, rampaged throughout the subway, terrorizing adults.

Somewhere in his criminal justice degree, earned after he had already been a cop for ten years, Morris must have taken a sociology course, but he genuinely couldn't remember it. His education was from a lifetime of observing people and trying to keep himself alive. Whatever the case, Crowd Management 101 dictated that the behavior of a group directly reflects the maximum assholery of any one individual. It only takes one jerk, and then ten others follow.

Whether you are talking political corruption or harassing a sausage cart vendor, the a-hole who starts it was a problem, but the others who join and buy into it were the real miscreants. They knew better but lacked the guts or compassion to do the right thing.

That's how you get from radical to riot, and Morris observed the phenomenon as he watched a gaggle of BC High students, freed from the shackles of Jesuit teachers, storm the train bent on malicious mischief. The ringleader's boisterous antics fit with the persona of being a rich son of a bitch from the South Shore who wanted to play bad-ass for a day.

Despite his current physical limitations, Morris contemplated stepping in when the kid started using the emergency intercom system to facetiously call in an order for fries and cheeseburgers. Then, when the gang blocked the doors from closing at the next station, effectively stopping the train in its tracks, Morris raised his walking stick and prepared to crack some skulls.

At that moment, however, a transit juvenile detective stepped into the train, shoving the student-punks away.

"Listen, this ride isn't interactive. So step away from the doors!" he shouted. "And stay off the intercom. It's for emergencies only!"

"Fuck off," responded the young cherub. "My dad's a state trooper."

Morris figured that was probably a bullshit bluff, but if his dad were a trooper, no doubt he would be quite upset with his darling son trying to name drop right now.

The juvenile detective approached the punk in a fury but froze. The kid was flipping him the middle finger. At first, Morris didn't understand why such a common, albeit profane, gesture halted his fellow T-cop. Then he noticed the punk's other hand. It was on his cellphone, pointed and recording the detective. As Morris expanded his gaze, he noticed the punk's minions were doing the same.

The detective must have realized that his next move could cost him his career if he became a Facebook star for manhandling an altar boy on the subway. Of course, it was a stalemate, though. The transit detective knew he couldn't back away. That would only give these jerks carte blanche to be assholes the rest of the day. Plus, there was no way the motorman would keep driving the train with these punks on it.

Just then, the unlikely duo of Father Michael McGovern, a local Catholic priest, and Reverend Eugene Lake, from the Center of Church and Prison, boarded the train. Morris didn't hear what either said to the teen. Father Michael was 6' 2" and, despite being in his 70s, still looked as though he could knock out someone a third his age in the ring.

Reverend Lake may have been slightly younger than Father Michael, but the rumor was that before he found God, the good reverend was one of the most feared gang members in Boston. Morris suspected the truth might fall short of the reputation, but Lake was a smart man who understood the value of street credibility.

In any case, the punk and his comrades had an instant change of heart, and the two clergymen decided to escort them off the train.

It was proof of one of Chief Stephanie Tam's initiatives on the T. She had recruited McGovern, Lake, and a few others as part of customer-oriented policing. The chief realized that kids were no longer scared of the police, but they still feared men of God.

Both men recognized Morris when he yelled, "Father, can you help an old altar boy and get this train moving?"

Reverend Lake smiled back. "If this was the Underground Railroad I would have been a slave forever." Morris laughed. He had heard Reverend Lake's joke before – it was easy to poke fun at the delays on the T as they were so frequent – but the train needed to hear some laughter right then.

The train doors slid shut, and the journey rumbled forward toward Fields Corner. Morris squinted at the young urban dweller who was using her seatmate's shoulder as a makeshift vanity table, poking herself in the eye with a mascara wand and curler.

As the doors slid open at Fields Corner, a young Asian mother and her daughter sat down and were towered over by two tall black females wearing red bandannas.

The young girl started to shake, and one of the ladies leaned toward the girl and said, "Child, are you OK? Is something wrong?"

The mother responded, "I'm sorry. Young black American teenagers wearing bandannas pelted the Vietnamese Community Center with rocks and called all the young kids horrible names."

The tall woman straightened up. "Child, stop shaking," she said. "We're not gangsters. We're lesbians."

The other chimed in, "Only on weekends."

She then pointed to a young man sitting in the priority seats and said, "Now, that's a gangsta." She looked at him and said, "Get your black ass up, you seat vulture, and let the old, blind, white dude with the funny cane sit down."

Morris realized she was talking about him. "I'm fine," he said. "I'm getting off at the next stop anyway. I'm catching the trolley to the cemetery."

"Damn!" she cursed. "You couldn't pay me to take that ride. It's Spooky World."

Morris laughed. Cedar Grove did occupy a unique reputation as being the only cemetery featured on *Ripley's Believe It or Not!* because it was bisected by a trolley line.

As the train doors opened at the Ashmont Station, a large cockroach scurried across the floor. Morris instinctively smashed the insect with his walking stick.

"Fuck Kafka," he said.

He looked up to the see the Vietnamese woman and the two lesbians looking at him.

"Pretty fly for an old, blind, white dude," he said with a smile as he stepped off the train and headed toward the stairs that would connect him with the trolley line.

Once at the top of the stairs, Morris saw a T-cop in a heated argument with two ladies on the Ashmont plaza by the Sleeping Moon statue. Even though the cop was out of uniform, he recognized him as Bill Feltrup. Everyone called him "Bulldog." Morris wasn't sure why and had never heard anyone ask for an explanation. The name just fit.

Morris gave him a slight nod and continued toward the platform for the Ashmont-Mattapan line, but he heard Bulldog shout toward him. "Morris, hey, wait up!"

He stopped and turned, but he wasn't looking forward to the typical onslaught of questions about how he was feeling and when he was coming back.

"Morris," Bulldog said as he caught up. "I need your help."

It was a pleasant surprise for Morris. "Sure, what's up, Billy?"

"We got a report of a couple of female panhandlers getting a little too friendly with some of the male patrons, you know what I mean?"

Morris nodded. The destitute were also the desperate and would deal in whatever currency they could.

"Anyway, I'm having a hard time getting anything on them because, well, they don't take any interest in me."

"Have you tried Match.com?" Morris quipped.

The Bulldog frowned.

"Sorry, so what's your problem, other than that crappy suitcoat and tactical shoes that scream plainclothes cop?"

"I'm out of ideas, and apparently the chief is getting an earful from some South Shore snob."

Bulldog then went on a rant, but Morris tuned him out and thought on a few things. Then he decided to interrupt his fellow T-cop's soliloquy. "Hey, you know Stretch — tall kid who plays basketball at Dot Academy?"

Bulldog nodded.

"Find him and ask him about your two panhandlers," added Morris.

"Why would he care?"

"He's always running some scam, selling candy bars to passengers to raise money for needy kids, stuff like that," said Morris. "If those panhandlers are cleaning out his customers, I bet you he'd be willing to help you out."

Bulldog smiled.

"Listen, I've got to catch the trolley. Let me know how it goes," Morris said, trying to hurry to the platform.

Bulldog headed in the other direction. The guy was a good cop even though he wasn't the sharpest knife in the drawer. One of the problems with community policing these days was that the cops forgot the value of knowing their community.

Morris managed to catch the distinct red-orange colored trolley just in time. The Ashmont-Mattapan line, which would bring Morris to Cedar Grove Cemetery, was the transit line that time forgot. As best could be determined, the last ten functional PCC streetcars in America were owned by the MBTA and comprised the fleet serving this antiquated line. Named after the

Presidential Conference Committee – a group formed in 1930 to develop better transit resources – these cars became the icon of public transportation for decades.

In truth, only eight of the PCCs worked. The other two were cannibalized for parts, and when the T couldn't find parts from those spares, they turned to transit museums for help.

The sensible thing would be to replace the old cars, but they were the transportation Fenway Park — something so old but so familiar to the city, Boston would be stuck with it forever. Every now and then, some naive city councilor might suggest replacing the cars, and he or she would get more hate mail than the manager of the Yankees during a homestand.

The trolley was empty for most of the short ride except for a young man who had an arm full of tattoos that were wildly incongruous with the skinny jeans and Cincinatti T-shirt he was wearing.

As the train pulled into the Cedar Grove Station, Morris stepped off the ancient car and slowly made his way to the cemetery's gate. He told himself that he should be using the walking stick he had taken along with him, but he was a stubborn man. Maybe it was that stubbornness, buried somewhere in his DNA, that told his cancer to go fuck itself while that which had attacked his wife prospered.

He sneered slightly, not for a particular reason, and certainly not at anyone because he was, for all purposes, alone here at Cedar Grove Cemetery. Still, he felt anger. He knew he hadn't lived the most righteous life, but now as he saw his 60s approaching, Morris felt in the balance of things he had done more good than bad.

"Stubborn," he said to himself as he stepped past the tombstones. Some might say having been raised Irish Catholic in South Boston, Morris' fate was cast from birth. There's a reason every Hollywood script involving someone from Southie features the same stereotypes.

"The truth hurts, don't it?"

Morris was startled to hear a voice. Raising his eyes from the graves he was navigating, he saw one of Cedar Grove's caretakers several feet away. He searched for words, but the confusion on his face must have said all he needed.

"Your leg there," said the caretaker, standing in soiled Carhartt overalls with a shovel in one hand. "We're all getting old, aren't we?"

Morris nodded. All he needed this morning was a chatty gravedigger. He continued his journey to his wife's grave, sensing the caretaker was still watching him, perhaps trying to engage in more conversation. Morris would have none of that.

Like many things in Boston, Cedar Grove occupied the overlap between historic and illogical. Opened right after the close of the Civil War, Cedar Grove remained a bucolic respite in the midst of a city. Too bad its occupants were all too dead to enjoy it.

The cemetery's surrounding neighborhood of Dorchester was originally an independent town that had long ago been absorbed by the encroaching city. "The Dot," as many call the area, actually predates the founding of Boston by a few months and witnessed many cycles of gentrification.

The 20th Century saw Dorchester grow into one of Boston's largest and most diverse neighborhoods. By the 1950s, the Blue Hill Avenue section of The Dot was predominantly Jewish, giving rise to the moniker "Jew Hill Avenue" that was still uttered by some of the old-timers.

However, as the 1960s arrived, the "white flight" out of Boston had begun. The enclaves of Jews, Irish and Italians who had taken root in parts of Dorchester, moved up and out of the city, propelled by rising education – thanks to the G.I. Bill – better jobs, and the opportunity of home ownership outside the city.

Still, many in the "white" demographic stayed behind, fiercely committed to their neighborhoods. They also carried plenty of political clout, and by the mid-1960s, public schools in these sections of Boston, by most accounts, were much better than those in primarily "black" neighborhoods.

Morris, however, had learned to loathe those labels. They were convenient, sure enough, fitting everyone into one of two categories. But as proven on a daily basis in Boston, just because two people looked alike, it didn't mean they came from the same class.

By the mid-1960s, the Massachusetts Legislature had passed a law prohibiting racial imbalance in the schools, bringing the state in line with federal civil rights movements. While the legislature moved in one direction, Boston's local politicians, especially the leadership of its School Committee, became the immovable object, refusing to be told what to do by the state and, eventually, the federal government. Finally, in 1974, a federal judge ordered the city to start busing kids from one neighborhood to schools in another.

That's when hell broke loose in the city, particularly in Morris' neighborhood of South Boston. Protests turned to riots, and the city became permanently branded as racist. Morris had long given up on determining whether or not the city was, in fact, prejudiced. On one hand, racism had to be viewed as a self-fulfilling prophecy. If you tell a group of people that another group hates them, regardless of whether it is true or not, you'll create animosity between the two groups. On the other hand, other than a six-year stint with the Marines, Morris had spent his entire life in Boston. He knew its prejudices well, but they ran much deeper than judging based on skin color.

Ultimately, Boston was a city of haves and have-nots, insiders and outsiders, those in power and those out of it. It had been that way since its founding, a constant contradiction that first took root in a group of Puritans promoting religious freedom but only granting it to those who shared their form of worship.

While the demographics of Boston had continually churned over the centuries, each generation perpetuated a culture that respected political power above all else. It wasn't necessarily a respect of government. In truth, some of the most powerful in the state, like the billionaire Eliot Franklin, had never held public office. But these ruling class elites, the Boston Brahmin as Oliver Wendell Holmes coined them, were the kingmakers.

Fortunately for many of the city politicians, these benefactors found day-to-day governing too dirty or boring for their interest. Such tasks would be left to the brilliantly corrupt liberals who treated the city and state as a fertile ground upon which to grow their personal fiefdoms. In Morris' old neighborhood, these were the likes of the Bulgers and the Barretts, but every corner of the city had their figures who owned a piece of every district attorney, cop, or criminal.

In the wealthy parts of the city and its well-to-do suburbs, the corruption may be more subtle – a fundraising check rather than an outright bribe – but the effect was just the same. Power was something to be preserved, handed down, and occasionally traded.

Those who didn't want to pay homage to such enterprises learned the smart play of keeping their head down before someone chopped it off.

Of course, Morris' problem was that he was never good at ducking.

After his honorable discharge from the Marines in the 1980s, he needed a job, and the MBTA police force was hiring. The son of a well-known and presumed dead criminal, he should have been rejected for employment by any law enforcement agency, but thanks to his godfather, Patrick "Sonny" Barrett, a powerful state senator, he found employment as a T-cop. Morris paused, recalling the last time he saw Sonny, bloodied and trying to cling to Morris' leg as rescue from a bus that had plunged into the Charles River. He smiled, recalling the kick he gave the son of the bitch that caused him to tumble to the bottom of the bus and eventually the depths of the Charles.

As Morris ambled between the graves, he caught sight of different plantings, and it triggered a reminder that his troubled cousin, Cathy, had left him a message not long ago. She and her brother were the black sheep of the Fitzgerald clan, each consumed by their own vices. Cathy, by far was the worse off of the two, fluctuating between homeless shelters and drug-rehab programs. Her voicemail was typical nonsense, likely delivered while high on heroin. She wanted him to investigate dying flowers in the city's parks or something.

He grinned and shook his head, but he suddenly stopped walking and winced. Another migraine was coming on. He had already taken two aspirin this morning. Since the St. Patrick's Day attack, his doctors had prescribed him various medicines, but he didn't want any of that crap. Tried and true aspirin and a glass of Jameson's was all the pain relief he believed in.

But, as he peered through his shaded migraine therapy glasses, he saw his wife's grave. The flowers he had planted months earlier had been torn up.

"What the...?" Morris started to shout, but his eyes suddenly told him to drop to the ground.

Hitting the disturbed earth, Morris rolled over to see the caretaker recoiling from having swung his shovel. Worse yet, he was now raising it over his head, preparing for another attempt.

Chapter 2

Morris looked up at the wooden handle in the caretaker's hands. Feeling for his walking stick with his right hand, he managed to seize upon the shillelagh and raised it over his head, grabbing the far end of it with his left hand so as to block the oncoming swing.

The caretaker's blow splintered the stick, caving it, but not fully breaking it. Morris was able to bend the ends together, ensnaring the shovel head, and gave it a yank.

His assailant stumbled forward as the shovel came free. Morris got himself to one knee and then fully stood on his feet as he flung the shovel away and turned toward the caretaker, now on the ground.

"What the hell was that!" Morris shouted.

"You senile old fuck," the caretaker retorted, rolling over onto his elbows. "You don't recognize me, do you?"

He gave the man a better look. He was scrawny and maybe no taller than Morris. His hair was too long for its thinning nature. His face was unshaven, and his general appearance was that of a stray dog, malnourished and beaten. But Morris' eye seized on something. At that very moment, some geek at MIT was probably writing software meant to recognize faces. But even with a headache and the red-tinted glasses, Morris managed to identify the caretaker and cross-reference him with his personal database of degenerates.

"When and how did you get out Jakie?" Morris asked, only half caring about the answer.

The caretaker got to his feet, more animated than before, his face turning crimson. "I was a victim, you fuck. You and that fuckin' Amtrak cop. I should have killed both of you."

"You were a drug mule, Jakie," Morris said sternly.

"Bullshit!"

"You were caught with a kilo of cocaine inside a leg cast while carrying your own crutches," Morris shot back. "You should have been arrested for stupidity, on top of assholery, on top of being a piece-of-shit drug mule for Wacko and the Squid."

Jakie became enraged and charged at Morris, who barely ducked a mean right from the caretaker. "You sent me to that zoo in Concord, and you aren't shit without a badge and gun!"

As correctional institutions go, MCI-Concord, no doubt, was a zoo. But if it wasn't Morris who put Jakie there, it would have been some other cop. That's the fact. Jakie certainly had a mother, and maybe she gave him every hug and encouragement. Maybe even to this day, she loved the cretin. That's what moms do. But to the rest of the world, Jakie was shit. Playing drug mule for the South Boston mobster Wacko Barrett, brother to the late Senator Patrick Barrett, was probably the least offensive role he had held in life.

The missed punch seemed to only anger Jakie more. "I'm going to fuck you up!" he shouted with spit coming from his mouth. He tried another punch, but his balance was all off. Morris easily evaded the attempt.

Like everyone who had come under Wacko's wing, Jakie was a mean-spirited sort who was all too happy to do the kingpin's bidding in Southie. Morris had never doubted that Jakie was part of the mobster's crew that beat a Vietnamese couple half to death so that Wacko and his right-hand man, the Squid, could take over their convenience store for money laundering.

But unlike Jakie, Wacko wasn't some shit for brains. His late brother rose to power in the state senate on a reputation of being a brilliant academic, but truthfully, Senator Patrick Barrett was no match for the genius of his older brother Tim. The life-long criminal was always two steps ahead of anyone trying to catch him. Whether you were a cop, prosecutor, or rival gangster, if you went after Wacko, you either ended up dead or indicted.

Jakie was in the midst of some profanity as he looked ready to charge at Morris, who figured it was time to end the confrontation.

"Hey!" Morris shouted in a commanding voice that grabbed the caretaker. He then shifted back into a normal tone. "You know Jakie, there's a reason why they separate the gazelles from the old cats at the Franklin Park Zoo."

Stunned by the comment, Jakie straightened up for a moment, and that was all the opening Morris needed. With an open right hand, he gave the grave-digger a much-deserved slap across the face, which then exposed his cheek to an ensuing left hook.

The sound of his knuckles against Jake's jaw was like a tray of ice being cracked. He dropped like the sack of shit he was. Morris then stood over the prone body and snorted. "Some free legal advice for you Jakie, those who play with mean old cats get scratched."

Jakie rolled over to his right a few times, trying to scramble away. He stumbled to his feet, dropped to a knee, but then managed to get up again. As he limped away, he swore something about suing Morris.

"Take a fuckin' number," Morris said turning back toward his wife's grave. While his knuckles hurt, the truth was Morris felt good. Maybe it was the adrenaline rushing through his body or maybe it was just psychological. He was old. He was broken, but he still didn't take crap from anyone. He hadn't felt this good in weeks.

He looked at his wife's name chiseled into the granite and let out a deep breath. He got down on both his knees and considered saying a prayer. He was never sure where to start. He knew the words well enough. He just didn't like them. If he had to choose, a Hail Mary always seemed best, but he wasn't here to hail anyone. He just wanted to talk to the soul of his dead wife.

Many thoughts came to his mind, as they always did on his weekly visits here. Their daughters had grown into women, both doing well at college. Occasionally one might check in on Morris under the pretense of needing something from home. Mary Ellen would be proud of them. Words and memories raced around in his head for what may have been a minute or even five, but in the end, his attempts at prayer faded to just two syllables. "Sorry," he said aloud, as he got onto one knee to pull himself up.

As opposed to moments ago, he could feel the aches in his body. With his right knee still on the dirt, he started to stand, hoping that his left leg would be up to the task. As he stood, he felt dizzy, all too common these days. He wondered whether it was just his age or the lingering injuries.

As he got both feet under him and straightened his back, his head cleared. He looked around for the remnants of his walking stick and found it still bent around the abandoned shovel. The sight verified the aptness of his single-word prayer to his late wife. Morris knew he was stubborn, at times as quick to anger as he was slow to sympathy.

His wife always managed to help him see past his mistakes, not that she wasn't aware of them. She'd be the first to let him know when he was being an ass, but she always had perspective. There were any number of times his climb up the transit police professional ladder was halted or reversed by his own questionable judgment. Her counter always was, "You came home alive tonight, and that's all I care about."

As Morris took a final look at his wife's headstone, he made mental note of the remaining space on it. No doubt someday his name would be there. His mother's name was already there, having passed away just a year ago. Noticeably absent, however, was the name of his father.

It was only recently, thanks to a classified FBI file a friend had passed to him, that he learned that maybe his dad was the source of his stubborn streak. When Wacko Barrett started bringing the scourge drugs into Southie, his dad stood his ground against his fellow gangster, and that apparently became his undoing. Still never a body. Never the closure. Never a name on a stone.

Somewhere in all that was also an explanation of why Morris could be a pain in the ass to his fellow T-cops. Transit police often deal with the most marginal of society. The runaways and homeless sought refuge in the subway. They were the forgotten, the disappeared, but they were still someone's child, sibling or parent.

Life expectancy underground could be brief. Among the drugs, dangers of the third rail, speeding trains, and their quasi-human fellow inhabitants of the tunnels, most who took up residence in the subway eventually died there. It would be easy to ignore them, but Morris never let it go. As he thought about it, compassion maybe didn't motivate him as much as just the opportunity to slap the rest of society in the face.

As he approached the exit of Cedar Grove Cemetery, he reflected that maybe he had always been a mix of good and bad, but for all his imperfections, his wife loved him as he was. Sometimes those flaws had been useful. His profession emphasized a decent decision made quickly was better than a great one made a second too late. Perfection was a liability.

At that moment, he saw a Boston Police cruiser round the corner and hop the curb in front of the cemetery. He could see a second cruiser, lights on, in the distance and also heading toward Cedar Grove.

Morris spun to see if there was chaos he had missed. His senses were usually more attune than this. He picked up his pace and headed toward the cruiser as the driver's door opened.

"On the ground!" shouted the cop.

Morris turned over his shoulder, expecting to see someone near him. Maybe the cops had come for Jakie.

"Stop and drop," the cop shouted again.

Morris was confused until he saw the cop unsnap his holster. The cops weren't there for Jakie; they were there for him.

Morris instantly went to his knees, wincing for a moment when he felt the hard pavement. He raised his hands. "I'm a cop!" he shouted.

The officer was wearing a fluorescent-yellow jacket and spoke into a lapel radio while keeping his eyes on Morris. For his part, Morris kept his hands up and tried to remain motionless. He still had on the migraine glasses, but the Boston cop looked like he could have been 12. They just seemed to get younger and younger.

The second cruiser was still coming, but then Morris saw an SUV with the familiar circle-T logo of the MBTA race toward the entrance from the other direction. The cruiser and the SUV stopped short of colliding. The first cop on the scene diverted his gaze from Morris and looked at the vehicles that just arrived.

The door of the SUV flung open and a broad-shouldered cop quickly stepped out and moved toward the front of the vehicle. Morris spied the short ponytail and then immediately glanced toward the back of the vehicle. The K-9 insignia confirmed his assessment as did the T-cop's voice when she went to address the two Boston cops who were on the scene.

"He's one of ours," she shouted.

The second cop answered something back. He must have been the shift supervisor checking on a rookie.

Whatever he was saying, Transit Police Sergeant Nancy Steiger would have none of it. Nancy had recently returned from her second tour in Afghanistan. She was tough as nails and meaner than her own junkyard dog, Kaiser, who when unleashed was more vicious than a land shark.

As the cops continued to debate, Morris saw Jakie run over to the scene. He couldn't make out the words, but he seemed to be saying he had made the 911 call. Nancy started moving back to the SUV even though it looked as though the discussion with the Boston cops was far from over. Jakie then pursued her, shouting something to her back.

Whatever he said, Kaiser took exception to either the words or the manner and started barking. That's when Jakie pounded on the SUV window, either threatening or teasing Kaiser. You don't mess with a K-9 cop's dog.

In one swift move, Nancy grabbed the gravedigger with her left hand and threw him against the SUV. She cocked her right hand ready for a brawl, but the two Boston cops quickly intervened, grabbing Jakie and throwing him to the ground. T-cops and the city police may have their differences. Certainly, the MBTA police force had a chip on its shoulder since it always seemed to play second fiddle to everyone. Still, there was nothing like the common enemy of a punk like Jakie to bring the two forces together.

A few moments later, the gravedigger was thrown into the back of one of the cruisers, and Nancy had taken Kaiser out of the SUV to calm him down. She and her four-legged fellow officer then made their way toward Morris, who only then realized he was still on his knees.

"I'm not sure I want to know what that was about," Morris said getting to his feet.

"What do you mean?" said the K-9 officer. "It was about you. That guy was a little bullshit that you took a swing at him."

"After he took a few at me," shot back Morris. "A couple of them with a shovel!"

Nancy laughed. "Listen, I know the guy had to have it coming. You were just lucky I got here when I did."

"Yeah," said Morris. "How did you end up here?"

"Your partner told me you would be here."

Morris' nodded. He and Elijah Poole had been friends since high school when their respective neighborhoods of South Boston and Columbia Point were merged together in the riot that was known as the desegregation of the Boston Public Schools. Elijah knew him better than anyone else on this earth. He knew where he'd be this morning.

"Well, I'll thank him for checking up on me," said Morris.

"He wasn't checking up," said Nancy. "I have to bring you over to headquarters."

Morris was frustrated. "Listen, he knows. I have my physical this afternoon."

"It's not about that," said Nancy. "Apparently you're not the only Fitzgerald tussling with the Boston PD these days. Your cousin had a run-in with them."

"Oh shit," sighed Morris.

"Come on, get in the car," said Nancy.

"Care to trade cousins with me?" joked Morris as he opened the SUV door.

Nancy smiled as she stepped into the driver's seat. "You know what? You should seriously consider going to see my cousin."

Morris laughed, but Nancy didn't join in. It wasn't a joke. Her cousin was Sergeant Brian Gregg, director of the Boston Police Stress Unit. The man was well known in the tight circle of police forces in the Greater Boston area. He had no formal training as a psychologist or any other kind of doctor, but he had nearly three decades working the beat as a city cop and was edging toward his 10-year sobriety chip with AA.

Gregg had been a rising star with the Boston Police. He started as a streetwise patrolman with a sense of humor and a knack for putting people at ease. If he hadn't chosen to wear a badge, he could have done stand up at the Comedy Connection in Faneuil Hall.

Gregg ended up working his own backyard, District E of West Roxbury. Geographically, the neighborhood was a transition zone, buffering some of the area's wealthier suburbs from the city of Boston. Parts of West Roxbury resembled Morris' home of South Boston, a heritage of middle-class Irish, the descendants of people who emigrated to the area in the 1800s and eventually sank roots where they could.

Morris never heard the full story, not to say that there had to be a story behind a cop hitting burnout, being divorced twice and drinking far more than he should. Morris' suspicion was that Gregg had been swallowed by the phenomenon of trying to police your own neighborhood. Community policing is great on paper. You hire men and women from the area. They have a vested interest and an instant rapport with everyone.

The model works great save for two major pitfalls. The first is that rapport also applies to the criminals in the neighborhood. The kid you played street hockey with might now be leading a car-theft ring and chop shop. Or worse, he's now part of a crew like Wacko Barrett's, and he knows everyone dear to you and where you hide your skeletons.

But most decent cops find a way to skirt that danger, mostly by minimizing their personal life or at least their emotional connection to it. The less you care, the less leverage anyone can get on you. The real reason cops who police their own neighborhood end up sitting in their basement with a bottle of booze in one hand, their service weapon in the other, and a tortured brain trying to negotiate a truce between the two, is the shit you wish you could unsee.

Morris was thankful that as a T cop his beat was basically the world. Boston was a gateway to America. Trains, subways, buses, even ferries were part of the transit fleet. His job was unpredictable if nothing else. But even as a T-cop, he occasionally had to work in his own neighborhood of South Boston and would glimpse what life could have been like for folks like Gregg who worked their hometown.

He remembered back to when he had only been on the job about a year. A call came in over the radio for a disturbance near the Broadway Station. Morris arrived on the scene and found an older gentlemen beating the shit out of someone. The first indication that the victim was a woman was the high-pitch of the wailing. Her face was so bloodied and beaten, it looked more like some horror mask than anything human.

Morris lunged forward and grabbed the guy's arm before he could deliver another strike. That's when he recognized him. Morris had to jog his own memory for the man's name because Morris had only known him as "Coach." It came to him though, Jerry O'Donnell and his wife Marie, now laying in a pool of blood on the sidewalk. They seemed to be the sweetest couple, and their kid Mikey had been a buddy of Morris. He probably ate at their house at least two dozen times, and his own mom and Marie worked church bazaars and youth hockey fundraisers together.

Over the years, Morris had a few incidents in his own backyard – too many times he found the son or daughter of a neighbor with a needle in the arm in the subway – but it was that moment that continually resurfaced in his head. It wasn't that it was terribly gruesome, certainly when compared to the high-speed or high-voltage faces of death he witnessed monthly on the nation's oldest public transit system. More than anything the memory represented the cold water to the face, the wake-up call, that as a cop he was now viewing life through the devil's looking glass. He would see people at their worst and most vulnerable. There aren't a lot of other jobs that can compare. Sure, emergency room doctors and firefighters saw some terrible things, too, but at least they were armed with the resources to pull people from the clutches of such inhumanity. Cops, on the other hand, were bound to rules and a revolving-door judicial system.

More than anything that was the stress of being a cop. Like an eroding beachfront, it wasn't some massive wave that would wash you away but rather a constant tide of helplessness, imperceivable at any moment, but over time, a force that could be as devastating as it was unstoppable.

The visible danger, such as crossing paths with some punk with a gun or knife, sure, that could get you killed in an instant, but that was the accepted risk of the job. The obvious things that could kill you weren't as much a worry as the darker, more hidden things, you had to live with. They could bury you a little each day. Most learned to bury it first before it could get to them. You learned to put the demons in their own room and shut the door quick so that you could get on with being a decent parent or spouse. Sometimes you needed help closing that door, and you turned to a few drinks. The key was not to let the alcohol do all the work.

Morris suspected that's what happened to Gregg. Whether it was the demons or the booze, one was too strong for him to keep under control. Still, something sobered him up, and with the help of a city councilor, he began the Boston Police Stress Unit.

Gregg was non-denominational. It didn't matter what force you served on, the stress unit always had an open door or an available phone line for you. Over time Gregg recruited doctors with certain expertise to work with him. He was still an active-duty cop, but at least three-quarters of his time was occupied by the unit. It was one of the few things in the realm of government work that politicians had yet to screw up. Maybe that was because the unit generally flew under the radar.

"Hey."

The voice jolted Morris.

"We're here," Nancy reiterated, apparently.

"Sorry," said Morris as he began to pull on the door handle. "Hey Nance, how busy is your cousin these days?"

"Busier than he wishes he was," she responded flatly. It was true. All cops had had a target on their back these days. "Why? You want me to give him a call for you?"

Morris searched for the answer. It couldn't hurt. "Nah," he answered as he opened the door and began to step out. "He needs to save his schedule for the real fuck-ups."

"Uh huh," Nancy said doubtingly.

As Morris stepped away from the SUV, her tone echoed in his head. He heard her clearly. He just wasn't sure whether she questioned Morris' rejection of her cousin's help or whether she questioned his exclusion of himself from the category of fuck-up.

Chapter 3

Morris looked at Elijah Poole, sitting in the chair to his left, outside the office of the MBTA police chief. Elijah didn't seem to be looking at anything. At 6' 4", he had never been a sheepish person, but he had his head down for some reason.

"What's wrong?" Morris asked.

"Huh?" he said, lifting his head, and looking at the man he had known for almost forty years. "Oh, it's my shoes," he said. "They're too damn nice."

Before Morris could follow up on the nonsensical statement, a voice interrupted them.

"Hello, sergeant."

Both Morris and Elijah turned and saw the face of Mark Turley, the assistant to the chief. Turley was a holdover from the administration of the former head of the transit police, Claire Barrett, who served as a puppet for her father-in-law, state

Senator Patrick Barrett. Both were killed when a madman crashed a bus into the Charles River. They should have left the bodies there to rot, but that wouldn't have been fair to the fish.

"The chief is quite busy this morning," Turley continued, speaking to Elijah. "Can I help you?"

Turley's official title was assistant to the chief. However, he had taken to leaving off the preposition, often acting as though he were second in command. The truth was the man had never done an hour of police work in his life. His skill set consisted of being a corruptible gossip that the late senator was able to plant to keep an eye on his daughter-in-law. Turley was a suck-up. His problem since the senator's death was that he had become a whore without a pimp.

"That's OK," Elijah said evenly. "I'll wait for Steph." Under most circumstances, Elijah probably would have given Stephanie Tam the respect of a full title, but Morris understood that his former partner wanted to emphasize to Turley that he and the chief were on a first-name basis.

"Certainly, as you wish. How's the leg by the way?" Turley responded.

"Fine," said Elijah with an expression that said the conversation was over.

Turley took the hint and turned away while Elijah went back to looking at his shoes.

"So what's the problem with good looking-shoes," asked Morris.

"They're three months old," he replied without looking up. "Normally they'd be worn out now. Too much time in conference rooms, buddy."

Elijah was a good cop, just as he had been a good Marine. Morris wasn't so proud that he couldn't acknowledge his friend had been better at both than he ever was. However, it wasn't until the aftermath of the bus crash that killed the Barretts, that Elijah ever got his due. Some might suggest what had held him back was the color of his skin. A black kid from the Columbia Point projects, growing up in the 1960s and '70s in Boston had certain hurdles, no doubt about that, thought Morris, but practically speaking the real detriment to Elijah's success probably had been his taste in friends, especially one in particular, Morris.

The fact that he finally got the promotion he deserved should have been a good thing, but Morris understood. Still, he hadn't anticipated the bittersweetness of an increase in prestige and pay had to come at the expense of not being on the streets, or in the case of a T-cop, below them in the subways.

At that moment, Elijah's phone rang, and he retrieved it from his coat pocket.

"Hello Herm," Morris heard his partner say. It must have been Elijah's cousin, Dr. Herman Poole, who was set to give Morris his return-to-duty physical that afternoon.

Technically, since Elijah's promotion and Morris being placed on restricted duty, they weren't partners anymore.

They originally met under the most inauspicious circumstances. Morris and a gang of kids, mostly of Irish-descent, but all absent any significant skin tone, on one side of Carson Beach in South Boston. Across from them were Elijah and an equal number of kids, most of whom traced their lineage through slavery, but all of whom were lumped into the ever-changing label that had progressed from negro to black to African-American. In between them were state troopers who had caught wind of the showdown between Southie and Columbia Point.

This was the 1970s in Boston. Of course, to understand the 1970s, you needed to understand the 1950s and '60s in the city. It was over those decades that as the city gentrified, the politicians grew fat and comfortable. That's the problem with democracy. With a monarchy or dictatorship, your leadership might have been pre-ordained, but it took a lot of the drama out of government. Democracies were sloppy, thought Morris. Power was a matter of popularity. Politicians sell people any sort of lie or crooked deal to keep themselves in their positions.

Post World War II saw the Great Migration of blacks from the rural south to the northern cities. Boston also saw an influx of Haitian immigrants along with Vietnamese and Taiwanese looking to escape strife in their homelands. To Irish politicians, however, this gentrification was a threat. It was too easy to categorize the fault as racism. Certainly, there were people throughout the city who had been bred to boot-stomp someone based just upon skin pigment, but if the problem were mere ignorance, it would have been so much easier to solve. No, racism was more the symptom than the disease, the disease of having more and wanting to keep it all to yourself. That's where the city stumbled. The politicians knew these enclaves of new residents would start electing people who looked more like themselves than Howdy Doody, and that just couldn't be tolerated. It wasn't prejudice; it was politics.

If a city council seat went to a different neighborhood, then so too would the patronage jobs, the bribes, and the public works projects. That meant also the unions and with them the political clout, and eventually the power. Government corruption was a tautology. The only way you could unseat a corrupt official was to become just as corrupt.

Therein lies the democratic flaw. It's a competition for power and all the trappings that come with it. You can't expect people to play fair. The Irish politicians looked after their own. The white neighborhoods ended up with better schools, and it got so bad to the point of being a federal lawsuit, claiming the city's school committee had a segregated Boston and provided sub-par resources to the black neighborhoods.

The proof that democracy is a pipe dream lies in the judicial system, which for all purposes functions like a dictatorship. So when Boston politicians stood in defiance of a court order to come up with a plan to improve the schools, federal judge Arthur Garrity swooped in with all subtlety of a blitzkrieg. He started busing black kids to white schools and vice verse.

Those who could, either moved out of the city or sent their kids to private school. Most of the kids Elijah grew up with ended up not going to school rather than face the literal riots. Elijah rode the bus from Columbia Point to Southie. Every day, it would be pelted by rocks and racial slurs from the neighborhood.

Since that time, Morris had heard the rumors plenty. It had been the likes of Wacko Barrett and Whitey Bulger who hired or riled up a few to fight the school integration. Even to this day, Morris resisted the labels that had been cast on Southie and other parts of the city. They were just protecting their turf or maybe being exploited, but deep down, he couldn't fight the conclusion that if it wasn't racism motivating the rock-throwers, it was the spinelessness of letting a few assholes speak for the community.

Once at school, things weren't much better, the sons and daughters of Southie took after their parents. Outnumbered and out of place, the Columbia Point kids stood their ground where they could, and one day, they were all supposed to have it out on Carson Beach.

So there Morris was standing, ready to crack skulls. On the other side of the beach, there was this lanky black kid with his fists raised. When he saw that kid break from the line, Morris ran right for him. The troopers rushed in to keep the groups separated, but Morris paid them no heed and neither did the kid running toward him. He could see him coming with rage in his face, but suddenly the kid looked away as he slowed his charge. Morris traced the sight line to a German Shepherd breaking toward his future combatant.

Apparently, the dog had broken away from a K-9 officer, or maybe the trooper had grown up in Southie and turned his partner loose on the Columbia Point side of the melee. The black kid had stopped as the dog rushed with its teeth bared. In a word, it looked like he froze. To this day, Morris couldn't fully explain what happened next. It wasn't so much a conscious thought as it was a natural reaction. Perhaps it was all the tutelage he had learning to box from Father Michael McGovern, who always stressed the importance of a fair fight. Whatever the case, when the dog leaped, looking to latch on to a neck or an arm, Morris stepped right, and turned beautifully through the punch, connecting with the canine and sending it to the sand several feet away. It still may have been the best left hook he ever threw.

Thanks to the remarkably well-timed and powerful punch, the dog landed on the beach with a whimper. When the black kid looked at his counterpart, all Morris could do was shrug with a smirk. Maybe all Southie and Columbia Point needed was a common enemy, but before either could say much or resume their battle, the troopers moved in. Morris quickly learned that K-9 cops didn't take kindly his form of animal control.

Even from his vantage point of having his face in the sand while the troopers, with the help of Boston Police, lunged on top of him, Morris could see his prior opposition getting the crap kicked out of him. He even noticed how one of the cops that grabbed him wore a pair of sap gloves. To most observers, they might seem to be regular leather gloves, but lead powder in the palms could turn a casual slap into a stunning blow. Lots of kids in Southie had a pair. Morris saw the cop give the black kid what was otherwise an imperceptible slap, but the kid's eyes rolled back. He was knocked out. It wasn't a fair fight.

He and the other kid spent the night in the Southie lockup, facing arraignment in the morning on an assortment of charges, including assault and battery on a police officer, albeit the four-legged kind. The judge offered them a simple deal: Either head on down to the Marine recruiting office or be hauled off to the Nashua Street jail, pending trial. He and the other kid took the Marines.

As the line goes, it was the beginning of a beautiful friendship as well as a lifetime mission of Elijah trying to keep Morris one step ahead of self-inflicted disaster. While Elijah happily yielded the role of primary ass-saver to Morris' bride Mary Ellen, since she passed away from cancer five years ago, he had reprised the role.

"You're all set," Elijah said, bringing Morris back to the present. "Herm will see you this afternoon at the clinic in the Transportation Building."

"Thanks," said Morris, knowing that a less-connected doctor might be more discerning of Morris' physical state.

"Yeah, he keeps on wanting to call you Fitzpatrick, though."

"Ah, you've met one Mick, you've met 'em all," joked Morris.

"Oh, I tried to explain to him that he'll remember this Irish asshole."

"Irish asshole?" shot back Morris. "You did tell him I had my prostate removed, right?"

The two laughed, but just then the chief's door flung open, and out stepped Chief Stephanie Tam, who stood all of 5' 1" but could be more ferocious than a bulldog in a butcher shop.

She looked right at Morris. "Your fuckin' cousin. He did it this time. He pissed off some BPD lieutenant." She took a brief glance toward her assistant who had just perked up his ears. "Come on guys. Get in here before Turdley starts taking notes."

With that, Elijah and Morris followed the chief into her office, being sure to close the door behind them.

"Steph, I'm sorry," said Morris. "I've told Happy not to drop my name."

"Jesus Christ, Morris," said Tam. "We're the fuckin' transit police. It's not like we have a lot of get-out-of-jail-free cards to begin with."

Stephanie Tam was a decorated combat Marine with nearly twenty years police experience. The daughter of Taiwanese immigrants who grew up in a tough section of Charlestown, she blended a tireless work ethic with street smarts and a bluntness that made her one of the most respected cops on the force. Steph didn't know how to pull punches or sugar-coat anything, which also made her a threat to the political infrastructure. She may have been the best chief the transit police ever had. The fact that a Boston Police lieutenant even took her call showed how much respect she had gathered among law enforcement, but the rumor was the MBTA's General Manager was feeling some heat because Tam's style clashed with a few city councilors.

Unknown to her and every other soul except Elijah, Morris called in a political favor with the governor after Claire Barrett was killed to get Steph the top-cop job. However, the governor had recently left office, accepting an ambassadorship. This put the state's Lieutenant Governor in charge, and Morris didn't have the same sway with her.

Tam had earned her position, but he also wondered if Steph was too good of a cop to waste in an office somewhere.

The chief looked at Morris and Elijah. "There's a lot of shit going on here." Her tone had shifted to confiding in her two friends. "The Feds already sent us this Terrorism Liaison," she said with sarcasm. "The General Manager made her a deputy director, and now I've got her peeking over my shoulder."

"That's bullshit," said Elijah. "You don't have to do that."

"Oh, absolutely," she responded without changing her tone. "And then we lose a federal grant, and then what happens? No over time. Good luck fuckin' runnin' a transit force like that."

Elijah looked at Morris for comment, but Morris had no retort.

Tam looked at both men. "This is shit you guys don't think about. And then, get this, I am supposed to leave for Israel tomorrow night. Some sort of US-Israeli transit task force or some such bullshit."

"Be careful over there Steph," said Morris. "There's been some terror alerts."

"Oh please, there all a bunch of pussies over there. You want terror? Try being the little Asian girl growing up in Charlestown. Girls in my neighborhood used to shoot bottle rockets at my head on my way to school, and those were the ones who liked me."

Elijah and Morris both let go a laugh. Tam eyed the two of them and broke into a smile too.

"OK, OK," she said raising a hand. "But it's true. That's how I got my fast reflexes," and she broke into a couple of moves that would have rivaled Bruce Lee in his prime. "Little Suzy didn't find it so easy to set off fireworks with a broken arm, I'll tell ya."

The three laughed along for a moment, but then Tam let out a sigh. "OK Morris, tell your cousin not to show up at BPD headquarters shitfaced again."

Elijah interjected, "He's harmless. The guy's name is Happy after all."

Morris laughed. "You know how he got the name, right?"

"Because he is happy-go-lucky, or whatever the fuck you Irish say?"

"No," laughed Morris. "We were like 12 or something. We used to shoot hoops with some other kids down by the projects. So, Eddie, that's his real name, used to freak out any time you fouled him. I mean, psycho freak out. A shit fit, right?"

Elijah and Tam nodded their understanding.

"Well, shit fit becomes Shit Fitz. That was his real nickname. The problem is you can't really say Shit Fitz around your mom. So we changed it to Happy Fitz."

"Kind of like the way you call the big guy 'Tiny'?" asked Elijah.

"Exactly," said Morris, who then turned to Tam. "But don't worry. That's years ago. Marines and booze tamed him a bit. He's a fuck-up, but he's family."

"Whatever," said Tam. "We just can't have him pulling bullshit like this."

"Understood Steph," said Morris.

"By the way," Tam added. "Who's this Rico Paulie with the State Police?"

"He's a good guy," said Morris, looking toward his partner to confirm the assessment.

"Yeah," said Elijah. "He works in the registry division, inspections and stuff like that."

"No, he got re-assigned to the marine unit, you know, down by the Charles River," Morris said, turning back toward Tam. "What's going on?"

"Well, he's been calling for you," Tam said. "When you never got back, he called me. You gotta start checking your messages."

Morris sighed. "Honest Steph, I've got a mountain of emails, phone calls, and other messages from the last year I'm never going to get to."

The chief looked at Morris and nodded sympathetically. "Just keep your bullshit from overflowing onto my desk, OK?"

"Yes, Steph," he said, as he reached into his coat pocket to retrieve his cellphone. He wanted to check he had the trooper's number. However, as he went to open his vintage flip phone, it nearly fell into two pieces.

"Oh shit," Morris mumbled, trying to keep the pieces together. In the tussle with Jakie, he must have landed on it somehow. After another moment, the T-cop looked up and saw Elijah and Tam staring at the electronic mess in his hands. "It still works," he pleaded.

Tam looked over at Elijah and just shook her head.

Elijah shrugged. "Have you seen his car? It's about in the same condition, and I think it was built in the same year."

"Don't be bustin' on the Ghetto Glider," shot back Morris. "It's a classic."

"Classic shitbox," interjected Tam.

Morris and Elijah laughed.

"OK guys," Tam said. "They should've brought your cousin up by now, and I've got a call with the GM and our new deputy director that I have to take."

With that, Morris and Elijah turned and exited the office to find Happy Fitzgerald sitting on a chair.

"Not a word," Morris said to his cousin as he pointed at him.

"But Mo," Happy interjected.

"Nada," Morris said, glancing toward Elijah.

Elijah caught the hint that his friend wanted to get out of the public setting. "Hey, let's head downstairs, and I'll get a cruiser," he said.

Elijah then opened the door to the stairwell, and as the three entered it, Morris started in on his cousin.

"Jesus, Happy, I told you. Don't use my name when you get nabbed by the Boston cops."

"I didn't get nabbed by them," shot back Happy. "I walked into the Brighton station."

"Shitfaced?" countered Morris, as all three descended the stairs.

"Yeah, I had some drinks."

"What the fuck, Hap," Morris said, sounding exasperated.

"She's missing," Happy said plainly.

Elijah and Morris stopped.

"She's missing," he repeated. "Cathy's missing."

Morris looked at Elijah. The two had known each other since high school. He didn't need to explain to him the insignificance of his cousin missing. She had struggled with drugs and mental illness for years and was essentially homeless.

"She does that," Morris said to Happy, and then he continued down the stairs.

"I know," said Happy. "But we were supposed to meet up three days ago at St. Anthony's shrine. It was dad's anniversary. We never miss it."

Morris stopped and looked back. He seemed lost for what to say, and Elijah decided to help him out.

"We can look into it," Elijah said to Happy.

"Yes, Hap," Morris added. "I promise. We'll find her."

Happy seemed satisfied, or maybe it was just that he had run out of things to say. He followed the two T-cops out the building and into a cruiser that Elijah had checked out. It was a short drive from headquarters at 240 Southampton Street to the Old Colony Housing Project, where Happy had a subsidized apartment.

Morris exchanged goodbyes with his cousin, and Elijah then performed a U-turn and headed toward downtown Boston.

"Where ya going?" asked Morris.

"Transportation Building," Elijah said, referring to the common name for Ten Park Plaza in Boston's entertainment district. "I'm taking you to my cousin so you can get your physical."

"Ah, yeah, right," Morris mumbled in agreement.

Morris' head was somewhere else, and it had been since the concussion, likely several of them, he sustained eighteen months ago. Given the intricacies of Boston traffic, Morris was thankful Elijah would be fully occupied for the next few minutes as he tried to get them into the city.

The beauty of getting anywhere in Boston was the seemingly infinite number of choices to your destination. The classic punchline of "You can't get there from here," with the New England kracker accent thrown in, was a myth. You could get there alright, just not in a straight line.

Yes, Boston's roads may have originated as wandering cow paths, and that could be one reason for their meandering nature. But few Bostonians realized just how little of the city was solid ground. When Boston was settled in 1630, it was essentially an island of a several hundred acres. Today, it's thousands of acres. It's not that the cows of Boston wandered. It's just that they didn't know how to swim.

Morris' mind returned to focus. "This is your cousin Herman, right?" he asked Elijah.

"Yeah, you met him once or twice."

"Glasses, the good-looking Poole?" he jabbed.

Elijah smiled. "Fuck you."

Morris felt his melancholy lifting, and Elijah apparently recognized it.

"So what was all that about with Happy?" Elijah asked. "I always get the sense he doesn't like me."

"It's not that he doesn't like you," said Morris. "It's just that he's scared shitless of you."

Elijah smirked.

"Come on," Morris followed. "You're a 6' 4" black man, with a gun and hands that could palm a coffee table. You can be a little intimidating, you know."

"How come it's never worked on you?"

"I'm too stupid to be intimidated," replied Morris.

"Got that right," Elijah said.

"Thanks so much for agreeing with me," he said sarcastically. Then his tone shifted a little. "I feel guilty, I think."

"What do you mean?"

"They're family," Morris said. "Hap and Cathy's dad died like when they were four and five. He was a Marine and got blown up when his jeep went over a mine in 'Nam."

"Oh, shit," said Elijah.

"Yeah, so we ended up being pretty close for a while. My dad kinda felt responsible for his brother's family. But then he disappeared a few years later, and my family had its own worries." Morris' voice trailed off.

"Well, you can't blame yourself for that," said Elijah.

"I know," said Morris. "It doesn't change the fact that they're family. Their mom kind of checked out. Hap ended up in the Marines, a little bit behind us. Then I think it was summer of '83, Cathy got mugged, or at least that's how my mom put it, and she was never the same."

"Mugged?" asked Elijah.

"Yeah, I mean it didn't register at the time. Hap was probably in basic training. I think we had just ended up in Beirut. I basically found out in a letter my mom sent."

Morris finished with a laugh even though it seemed inappropriate, but Elijah had known Morris' mom. He seemed to understand the implication. The Irish could talk anyone's ear off about the weather or how to cook a roasted potato, but if it was something that could trigger human emotion, best not trouble anyone with a word.

"I'm sure that ate at Happy, too," Elijah offered. "He wasn't there."

"Exactly," acknowledged Morris, contemplating the same thing. "Back in the day, he'd have grabbed a bat and throttled anyone who touched his sister. But as far as I know, no one ever said anything."

Elijah then shot Morris a look, and he read it. Southie wasn't much different from Columbia Point after all. The two T-cops had both been raised in neighborhoods where you often had to think before you threw a punch because the guy on the other side of it might have a friend or brother who was tight with someone who had a gang behind him. That's not to say Morris always thought before taking a swing.

"There were a few times I thought it must have been one of Wacko's guys, and Hap's mom, my mom, knew we'd be dead if we went after them," explained Morris.

It was a somber topic that halted most other conversation between the two friends. A few minutes later, Elijah pulled up outside the block-long red-brick Ten Park Plaza. "OK Miss Daisy, here we are," he said.

"You know I've always thought of you more as a Samuel L. Jackson than a Morgan Freeman," joked Morris.

"Well, I have always thought of you as a Jessica Tandy," quipped Elijah.

"Great," Morris said, looking out the window. "You know I hate doctors."

"I know. Don't worry. Herm's good."

He couldn't understand why, but Elijah was always looking out for him. "Thanks for the ride," he said as he opened the door. Stepping onto the curb, a thought struck him. As much as he had loved his mother, it may have been time to separate from his emotional heritage. "Hey, seriously," he said with sincerity as he stuck his head in the cruiser. "Thanks for everything."

With that, he shut the door and took a step toward getting his life back to normal.

Chapter 4

Morris walked into the eight-story building at Ten Park Plaza that no Bostonian called by its address. Throughout the city, the red-brick structure was known simply as the "Transportation Building."

Built in 1983, it stood as one of several reminders throughout the city of the aesthetics and politics of Boston's urban renewal. Starting in the 1950s, the politicians got it in their collective heads that the city just wasn't modern enough for the 20th Century. What they hatched was a collection of public and private projects, many of which involved bulldozing neighborhoods in order to build highways, luxury towers, or atrocious-looking facilities that often were mistaken for prisons.

The Transportation Building began as a potential private development under the auspices of the mayor's office. It would link the city's entertainment district with Boston Common through a facade that was as bland as boiled potatoes. However, when private interests balked, the city's politicians turned toward the state to bail it out. The state took over the project with the goal of housing several transportation departments in the mixed-used facility.

As Morris walked through the first-floor food court, he couldn't help but agree with the general assessment that the structure turned out to be a useful building in the wrong location. As he scanned the directory for the MBTA medical clinic and felt his shoe stick to the brick floor, the consequence of some careless discard of chewing gum, he revised his thought. The building was as ugly as it was out of place.

A hundred feet in front of him were historic theaters. A hundred feet behind him were some of the oldest buildings still standing in the city, a stone's throw from the Boylston T stop, which served as a bookend for the ancient Tremont Street Subway, the first public subway in the country.

Here he was standing in what felt like the set of some failed sci-fi flick from the 1970s. All he needed was moon boots and a silver jumpsuit. Still, this is what progress and urban renewal felt like a few decades ago. There was no accounting for taste.

As he stepped in the elevator and pressed the button for the sixth floor, he felt his foot stick to the ground. He groaned and checked his watch. He still had a few minutes before his appointment. When the doors opened, he exited looking for the bathroom in the hope he could free his left heel from its sticky predicament.

As he spotted the men's room door and made his way toward it, he tried to keep his left shoe from fully touching the ground. He could only imagine he must have looked like Quasimodo, dragging a foot behind him.

"Who's that?"

The voice surprised Morris as he entered the men's room. It seemed equally startled by Morris' presence. As a T-cop, he had learned there could be a certain risk to entering public restrooms. He looked up and was relieved to see the tall, thin frame of Bob Sosa, the T's deputy director of real estate.

"Hey, Bob. How ya been?"

"What do you want?" he replied in an unusually jumpy tone.

"It's me, Morris."

Sosa leaned down as Morris straightened up. While it took a moment, he apparently recognized him. The two had grown up together in South Boston and as adults played together on the Southie park league football team, the Chippewas. Bob was better known in that circle as "The Mantis" due to his skinny physique.

With the recognition, Sosa immediately grew less anxious. Morris didn't want to ponder why.

"So what are you doing here?" Sosa asked.

"I have a physical next door," Morris answered.

"So you're alone?"

"Aren't we all?" Morris replied with a grin, but he noticed Sosa wasn't smiling, his dark eyes darting around the restroom. Something was going on, but then Sosa's expression shifted. It was as though he had convinced himself to say nothing.

"Bob, is something wrong?" Morris pressed.

The Mantis seemed to weigh something. "You'd probably be a good one to ask," he began. "If you had to trust someone in the AG's office, who would it be?"

"Oh Geez," said Morris, trying to remember anyone he knew at the Attorney General's Office. "I don't know." He then started trying to assemble the equation from the little information Sosa had volunteered. The deputy director for real estate was a good guy. His parents had been Portuguese immigrants. Morris never met the man's father. Apparently, he had worked himself into an early grave a couple of years before Bob and his mom moved in with relatives in Southie.

Sosa had done alright for himself. He was always smart, but some might say he lacked ambition. It's not that Bob was lazy, but he tried to be fair to a fault. That explained why he couldn't cut it in the city's investment community. He just wasn't enough of an asshole. But he knew money and numbers, and it didn't hurt that Sonny Barrett had been in his corner. That's how he landed a nice management job with the T.

Not long after Sonny met his untimely death, Sosa discovered the late Senator's role in some questionable real estate dealings, including the construction of a new lobster dock on the waterfront using federal transit money.

Sosa had probably come across something more significant – after all the informal full name of the MBTA was Mr. Barrett's Transit Authority. Sonny was a bastard, but he had a code, albeit a corrupt one. There was the time he diverted subway funding to help a veterans group in Quincy. Another time, the MBTA ruined some guy's backyard when they were re-building the Ashmont Station. Sonny straightened the whole thing out, had the T redo his yard, and saw that the guy got a cash settlement.

Quietly, Morris always suspected Sonny had put Bob in the T's real estate office because he knew the man was gullible enough to go along with whatever the corrupt politician fed him, but since Sonny's death, Boston politics had become ruthless. With so much influence wiped out, everyone was trying to muscle in for a corner. You had to watch yourself these days, especially if your morals inclined you to be a whistleblower.

"You know Bob, what I'd do is find the most junior one there and reach out to them," Morris advised. "The young ones don't know any better, and they don't owe anybody."

Sosa nodded. "It's probably nothing anyway."

"Seriously," Morris continued. "Give me a call next week. We'll meet at Bobby Greene's. In the meantime, never write if you can speak. Never speak if you can nod. Never nod if you can wink, and never use email or Facebook!"

Sosa laughed but didn't add another word as he turned and exited the bathroom, leaving Morris to return to extricating the gum from his shoe bottom.

After doing as best he could, he left the men's room and entered the offices of the MBTA clinic, which in all respects looked and functioned like a normal doctor's office. While it was staffed with regular T employees, the doctors were independent contractors, pulled in on a rotating basis from area hospitals.

Morris crossed the small waiting area to reach a desk behind which sat an older woman – on second thought, she probably was about his age – who was engrossed with doing some sort of work on her computer. He edged a little closer and leaned to get her attention.

Without diverting her gaze, she reached for a clipboard. "Write down all your prescriptions," she said, handing the clipboard to Morris.

She conveyed all the warmth of a package of frozen fish sticks.

Morris looked at the form. "I don't know. I can't even remember where I put the TV clicker," he said with a smile. "How am I supposed to remember all the prescriptions I'm on?"

She then looked at Morris for the first time. "Well, do the best you can," and then she turned back to her computer.

So much for my charm, thought Morris, and he needed to make sure he was going to be seen by Elijah's cousin.

"Excuse me," he said. "I think my appointment is with Dr. Poole. I'm …."

"You're Fitzgerald, right?" she said.

"Yeah."

"You're the only appointment we've got this afternoon. I don't know who the doctor is today. It's not like we're a doctor's office or something."

Morris wanted to point out that, in fact, the clinic was some sort of office, and there were doctors who worked there. That would make the facility a doctor's office, but he probably had pushed his luck with Broom Hilda to begin with.

At that moment a door behind the woman opened, and Morris was relieved to see a tall man that looked a bit like his partner Elijah walk into the area.

"Sergeant Fitzgerald?" the doctor queried.

Morris had met Herman Poole a few times over the years, but he wasn't sure if he was supposed to play along with some ruse of not knowing the man.

"Yes, doctor, right here," he said stepping around the medical officer's desk.

"Hey Morris, good to see you," Dr. Poole said extending a hand and dropping all sign of formality.

As Morris shook the doctor's hand. Broom Hilda turned to hand him the clipboard and a folder. "Make sure you fill out the physical form, or he'll have to come back."

Dr. Poole took the clipboard and folder, and Morris glanced toward the seated woman. He could now see what had kept her so engaged – online poker. What a wonderful way to spend the paycheck you were earning.

"Oh," said the medical officer as she turned back around. "He said he couldn't remember any of his prescriptions."

Dr. Poole laughed as he put an arm on Morris' shoulder to guide him toward an exam room. "Yes, my cousin tells me you suffer from Irish Alzheimer's," he said. "You only remember grudges."

Morris laughed. It was far from the first time he had heard the joke, but he appreciated the doctor's choice of humor.

Poole was dressed in a square-shouldered tweed jacket, plain oxford shoes, and a paisley tie. He served as the grand master of the Prince Hall Grand Lodge, the oldest and most powerful black fraternal organization in the United States.

While he wasn't as imposing as Elijah, his handshake had been every bit as powerful as his cousin's. "Morris, we just have a few tests we need to do, nothing too out of the ordinary."

Morris glanced around the room and mumbled, "Doc, I didn't have time to study for my piss test so it could be a while."

The doctor chuckled and commenced with a short battery of exams that lasted about twenty minutes. Afterward, the doctor offered his assessment. "Morris for a guy who has been blown up and gassed, you're not in bad shape. Between the migraines, diabetes, sleep apnea, you also suffer from color-vision deficiency."

"Your cousin always said I was the only guy from Southie who didn't see color."

Doctor Poole laughed. "Not that type of color blindness. I have to ask, how did you get your driver's license renewed?"

"The same way I got my inspection sticker," Morris said matter of factly. "I called Trooper Paulie down at the registry, and he took care of everything."

"Low friends in high places?" commented the doctor.

"More like low acquaintances in high places," answered Morris. "Unfortunately, he got transferred out of the registry. Paulie is a typical statie. Full of himself and a bullshit artist, but if you need Patriots or Celts tickets, he's the guy to call."

"For a price I am sure," said Dr. Poole.

"Well that's the way, doc," said Morris. "Favors are like the stock market. You scratch someone's back, and you hope by time you need to cash it in, that guy's gone up in value. Sometimes that happens, sometimes it don't."

"I see," said Dr. Poole. "And what kind of an investment have you been?"

"I'm pretty much a Ponzi scheme, doc."

"Mhmm," Dr. Poole said, nodding along. "Well, from what I can tell, you pretty much are a typical cop," he continued. "You're hooked on adrenaline, and you treat danger as an aphrodisiac."

"I wish," said Morris. "My love life has kind of hit the skids."

He then could see the doctor's expression shift, as though he just remembered something and wanted to retract his words. It had been five years since Morris' wife died. "Anyway doc, the next time the environmental police nab you on your boat down at Inkwell Beach, give your cousin a call, not me. He's the one with pull these days."

The doctor laughed, pushing past the awkward moment. "Yeah, I'll have to remind myself maybe to have a little more discretion when I tell him about being cited for boating violations."

"Come on doc, you don't have to worry about me. My brain has been gassed and then concussed. I'm lucky that I can remember your name, Fred."

Dr. Poole smiled and raised an eyebrow. "Actually of all the things that are broken in your body, as best I can tell, your brain is the one thing that works right."

"Must be my thick Irish skull."

"You're not still boxing are you?" asked the doctor.

"Best way to stay in shape," shot back Morris.

Dr. Poole shook his head back and forth in disagreement. "Seriously, you sustained a brain trauma. No more sparring, anything."

"Listen, I'm a fool, not an idiot. Heavy bag, speed bag, stuff like that. It's therapeutic for me. Plus, I can hop in the harbor for a swim right at L Street."

"Oh that's right, you're a Brownie," Dr. Poole said referring to the famed L Street Brownies, a century-old swimming club based at the L Street Bathhouse in South Boston. The group was best known for their penchant for year-round swimming. While a relative handful of the members kept up the tradition, every January 1, their numbers would swell by the hundreds as people would be drawn to join in their New Year's plunge. It was clean fun, but Morris always got a kick out of watching yuppies run into the water in body suits that cost more than what some of the old-timers paid for their triple-deckers in Southie.

"You know," Dr. Poole continued. "I've got a swimming group down on the Vineyard."

"Oh, the black Hamptons," countered Morris, followed by a laugh from the doctor. About seven miles off the coast of Cape Cod, just a little over an hour drive and short ferry ride from Boston, lies Martha's Vineyard. In the early 1900s, the son of a former slave had the idea of renting a cottage to those who shared his ancestry since, due to segregation, many were denied access to such accommodations. From that point, the town of Oak Bluffs, and then eventually the entire island, gained the reputation as a respite for people of color, particularly the elite who could afford island living or at least island vacationing.

"Come out with my cousin some time," said Dr. Poole. "You can go for a swim with us."

"You're shittin' me if you tell me you call yourselves the Oak Bluffs Brownies," Morris said.

The doctor smiled. "The Black Polar Bears."

Morris nodded.

"Seriously, stick to swimming over boxing. It's done wonders for my arthritic knee."

"What happened to your knee?" asked Morris.

"Oh, it goes back to when I was at Boston Latin."

"High school football?" he asked.

"No," Dr. Poole answered. "I was kneecapped by a salt-and-pepper duo from English High one day while walking through the Fens."

"Shit," said Morris. "Back then, you had to be careful in the Fens. Still do, actually."

The Fens were part of the Back Bay section of Boston and also give Fenway Park its name. The neighborhood represented a scenic link between Back Bay, which ran along the Charles River, and other parts of the city. Designed by Frederick Law Olmsted, there were a series of gardens and plantings that could offer Boston residents and visitors a break from the city landscape. However, the same features provided cover for unsavory activity, including a pair of thugs looking to beat up someone from a rival high school.

"Yeah," continued the doctor. "Maybe it was a blessing in disguise. It laid me up and forced me to take school more seriously. Still, my blood boils every time I see the guy who did it."

"No kidding," said Morris. "You know who he is?"

"Like every thug, he was destined to become a cop or criminal," said Dr. Poole. "He went with the former. He ended up as a chief of police on the Vineyard."

Morris shook his head. "You're not talking Hero Jordan, are you?"

"Hero?" asked the doctor.

Morris laughed. Apparently, he didn't intone the nickname with enough sarcasm. "Jim Jordan, I think his name is. He was a Boston cop."

Dr. Poole nodded along.

"Yeah," continued Morris. "Pretty much everyone I know who ever came across the guy thinks he's an asshole. He ended up getting nominated for a Hanna Award because he burned his hand trying to save some kid working in a manhole."

"An electrical fire or something?" asked Dr. Poole.

"No, this was pretty gruesome, doc. The kid was soldering spliced lines and a couple of solder pots got dumped into the manhole. Jordan was working a traffic detail nearby and tried to save him."

The doctor had a shocked look on his face. "Maybe I got him wrong? Maybe he turned a leaf after high school?"

"I wouldn't bet on it," Morris said. "The real story is Jordan was sleeping in a cruiser, and he milked the injury for all that he could, just to cover his ass. That's where the Hero Jordan thing comes from."

Dr. Poole shook his head with a sigh.

"In any case," said Morris. "I don't think you'll see me down the Vineyard any time soon. You can ask your cousin, but he'll tell you. I'm a scared paleface. I don't do well around asshole police chiefs or black polar bears. I think I'm going to have to decline that invite."

The doctor laughed. "Your brain and your mouth are working fine. The rest of you? Ah, what the hell." With that, he opened the folder and began to sign the medical form. "You're officially cleared for full duty starting tomorrow."

"Thanks, doc," Morris said.

"But if anyone questions my judgment," the doctor said, pulling back and waving his hand in a circle in front of Morris. "All this? That happened once you left here."

Morris laughed. "That's the same thing Trooper Paulie says when he gives me my sticker."

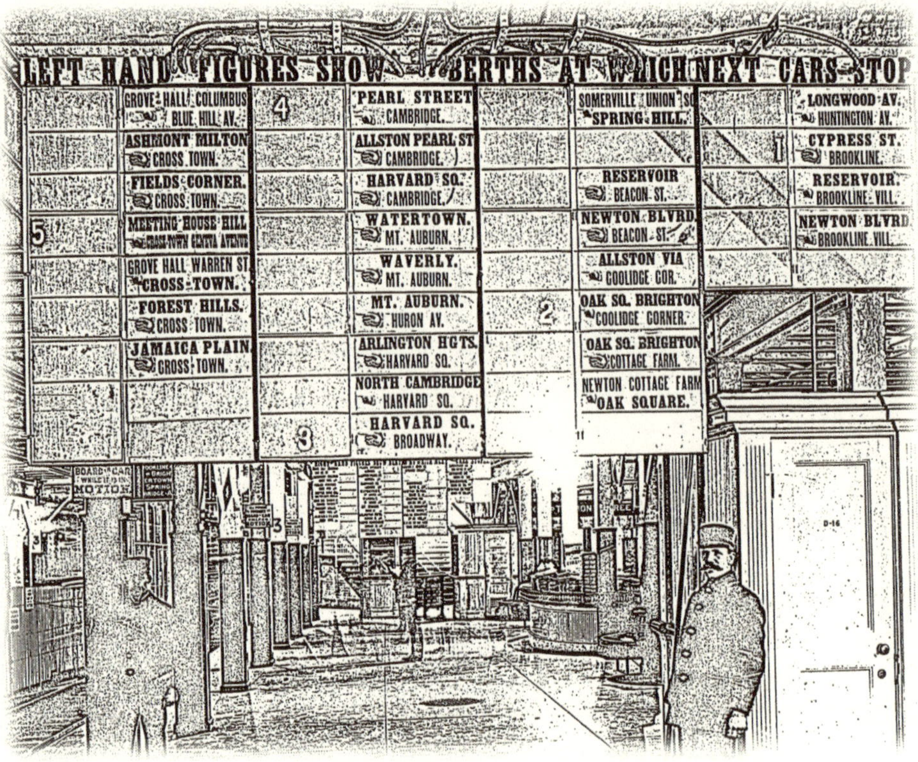

Chapter 5

Morris made it home from downtown Boston just before the crush of rush hour in the city. His journey was a fairly simple one. Exiting the Transportation Building, he walked the short distance to the Park Street subway station and picked up the outbound Red Line to South Boston.

While he could have taken a bus down South Boston's Broadway, he decided to walk the mile. It was a decent November day, and the exercise provided an opportunity to observe his changing hometown.

Rows of three-story buildings that had been homes to the working class had been wiped out and replaced by condos catering to the upper class working in the city's financial district and nearby waterfront. Southie always had the clout to resist politically imposed change, but every neighborhood had its price.

After the rest of the city went through its waves of gentrification, the developers eventually came knocking in South Boston.

As Morris stepped up the stairs of his triple-decker, he concluded there was a lot he missed about the old days but not enough. The Southie Pride culture that made his hometown so special had also given rise to the blind eye his neighborhood turned toward gangsters like Whitey Bulger and Wacko Barrett. Maybe it was time for a change.

"Oh hello there, Mr. Fitzgerald."

Morris turned to see his neighbor, Fillmore, who had moved into the triple-decker next to him last spring, coming toward him. It's not that the two were friendly, but they did exchange neighborly chit-chat, none of which gave Morris much of a clearer picture of the man other than he was a fish out of water.

The mailbox read Fillmore Drummond-Fox and Lavender Pitt-Lane. They seemed to be a couple hovering in their mid-30s, Fillmore perhaps slightly older. British, that much Morris could figure from the accent. Fillmore always introduced Lavender as his "partner" as opposed to his wife or girlfriend. For the first couple of months, Morris wondered if she might be a cross-dresser, but then the couple's 12-year-old boy, Gaylord, appeared mid-summer, apparently having finished at some overseas boarding school. It's not that he doubted modern medicine couldn't somehow yield offspring for a biologically male couple, but Morris eventually concluded that it wasn't a matter of gender-bending. They were just European.

"Hey, what's up Fillmore?" Morris said as the man came up the stairs.

"I just want you to know that the contractors will soon be doing the renovations on our condo," Fillmore said. "I've told them to be conscious of the parking situation, but I wanted to alert you all the same."

Morris nearly laughed at the term "parking situation." Having grown up in the neighborhood, he had learned to take for granted the art of double-parking, which was exercised quite liberally in Southie.

The original housing stock in the area served multiple generations, few of which owned a single car, never mind more than one. However, as times changed, more cars came to the neighborhood. Also, many of those triple-deckers had now been converted to apartments and condos, but Southie, like all of Boston, suffered a parking shortage.

So the pragmatic solution was to double park. You'd have the line of cars on either side of the road, and then another line next to one of those, usually leaving just enough space for a car to pass by. It worked because, back in the day, everyone knew each other and their schedules. If a mix-up happened, you knew the car and which house or pub to find the owner at.

"I'm sure it will be fine," Morris said to his neighbor. "How much work are you having done?"

"We're re-doing the roof deck. Lavender wants her own space there to relax in the good weather, and then we need to re-do one of the bedrooms as an au pair unit."

Fillmore and his wife both worked in the city's financial industry. Obviously, they weren't part of the Keno crowd who hung out at Tom English's pub hoping to make next month's rent by pissing away this month's.

"Au pair?" Morris queried.

Fillmore instantly laughed. "Oh yes, you call them nannies around here."

"In my day they were called baby sitters, but take your pick," Morris said.

"Yes, well our son can be a bit to handle still," Fillmore said. Even though the two men seemed worlds apart, there was something in Fillmore's tone that resonated, perhaps a subtle acknowledgment that his son was pampered. "Oh but that does remind me," continued Fillmore. "Lavender wanted me to ask you if you thought it safe for Butterfly to ride the tube at night."

"Butterfly?" Morris asked.

"So, sorry," Fillmore said. "That's our au – I mean nanny – she's one of Lavender's relations, a bit aimless I guess you could say. I think her family thought it might do her some good to be with us."

"Oh, so Butterfly's a bit flighty," Morris deadpanned, wondering if Fillmore would pick up on the humor.

"She's bright enough alright," he said, apparently missing the pun. "Just not quite attuned to the world just yet."

"Well, riding the T will fix that for her," Morris said with a laugh. "And it's the 'T," not the 'tube.' That's what we call a TV in these parts. You see, a lot of the system is above ground. It's right in the city where it goes underground, at the portals."

"Pardon?" interjected Fillmore.

"Portals," Morris repeated, being sure to block any of his Boston accent. "They're the holes the trains go into, in and out of the tunnels."

Fillmore nodded along.

"Anyway, the T is safe most of the time. Just tell her to avoid the guys playing pocket pool with themselves and anyone with an ankle bracelet. Oh, and always be on the look-out for apple pickers."

"Really?" asked Fillmore. "Where are the orchards around here?"

Morris grinned "Apple pickers, it's cop lingo for cellphone stealers."

"Oh, I see," said Fillmore.

"Yeah, pickpockets come and go. Usually, it's the worst in the fall with all the kids back in the city for school," explained Morris. "Same thing for the perverts. Each new wave of coeds is like herded hottie cattle for them. Never get on a train when its empty, but you don't ever want to get on when it's packed either. That's when they get their jollies, bumping and grinding. Guys get off the T and reflexively check to see if they have their wallet. Women get off and check bodies."

Morris caught himself from saying any more, realizing he may have been too blunt already.

"Well, thank you for that advice," Fillmore said. "By the way Lavender and I …."

Morris continued to hear Fillmore, but his eye had caught sight of a black Cadillac Escalade making its way down the street. The side windows were blacked out, but through the windshield, Morris thought he could make out the driver. He didn't like what he saw.

"Hey Fillmore, I wonder if you could do me a favor," Morris said as his neighbor stopped in mid-sentence. "I've been having this problem with my land line in my basement. If I let you in, you think you could just wait by the phone while I gave a call."

"Well ..."

Morris didn't wait for an answer. He opened the door and ushered Fillmore inside just as the Cadillac slowed out front. Morris moved down his steps, and stepped to the side, keeping a car between him and the encroaching vehicle.

He exchanged looks with the driver, who seemed to have no change of expression or agitation. Morris slowly walked around the car, lining himself up with the back of the Cadillac while keeping his eye on the driver's side mirror.

Suddenly, the backseat window lowered. A hand reached out and waved forward. "Get in."

Morris was instantly relieved, recognizing the familiar voice of Robert Powers, but as the door opened, he remained confused by Powers choice of driver. He looked into the backseat. "BoBo, how the hell are you?"

There weren't a lot of people who called Robert Powers "BoBo" any more. It's not that Powers shirked his childhood name, but the man was now worth a sizable fortune as the "Parking Lot King of Boston," as he used to refer to himself. He had come a long way since the days when he and Morris grew up together in Southie.

"I'm doing well my old friend," Powers said, his dark hair slicked back back in an attempt to hide a bald spot. "Get in. I have a business proposition for you."

"BoBo, we go back a long way, but I don't care for your taste in upholstery these days," Morris said, throwing a glance toward the front seat.

"Hey, fuck you," interjected the driver.

Morris looked up, and his eyes met those of the driver in the rearview mirror. It had been a couple of years since Morris had seen John Joseph McHugh. As kids in Southie, everyone took after his mother, calling him JJ, a cute-sounding nickname that belied the evil inside. Despite the years, JJ's ice-water gray eyes and mortuary pallor hadn't changed. It was another feature though – his seemingly long arms – that had earned the man another nickname in a neighborhood known for nicknames. He was the notorious Squid, whose secret to staying out of prison was injecting fear into witnesses so they would never testify against him or his boss, Wacko Barrett.

He would eliminate anyone who was dumb enough to talk – stool pigeons, tattletales, rats, squealers or Southie Snitches. Sometimes the technique, especially if the target were a known junkie was to inject them with a shot of heroin or Vitamin K, but for a more direct approach, he favored a pair of Louisville Sluggers, one in each hand, and those long arms would wind around, beating a potential witness into submission if not the after life.

Morris felt a ripple of unease go up his back, but he couldn't help himself. "Hey, Squid, how's Jakie the gravedigger doing? You know he got the shit beat out of him this morning by a girl cop?"

"Fuck you."

"Time to expand the vocab, JJ, and maybe your hair-care products, too, or did you just decide to stick a finger in a plug socket rather than use a hair dryer."

The driver turned with a cavernous smile that flashed hints of the monster underneath. There was no humor in his expression, only a deadly serious glare. "Fuck you, Mo the Fist. I'll be reading about you in the Irish sports pages soon enough."

The threat wasn't even veiled. Morris wasn't going to the let the Squid reference a forthcoming obituary for the T-cop, but Powers intervened.

"Enough with your Tourette moments gentlemen," said Powers with a hint of frustration. "I don't know what your blood feud is about, but it doesn't involve me. So John Joe, just get us out of here. Eyes on the road, mouth shut."

Morris looked around at the interior of the vehicle, black leather seats, maroon carpeting. "Jesus, BoBo, you travel in class these days."

"I also eat in class. You care to grab an early dinner in Chinatown?" asked Powers.

Truthfully, Morris had been hoping for a good nap, but if BoBo Powers was buying him a meal, he could stomach it. Just then

Morris remembered Fillmore. "Shoot, I gotta make a call," he said, pulling out his tattered cellphone.

"What? Do you have to cancel dinner plans or something?"

"Yeah," answered Morris. "I was going to order some deep-fried calamari." He didn't break his expression but saw Powers glance to the front seat. The Squid didn't make a sound. Morris loved getting in the last word.

The remaining ride to Boston's Chinatown neighborhood reminded Morris of standing on a deserted subway platform in the cold darkness, hearing distant creaks and whistles wondering if every sound is your train pulling in. Most people only ventured into the subway as part of some crowd, heading to work or escaping the city. But absent all the periphery, the tunnels could be the creepiest of settings, and every squeak of a wheel could just as easily be the tormented screams of the damned.

As they pulled in front of the Genghis Khan restaurant, Powers exited the car first. Morris stepped out and then leaned into the driver's side window, looking directly into the Squid's eyes. "Keep your hands off that bat under the seat unless you want me to shove it up your ass and turn you into chicken on a stick."

The Squid just flashed a smile of evil and said, "You may think you represent Boston strong, but I play for Boston wrong, and in this game, it doesn't matter who's right. It matters who's left."

The Squid then drove off, leaving Morris shaking his head. "What a tool," he said stepping toward the restaurant entrance.

As he entered, he looked for Powers, but apparently he had been seated already. Just as he was about to track down the hostess, he spotted the smiling face of the owner Henry Chin, better known as Dragonhead, the unofficial ruler of Chinatown.

"Mr. Fitzgerald, how are you?" Chin asked, extending both hands to greet Morris.

"Good," Morris said, caught a little off guard.

"You might remember, you were seated at my table at the annual Jade banquet along with Detective Moy," Chin explained. Homer Moy was an Asian T-cop who long ago had been nicknamed the Flyin' Hawaiian. "He says you're a good man," continued Chin. "You say hello to him for me?"

"Yes, Mr. Chin, will do. It's an honor to be in your establishment and also be a member of Jade."

In truth, Morris was more an honorary member of the Benevolent Asian Jade Society given his lack of Asian-American heritage, but his style of policing always seemed appreciated by the Chinatown community.

"Here, I'll take you to Mr. Powers," Chin said, ushering Morris toward a private room at the back of the restaurant.

Chin played no favorites in his establishment, and that was evident as Morris passed several tables, recognizing members of both law enforcement and crime syndicates, several seated together. Despite his affable persona, Dragonhead had a reputation that was both notorious and honorable. You could be assured that no word of any conversation you had inside his restaurant ever left the premise, whether by word-of-mouth or electronic means. Not even the FBI would dare bug the place. Plus, the General Gao's chicken was so good that no one would want to risk a lifetime ban.

Still, as Chin led Morris to the private room, the T-cop was certain he had spotted one of the city's most detestable figures heading toward an exit. The plump frame with the distinct white mustache gave away Charles Shanley, a former priest turned liberal talkshow host.

Chin escorted Morris into the room and excused himself, leaving the two men to their meal and conversation.

"BoBo, tell me that wasn't Charlie Shanley leaving this room," he said taking his seat.

"Don't worry yourself about it," the parking king replied.

Morris rolled his eyes. "Come on. The guy is like the Whitey Bulger of perverts. There's got to be so much dirt on him, and yet nothing sticks."

"Hey, even perverts need parking lots," quipped BoBo. "Come on my old friend, liberalize yourself a bit. So his sexual interests are different? Don't persecute him for it."

"I don't give a shit about his sexual disorientation," shot back Morris. "I couldn't care less. It's that he's a sleazebag. First the Squid and now Shanley, what the fuck are you into, BoBo?"

"Yeah, about that," said Powers. "I need you to bury the hatchet with JJ."

"He's always been a piece of shit," counseled Morris. "The Squid still controls the third rail mob, bunch of punks that loot T parking lots. Stereos, airbags, laptops, Xenon headlights, catalytic converters, you name it."

"Well, he's working for me now," said Powers. "He'll keep his nose clean."

Morris shook his head. "How did you end up with garbage like him?"

"Consider it a strategic alliance. JJ and his crew were so good at stealing from T lots, the Secretary of Transportation decided to privatize the worst of them. Crime reduction by outsourcing."

"You are a goddamn opportunist BoBo," Morris said with a laugh as a waitress brought over an appetizer.

"You got that right," Powers answered, glancing at the young Asian woman's figure. "So I pick up the contracts, and I figure rather than trying to fight the crooks, I'll hire them."

"I don't know BoBo. Be careful about inviting stray dogs into your house."

"Ahh," Powers responded, lifting a hand up to swat away the comment. "JJ is nothing without Wacko around to protect him. The guy is a half-wit. Malicious, I'll give you that. Let's just say that in my business, a man of his skills comes in handy from time to time."

Powers was right on one account. About a year ago, Wacko went into hiding after a series of indictments surfaced. Once his politically connected brother was no longer around, it turned out judges and prosecutors had finally found the guts to go after the gangster. Wacko skipped town leaving his deviant minions without any cover.

"I don't know," Morris said with sincerity. "It's just that Squid and me, we've got a lot of history. Actually, more like Squid and my cousins, but it's all the same. He was always chasing Cathy, and Happy, being the older brother and all, wouldn't have any of that."

Powers seem fixated on the appetizer and never gave a look at Morris, which led the T-cop to believe his host wasn't interested in hearing more.

"Well, what happened?" Powers eventually said, causing Morris to think he misread of his old friend.

"He's a creep, BoBo. A real pervert. You know how him and Wacko were. When they came around, you kept your girls off the street."

Powers nodded and reached for his water glass.

"The whole thing came to a head – no pun – at L Street one summer," Morris continued. "So you got the fences at L street...."

"The ones that give the nudes their privacy from the M Street beach on down," chimed in Powers.

"Exactly," Morris continued. "So Cathy is on one side, and the Squid is over on the other, and apparently he gets the idea that it would be funny or romantic or whatever to stick his dick through the fence. We're talking there are women and little girls on that beach. The guy is a piece of work, I tell you."

Powers shrugged.

"Anyway, the next thing you know, the Squid is howling." Morris started to laugh. "Cathy had grabbed her lighter and started roasting his wiener."

"You're shittin' me," said Powers.

"God honest truth. She yells, 'Does anyone else suffering the Irish Curse want to have his dick Bicked.'"

Powers laughed and then caught himself. Morris was a little surprised. Normally the jocular BoBo wasn't afraid of making such a scene.

"Anyway, ever since then, the Squid and my family have had issues. He tried to go after Cathy a couple of weeks later, and her brother pounded the shit out of him. So then he goes and gets a bat and cheap shots Happy. That was back when Sonny Barrett was an assistant DA. So Sonny got him put away on assault with a deadly weapon. Of course, he didn't serve much of it and ended up working for Sonny's brother."

"Funny how that happens," said Powers.

Morris could sense himself nodding, but let the discussion die at that point. Powers had something going on, and it was time to change subjects.

"Well, here's the deal my friend," Powers began after the pause. "I hear you're retiring, and I could use an old T-cop like yourself."

"You heard wrong BoBo. I was cleared to go back full duty, just a couple of hours ago as a matter of fact."

Powers smirked. Morris wondered where he was getting his information, but he was also curious just what the parking king of Boston had up his sleeve. "What have you got going on, BoBo?"

"I have a development project," Powers said cautiously. "I need people who know security, and it also helps if they have few connections here and there."

"BoBo, you're more connected these days than a Millennial with a smartphone," Morris shot back. It was true. Powers quietly had been donating significantly to local and state politicians for years. Rumor was he had significantly bankrolled the Lieutenant Governor's last election.

"You can always have more friends in your corner," said BoBo. "Hey are you still tight with Father Mike, the patron saint of the homeless?"

"I wouldn't say we're tight," said Morris. "Just what the hell you have going on?"

Powers laughed. "Let's just say I wouldn't *bet* against me."

Interesting choice of words. "Are you saying a casino, BoBo?"

"Maybe."

"Where? In Maine? How are you going to lock up the amount of land you need for something like that?"

Power's laughed. "You just have to be creative, Morris. If you worked for me, you'd take the T to work."

Morris ran through a few different locations in the city that might be ripe for a large development. None seemed to make much sense. "Where are you talking?" he asked finally.

"Let's just say I recently acquired some property, and I anticipate with the right negotiation, I'll be able to reach an arrangement on everything else. You let me worry about that. I just need people I can trust and who might be able to get a few others on board."

"Yeah, well, given your choice of driver, I'm not sure I should feel comfortable with your judgment."

"I thought you were going to drop that?"

"Sorry, BoBo. I'll tell you what. I'll submit my resume," said Morris. "But if you're looking for animal control, may I suggest you hire any of the old bus drivers who did the Boston school shuttles. That's someone who knows how to tame lions and tigers."

Powers smiled dismissing the advice, and then his expression changed quickly, as though an idea just came to him. "Hey, I'm having a little party Friday night at the SideCar Lounge in South Station," he said. "You ought to come by for a drink or two."

"I'll consider it," said Morris, but the truth was he doubted he would make it to any party hosted by BoBo. It wasn't that he'd turn down a free drink, but while the parking king may have grown up in Southie, he rubbed shoulders with a different crowd these days. In Morris' eyes, that's probably the way Powers preferred it. He was always working an angle, trying to get himself up and out of the neighborhood.

As a kid, Powers worked the stands at Fenway Park, selling popcorn. He and the other vendors would be given a set stack of buckets. They'd fill the buckets from large bags of popcorn and then sell them. At the end of the night, the concession manager would count up how many buckets they had left, subtract that from the total they had been given, and then he'd know how much money he was owed. He took the park's cut, and the vendors had what was left. Powers and a friend, Ed Walsh, figured out all they needed to do was round up the slightly used buckets that people had thrown out, use those for the popcorn they sold to fans, and they could pocket 100 percent of the sale.

"Hey BoBo," Morris said, taking a break from the Asian cuisine. "How is Edso Walsh these days?"

"Dead," Powers said, without looking up.

"Ah, sorry about that," Morris said. "I knew he fell on hard times."

Powers shrugged. Maybe it was money. Maybe it was age, but the parking king was no longer a benevolent ruler it seemed. Back in the day. Powers could be a bit of punk, but he always had your back. He and Walsh were as tight as brothers. By their early-20s they had moved on from scamming their bosses at Fenway Park to looting rail cars in the Lower Mills. A $10 set of bolt cutters was all the investment you needed to access some of the best merchandise coming into the city. Powers was always thinking a step ahead too. The story was he outfitted the entire Boston Police softball league with gloves and other equipment he and Walsh had swiped.

One night, though, a couple of the original T-cops chased them through the rail yard. Powers got away, but Walsh got clipped by a freight train and ended up losing his leg and two and a half years of his life at the Nashua Street jail. The word was he tried to rat out Powers, but the DA's office felt like it couldn't make a case. Morris occasionally used to see Walsh wandering the tunnels near the Prudential Center. Like so many others who had fallen to the bottom rung of society's ladder, he had been relegated to begging to stay alive.

In the meantime, Powers had gone legit. Thanks largely to his marrying into one of the city's wealthiest families, BoBo had the cash to find opportunity in Boston's longstanding plague of limited parking. He bought up a couple of lots near the financial district, realizing the suited transients of the city would pay anything to avoid having to take public transportation to work. From there, he worked more deals, and eventually amassed more real estate than the investment banks, law firms, and government agencies that spawned his clientele.

Along the way, Powers rose in wealth but not necessarily stature. He was what the locals called a K-Mart Kennedy. Boston's elite would never welcome him as one of their own despite his marriage. He didn't go to Harvard or any college for that matter. He was a scrapper from Southie who had done alright for himself, but now as he gave the waitress yet another lascivious look, Morris wondered if maybe BoBo wasn't so distant from the Squid after all.

"What's with that?" Morris asked

"What?"

"How's your wife Debbie doing these days?"

Powers rolled his eyes. "She's fine."

"Uh huh," said Morris. "I don't think she'd approve if you came down with a case of yellow fever."

"I'm just looking," said Powers. "No touching or our pre-nup gets triggered, and I'd be fucked – figuratively and literally," he added with a laugh.

"Yeah, well be careful where you look or next week Henry Chin might put BoBo Balls on the menu."

The two laughed. As much as he didn't trust Powers, he might be a better employer than the MBTA. Morris was getting too old to be running through tunnels and wrestling with pickpockets. Maybe it was a good idea to join Powers.

"Hey BoBo," Morris said. "Just don't underestimate the Squid."

"Harmless," Powers replied.

"More like ruthless," responded Morris.

Chapter 6

Morris couldn't sleep. He didn't feel physically sick, but mentally his mind was twisting in so many ways his head ached. Yes, he had been cleared for full duty, but once he got home last night, he gave into the prescription medication to make his brain feel better, and then, as had become his routine, he had a couple drinks to settle him for sleep.

He was worried that the little pills that he took were more dangerous than a loaded gun pointed to his head. At least one to the temple would take the pain away, but as his wife always surmised, long before she was diagnosed with breast cancer, it's not the deceased you worry about. It's the ones who are left behind. He couldn't leave his daughters just yet. Between the two of them, he had four more tuition payments to make. He had borrowed against his retirement and his triple decker. He might have to work until he was 80, but he'd fulfill the promise he and his late wife made to each other.

BoBo's job offer was attractive, but the truth was, even as a kid, you wouldn't trust Powers. He was always playing an angle, and if that angle happened to be a friend, so be it.

Morris rolled over and felt the familiar pain in his head. He wondered if the doctors misdiagnosed the concussion. Maybe the migraines were a chronic hangover or just his conscience finally catching up to him, propelled by his latent Irish Catholic guilt and his inability to shake the faith that shaped him. Still, he doubted he could tell the difference between the sacred and the sordid anymore.

His destiny had been shaped by the streets of Southie, which was ruled by wise guys who handed out their own form of justice and demanded loyalty. They punished the heretics by putting two bullets into the back of the head. His Irish Catholic faith was ruled by wise men who handed out wafers and who punished sinners by banishing them to a place called hell. In both cases, you either became a member of the faithful or you learned to fake it.

Funny though, Southie was changing. He'd have bet the neighborhood would've outlasted Catholic dogma. Still, his faith didn't scare him much. At least if he went to hell, he'd be among friends, he thought.

Over the past eighteen months, there were times the pain in his head was so severe that he had to crawl up the stairs to his triple-decker. He needed help, but like most stubborn ex-Marines from South Boston, the only psycho shrinks available were your drill instructor, original gangsters, or Bruins chicks from the Old Harbor projects, posing in their bathrooms, chanting "Mirror, mirror on the wall who's the biggest bitch of all?"

He had to keep working. He wasn't going to let down his daughters and late-wife.

Suddenly, his reverie was disturbed by a blast of rap music blaring from the kitchen. He couldn't make out all the lyrics except "rage of the renegade" and "the white man is the devil."

Morris got up from his bed screaming, "Turn that rap shit off!" Despite the disturbance, a sense of relief came over Morris. His daughter Ellen must have stopped by to check on him. As he threw on a pair of sweatpants and a T-shirt, he yelled down to the kitchen, where the music had softened slightly in volume but not in content. "Ell, you know that stuff's a poor excuse for music. How about some Standells?"

With that, the lyrics got louder, and he hurried down the stairs into the kitchen to see his daughter having coffee, and his friend, Elijah, standing near a Bluetooth speaker with his cellphone out.

"Very funny. If you two are trying to kill me with black rap music, you have succeeded."

With that Ellen looked at Elijah. "Whoa! Did you hear that? Dad called it 'black!'"

"What do you mean?" asked Morris.

"You never call anything black," said Ellen. "Because that means someone will call you 'white,' and you hate that."

"I don't hate it," said Morris. "It's just not accurate."

"Seriously, Ellen," chimed in Elijah. "I've seen him turn an ethnicity checkbox into an essay."

"Maybe he has a point," Ellen said, going back to her coffee. "He's kind of more pinkish than white."

"Almost red if he's been drinking or mad," added Elijah.

It was too early in the morning for Morris to match wits with his daughter and friend. "What are you doing here?" he asked Elijah.

"I'm here to see if you wanted a ride to work."

"What do you mean? I'm not back on full-time until next week," answered Morris.

"Not work work," said Elijah. "They're dedicating the Barrett training facility this morning."

"Oh Jesus," said Morris. "Barrett training facility? What do they train you to do there? Be an asshole?"

"You're awfully cheery today," Elijah said. "Come on. Put a suitcoat and tie on. Steph's going to introduce the new deputy director Homeland sent our way."

"I can't," said Morris. "I'm meeting Goldi at the Aquarium Station."

"Goldi?" responded Elijah. "What does she want?"

"Nothing. I called her last night. I figured she might help me find my cousin."

Elijah nodded. "She's a good place to start."

Officer Susan Sann was the MBTA's homeless liaison. She was the Mother Theresa of the tunnels. That is if Mother Theresa were a 5' 4" blond who swore like a truck driver and could fight like one too. Sann had a big heart that went along with her cop sensibilities. She earned her street credibility and nickname, Goldilocks, when she broke up a robbery crew who relied on the wolfpack approach, surrounding their victims and then intimidating, if not beating, them into giving up their valuables.

Sann volunteered to go undercover and managed to single-handedly arrest all of them. Of course, that was after two of them required medical treatment, one for a broken nose and the other for a ruptured testicle. When word got around that the crew was Russian, the story turned into a tale of Goldilocks and the Three Bears. In truth, only one of the three was Russian, but no real T-cop would let facts get in the way of a good nickname.

Morris arched his back. "Hey maybe on the way, we can swing by Sullivan's over at Castle Island for some hot dogs and fries."

Ellen shook her head. "No way, dad. You have to start taking care of yourself. Stop eating that crap."

Elijah laughed. "Ellen, you don't understand. Your father loves hot dogs because it reminds him of his style of policing. He just wants to see the end results without having to know the ingredients."

"Very funny," said Morris.

Elijah shook his head while looking back to Ellen. "You know your father works like a mule."

"He thinks like one too," she said. "Should you tell him about that 'black' rap?"

The two laughed, and Morris felt he had been left out of a joke. "What?" he asked.

"The rapper is a white kid," said Elijah. "Oh pardon. He is American of western-European descent," he corrected himself with sarcasm. "His name is Slaine. You'd like him. He's got a song about the opioid crisis in Southie."

"I think I'm having an opioid crisis in Southie," responded Morris. "My best friend and daughter are giving me shit, and I haven't had my morning coffee yet."

"Coffee, I can do," said Elijah. "But I'm with Ellen on the hot dog. You've got to start taking care of yourself, buddy."

With that Morris grabbed his coat, gave his daughter a kiss, and then joined Elijah in leaving the triple-decker for a double-parked MBTA cruiser.

The two T-cops picked up some coffee at a drive-through. On the way over to the Aquarium T stop, the two talked about their families and the potential for getting together over the forthcoming holidays.

When Elijah pulled the cruiser off to the side of Atlantic Avenue so that Morris could get out, Morris thanked him for the ride.

"Tell Steph I'm sorry that I can't be there," he said.

"She wasn't expecting you to be. I don't think anyone was," Elijah said with a smile.

Morris nodded and stepped out of the cruiser. He shut the door, gave a wave, and then headed toward the Aquarium T stop, which sits on a section of waterfront adjacent to Boston's historic Long Wharf.

The brisk morning foretold of another Boston winter that would soon be upon the region. The skies had cleared overnight, but there were still puddles on the street from the recent rains. Morris turned the corner and glanced at the New England Aquarium, which gives the T stop its name.

While this part of the city was geographically removed from the density of the financial district, it remained one of the most active sections of Boston, echoing to the days when the harbor served as the city's commercial lifeblood.

What most Bostonians didn't know was that Long Wharf used to be much longer. At one time it stretched nearly a half mile into Boston Harbor, but it had shortened over the years, not by being lopped off at its sea end, but by having the land enlarged on its shorefront.

The filling of the Boston Harbor since the early 1700s had brought land closer to its tip, but it was the construction of the elevated central artery in the 1950s that cut it and much of Boston's waterfront off from the rest of the city. Even before completion of the central artery, city leaders realized their own folly, and put the last section of the highway underground, and thus began a movement that eventually led to Boston's $15 billion boondoggle, the Big Dig, which saw the elevated Interstate 93 replaced with an underground tunnel.

The politicians sold the public and the federal government on its necessity as a traffic project, but truthfully it was about aesthetics, reconnecting the city with its waterfront.

As Morris stood at the Aquarium T stop entrance, he noticed a collection of silt and debris piled up against the side, no doubt remnants of the last storm. In Boston's suburbs at this time of year, the falling leaves would raise concern about clogging street drains. In Boston, the foliage was of a different sort – the discarded urban refuse – but the impact was just the same. Trash in the gutters could turn a downpour into a small flood.

Morris proceeded down the long escalator, ending up on the outbound platform of one of the MBTA's prettiest, but deepest, stations. Designed with a vaulted ceiling, intended to evoke parallels to the Paris Metro, the Aquarium stop was the jewel among the T's typically utilitarian subway stops.

Originally the station was known as Atlantic Avenue, but in the 1960s, it was renamed in anticipation of the new aquarium being built. At that time, the section of the transit system was already nearly 70-years-old and featured the engineering marvel of the East Boston tunnel.

As Morris walked the platform, he saw an older couple trying to make sense of the T's color-coded map, which the transit police referred to as a spider map given the way the T lines appear to radiate out from the center, downtown Boston.

"Need any help?" Morris asked as he stepped within earshot of the couple.

"Oh, well, thank you," said the elderly man as he turned toward Morris and appeared to size up his intentions.

"Yes, we're a bit lost," chimed in the woman without hesitation.

Morris laughed slightly. "Well, I've been working in these tunnels for thirty years. I'll see what I can do for you."

"Oh do you drive the trains?" asked the woman.

"No, I'm a transit cop," Morris said, detecting some ease come over the gentleman's face.

"Oh lucky for us!" said the woman. "We're down here from Kennebunkport, you know, Maine."

"Yes, I'm familiar," said Morris. "You have the Seaside Trolley Museum there."

"Yes," said the man.

"Yeah, we know it pretty well here," said Morris. "Occasionally, we have to call them up to get spare parts for some our trains."

The coupled laughed heartily.

"I'm not kidding," said Morris. "If you get a chance, get out to the Ashmont-Mattapan line, off the Red Line, you'll see some antiques running there."

"Red," said the man with some confusion while looking at the map.

Morris took a step toward the map. "Here," he said pointing at the Aquarium stop. "You're on the Blue Line right now. It's the shortest line in the T system." He moved his finger to the left and began tracing the line. "Here, it starts at Bowdoin Square in Beacon Hill and goes up to Wonderland in Revere." He looked at the two. "Did you ever see the movie *Next Stop Wonderland*?"

The couple shook their heads.

"Ah, so-so movie, but some good shots of the T and the Blue Line."

"So all the lines here are by color?" asked the woman.

"Yep, pretty much," said Morris. "We picked blue for this line for water. We were the first subway to stick a tunnel under a body of water, namely the Atlantic Ocean. You'll get a kick out this, the Blue Line cars are unique in that they use both the third rail and an overhead catenary pantograph."

The couple gave each other looks of surprise and delight. Morris smiled along and noticed some others had gathered to listen to his insight.

"OK, so the other lines," he continued. "The Red Line at one time ended at Harvard Station. Crimson is Harvard's color, so that was an easy one. The Orange Line originally ran overhead along Washington Street, which had a section named Orange Place or Orange Way, something like that. Now, the Green Line, that goes through the so-called Emerald Necklace. Frederick Law Olmsted, the same guy who did Central Park in New York, he had this plan for all these parks surrounding Boston, you know, like a necklace."

The couple nodded, and by now a few more T patrons had turned toward Morris.

"So the Green Line runs through Boston and Brookline, where a lot of those parks are. So that explains that color. The Purple Line is our commuter rail servicing the suburbs. Purple is the color of royalty, luxury. So you figure that's a good color for those folks who think the commuter rail is their own private train or something."

He could hear a few snickers and saw one yuppie-looking gentleman appear offended. "OK, that gets us to the Silver Line, which really isn't a subway line. It's just a bunch of buses painted silver. I'm not sure why they picked the color, but pretty much all the community leaders call it the 'silver lie' because it basically cost a ton of money and took forever to get running."

"Well, we stay clear of buses," said the elderly gentleman.

"The good news is it's November. In the summertime, they turn off the AC on the Silver Line and passengers roast like popcorn kernels. It's getting better, and it's pretty much the future of public transit. It just costs too much to dig new tunnels."

"And how old is this tunnel?"

Morris heard the voice, but it didn't come from the couple or anyone in front even though it sounded familiar.

"You don't want to know," Morris said looking at the crowd as the squeal of a subway train drowned him out. The small crowd quickly dissipated and the couple waved goodbye to Morris as they moved toward the train.

As the crowd thinned, Morris was finally able to place the voice. "Jesus Christ, Goldi, I thought that was you."

She stepped toward Morris. Her dirty blond hair was tucked up under a worn Red Sox hat. She was wearing yellow Grundens waterproof overalls, Sperry boots, and a Carhartt jacket. She could have just stepped off a lobster boat. "Sorry, I was just giving you shit!"

She then gave him a hug. Sann was a friend to all unless you gave her a reason otherwise. "I was hiding behind the welfare mom with the six bags of groceries and the kiddie carriage bigger than Old Ironsides."

Sann then shifted her expression. "So what's new with you? I thought you retired or something."

"No, not yet, at least."

"Good, you're one of the few people I can fuckin' stand on this job."

"Really Goldi?"

"Oh, I love the people. It's the bullshit bureaucracy I can't stand," she said.

Morris had known Sann long enough to understand that when she said 'people,' she meant the homeless of the city, not necessarily her co-workers. Sann preferred to work alone. As homeless liaison, she held a job no one else wanted, and as she pointed out, if an officer with male genitalia had wanted the position, he would have been selected, in part due to the screw up on her last assignment. She had been patrolling the South Station bus terminal, better known to T-cops as 'Terminal Illness' when she spotted a pimp trying to recruit young girls. She arrested the Mack Daddy, but the case was eventually thrown out. She was now being sued by the pimp in federal court.

Such was the life of a female cop. Males wouldn't be considered a screw-up until they made ten times the mistakes a female did. Of course, the exception was the former chief, Claire Barrett, but that was only due to the fact that the most corrupt and powerful politician in the state was her father-in-law. As the new chief, Steph Tam found herself on thin ice with the state leadership even though she was a world better than Barrett ever could have been.

Sann had learned the hard way that in policing, females had to work twice as hard to prove themselves to be accepted while male officers gained acceptance by showing up.

"So what's up?" asked Sann. "Your message said you're trying to locate someone."

"Yeah," answered Morris. "I'm looking for my cousin Cathy."

"Oh, right," said Sann. "I think I met her before at St. Anthony's. I remember her dropping your name once or twice."

"Yeah, that sounds like her," Morris said with an eye roll.

"What's that about?"

"I shouldn't," said Morris, feeling guilty. "It's just that side of my family tends to be a pain in the ass. Honestly, though, I really should check in on them more."

"I get it. You can't pick family," Sann said.

Morris then pulled out his phone, trying to scroll through his pictures for one that included his cousin.

"What the fuck, Morris?" Sann said looking at his broken device. "The '80s called, and they want their technology back."

"Come on, Goldi, you weren't even alive in the '80s."

"Yeah, but I've heard rumors. Serious, you need to upgrade," she said pulling out her phone. "They call these 'smart' for a reason."

"Well don't be a smartass," Morris said, closing his phone, realizing he didn't have a picture of his cousin on it.

"Don't worry, it's not so smart these days," she said. "Last storm, I was chasing some bag-opener off the Green Line, down by BU, and it ended up in a puddle the size of the Quabbin Reservoir."

Morris grinned, not at the reference to the state's largest body of water, but at picturing Goldilocks tackling some pickpocket.

"Anyway, it's all fucked up now," she said still holding her phone. She then tucked it away and said, "Listen, let's go up top and cut over to the emergency exit. Most of the homeless don't come down here anymore."

"Gotcha, Goldi. They probably prefer up top and the fresh air and sunshine."

"Not so much that," said Sann, "They've been getting hassled a lot in the tunnels. The emergency exit is harder to get to, but no cops go there either."

"Which cops?" asked Morris as the two climbed on the escalator back to street level.

“To be honest, I’m not sure. Supposedly it’s not the T. The BPD says it’s not them, but someone is rousting the homeless.”

“Who knows?” responded Morris. “Probably some politician who got tired of looking at the problem caused by their own politics.”

Sann grinned and looked at Morris as the two stood on the escalator. “I’ll make a liberal out of you yet.”

“Who says I’m not? I just have a low tolerance for bullshit.”

The two left the entrance to the Aquarium T stop and turned to head toward the Chart House restaurant, a city institution that began life as a brick warehouse. Morris noticed the silt and debris piled up next the T entrance.

“It looks like someone has been dumping their shit here.”

“King Tides,” said Sann.

“King who?” responded Morris.

“King Tides. There’s a couple of high tides in the fall that are stronger than the others. The last one pushed water up over the bulkhead. We were probably half a foot away from flooding Aquarium.”

Morris remained silent but did the calculation in his head. As one of the deepest T stops, Aquarium would have been like a floor drain in a flooded basement.

“Yeah, they’re talking more rain on Thursday,” continued Sann. “Lieutenant Fredette is already freaking out, trying to cover extra shifts.”

As they made their way down the block, Morris spotted the huge puddles of water. “It looks like Long Wharf is getting shorter,” he joked. Just then a food truck made a wake through an adjacent puddle, splashing the two T-cops.

“Fucking food trucks,” grumbled Sann. “They’re ice cream trucks for fat people.”

Morris turned and grinned at Sann. “I’ll make a curmudgeon out of you yet.”

When they reached the door to the Blue Line emergency exit, Sann unlocked it with her key. The two each pulled out a flashlight as Morris stepped aside. “After you, Princess of Tides.”

Sann sneered back and then proceeded inside. They descended the steps toward the Aquarium stop below. The steps were damp and slippery, and Morris could feel his sneakers getting wet with the frigid water. Just then, he felt a powerful hand grab him from behind. He tried to break the grip, but it was futile.

"Leroy, don't hurt him," he heard Sann say in the darkness. "He's with me."

Morris felt the hand let go. At the mention of the name, Morris immediately recognized who had grabbed him even though he had yet to see his face. Leroy was the given name of a homeless man better known as the Tin Man to those in the subway. A former linebacker for the New England Patriots, he fell on hard times due to injury. A shady agent and Leroy's ex-wife stole most of his money. That which was left, Leroy wasted on crack cocaine, which became his one-way ticket to the tunnels of the MBTA.

He was no longer welcome in most of the city's homeless shelters. His size and strength alone terrified most of the inhabitants, but supposedly he had been prone to violent outbursts, possibly linked to a history of steroid use. There was also rumor that he had a metal plate in his head due to a football injury.

While Morris couldn't confirm that rumor, he did know that Leroy got his moniker from the elder member of the city's homeless population, Beetlejuice. Beetle was the Keith Richards of the subterranean population. A lifetime of drugs and abuse only seemed to make him stronger. Even when Morris first came on the force more than thirty years earlier, Beetle was already well established in the subway.

The Tin Man name came from the fact that Leroy had no qualms about smearing grease on his face and exposed skin to keep out the cold in the winter. It wasn't quite Oil of Olay, but truthfully, the old football player didn't seem to age. His strength certainly hadn't weakened.

"Oh, Mo the Fist," the Tin Man said as Morris turned.

"Hey Tin," he said trying to take care not shine his flashlight in his face. Morris had three decades working in the tunnels. Most of the new T-cops were hesitant to venture too far off a subway platform. The labyrinth of abandoned tunnels mixing with those in use was dangerous enough, but the inhabitants of the underground could be like wild animals.

Goldilocks didn't necessarily understand that. She wanted to pet them and take them home. Morris had learned that even the cutest and cuddliest of the subway homeless could turn rabid in an instant. That's what happens when you've been deprived of sunlight, fresh air, and normal social contact.

"How have you been Leroy?" Sann said in a pleasant voice.

"I'm good Susie," he said breaking into a big smile. Then he turned toward Morris and grabbed his hand to shake it. "And good to see you Mo the Fist."

Sann had a way of putting people of all sorts at ease. Of course, as Morris felt his hand engulfed by Leroy's massive paw, he recalled his first encounter with the Tin Man. A deranged mountain of a man had thrown a female passenger into the path of an inbound train at Downtown Crossing. The woman survived with two broken legs but suffered major trauma. Transit police dispatch reported a suspect with – of all things – war paint on his face. Morris ran down the stairs at Park Street and spotted the Tin Man. He tried to take Leroy down, grabbing him by the throat. Instead, Leroy picked up Morris and body-slammed him to the platform. Several T-cops came to his aid and managed to overpower the former NFL linebacker.

It turned out that the real culprit was in a brawl with Boston Police on the Common. He, in fact, was wearing war paint – and buckskins. Morris apologized to Leroy, and from that day on, he made a point of saying hello to the man. Over time, Tin Man trusted him, and that proved valuable in helping Morris understand the complex subway ecosystem.

Now as Morris glanced down the emergency stairwell of the Blue Line, realizing how easily Leroy could have tossed him over the side, at least a hundred feet to his death, he wondered how secure their trust was.

"Leroy, we're wondering if you could help us find someone," Sann said as Morris' flashlight caught the Tin Man's profile, his ebony skin hidden behind layers of grime and his long hair matted like a tangled mop.

"Her name's Cathy," said Morris. "Blond, gray hair. She usually hangs out down near the Common or Prudential?"

"No one is down there anymore," said the Tin Man bruskly. He then stepped past Morris and started down the stairwell.

Morris tried to think of something to say to retreat from the nerve he apparently just struck, but the Tin Man spoke first.

"Come on," he said looking back. "We need to see my friend. He might know, but not many of us hang out down there anymore." Then he looked back. "Bad cops."

Morris and Sann continued down the stairwell until they reached the tier directly above the Aquarium stop. It looked as though it was an abandoned storage area with several boxes tied to the ceiling. As Morris was trying to make sense of the scene, he saw the boxes start to shift, and a diminutive figure jumped out from behind them.

"What? What!" shouted a fastidiously groomed man, who Morris instantly recognized as Gary the Gnome, one of the shortest adults known in the tunnels.

"Relax," said Leroy.

"Hello Gary, remember me?" Sann said reaching out a hand. Gary's expression changed immediately upon seeing Goldilocks. "Gary this is my friend," she said, preparing to introduce her fellow T-cop.

"No need, Goldi," Morris said. "Gary and I go back a long way."

Suddenly, a black cat leaped from the darkness, and Morris stumbled, but before he lost his balance, the powerful grasp of the Tin Man seized him.

"So sorry about that," said a voice in the darkness.

Morris gave the Tin Man a look of appreciation as he got his feet back underneath him. The Tin Man quietly acknowledged it as he loosed his grip on Morris' shoulder. At that moment, he saw another figure step from the shadows and gain illumination from the flashlights the two T-cops held. He, or maybe she, had reddish hair.

"Ginger, your cat nearly scared the shit out of us," said Sann.

"My apologies," said the feminine voice. "Here, Nightmare, here," and she let out a little whistle to which the black cat responded.

"Yes, Ginger, Officer Fitzgerald and I were just being reacquainted," Gary said.

Morris took a moment to gather himself. Then he let out a small laugh. "I haven't seen you since your Wung Fah bus days," he said.

Gary smiled, but Morris couldn't tell what emotion the man might be feeling. He was trying to break the ice, but right now he and Sann were out-numbered three to two, and one of those three was Leroy.

"I could have been a millionaire were it not for you meddling T-cops," Gary said playfully.

"Oh, I have to hear this," said Sann.

"Yeah, this was before your time," Morris said to Sann. He then looked at Gary.

"Go ahead," said the tiny thief. "I paid my debt to society. I have nothing to hide."

"Stop me if you've heard this one, Goldi," Morris began. "Remember the Wung Fah bus?"

"You mean that bus line that got shut down because they were losing axles and shit on the road?" she asked.

Morris shot a glance at Gary and the Tin Man. All saw the humor in Sann's choice of expletive. "Yes, well our friend here and a partner, who we never nabbed mind you, would work together." Morris' eyes then settled on Ginger. "He or maybe she would stuff Gary into a suitcase and put him and an empty suitcase into the hold of the bus. Once on the road, Gary would rifle through the other passengers' stuff, put any good loot in the empty suitcase, and then zip himself back up."

"Not the most luxurious way to travel, but it did have its perks," Gary added.

Sann was laughing. "Gary, you hot shit."

Morris tried to contain his own laughter. "Gary, how long had you and your partner gotten away with this? Months? Years?"

"A true artist doesn't reveal such things."

Morris chuckled. "Anyway, passengers complained, and it gets back to us. So Elijah comes up with the idea of putting a camera in the cargo hold."

"Oh so that's how they bagged you, Gary," said Sann.

"Not entirely," said Morris. "That bus company sucked so bad, that when they were putting the camera in, they accidentally cracked the tank holding all the shit from the bathroom. So when Gary gets out to do his thing, he is sloshing around in all the stuff from the passengers having done their thing."

"Awww disgusting!" groaned Sann.

"Exactly. So Gary starts pounding on the cargo hold. Finally, the bus driver pulls over, and out comes Gary the Gnome covered in shit."

"I could have died in there."

"In any case, the judge sentenced him to a couple of months at South Bay. He never did give up his partner even though he could have gotten off with just probation."

"What can I say," said Gary. "Snitches get stitches."

The entire group laughed along.

"So we need some help," said Sann shifting the conversation.

"They're looking for Chaffy," said Tin Man.

Morris paused on hearing the derivation of his cousin's name. He didn't know that's what she was called among her peers in the subway, but there was something oddly comforting about the fact that she was known and had her own name.

Gary remained silent.

"She's got gray hair, maybe a little blond, been known to use needles," said Morris.

"We know her," said Ginger sharply.

Gary looked at his accomplice as if to admonish her for being rude. "She comes and goes around here, but she's not shy about mentioning her T-cop relative."

Morris was at a loss for words.

"It's OK," said Ginger. "She's lucky. You're one of the good ones."

"Hey, we're all good ones," said Sann, looking at the three homeless in front of her. She paused. "Fuck that, you're right. Some of us are assholes."

The group laughed again. Sann's diplomacy was unique but effective.

"The last I saw her, she was down near the Fens," said Ginger.

Morris nodded. The homeless of the city, especially those that used the subway as their primary domicile had a migratory pattern. It fluctuated with the weather. Winter was the peak occupancy for the tunnels, often near the major stations like Park Street, where there could be an assurance of ample warmth.

In the better weather, the homeless weren't much unlike the better-off residents of Greater Boston. On their own schedules, they would venture to more distant places. While Bostonians might vacation among the vistas of Cape Cod or Maine, the homeless would venture to scenic shores of the waterways in Boston, finding a convenient overpass under which to set up camp until they were tossed by police. While the Charles was the best-known river in the city, one of its tributaries, the Muddy River, was really a series of brooks and streams that wound its way through the Emerald Necklace, including the Back Bay Fens.

It was a pretty stretch, and one the Fitzgeralds would occasionally visit alongside their cousins in the day. Again, guilt fell over Morris for looking at Happy and Cathy as baggage more than family.

"Morris, what size boot do you take?"

Morris shook his head to stir him from his reflection.

"What's that Gary?"

"I've got a pair of Timberlands, retail value two-twenty."

Morris laughed. Gary was a capitalist through and through.

"You ought to take it Morris," said Sann. "Your sneakers are soaked."

"In that case, I'll throw in a pair of socks," added Gary.

"What do you think you're doing?" Morris said, allowing a touch of anger to show in his voice. "I'm a cop, and you're trying to sell me hot merchandise?" The three homeless and Sann held blank expressions. "And you're expecting me to pay retail?" he added breaking into a smile.

Gary turned to Ginger. "What kind of police discount do we have for T-cops?"

"There is no police discount," Ginger said flatly. "But for Mo the Fist, let's say thirty dollars for everything."

Morris looked at the redhead. Something seemed familiar, and he wondered if between age and concussions, his brain wasn't beginning to slip.

"Come on, Morris, you cheap shit," Sann said. "You're not going to get a better deal."

Morris blew out a sigh and agreed to the payment. "I should notify the real estate department to increase your rent," he joked as he fished through his pocket for his wallet. As he did so, he took out his cellphone.

"Oh sergeant," said Gary. "We can get you a good deal on a cellphone, too."

"I don't know," said Morris, holding his broken flip phone. "This guy has been pretty reliable for me."

But the undersized hustler was already moving some boxes around, finally emerging with a container filled with several small cartons in them. "Here," he said. "The latest from our supplier in Asia."

"Supplier?" queried Morris.

"See for yourself," said Gary. "All unopened. We're not some pickpockets, you know."

Morris looked them over. It was probably time he gave up on his flip phone, and he doubted he would get a better deal. He took at look at Sann, whose expression said she agreed.

"We're talking 5G technology, GPS, WiFi, LTE-direct," said Gary.

"LTE-direct?" said Sann. "That's pretty cool."

"I used to drive a Ford LTD," joked Morris. "Is that the same thing?"

Sann smirked. "LTE direct, it lets two phones work like walkie-talkies. They can talk to each other even though they can't get a cell signal."

"As I said, the latest technology from the Far East," interjected Gary. "I'll even work a two-for-one deal."

"How much?" asked Morris.

"A hundred dollars for two of them," said the Gnome.

Morris looked at Sann, who nodded enthusiastically. The two T-cops then managed to cobble together the cash.

“How do I set this thing up?” Morris asked as he handed over the money.

“Here,” said Ginger, reaching out her hand.

With that Morris and Sann gave their old phones to the redhead. Within moments she had them apart and had opened the shrink-wrapped cartons containing the new phones. A few moments later, after moving a tiny card from the old to the new, she powered them on and handed them back to the two T-cops.

“You should be all set now,” she said.

Morris admired the service and reminded himself that the homeless, despite their limited resources, generally were quite technologically adept.

The Tin Man then guided the two T-cops back to the emergency exit, Morris carrying his soaked sneakers and socks all the way. They exchanged goodbyes, and the two T-cops exited the emergency stairwell and headed back toward Long Wharf and the Aquarium Station entrance.

Morris turned to Goldilocks. “I’m old, and my bones are creaky. I think I’m going to head home and take a nap.”

Sann laughed.

“Seriously,” said Morris, “I don’t know whether I’ll be able to sleep without dreaming of that red-headed grim reaper and her cat.”

“Ahh Ginger, she’s nothing. She seemed to like you,” said Sann.

“Listen to me Goldi,” Morris said. “The Tin Man, you can trust him, but those other two, they’re subway vermin who will someday paint the tunnel walls with your guts if you’re not careful.”

Goldilocks gestured with both hands “I’m always careful. I’ll tell you what the most dangerous part of my job is. It’s going into headquarters and dealing with all my fucking bosses.”

“All?” queried Morris.

“Oh, you don’t understand the shit of it. So I’ve got a lieutenant that I report to, but then I’ve got the assistant General Manager for community outreach, or some fucked up title like that, and then I also report to Turley or at least he thinks I do.” She paused for a breath. “And they’re all fuckin’ men. No offense.

But I mean, really, what is it with guys and tits? I mean you never check out my boobs, but like all of them always do."

Morris felt a little trapped as to whether Goldilocks was asking him to look at her body.

"I'm wearing a fuckin' flannel shirt. It's not like I am out clubbin' or something. Those fuckin' creepy guys. It's like you've never seen boobs before? What the fuck?"

"Geez, Goldi, sorry." Morris wanted to say more. The truth was underneath that worn Sox hat, unkempt hair and lobsterman wardrobe, he was sure there was an attractive woman. Maybe it was his age or Goldilocks' personality, but he always looked at her as just another T-cop. Granted, he much preferred her company over the likes of a cop like Claire Barret.

"It's not like I'm a lesbian or something," Sann continued on her rant. "I like guys, but I am not going to run around in heels and a skirt, and be all fuckin' Barbie. The right ones never notice you anyway. It's just all the fuckin' creeps."

Morris contemplated telling Goldilocks that when he and Claire Barrett first joined the force, she had hit on him quite a bit. Of course, while it passed a definition of harassment, he knew it wasn't the same thing that Goldi and other women like Steph Tam dealt with. It probably wasn't until his own daughters were born that he gained perspective on the male persona. Goldi stayed on her rant, though.

"And I'll tell you. This isn't some metoo shit. I'm a tough fuckin' broad, you know that."

Morris nodded and figured the best strategy was to wait until Goldi ran out of fuel.

"But I'll tell you, the dumb-ass thing is when everyone talks sexual harassment, it's like let's give money to these women's causes and do all this shit. Supporting breast cancer research isn't going to fix what's wrong with creepy guys!"

She had a point, thought Morris.

"The guys have to fix the guys. They should be creating the Don't be an Asshole Foundation rather than buying teal ribbons or whatever the fuck. Morris, you got a son?"

He could feel the synapses cross-fire. His brain settled on the words "It's complicated," but there was no way his mouth was going to agree to say them. Just then, Morris spotted a blue and white transit police cruiser with its lights on, weaving through traffic. Saved by the siren.

Morris ran toward the street to try to wave down whoever was driving. "You got your radio?" he asked Sann.

"No, they don't give me one."

He was still holding his wet sneakers. As the cruiser passed, he threw one at the driver's side door.

The cruiser screeched to a halt. Morris could see the driver, Detective Bruce Donohue, turn furious as he looked out the window, but his expression changed upon seeing Morris.

"What's up, Bruce?" Morris shouted.

"Someone got nailed by a train down at Medical Center. Here, hop in."

Chapter 7

Bruce Donohue pulled the cruiser up to the front of Tufts Medical Center Station. It was less than a block away from the Genghis Khan restaurant where Morris had eaten with BoBo Powers the day before. The station was known for its art, especially the four abstract pieces, collectively titled *The Caravan*, and for the granite monument outside the head house with a poem of peace titled "Mr. Yee is in the Garden."

As Morris, Sann, and Donohue ventured toward the entrance, they had to make their way around numerous police vehicles, fire engines, black SUVs, and an EMS ambulance all blocking traffic on Washington Street, crippling the Silver Line.

Morris also saw a truck of T laborers. The foreman was on the phone and shouting.

"They're all bullshit about overtime," said Sann, who must have noticed where Morris was looking. "They've been running around like crazy with the last two storms, but the General Manager wants to cap overtime."

"You can't budget the unexpected," Morris said plainly as he noticed a familiar face at the station entrance.

In all likelihood, Elvis Norton wasn't born with his first name any more than his hair was naturally jet black, but both were a combination of an ode to The King of Rock 'n' Roll and good marketing. Norton frequently moonlighted as an Elvis impersonator. Of course, it had been suggested once or twice that his imitation skills also covered being a T-cop. While Elvis may not have been the most vigilant of police officers, Morris appreciated his laid-back style. It was far more suited to the range of MBTA patrons than some of the Dirty Harry characters found among many of the new recruits.

"Hey, Elvis," Morris said at the entrance. "What's up?"

"Be careful. There might be peace up here, but there is a war going on downstairs," he said. "I volunteered to be the recorder of anyone who enters the scene, anything to get away from that pissing match."

"How bad is it?" Morris responded.

Norton snarled his lip and channeled The King. "You only pass through this life once, and you ain't coming back for an encore!" Then he returned to his T-cop demeanor. "It looks like suicide by subway. Some son of bitch just plopped himself in front of an Orange Line train."

"Shit," said Sann "Homeless?"

"I doubt it, Goldi," said Norton. "The guy's wearing a suit. Not a good one mind you, but a suit."

Sann then spotted a community leader in the gathering crowd. "I'll meet you guys downstairs. I've got a little 'liaising' to do."

Morris and Bruce Donohue made their way down the escalator to the outbound platform where they met Boston Fire Deputy Chief Jay McKenna and Elijah. Both men had their eyes fixed on two well-dressed women engaged in a heated argument on the other side of the yellow crime-scene tape.

One looked familiar, but the other had her back turned to Morris. Both had dark hair, the familiar one, short and curly, and the other, straight, pulled into a pony tail. Neither could have been more than 30 years old. Just as Morris was about to make a comment, the second woman turned.

"Holy crap," said Donohue. "What's with the boo –"

"Don't say it," Elijah wisely interrupted.

Still, Morris had to acknowledge that the woman's choice of a white top with a plunging neckline framed by a black jacket did call attention to certain aspects of her figure.

"I don't know, Bruce," he said. "Maybe we started a cross-training program with the Foxy Lady."

Morris expected to hear at least a snicker from his male colleagues, but they remained silent, looking not just back at Morris, but past him. It was a gesture that convinced the T-cop that there was someone standing behind him, likely not appreciative of his humor.

Morris turned to see a woman glaring at him. "You better be a cop and not some T asshole trying to get your choo choos moving," she said sternly. "This is a crime scene, and the DA's office is in charge before we say otherwise."

Morris tried to find words, but Elijah intervened.

"Assistant District Attorney Anne Marie Melia, this is Sergeant Morris Fitzgerald, transit police."

"I see," Melia said, not softening her tone at all. "Where's your badge, and what do you do at the MBTA?"

Morris paused. "As little as possible?" Morris could see his friends suppress a giggle. It was just too hard for him to pass on that setup.

"Very funny, you Neanderthal," said Melia. It had been a while since Morris had been likened to a caveman. He doubted that Melia would understand why he viewed the name as a term of endearment. She then broadened her gaze at the three other men, placing a hand upon her hip. "You're all so damn smug, in your little boys' club here. When you see strong women, the only thing you know how to do is make fun of it. Well, get used to it."

Melia then lifted her head and pointed toward the woman Morris thought looked familiar. "That's Sergeant Joanne Manning from Boston Police Homicide. She's in charge even though your boss over there doesn't think so."

"She's not our boss," said Morris.

"I'll fill you in later buddy," said Elijah.

"Now make yourself useful," Melia said to the men. "And someone figure out how the hell we can get the body out of here!"

The confusion on Morris' face must have been evident.

"He's pinned between the train and the platform," explained McKenna.

At that moment a group of firefighters came down the stairs, and Morris noticed Melia suddenly became more composed. Two of them came over to McKenna. They were young, ruggedly good looking and in prime shape. The taller of the two spoke.

"Chief, lift team is on the way." He paused and stared at the woman arguing with Sergeant Manning.

McKenna cleared his throat loudly and the firefighter refocused. "Yeah, the team is on the way."

A few moments later, Melia stepped up to the gathering of firefighters. "Hello gentlemen, Anne Marie Melia Assistant District Attorney," she said while extending her hand and a smile to the tall one.

Morris looked over at Elijah and whispered. "You know I was a stud once, too."

"A dud?" Elijah asked facetiously. "Have you tried Viagra for that?"

Before Morris could offer a retort, the cat fight on the platform boiled over. "Bitch get off my crime scene," shouted Manning. "You ain't a cop, and I don't give a fuck what your title is."

With that she raised a hand, and Melia sprang toward Manning. Elijah responded by swooping in to hold back her buxom counterpart.

Morris' eye then caught Officer Sann bounding down onto the platform from the stairs.

"Hey guys," she said as she saw Morris, Donohue, and McKenna. Then her eye caught the scene in front of the stopped train. "What the fuck's going on, and who's the tits?"

McKenna laughed. "One of yours apparently."

Morris then noticed Sann look toward one of the firefighters who had been talking to McKenna a moment ago.

"Holy shit. It's February," she said quietly.

"What?" said Morris.

Before he could get an answer, he felt Elijah tap him on the shoulder. Morris turned to see him standing there with the woman that had been arguing with Manning.

"Sergeant Fitzgerald, this is deputy T director Dyani Swan."

Morris quickly assimilated the details. Steph Tam had talked about some new director coming on board. However, Swan never looked at Morris. She was furiously working her phone.

"At Homeland we never had to deal with this bullshit," she grumbled.

Morris decided to get himself on decent terms with at least one person at the scene. He stepped over to where Melia had been talking to Manning but judiciously waited until the assistant district attorney hurried off somewhere.

"Sergeant Manning, let me introduce myself, I'm Sergeant Morris Fitzgerald, MBTA police."

She looked at him, and Morris couldn't figure what he might get for a greeting. "You Irish asshole," she said slowly. "I never forget a face, but in your case, I wish I could make an exception. You don't remember me, do you?"

Morris began to feel envious of the dead guy on the tracks next to him. All he could do was look dumbfounded.

"Sam Albany's retirement party," she said.

"Oh shit," said Morris with no specific recollection, just a recognition that when the Boston dectective retired, Morris may have had one drink too many.

"You and your drunken friends were all singing the Irish Belly Dancer song, and you started destroying the buffet centerpiece, tossing apples, oranges, and shit onto the floor."

OK, Morris thought to himself, it may have been ten drinks too many. "I'm sorry that wasn't one of my better moments."

"Yeah, well I ended up wiping out on a fuckin' pineapple. Sprained my ankle."

Morris searched for words or at least an excuse to back out of the conversation, but he was at a loss.

"You're lucky Sam liked you," she said.

"Oh, you knew him well?"

"I hope so," said Manning. "I'm engaged to his son."

"Oh, Mikey," Morris said. "Great kid, good ball player in his day."

"Yeah I realized I shouldn't make the mistake my mom made and marry some Irish drunk. I'm going to marry a real man, Syrian."

Despite the insult, he laughed. She sounded just like Sam, who had passed away from pancreatic cancer just a couple of months earlier. "Sorry," Morris said, gathering himself. "Back in those days my motto was one drink was too many, and a hundred is not enough."

She was slender, maybe average height, with delicate features that perhaps belied her personality. Much to Morris' concern, her plain expression did not readily move into a smile. "Forget it," she said finally. "Like I said, Sam thought you were a good guy. Plus he told me about your wife."

Morris would never have played that card as an apology, but at the moment of Sam's retirement party, Morris' wife was in the final stages of her battle against cancer, and the toll was clearly too much for him to shoulder. He caught himself growing melancholy.

"Come on," said Manning. "Let's check out the poor bastard that was killed by your Orange Line train."

Morris smiled and noticed she had lost some of her sternness. As they approached the third car, Morris was expecting what one of his T-cop colleagues had coined "hamburger helper." When a human body hits a speeding subway train, it's not really a collision as much as it is an explosion. However, in this case, he was stunned by one of rarest versions of subway-cide – the corkscrew.

Given the dimensions involved, a corkscrew was like drawing to an inside straight. There were only a few inches between the platform and the train. Someone needed to be on the tracks, right up against the edge of the platform, and of a physique slight enough. When the force of the train met the suppleness of their body in that tiny window of opportunity, what would happen is the torso on up would be spun around while the lower body remained pinned – a gruesome way to go.

He bent down to take a look at the sorry soul whose back was to the open doors on the train. Morris glanced at the white-knuckled fists sticking out and then looked at the face of death staring back at him.

"Oh my God, it's Mantis."

"What's that?" said Manning, who proceeded to try to answer her own question. "Well, I guess he does look a little like a praying mantis."

Morris continued to stare at the eyes of a man confronted with his own mortality. "It's Bob Sosa," he said finally. "He's deputy director of real estate for the T."

"Oh," said Manning. "What was he doing here?"

"No idea," said Morris. "I grew up with him. We played park league football together. That's where he got his nickname Mantis. You know, skinny guy."

"Did I hear you say it was Sosa?" chimed in Elijah.

"Yeah, look at him," said Morris.

He then imagined the obituary in his head. It would say "died suddenly," the code phrase for some sort of unnatural death. Would they mention he was a friend of the cardinal of the Archdiocese of Boston, or was that still taboo? Choir member at the Gate of Heaven Church, volunteer at Saint Cecilia's where he also did homeless outreach. A good family man, well liked by anyone who knew him. Gregarious, a member of the L Street Runners Cub, a mentor to troubled kids at the Boys and Girls club, a solid citizen who will be missed.

"I'll contact Father Michael to perform last rites before we move the body," Morris said.

"What's that?" Deputy Director Swan interjected. "The Silver Line is already backed up. This is a mess. We can't delay for some medieval ritual."

Before Morris could say anything, Manning spun around. "Listen, I told you, this is my crime scene, and it will be until I tell you when you can resume service."

"We'll see about that!" Swan shouted back as she turned to her phone.

Manning looked ready to launch into a tirade, but she was suddenly distracted as the firefighters moved in with the lift team. "I think that's February."

Morris shook his head. He wasn't sure he was hearing right. Just then Bruce Donohue came up to the train, talking with another officer.

"I know," Bruce said to the other cop. "It looks like a full-grown ass was stuffed into her shirt. I mean it's like butt cheeks squeezed together and were ...." The two officers stopped and were looking at Manning, Morris, and Elijah.

"We should probably go find witnesses," Bruce said.

Morris nodded.

"I'm going to get in touch with operations," said Elijah. "You make that call to Father Michael."

Morris reached for his new phone, but it was already ringing. It was Chief Stephanie Tam. He was momentarily delighted to find out that Gary sold him a working phone. He answered and told her that the victim was Sosa.

"The scene is pretty gruesome chief. It's going to take some time to figure out what happened. We're trying to find witnesses. A few other guys are working with BPD on processing everything. Any idea about getting the surveillance video?"

"It's a damn nightmare," said Tam. "It all gets sent out to the cloud or whatever. So now we gotta call the nerds to get access to it, and they don't do shit if it's not a work order in triplicate."

"And the geeks shall inherit the earth," said Morris sarcastically.

He recalled that over the past several years, the T had been adding security cameras at an astounding rate, thanks largely to federal grants. Of course from a policing standpoint, more wasn't always better. Adding a few thousand video feeds was like going from trying to follow one conversation to trying to follow every conversation happening inside Fenway Park on a Red Sox home stand.

Part of the solution was to back up all video to Mass. Department of Transportation data centers.

"I'll call MassDOT and get the ball rolling on video," Morris suggested.

"Fuck that," said Tam. "Have Swani do it."

Morris laughed. "You're not a fan of the new deputy director are you?"

"I don't know, but basically the GM had to hire her as part of the federal grants. You know how required hires usually go."

"I know, Steph," Morris said.

"Anyway, have her do it. She's supposed to be in charge of all that shit."

"OK."

"Just watch your back," Tam added. "I already heard from the Lieutenant Governor's office that we need to get the trains moving. I can only guess how they found out. That bitch is connected, I tell you, and remember I'm gone for a week starting tonight."

"Oh shit," Morris said, making the connection. "Who's running the show while you're gone."

"Guess," said Tam.

Morris looked down the platform and spotted the T's new deputy director. "God help us. On the plus side. If she keeps dressing like she shops at Frederick's of Hollywood, press conference ratings should skyrocket."

"Fredrick what?" asked Tam.

Morris had to lose the grin that came from his own joke. "Nevermind Steph, before your time I guess."

Morris then wished her a safe trip and said goodbye. After hanging up, he walked over to Joanne Manning. "No video yet."

"Now what the hell are we supposed to do!" she said.

"We do it the old-fashioned way," said Morris, as he tried to find Father Michael's number in his new phone. "We follow evidence, talk to people."

"Oh that reminds me," said Manning, cutting Morris off. "Your deputy director, Swan or whatever her name is, fucked that up too. She came down here and started kicking everyone out of the station."

Morris couldn't deny that error. "Hey, the T's got the same problem that I'm sure you do," said Morris. "You give people a title, and all of sudden, they think they gotta do something."

Manning laughed.

"Seriously, I blame the Spotlight Team and all those other news hacks. Give me the good old days where political patronage resulted in no-show jobs, and middle management only put in a half-day. That way they couldn't be around to fuck things up."

"Yeah, and who was this guy again?" Manning said, looking at Sosa's twisted figure.

"Bob Sosa, deputy director of real estate."

"Wait, he's a director. She's a director. How many directors do you have at the T?"

Morris shrugged.

"And just what the fuck do they do?"

"They direct." said Morris.

Manning sneered.

"Oh please, you know how it is. Julius Caesar built a bridge over the Rhine River in ten days," said Morris, as he finally managed to dial Father Michael's number. "Two thousand years later, if you are dealing with a state agency, even a simple idea has to be discussed for a month – by directors – before anything even starts to get done."

She shook her head. "A management team that concentrates on preventing failure usually forecloses success."

"Exactly," said Morris. "I knew you weren't all bad."

"Watch it, my ankle still hurts thanks to you and your drunken buddies."

Morris decided not to push things any further, but he and Manning were actually seeing eye-to-eye. In any organization, the rank-and-file usually have the best idea of how to get the job done. Management's job should be to make the workers' jobs easier, but when you don't trust your basic resource, your workers, it's hard to perform your basic business, which in this case was moving the damn trains safely.

As Morris left a message for Father Michael, he spotted Elijah coming back.

"Well, that's a mess," he said to Morris and Manning. "The motorman – motorwoman, I guess – is a 20-year driver, Kristine. She's got no idea how Sosa ended up on the tracks."

"Let me talk to her," said Manning.

Elijah shook his head. "EMS is taking her straight to the hospital. Here, I'll text you her contact info. Maybe you can grab her in the emergency room."

Manning frowned as she pulled out her cellphone to receive the information from Elijah, who began texting while giving a subtle nod to Morris. As Manning received the information, the two T-cops quietly stepped away from the homicide sergeant.

"She's upstairs," Elijah whispered. "EMS is checking her over, but I'm trying to find her a ride home. She's a disaster. Apparently some 16-year-old girl jumped in front of her train last year at Andrew Square, and she's still getting over that. She told me she's on medication for migraines, nightmares, all that shit."

Morris shot Elijah a look.

"Yeah, I was thinking the same thing. No way she'd pass a drug test right now. I doubt she'll be back in a motorman's cab any time soon, anyway. It's a personal hell for her."

"No kidding, sitting in a three-by-nine box with a hard plastic chair and working a cast-iron handle," said Morris. "Then you gotta add to that seeing some girl smashed to death right in front of her. Now this. She's going to be seeing ghosts if she ever gets back in there."

"Listen, I talked with the train guard, and he basically said the same thing. He never saw Sosa. He's got no idea how he got on the tracks," Elijah said. "This isn't on the driver."

Morris nodded. "Yeah, definitely keep her away from Manning." Then he turned toward the tracks. "He had to end up there somehow."

"Yeah, what was he doing there?" queried Elijah.

"I don't know," contemplated Morris. "Something real estate related? I actually bumped into him yesterday. He seemed to have something going on, but he didn't seem like he wanted to off himself or anything."

Suddenly a third voice spoke, "I don't think it was that."

Neither Morris nor Elijah had noticed Bruce Donohue had stepped up to them.

"Yeah, take a look at him," said Bruce. "I think he was trying to climb out. His hands are up over the platform. I think he was on the tracks trying to get out. The driver comes around the bend, she'd never see him down there."

Morris and Elijah nodded and exchanged looks of pleasant surprise. It took Bruce multiple attempts to pass the detective's exam, and both men had witnessed Bruce use his cellphone to compute a twenty percent tip on a $100 dinner tab – and still get it wrong. However, what he lacked in intellect, Bruce made up for with stubbornness and plain talk.

"What else you got?" Morris asked.

"Goldi is talking to a couple of the mole people right now. They were on the platform panhandling. There was another guy when I first got here. I thought he might have seen something, but he also seemed pretty fucked up."

It wasn't an uncommon occurrence that the best witnesses to some incident on the T were the homeless who lived in the subway, but it also wasn't uncommon that their recollection was skewed by a combination of their distorted mental state and the influence of some narcotic.

"What makes you think he saw something?" asked Elijah.

"He was ranting about shit," said Bruce, flipping through his notes. "Let's see, 'I seen it, I seen it, crime on the subway. Redrum, redrum. The douche did it, nine of spades. The douche.' I have no idea what the fuck that means."

"You never saw *The Shining*?" asked Elijah.

Bruce shrugged.

"What's 'redrum' spelled backward?" asked Morris.

Bruce paused. After a moment, he asked, "you mean if I put the letters in reverse?"

"Yes, backward," Morris said impatiently.

"Oh OK, I thought you meant, like, the other way."

Morris and Elijah both looked at each other as Elijah mouthed 'other way?'

"Murder," Morris finally blurted.

"Oh right, yeah," said Bruce with a smile. "Like I said, he seemed pretty fucked up."

Just then Sann came rushing up to her three fellow T-cops. "Beetlejuice," was all she said. "He saw it, apparently. I was talking with Kenny the Clown, and he said Beetlejuice was down the other end of the platform and saw the whole thing."

"Where's Beetle now?" asked Morris.

"Gone," said Sann, turning toward Bruce. "Kenny said he talked to you."

"Who?" asked Bruce.

"Beetlejuice."

"Is he the tall one, looks like his face is being attacked by flesh eaters?" asked Bruce.

"Yeah, you ever see the movie *Beetlejuice*, Michael Keaton?" interjected Elijah.

Bruce shook his head. "You guys must have shitty movie collections."

Morris and Elijah rolled their eyes.

"Yeah, but he's the guy, the fucked up one, I was talking about," said Bruce. "Looks like he's got those skid-row cooties."

"Be careful," said Goldilocks. "That's a staph infection. It's getting bad, resistant to antibiotics, too."

"Whatever," said Elijah. "We've got a witness at least."

"What's that?"

The four T-cops turned to see Dyani Swan, with her phone in one hand and looking at them.

"We think someone saw what happened," said Morris.

"Good," said Swan. "I want to talk to them."

"They left the scene," said Elijah.

"Name and picture then," she said turning back to her phone.

"What crawled up her ass," said Goldilocks, recognizing Swan's curt tone.

Sann suddenly stopped talking, and Morris noticed her step back with a slightly nervous expression. He turned to see Deputy Chief Jay McKenna coming his way with one of the young firefighters next to him.

"I've been thinking about this," began McKenna. "If we jack the train up as we usually do, half this guy will untwist and spill out all over the place, and that doesn't sound like it will be good for anybody."

Morris could feel the group nodding.

"So I figure if we are able to push the train back a few feet, maybe we untwist the body, and he can be pulled out in one piece. You get your evidence, we get out of here quicker, and you can get these trains running again."

With those words, Dyani Swan stepped into the group. "What's that about getting the trains running?"

"Jay was just saying he's got an idea for getting us out of here quicker," explained Elijah.

"Do it!" said Swan authoritatively. "You know, when I was with Homeland, our priority was always getting the scene back to normal as soon as possible."

"We'll get going on it," said Morris. "By the way, Steph Tam said to go through you for video."

"I'm already on it," Swan replied holding up her phone, apparently signifying she had made some call or text on the matter.

As the group started to move, Manning interjected. "Hold on a minute. What's happening here? We still have a potential crime scene."

"Well, that's the point," said McKenna. "If this works, it should be a lot less disruption to the body and evidence."

"Plus, I am sure Barbara Sosa would appreciate having her husband back in one piece, even if he is a corpse," added Morris, who noticed Manning look at the young firefighter.

"All right, then Boston Police is on board," she said, continuing to look at the firefighter and using a tone that seemed less crass than that which she apparently reserved for transit police.

McKenna led the group over to the tracks to set up the plan. Morris trailed behind and heard Manning and Goldi whisper to each other. The only word he could make out sounded like "February."

He turned around. "What the fuck is February?"

Manning paid no heed, and Sann just raised her hand. "It's nothing. Come on, let's move this fuckin' thing."

The firefighters gathered around the front of the cab. Morris and Sann jumped down onto the tracks as McKenna directed the group. As they moved into the different positions, Morris felt someone bump him on the left side. It was Goldilocks squeezing in between him and the tall firefighter that had been with McKenna.

"Hi, Officer Susan Sann," he could hear her say. Morris looked over his shoulder to see Sann gazing at the firefighter, but the young man's focus seemed elsewhere than on the blond lobsterman next to him. Morris then looked in the other direction and saw, Dyani Swan on the platform, leaning over to speak to the team about to push the train.

"I don't see how this can work," she was saying.

Morris looked at her. Bruce was right. With that top, it did look like an ass stuffed into her shirt.

"There has to be more suspension on that bra than the Zakim Bridge," Morris mumbled to himself.

"What's that?"

Morris turned to see Goldi looking at him. "Nothing Goldi."

"I guarantee you they're fuckin' fake," she said.

"Hey, you got the right boots for this," said the firefighter next to Goldi.

Her expression changed as she looked away from Morris toward the tall gentleman next to her. All Morris could hear was the forced but polite laughter from Goldi.

McKenna then instructed them to push, but the train didn't budge an inch.

"I told you this wasn't going to work," Swan yelled down to the tracks. "Just jack the thing up. We've got to get the trains running."

"Hold on," shouted Morris. "Is the emergency brake on?"

"You mean these things have a parking brake?" shouted back Swan.

In the meantime, McKenna had gone around to the cab. A few seconds later, he was back on the platform.

"OK, try it again, 1 – 2 – 3 …."

Slowly the train began to move back. As the body untwisted, another group of firefighters, under the supervision of Manning, was able to pull out Sosa and place him on the platform. As they continued to push the train, Morris looked up. There he was, the Mantis, looking every bit his namesake getting ready to perform the dance of death.

Something suddenly caught Morris' eye, and he turned to see Goldi lying face down on the tracks. He turned to help her, but the firefighter had already leaned over and was pulling her to her feet.

"I guess those boots didn't help you that much," he said.

Goldi laughed hysterically, her face covered in mud and grime. Still, Morris thought he could detect her blushing from underneath her improvised veil. The group pulled themselves up onto the platform as Manning came over.

“He’s got his wallet. No suicide note or anything, but we’ll send people over to his office, see what we find there.”

“What about a cellphone?” asked Morris.

“No,” said Manning who seemed to recognize that its absence might be significant.

“I don’t know, did he even have one?” added Elijah.

“Hard to think that he didn’t,” said Morris.

“What’s this I hear about one of the homeless maybe seeing something?” asked Manning.

“Yeah, one of our detectives got a statement,” said Elijah. “We need to track the guy down and follow up.”

“Go do it then,” said Manning.

“It ain't that easy,” said Sann. “The homeless population in Boston surged twenty-five percent last year. We closing in on maybe nine-thousand men, women and children living on the streets.”

“Jesus,” said Manning.

“Athens of America,” Morris added referring to one of Boston’s many monikers.

“Yeah, and they’re getting harder to find,” continued Sann. “The collapse of the Long Island bridge basically shut down the shelter there, so what we’ve seen since is they’re all going into the tunnels of the T.”

Morris could see the exasperation on Manning’s face. “Don’t worry,” he said. “We’ll find him.”

Manning left with Sosa’s body on the way to the morgue but not before Father Michael McGovern arrived to issue last rites. The priest and Elijah then left to inform Sosa’s widow. Jay McKenna also took off, leaving his crew behind to gather their gear while Bruce and the remaining T-cops dissipated.

“Where did tits go?” Sann asked, looking around.

Morris laughed. “No idea, Goldi.”

“Seriously, who the fuck wears an outfit like that?”

Morris remained quiet as Goldi began another rant, but suddenly he heard her change tone and noticed her Boston accent, not to mention proclivity for expletives, had diminished.

He turned around and saw her talking to the tall firefighter.

"Oh, well thank you, officer," she said. "You and your crew were very helpful."

"It's not officer," said the young man. "I mean I'm not a cop or anything."

"Oh right, I'm sorry," said Sann, her face still covered in dirt. "What is the correct term?"

Morris wondered who had stolen Goldi and replaced her with this fraud.

"I'm a firefighter," said the man. "I guess you can call me Pat though."

"Pleased to meet you, Pat. Is that short for Patrick?"

Morris rolled his eyes.

"Yeah," said the firefighter with a laugh.

Goldi then stuck out her hand. "Well I am Susan," she said. "You can call me Sue if you want, or Suzy. Really anything. I am fine with that."

"OK, then," the firefighter said slowly glancing at Morris, who nodded as if to say "It's OK, she is not insane."

Goldilocks then apparently noticed her own awkwardness and turned toward Morris. "Well, Sergeant Fitzgerald. We should follow up tomorrow and determine a plan for the investigation."

Morris just nodded, wondering when the aliens who abducted Goldi would return her.

"We should probably have a debrief," she continued, turning back toward the firefighter in front of her. "We should probably follow up with you as well since you were so integral to the scene."

She extended her hand again to shake Pat's. "I'd like to thank you on behalf of the entire MBTA orgasm – organization – for your assistance." She then turned and darted up the stairs.

As Morris watched Goldilocks scamper away, the firefighter stepped up to him. "So you're Sergeant Fitzgerald?"

"That's what they tell me," replied Morris.

"My dad says you're a hot shit."

"Who's your dad?"

"Jay, Jay McKenna."

"No shit," Morris said recalling that perhaps the last time he saw Patrick McKenna was at a Mite hockey game when the grown man in front of him was probably 7 or 8. "Following in the old man's footsteps?"

"Something like that," said Pat.

The two laughed, and Pat returned to the other firefighters, gathering their belongings. As he looked at one of the loadout bags with a "42" emblazoned on it for their engine company, a thought struck Morris. He pulled out his phone and left a message for Goldi to see if she could dig up a copy of the survey that gets distributed to the homeless every year as part of the census.

As he looked back at the bag, he noticed a bunch of what looked like glossy photos. "What's that?" he said as the firefighters started walking by.

They laughed. "Men of Boston Fire calendar. We do it every year for a fundraiser."

"No kidding?"

"Here, want one? It's November, we've got to give them away at this point," said the firefighter, handing the calendar to Morris.

"Sure," he said. "I'll give it my boss. She'll love it."

As the scene cleared, and the T prepared to re-open the station, Morris waited for a train that would take him to Downtown Crossing where he could make the short walk to Park Street and pick up a Red Line back to Southie.

He started thumbing through the calendar and stopped on February, which featured a large color photo of a shirtless Patrick McKenna. He nodded to himself. "OK, that all makes sense now."

Chapter 8

Morris stood on the platform, watching the several T employees go through the motions of bringing the service back online. Leaning against a column, he began to let his eyes close. Not that he would fall asleep standing up, but it was soothing to shut out the world for a few moments.

"Hey Fitzgerald!"

The voice brought Morris back into the chaos of the subway. He turned to see the uniform of a state trooper. He blinked twice to clear his eyes and then smiled.

"Rico!" he shouted as the trooper neared. "Sorry, I haven't been dodging you. I've just been swamped."

Rico Paulie extended a handshake as he greeted the T-cop. "No worries, but I need your help finding some of your graffiti punks before my major banishes my ass to western Mass. He's bullshit at some gang of aerosol artists – or whatever you call them."

"Taggers," interjected Morris. "They call themselves taggers."

"Yeah, well anyway, they've been spray painting the locks next to the marine unit, and he says 'If we can't catch some vandals under our own nose, how are we supposed to keep the harbor safe from terrorists!'"

"Geez," Morris shook his head. "It's always the fuckin' terrorists these days."

"Yeah, well, I'm already in the doghouse with him, and I don't want to end up patrolling the MassPike out in the middle of nowhere."

"Sure thing, Rico. I probably owe you anyway from the last time you helped me get the Ghetto Glider inspected."

The two men then made their way up the station stairs and onto street level where Paulie had parked his Ford Explorer among other emergency vehicles. They climbed in the SUV, and Paulie made his way through the evening gridlock of Boston traffic to Atlantic Avenue, which runs along the Boston Harbor, past the Aquarium Station, where Morris had been hours earlier.

Paulie and Morris went back at least fifteen years. Both were native Bostonians. Morris had his roots deep in South Boston. Paulie, on the other hand, was the fourth generation of his family to live in the city's North End, which historically had featured enclaves of Italian and Irish immigrants, who struggled against each other for housing and jobs. To the 19th Century Protestant establishment, it must have appeared to be some religious schism as both populations shared a Catholic faith. They didn't understand the gaping difference between Roman Catholic and Irish Catholic. More critically, however, was that both Irish and Italians waged battle for control of city hall, organized crime and the police departments.

Those times, however, had faded. The ethnic roots that at one time had so strongly shaped the city, reflective of the waves of immigration coming to America, ran more shallow today. The modern gentrification was the working class giving way to the liberal null generation, who eschewed all categorizations of gender, race, and creed.

In some ways, these new immigrants, many of them drawn to Boston as the mecca of higher education, were like the Puritans of centuries ago. They arrived armed with a hubris and a righteousness bred from superior schooling. They were here to save the natives, not assimilate with them. Their message was that of tolerance while their actions were to banish any who philosophically differed with them.

A bit like Morris, Paulie's career with the State Police had encountered a few sidetracks. As they traveled along Atlantic Avenue, Morris looked out the window. Given the time of year, it was already dark in the city, but the lights of the buildings reaching high into the sky helped emphasize to Morris how much the city had changed from his youth.

Paulie pulled into the nondescript entrance of the marine unit, crammed among the city's constant construction projects at the tip of the city's North End. Land only became more scarce in Boston with each passing decade. For the city, developers played a real-world game of Monopoly. A block of four-story brick buildings would be bought up, knocked down and a forty-story hotel or office complex put up, increasing the revenue potential of the land by more than an order of magnitude.

The current marine unit building had been built by the U. S. Army Corps of Engineers as part of a flood control plant managed by the state's Department of Conservation and Recreation. It sat where the Charles River flowed into the Boston Harbor. From there, the State Police could get anywhere in the harbor or upstream on the heavily trafficked river.

In another setting, the massive complex may have generated more interest. However, the mostly brick structure was dwarfed by Boston's Zakim Bridge and the adjacent TD Bank Garden.

The barracks included a three-story indoor heated boat bay and a complete fuel and maintenance facility. Morris marveled at the variety of specialized vessels and support equipment, which included a twenty-foot Teflon-hull airboat for ice and swamp conditions, a couple of Boston Whalers. A thirty-foot Defender class vessel, a forty-foot catamaran with water-jet propulsion, several forty-foot utility boats, and a few Kawasaki jet skis.

"Rico, what kind of a budget do you guys have here?"

Paulie chuckled. "Most of this stuff was seized from drug busts or cast-offs from the Coast Guard."

"Great, at the T, we occasionally seize a busted shopping cart."

Paulie rolled his eyes and grinned. "Come on, we have this multi-jurisdictional Operation Urban Shield coming up, and the major will be pissed if there's any more graffiti."

"He's a real hard-ass, huh?"

"You should know," quipped Paulie. "Major Jack Walsh, he's one of you Hibernian pricks, always threatening to banish my Italian ass if we don't catch these anarchist bastards."

"OK, well then, tell me about these vandalized padlocks," said Morris.

"Locks," shot back Paulie. "Locks not padlocks. I thought you were a boater."

"No, I'm a boatee," he answered. "I've got friends who have boats. Why would I need one?"

In truth, Morris was only playing along with the trooper. He knew the basics of navigating on the water and the function of a lock even though he had genuinely misspoken a moment ago. Typically, locks were found in places where bodies of water met but were at uneven levels. A vessel would enter the chamber. The doors would close, turning the lock into a giant bathtub that could be filled or drained to the level of the adjoining river, canal or harbor. The door on the other end would open, and the vessel would continue on its way.

"Yeah, well the locks, they help separate the Charles River from the harbor," Rico lectured. "Along with the new dam ...."

"What new dam?" Morris interrupted.

The trooper laughed, leaving Morris to wonder what joke he missed.

"Everyone calls it the new dam even though it was built in the 1970s," Paulie explained. "That's Boston for you. The real name is the Gridley Dam, named after Richard Gridley, the father of the Army Corps of Engineers, wounded at the battle of Bunker Hill."

"Thank you Cliff Claven," Morris cracked, referencing the fictional Boston postal worker with an endless trove of trivia.

"Well, this will make more sense to you," said Paulie. "Sure, Gridley is remembered as a patriot, but he supposedly filled his ranks with friends and family, many of them considered somewhere between incompetent and cowards."

"Now that's Boston politics for you," said Morris. "Somehow I am sure Gridleys must have married into Sonny Barrett's bloodline."

"Anyway," said the trooper, looking out the window toward the large brick building across the way. "That's the new dam. It can pump nearly four million gallons of water a minute."

Morris let go a whistle. "That sounds like overkill. I mean aren't rivers supposed to flow into harbors anyway?"

The trooper shook his head. "You sound like my major. Every time I tell him the locks are fucked up, he's like 'So what. That's DCR's job.'"

"All right, all right," Morris said. "Show me the paint. I'll see if I can figure out who's screwing with your bathtub here."

Paulie grinned. "Come on," he said, grabbing a pair of flashlights and handing one to Morris.

The trooper then threw open a door and stepped onto a steel walkway that spanned the river. Morris made note of the sign on the railing that said "pedestrian traffic only" and "moving walkway" as a blast of salt air hit him from the harbor to his right.

They were able to cross over all three locks. Two were identical, the third, as Paulie explained, was a little wider to allow larger boats to pass between the harbor and the Charles River. Along the way, the trooper pointed out the areas of vandalism. Morris nodded, moving the flashlight over the paint. However, it didn't strike him as anything remarkable. He had spent three decades in the transit system. For the gangs of the city, particularly those who frequented the subway, graffiti was their primary medium. It's how they marked territory, recruited new members, taunted rivals, or just entertained themselves.

Just then, another breeze kicked up, Morris could feel the chill run through his bones. "It's beginning to feel like November," mumbled Morris.

"Wait two days," responded Paulie, as he stopped on the walkway. "We've got a warm front coming in. It's going to be a mess on Thursday." Then he moved the beam of the flashlight toward the inside wall of the lock. "There, you see that? Someone painted that over the weekend."

Morris moved his own flashlight to illuminate the graffiti, but he nearly missed it with his first pass. "This is what you mean?" he asked, holding the beam steady on a sloppily painted circle with an "A" in the middle.

"At first, I thought maybe it was someone trying to do the Aerosmith logo," said Paulie.

"Jesus, Rico, you are a homer. Unless we've got some geriatric tagger, these kids don't know shit about Aerosmith. No, what you've got there is a piss-poor attempt at the anarchy A."

"See, I knew you were the one to talk to," the trooper said. "And over here it says 'Homeless Lives Matter,' but the water's too high to see it right now."

Morris looked more closely, but shook his head as he did so. "I'm not sure I can help you. This isn't really the work of some graf. I mean, the first thing someone would have done is paint a base, usually white or maybe black, and then they paint on top of that. And do you see how it drips right there? No real tagger would do that."

"Yeah, but you figure they have to be standing on the edge of the lock or maybe in a boat. They don't have a lot of balance."

Morris grinned. The MBTA, with its massive amount of rolling stock, bridges, tunnels and other infrastructure, was like a canvas for the graffiti artists of the urban areas served by the system. Most of them were affiliated with some gang. Really, it wasn't any different from the country club crowd who walked around with logos emblazoned on their polo shirts and ties or the suburbanites who plastered the rear of their Range Rovers with prep school stickers. Everyone has a need for affiliation.

So too, everyone has a tendency toward pride. Just as you usually don't see a Harvard sticker thrown askance on the rear window of a rusted out Impala, if a tagger was going to deface public property, they wouldn't be sloppy about it.

"Rico, I know a kid who painted Muhammad Ali knocking out Sonny Liston – it must have been ten-feet tall – right where the commuter rail goes into Back Bay station. Not only was the thing perfect, but you figure in order for him to do it, he had to be hanging upside down at some point. This," he said, casting the beam of the flashlight toward the locks, "is child's play."

Paulie exhaled a sigh. Morris couldn't see his face in the darkness, but he sensed the disappointment.

"So what you're saying is you can't help me nab these fuckers?" the trooper summarized.

"I don't know. I can ask around," said Morris. "What's the big deal anyway?"

"Well, besides the fact that my major is a pain in the ass, I don't think this is the only vandalism. The lock next to us doesn't seem to close all the way. I told DCR about it, but I'm not sure they even still have people running this stuff any more. It's all getting automated."

"You don't have to pay a computer a pension and benefits, Rico," Morris said. "There's an app for everything now, even us."

The two made their way back across the connecting walkway and re-entered the marine unit.

"Well, thanks for taking a look anyway," Paulie said. "Any chance you could shoot me an email, saying you're looking into it or something?"

Morris nodded. He understood the trooper was trying to get some breathing room with his boss. "Yeah, no worries, Rico. I'll ask around. Who knows, maybe someone has seen this somewhere else?" Still, he remained certain of his original assessment. Not only was the paint poorly done, but the gangs who lived in the subway weren't the boating type. Plus, there were plenty of other, more visible, places to make some statement.

"Yeah, this Urban Shield thing has everyone on their toes," said Paulie. "Rumor is they might be looking to reorganize the State Police."

"We hear that all the time at the T," said Morris sympathetically. "They'll roll us into you guys or they'll hand over the major stations to the city cops. It never goes anywhere. People forget. That's how the T-cops started in the 1960s, a bunch of Boston Police assigned to ride shotgun on the buses. It didn't take BPD long to realize they didn't want to have anything to do with the transit system."

Paulie laughed along and then paused. “Speaking of BPD, you’re never going to guess who is heading up Urban Shield.”

Morris shrugged his shoulders, prompting an answer from the trooper.

“The hero himself, Jimmy Jordan.”

“No shit, I was invoking the name of that bastard yesterday,” replied Morris.

“Yeah, apparently he’s got his own consulting gig going on. He’s the one whispering in the ear of the Lieutenant Governor about reorganizing.”

Morris laughed, making a connection in his mind.

“I bumped into Sammy Albany’s soon-to-be daughter-in-law a couple of hours ago. She’s a homicide detective with Boston Police.”

“Good for her,” said the trooper. “Shame about Sammy,” he added. “He was one of the good ones.’

Morris nodded. “You know Sammy was always pretty certain that Hero wasn’t the hero in that whole thing.”

“What do you mean?”

“The kid in the manhole, his name was Horton,” Morris began. “He supposedly had fingered one of Wacko’s guys in a murder down by the Fens. Sammy was going to talk to him, but then this tragic accident happens.”

“Yeah but Hero got himself burned pretty bad in the whole thing. Didn’t he take partial disability?”

“That’s the story. I guess Jordan claimed he suddenly heard the kid screaming, ran over, and reached down to him while hot solder was dripping all over.”

“So what did Albany doubt about that?”

“Have you ever worked a detail at a construction site?” asked Morris. “You can’t hear someone two feet from you, never mind a hundred yards away in a manhole. On top of that, the douchebag was supposedly asleep in his cruiser.”

The trooper remained silent.

“That solder only remains hot for a little bit of time. So even if Jordan was Usain Fuckin’ Bolt, he supposedly wakes up, gets out of his cruiser, runs to the manhole and manages to burn his hand almost as bad as Horton’s whole body?”

“Holy shit,” Paulie stated plainly.

Morris nodded in agreement. "Sammy was pretty sure there was only one way he could have gotten burned, and that was if he was there right when the pots got dumped on the kid." He paused to let the assertion sink in for the trooper. "Sammy was a tough cop," Morris continued. "But you can imagine how hard it was to chase after a fellow cop who the media had canonized. I don't remember a lot from his retirement party, but I do remember him telling me that Hero was the one case that still bugged the shit out of him."

Paulie exhaled heavily. "Clowns to the left of me, Jokers to the right."

"No kidding, Rico," Morris said. "Between your major and Jimmy Jordan, I'd take the first early retirement package they offer."

The state trooper chuckled and then regained his composure. "To Sammy Albany," he said, raising an imaginary glass.

"To Sammy," responded Morris imitating the gesture. As he did so, he spotted a wall clock that indicated it was nearly 9 o'clock. He could feel a headache beginning to swell. A lot had been thrown at him today, and he needed to give his brain a rest. "Hey Rico, any chance I could bum a ride off you?"

"Do I look like Uber?'

Morris laughed. "I tell you what. You give me a lift, and I'll talk to DCR about covering the graffiti."

"You know someone who can grease a work order?"

"No, but I figured I'd offer."

"Great," said Paulie, pushing back from his desk. "Come on, I need to grab some food anyway. I'll tell you what, you buy me a coffee, and we'll call it even?"

Morris nodded in agreement and then followed the trooper out of the building. They climbed back inside the Explorer, and Paulie pulled into the middle of more gridlock.

"Did the Bruins play tonight?" he asked noting the heavy traffic.

"No idea," said Morris. "But with the way they're building in this city, this might just be the new normal."

The trooper hit his siren and turned on his lights to push through the traffic jam, eventually working his way down Atlantic Avenue. In a few blocks, Paulie spotted a coffee shop.

"Here, let's try this place. I hear it's good coffee."

As the trooper double-parked in front of the trendy-looking corner shop, Morris had his doubts. "Not quite your Dunkin Donuts, here, Rico?" Morris commented as the two got out of the Explorer.

"Come on, coffee is coffee. They can't screw it up too bad."

The two cops stepped into the dimly lit store that looked like the living room of a pretentious college sophomore. They exchanged looks as Morris sought what he thought was the counter.

He tried to catch the eye of one of three workers behind the counter. He cleared his throat. "Excuse me, a couple of large coffees, please."

The nearest worker kept her woolen hatted head down, but her co-worker, who had similar knit cap on despite the fact that the building appeared to be a comfortable temperature, spoke up. "Oh, you order down here," he said pointing toward a cash register several feet away.

Morris and Paulie then made their way to the location. After a few moments, the young man sauntered over to meet his customers.

"Yes, two large coffees, please," Morris reiterated.

"Oh, you mean a sedici?" responded the worker.

Morris was at a loss.

"Sedici," he repeated with a hint of condescension. "It means large."

"Actually, sedici is Italian for sixteen," interjected Paulie.

"I never heard that," said the worker, as if to say the great-grandson of Italian immigrants perhaps didn't know what he was talking about.

"Two sedicis, whatever," said Morris, trying move along the order.

"Any pumps or shots?"

"No, just coffee."

"Nothing?" asked the worker, seemingly confused by the blandness of the request.

"Just two large coffees," said Morris.

"Cream and sugar," added Paulie.

"OK, two sedicis," the worker said with an emphasis.

It then took the woolen hatted barista another thirty seconds of typing on an iPad-like device to complete the order, which came to just under ten dollars. Morris looked in his wallet and remembered he had exhausted his cash earlier in the day with Gary the Gnome.

"Here," he said handing a credit card to the employee.

The action then prompted another series of events. First, the swiping, followed by the inserting of the chip, followed by the kid having to void the original order. Finally Paulie stepped in with a ten-dollar bill.

"Serves me right for picking this spot," he quietly mumbled to Morris.

As Morris and Paulie waited for their drinks, Woolen Hat 1 started talking to Woolen Hat 2, complaining about how someone named Steve was cutting back her hours. Woolen Hat 2 shared a similar frustration as he continued the conversation while holding an empty coffee cup, apparently a sedici-sized one, in his hand.

Finally, the pair managed to complete the order of two coffees, and Morris and the state trooper left the shop twenty minutes after they had entered.

"Jesus, Rico, you picked a winner there," said Morris as the two climbed back into the SUV.

Paulie laughed as he put the vehicle in drive. "I know, but supposedly the coffee is good." He then continued down Atlantic Avenue. He took a gulp out of the cup and nearly spit it out. "Fuck! It tastes like blueberries!"

Morris laughed. "Here, try mine. Caffeine isn't good for the migraines anyway." He then spotted the harbor off to their left, and a thought struck him. "So why do you need a dam anyway?" he asked. "I mean, aren't rivers supposed to flow into harbors?"

"Such ignorance, my friend," Paulie chided, his voice still recovering from the bitter taste of the coffee. "Don't you know your city history?"

Morris was at a loss.

"The dam's not there to keep the Charles from flowing into the harbor. It's to keep the harbor from flowing into the Charles," Paulie said, hitting the sirens to get around a blocked intersection. "Yeah, you see the problem is if you get a lot of rain in the river, a storm surge from the harbor, and you throw in a high tide, the harbor basically blocks the river from emptying."

"No kidding?"

"Well, no one has seen that happen in 60 years," explained Paulie. "Back in 1955, a couple of back-to-back hurricanes dumped a bunch of rain in New England. The Charles overflowed its banks. That's when they decided to build the new dam."

"The Gridley Dam," Morris added.

"There you go," said the trooper. "You've basically got this one thing that, if it breaks, we're all screwed. People forget. Boston's a filled-in swamp. All that pricey real estate can change in value in a hurry thanks to a natural disaster."

"Or an unnatural one," added Morris.

Paulie didn't answer, but nodded as he cut around some construction in the seaport district. "I don't see that happening," he added after the pause. "Too much technology. We'll never be caught off guard again."

"Yeah but it doesn't matter how much technology you have behind a button if some idiot or evil genius is the one who has a finger on it."

The trooper rolled his eyes as he drove into South Boston. "Conspiracy theories, my friend. Come on, Morris, embrace the 21st Century."

"It's not a conspiracy. I mean, all technology does is make things happen faster with fewer people involved. So that just means government can fuck shit up more quickly and with less accountability, right?"

Paulie grinned and shook his head.

"Tell me, what if your coffee artisan back there happens to be the DCR's next chief dam officer or whatever? Are you going to trust them to hit the right button at the right time? I mean, these kids all have SAT scores that sound like they're on the metric system or something, but they don't know shit about working."

Paulie was quiet for a moment. Morris couldn't tell if that was a sign of agreement or whether the trooper was just pre-occupied with weaving through the Southie double parking.

"Listen, I can only deal with one asshole at a time," he finally said. "Right now, that asshole is my major. So, if you can break out an email, or maybe it's Morse Code for you, saying you're looking into this, I'd appreciate it."

Morris laughed as Paulie pulled up at the corner of G and 8th streets.

"OK, I'll take care of it," he said as he stepped out of the SUV. "Thanks for the ride."

He gave a wave to Paulie as he drove off. A brisk wind blew its way down the street grid of South Boston, and Morris heard a sound to his right. He turned to see his neighbor carrying his recycling bin to the curb.

"It could be more rain, they say," Fillmore said as he gingerly placed the bin on the sidewalk.

"I don't know," said Morris. "I haven't trusted a weather report since the Blizzard of '78."

Fillmore chuckled. "Well, any more precipitation, and it might ruin Lavender's roof garden. That's for sure."

"We mustn't have that, now," Morris said with a grin as he let himself into his triple-decker. His mind already was in more places than it should be right now. A prolonged conversation with Fillmore would have been hazardous. He pulled out his new phone, thumbed over to contacts, and found Elijah's number right where it belonged. He smiled. Ginger and Gary had better customer service than the Apple store.

Then he called his old partner to find out how Barbara Sosa was doing.

As the phone rang, Morris' mind was stuck on how he had bumped into Bob Sosa the day before. Something seemed off about him, but he couldn't place it.

"Hey," Morris said into the phone after Elijah had offered his greeting. "How's Barbie Sosa doing?"

"She's OK. She's a lady of beauty and grace, but still, she's pretty shocked." Then there was a pause. "By the way, did you see Bob yesterday?"

"Yeah, like I said, I bumped into him on the way to see your cousin."

"Did he say anything to you?" asked Elijah.

"Not a lot."

"Interesting," said Elijah.

"What?" asked Morris.

"Barb was under the impression you two had met, talked a lot about something."

"It was like a ten-second meeting in the men's room in the afternoon," said Morris.

"Yeah, well, he said something to Barb about it," said Elijah. "According to her, he was kind of a mess lately. Something had him worried, and she had the impression you were going to watch out for him."

"He did ask me if I knew someone at the AG's office, but he didn't say why. I figured he was cleaning up more of Sonny's shit."

The two friends were silent for a moment.

"Are you thinking some kind of foul play?" Morris asked.

"I don't know," answered Elijah. "Maybe Bob was depressed about something and jumped onto the tracks only to get cold feet? Or how about this? Let's say he was into something dirty and was thinking of coming clean to the AG, but couldn't live with himself."

Both paused for a moment, weighing different possibilities.

"If we start poking around, Barb might not want to know the answer," said Elijah.

"I know," said Morris. "Maybe the video will tell us something. I just don't see Bob jumping onto the tracks."

"Yeah, well, you might want to skip the wake," said Elijah. "Barb had a few choice words for you."

"I haven't seen in her years," countered Morris.

"I don't know, somehow she was convinced Bob thought you were on his side. I think her comment was something like 'Bob should never have put his faith in that drunk asshole,' her words, not mine."

Morris contemplated the news.

"I mean I would have said drunk Irish asshole," said Elijah. "But there's a little redundancy to that."

Morris laughed. Then a thought crossed his mind. "Did Manning talk with Barb?"

"Not sure, but I assume at some point, she'll hear her side of things," said Elijah.

"Seriously," said Morris. "I forgot about bumping into Bob. It wasn't that big of a deal. Maybe I am slipping or something."

Elijah remained silent, and Morris wondered if his old partner hadn't reached the same assessment.

"I'll call Manning and tell her what I remember," said Morris. I should get ahead of this."

With that, he exchanged goodbyes with Elijah, who reminded him that he had Police Command School training the next two days.

After hanging up, he called Manning but got her voice mail. He left a succinct message that he had bumped into Bob Sosa but didn't think there was anything significant to the conversation. Sosa's wife apparently felt otherwise for some reason.

He then dropped his phone on the table and collapsed on the couch.

Chapter 9

The next morning, Morris awoke to the ringing of his cellphone.

"Hello," he said groggily.

"Fitzgerald, this is Joanne Manning."

Morris tried to clear the cobwebs.

"What the fuck is going on here?"

He sat up on the couch and felt dizzy. He struggled to collect his thoughts. "Yeah, I saw Bob Sosa the day before yesterday, literally bumped into him. The only thing I remember is he asked me if I knew anyone at the AG's office. It slipped my mind, but apparently, his wife thinks we had a bigger conversation."

"Yes, she does," said Manning. Morris grimaced. It sounded as though Manning had spoken with Barbara Sosa. "What aren't you telling me?"

“Nothing. Honest. Maybe Bob said more than I realized, or maybe I said more than I realized. I was on my way to a physical for shit’s sake.”

“I’ll tell you what,” Manning said. “Meet me at the Red Fez for lunch. I am going to want to hear what you say in person.”

The Red Fez was an upscale Middle Eastern cafe in Boston’s South End. Manning apparently was taking her engagement to someone of Syrian descent seriously.

“How about meeting me over at Castle Island, at Sullivan’s, instead,” said Morris. “My treat.”

“Sullivan’s? A hot dog joint? Such a big spender. What do you have against Middle Eastern food?”

“Nothing,” said Morris. “It’s the customers.”

She gave a snappy comeback. “That’s pretty racist, don’t you think?”

“No,” winced Morris as if he had been stung by a politically correct hornet. “If you’ve been to the Red Fez lately, lunchtime is for the alphabet agencies – FBI, TSA, all those guys – all looking for undocumented immigrants. I get nervous around suits and sunglasses.”

“Whatever,” Manning groaned. “OK, I’ll meet you at Sullivan’s at noon.”

Morris set an alarm for 11:30 and then fell back to sleep, trying to chase away the migraine that he felt coming.

Despite ignoring the alarm for five minutes, he managed to put on a coat and make it down to Sully’s by noon. Clear but cool skies. Boston meteorologists all sucked since Don Kent retired in the 1980s. There was a guy you could trust. Bushy eyebrows and a plain sportcoat and tie, the man’s hair always looked combed but never groomed. Today’s forecasters more looked like the cast of a reality TV dating show.

Still, the weather remained a nice break from the recent downpours. On the short walk down to Castle Island, Morris felt good. Maybe it was the extended sleep he managed or maybe his brain and body were finally healing. He felt clear and sharp and a thought crossed his mind. He texted Goldi about visiting some spots around Back Bay. He needed to find Cathy and resolved to be a better cousin to her and Happy.

As he crossed the parking lot at Sullivan's at the edge of South Boston's Castle Island, he spotted Manning and could tell she was in a foul mood. Morris was unsure if he was the source of her consternation and tried keep his greeting pleasant and simple.

They proceeded to order hot dogs, fries, and shakes, and Morris decided to break the ice first.

"Rough day?" he asked.

"Just a little exhausted," said Manning. "After I got off the phone with you, I got stuck with a robbery call from the Japanese Consulate's office."

"No kidding? Someone broke into the consulate?"

"No, some Japanese company was at the convention center for a trade show, and someone swiped a bunch of cellphones. The robbery detectives weren't around, so I got it."

Morris stayed quiet, thinking of a way to shift the conversation, but Manning beat him to it.

"So what was Bob Sosa into?" she said bluntly.

Morris shrugged. He had the same question.

"Let me be clear with you," she said. "I'm going to find out, and when I do, I won't give a shit about him, his wife, you, any of your buddies, any of your pensions."

"Listen, Joanne," Morris began.

"Stop the bullshit," she interjected. "Tell me about your meeting with Sosa. What did he ask you to do? "

"Honest, I walked into the men's room at the Transportation Building, and there he was coming out."

"Well, what did you two talk about?"

"What do two straight guys talk about in a men's room?" responded Morris. "Not much." He could tell Manning thought there was more to the story, but their order was up, and it gave Morris a momentary reprieve.

He took a few bites of the hot dog and a sip off his shake.

"Honest, I've been wracking my brain," he said, recalling the last time he saw Sosa alive. "We said 'Hi,' and he asked if I knew anyone at the AG's office."

"You didn't think to tell me that yesterday at the crime scene?"

"Jesus Christ, give me a break. It was a pretty busy day," Morris said, turning and starting to walk the path around Castle Island.

Manning followed, matching his pace. "Listen, I'm a female homicide detective. That means I have to work twice as hard for the same pay and three times the bullshit," said Manning. "You have no idea what it's like to be a woman in this job."

"Yeah, well you have no idea what it's like to be a man in it, either," Morris replied casually.

"What's that supposed to mean?"

Morris shook his head. "Trust me, I'm not oblivious to all the crap. I'm just saying if I can't know what it's like to be you, you can't know what it's like to be me." He paused, not sure the words made sense even to him. "I'm just saying, don't assume everything is a walk in the park because you have a penis, that's all."

"Yeah, well at least you can walk in the park," shot back Manning. "When I was at Northeastern, I wouldn't dare cut through the Fens or the Common at night. And your Green Line, that was the worst. I was groped by the perverts all the time, never a cop in sight, mind you."

Morris contemplated a few replies while he kept walking. Finally, he decided to rebut her generalization.

"The T is safe," he said in an even tone. "It's the passengers that make it unsafe. The MBTA is a moving monument to Yankee frugality. It's sturdy, cheap and quirky. It's not as elegant as the systems in Paris or Moscow, and it's got a funky smell."

He stopped and looked at her. "Everyone in Boston has been victimized one way or another when riding the rails, but everyone depends on the MBTA. The perverts aren't much different from the politicians that run everything. They do what they do because they know they can get away with it."

He then turned and took a few more steps, stopping at a red bench.

"What is it then?" asked Manning. "What did Sosa think he could get away with?"

Morris looked at her and let go a laugh.

“Come on,” she insisted. “Don’t give me some sort of Southie Code bullshit. I have no problem going after dirty public employees.”

“Bob wasn’t dirty,” Morris shot back. “And he wasn’t a public employee. We’re the T for fuck’s sake.”

“Fine,” said Manning between sips of her shake. “Quasi-public employees or whatever you want to call them.”

Morris sat down on the bench.

“Good. It’s too cold to do the loop,” Manning said referring to the two-mile path that leads out and around Fort Independence, one of United States’ oldest military fortifications.

“Did anything come from the video?” Morris asked.

“Your deputy director’s still stalling on that.”

Morris didn’t look at Manning, but as he sat, he raised his hand and pointed toward the statue in front of him. “Robert Greene,” he said with his eyes fixed on a bust of a firefighter. “Former Marine, fallen firefighter. It says there he died November 27, 1978, but most folks probably don’t know he was actually injured two days earlier, the Saturday of Thanksgiving weekend.”

Manning remained quiet.

“He fell from a building on Alpha Road fighting a fire. I was friends with his kids, Peter and Robbie.” Morris shook his head at the recollection. “A lot of tragedy, I’ll tell you. Both boys wound up dying young, one at the hands of a coward with a knife and the other by a drunk driver.”

“You forget I’m a cop,” said Manning. “I get it. Good people die. Shit happens. Prove to me Bob Sosa was a saint or martyr, and I’ll put up the statue myself.”

Morris sighed. “No, that’s not my point,” he said. “But it does make you wonder what they might say on our memorial some day, right?”

Manning seemed unmoved.

“Sorry, I’ve just been staring at a lot of names in granite lately,” he said. “My point is Bobby Greene was the best ladder man in Boston. They show up at this nothing fire. He goes up the ladder as he had probably done a thousand times. Somehow he falls. No one saw it. Two days later, his wife’s a widow.”

Manning looked at Morris. Her expression had shifted, but she still held a hard exterior.

"Listen," Morris said. "Maybe Bob Sosa just fell."

Manning looked exasperated. "His wife doesn't think that," she said finally.

"I gather," said Morris.

Manning gave Morris a look and then spoke. "Your Dyani Swan, there, she also told me this morning that some anonymous tip came in. They said Bob Sosa was mixed up in some underground sex ring."

"What?" said Morris incredulously. "You're fuckin' kiddin' me."

"You ever hear of a group of black kids they call the Lost Boys?"

"Yeah," said Morris "Land pirates, they pickpocket and mug folks on the Common. I think most of them are actually Somali."

"Supposedly, they also turn tricks," she said.

"I heard that too," said Morris. "Not uncommon. You're dealing with the ostracized of the ostracized. Seriously, most of them have been banned from the homeless shelters. They shack up in the Boylston tunnels. They gotta get by somehow."

"Yeah, well, according to the tip at least, Bob was one of their Johns."

"No fuckin' way," said Morris. "The Mantis was as straight-laced a guy as you would find."

"Yeah, and they always end up being the ones with a few gigs of child porn on their computers," said Manning.

"You're not taking it seriously are you? Tell me you didn't say anything to Barb Sosa."

"No," she replied. "Not yet. Honestly, I was hoping you were going to tell me he had a gambling problem or something."

Morris just shook his head. Perhaps as the incident with his old hockey coach taught him, you could never be sure that you really knew people, but Bob Sosa's idea of breaking the rules was failing to declare Bingo winnings on his tax return.

"Joanne, trust me," he said. "Sosa was squeaky clean."

"For the sake of his wife and kids, I hope that's true," Manning said. "But everyone I talked to made a big deal out of the fact that your guy Sosa was always volunteering at homeless shelters."

Morris was about to object, but Manning cut him off. "I know, I know," she said. "That doesn't mean anything on its own. I'm just saying, whatever you come across, the sooner you share it with me, the better for everyone."

The two sat quiet for a moment, and Morris contemplated all the possibilities. A stiff breeze then whipped up off the Boston Harbor.

"Shit, it's cold here," Manning said. "I shouldn't have let you talk me into meeting here."

"Oh come on," pleaded Morris. "Castle Island, I have the ocean to my back. I can see anyone on the walking paths, and the roar of jets as they're coming into Logan drowns out anyone trying to bug me."

"Paranoid much?"

"No, I have just learned to be cautious," Morris replied. "You know Edgar Allen Poe served as a private here at Fort Independence?"

She seemed unfazed by the trivia.

"Supposedly his time here served as inspiration for his *The Cask of Amontillado*."

"What?" she said.

"*The Cask of Amontillado,* short story, a guy gets buried alive?"

"I'm going to bury you alive," Manning blurted out.

Morris laughed.

With that, Manning stood up. "I need to get some real work done." She then eyed Morris, who felt like he was being sized up. "You wear your food well," she said, nodding at a mustard stain on his sweatshirt. "You might want to change that before you go into work."

Morris smiled broadly. "Thanks for the tip."

"Consider it a free piece of police intelligence."

"You know that's an oxymoron," he shot back, as Manning started to walk away. He wasn't sure she had heard him until he saw her extend her middle finger toward him without even turning around.

At that moment, he pulled out his cellphone and dialed Goldilocks. After the customary hellos, he asked Goldi if she had found a copy of the homeless survey.

"Yeah, I have one right here," she said.

"Under race, each box is numbered, right?" he asked.

"Yeah."

"What's listed as number two?"

"Black."

Morris paused, and Goldi chose to fill the silence. "What are you getting at?"

"Nothing, Goldi," Morris said, trying to avoid a conclusion he had already drawn. "Hey, I think we should try to find Beetlejuice, talk to him about the whole Sosa thing. While we're at it, maybe we can look for my cousin?"

"Sure," said Sann. "I have to head over to Back Bay later today. Maybe around there is as good a place as any to start."

"Sounds good. Let's also keep an eye out for the Lost Boys, too. I've got something I need to ask them."

Chapter 10

That afternoon Morris rode the Red Line to Downtown Crossing and switched to the Orange Line outbound to historic Back Bay Station, where he had agreed to meet up with Goldilocks. Back Bay was just one stop past Tufts Medical Center, and as the train performed its improvised dance of herks and jerks, Morris could imagine Bob Sosa being corkscrewed and pinned against the platform.

He shook his head. If you were going to kill yourself, there are a lot easier ways of doing it. Bob would have known that. Beetlejuice supposedly saw the whole thing. Beetle was a brilliant pickpocket, drug dealer, and meth user. He may have been full of riddles, but rarely was he full of shit.

Morris had arrested the man enough to have seen a glimpse of his former identity. It was sometime in the 1980s that Alex Scott broke from his reality of being the son of two Endicott College professors. He had grown up in the well-to-do and sheltered Cape Ann community of Manchester by the Sea, about forty-five minutes north of Boston.

Morris remembered meeting Beetlejuice's parents in court a couple of times. They seemed to be nice folks. They had set him up in an apartment in Kenmore Square, convenient for his classes at Boston University. Somewhere along the line, he stopped going to school. Then he started hanging out with the street crowd. From there, things spiraled down quickly.

Meth addiction could unravel anyone in a hurry. His parents may have been confused, but Morris had seen it enough that it made sense. Still, Beetle had his moments of clarity when his natural intellect would shine through. He had to be smart because he now had to be into his 50s, probably close to Morris' age, and had somehow managed to survive at least three decades on the city's streets where life expectancy was typically much shorter.

Beetle's ramblings, at least as Bruce Donohue had heard them, made no sense, but in spotting the number 2 on one of the fire department's load-out bags yesterday, a thought struck Morris, and he recalled a conversation with the drug addict about how the homeless were being turned into numbers, just like the Nazis did to the Jews.

That was Beetlejuice's response to the annual homeless survey, and Morris had to admit he shared the man's disdain for ethnic checkboxes.

The train entered historic Back Bay station and Morris took the escalator up to the main lobby. The complex served as an intercity rail, commuter rail, and rapid transit station located just south of Copley Square in the Back Bay and South End neighborhoods of Boston. Morris looked around the lobby and the waiting area of the station, past the nine-foot bronze statue of civil rights and labor icon A. Philip Randolph.

Morris felt himself smile. It was at this very location in December of 1990 that he and Elijah earned transit police notoriety. A northbound Amtrak train, it's Night Owl, doing an overnight run from Washington, D.C., came flying into the station at twice the posted speed. The train derailed, slamming into an adjacent commuter rail train with nearly one thousand passengers on it.

The force of the collision in the bowels of the station was so strong that it caused damage to the street surface above. All together, four-hundred-fifty-three passengers were injured, but there were no fatalities thanks to the quick response of multiple public safety agencies. Morris and Elijah were among the first on the scene, rushing into the chaos of twisted metal. For their actions, they were recommended for the prestigious Hanna awards, named in honor of a Massachusetts state trooper murdered in the line of duty in February 1983. During the ceremony, the then Lieutenant Governor leaned over and asked the two T-cops, "who do you work for?" When Morris replied, "the MBTA," she responded "Oh" and turned back to the speaker on the dais.

From then on, their fellow officers throughout the state referred to transit police as the "Oh" police. It was the perfect moniker that summed up the general outside attitude toward the department since its founding in 1968.

Morris loved Back Bay. In a city spoiled by gentrification, the station was a throwback, dim and grim with a smell of urine and diesel fuel, which Morris found charming in a dirty, filthy way. He appreciated that there were two Dunkin Donut shops in the lobby, providing a constant staple of fridge-to-microwave nourishment for the commuting public.

As Morris passed through, he gave a nod to Ahmed, the owner of the small convenience store in the station. Business had been booming since he started stocking vintage World War II gas masks, which fell into high demand every time the odors of the subway shifted their way toward the station.

Morris hadn't realized that his cellphone had been vibrating since the Chinatown stop. He took his phone out of his coat and noticed he had missed calls from Boston Police Sergeant Joanne Manning and Goldilocks.

He returned the call to Sergeant Manning and was greeted with "Did you get my texts? Have you seen the Tweets?"

"No, I don't text or Tweet."

"So you haven't seen what they're reporting?"

"Who's reporting?" replied Morris

"Everyone!" she bellowed "Thanks to you assholes, half of the Twittersphere is claiming Bob Sosa was pushed, and the other half says he was some kind of a sex offender."

"Where are they getting that?" asked Morris.

"MBTA sources supposedly!"

Morris cringed.

"Your security director over there just had a press conference on her own. The police commissioner, the mayor, the DA are all bullshit," said Manning.

There was an understood rule that whenever you had overlapping jurisdictions, you released statements jointly. In Boston, there was the added requisite of including the mayor's office. Heaven forbid the mayor miss some camera time.

"Maybe the leaks came from Baghdad Bob," Morris said.

"What?"

"Bob Mackay, he's the T's public affairs guy," explained Morris. "Remember the first Gulf War, Saddam's PR guy, everyone called him Baghdad Bob?"

"I was in preschool," said Manning. "But I think it's all your new director. Diane whatever the fuck her name is."

"Swan, Dyani Swa–"

"I don't give a shit! Just what's her game?"

"Joanne, seriously, I am clueless on this," said Morris.

There was a pause. Manning seemed to have exhausted herself and took a breath. "Well, she said you have two people of interest. One is a sex offender, and the other has a pretty long list of run-ins with the law, drugs mostly. She has a few screen grabs from video. You ought to check them out."

Morris didn't need the photos. The descriptions matched Kenny the Clown and Beetlejuice.

"Did she say something about a sex ring?" asked Morris.

"No, but she said the MBTA police were pursuing 'a number of possible motives.'"

Morris shook his head.

"Help me out here," said Manning. "I need to talk to those guys before anyone else does. Have you got any idea where they are?"

“I’ve got a few ideas where to find them,” said Morris.

“What about the shelters?”

Morris grinned. “These guys don’t hang out in shelters. They don’t take them. Drugs, sex offenders aren’t welcome.”

“Oh great. This whole thing is turning into a cluster fuck.”

Morris considered a reply, but he looked up and saw a familiar but out-of-place face coming toward him.

“Listen, Joanne, I have to run. I’m already on it. I’ll find them for you.”

Morris hung up and put away his phone as the young man approached.

“Fitzgerald, right?” said firefighter Patrick McKenna extending his hand.

“Yeah,” Morris said, extending his own. “How are you doing?” He noticed Patrick was carrying a forcible-entry tool – a giant crow-bar-like device designed to help firefighters pry open doors.

As he considered asking Patrick what he was doing at Back Bay with such a thing, his eye caught an attractive blond woman hurrying in their direction. Then to his surprise, the woman waved toward him.

Morris turned around to see who might be behind him. No one.

He blinked twice and looked more closely at the woman who was now only fifteen feet away. She was dressed in leggings, a skirt, an Irish knit sweater, and knee-high boots with heels that seemed a bit higher than she was used to.

“Sergeant Fitzgerald,” she said, and Morris instantly placed the voice but had to do a double take at the face that he normally had seen hidden behind curls stuffed into a baseball hat.

“Gol – Susan,” Morris caught himself, assuming Goldilocks had some motive for her shift in wardrobe. “Good to see you.”

She smiled, and turned toward Patrick. “Firefighter McKenna, thanks for being able join us.”

“Hey, it’s just Pat,” he said breaking into a smile.

She turned back toward Morris. “Yes, I connected with Pat yesterday evening, looking for more information about the incident at Medical Center.”

She continued, occasionally glancing at McKenna. Morris nodded along and tried not to grin.

"I see," Morris interrupted. "Well, it's a good thing Pat was able to join us and bring his tool."

Goldi picked up on Morris' crass double entendre and shot him a look, but the comment seemed to fly right by McKenna, who began to speak.

"Yeah, Officer Sann, here –"

"Please, Suzy," Goldilocks interrupted.

"Well, yeah, Suzy, texted me you guys could use some help getting into some of the tunnels, looking for those homeless guys. I figured what the heck. I'm off today anyway."

"You don't say?" said Morris. "Texting, huh?" he added, looking at Goldi. "That's what you kids do these days."

McKenna laughed, apparently oblivious to the ribbing Morris was trying to give Goldilocks. "It's OK," he said. "My dad is the same way, hates anything with a screen on it."

Sann smiled at Morris and then looked back at McKenna. "Old timers. What can you say?"

"Yeah, well this old timer thinks we should get started," Morris said. "I was thinking we head over to Carleton and Yarmouth."

"Good idea," Sann said as the three turned to head toward the exit. "That's a pretty popular spot for the homeless. I've never seen Beetlejuice there, but I bet someone he knows will be around."

As the three walked with Patrick McKenna leading, Sann caught her heel on something and braced herself against Morris.

"Careful, there, officer," Morris whispered.

Goldilocks glared at him. "What?"

"Nothing," answered Morris. "Just this doesn't seem to be your usual pragmatic fashion."

"Oh fuck you," she said out of earshot.

"There's the Goldi I know."

"Listen, can't a girl dress a little nice from time to time?"

"Hey, I think it's great," said Morris, as Patrick McKenna went through the door ahead of them, holding it for Morris and Sann.

"Enough," she said under her breath while she smiled and said "thank you" to Mr. February.

As they stepped onto the sidewalk and waited for the traffic to clear so they could cross Dartmouth Street, Morris heard the familiar shout of Bruce Donohue.

"What's he doing here?" Morris said quietly as Bruce walked toward the three.

"Hey there, Morris," Bruce said shaking his fellow T-cop's hand. "Geez, this is turning into some shit show, huh?"

Morris could see Bruce's eye glance over to Goldi and do a quick and not-so-subtle up and down.

"Hi, Detective Sergeant Donohue, MBTA police," he said gathering what charm he could.

"Fuck you, Bruce," Goldi responded.

As happened with Morris, Goldilocks' change of wardrobe and use of hair and beauty products apparently confused Bruce to the point where he didn't initially recognize the T's homeless liaison.

"Pat McKenna," cut in the tall firefighter. McKenna didn't quite have a glower, but even in his state of surprise, Bruce registered the mannerism.

Morris decided to move the conversation forward. "What are you doing here?" he asked.

"Oh," said Bruce gathering himself. "I'm grabbing a couple of uniforms. We gotta help out BPD. They just pulled a body out of the Muddy River."

"Why do they need you?"

"I have no clue," replied Bruce. "But our new security czar, Ms. Swan, wants us butting into everything we can. She says that's the way they did when she was at 'Homeland,'" he finished, using air quotes to add disdain.

"Did you see that news conference?" Goldilocks interjected.

"See it? I had to be there," answered Bruce.

"Did you see the video?" Morris asked.

"Yeah, you never see how Sosa got on the tracks, but Beetlejuice and Kenny the Clown were right there. I'm not sure that means they were involved."

"Well, our fearless leader thinks they were," said Morris. Things seemed to be unraveling fast. He considered giving Chief

Stephanie Tam a call, but there wasn't much she could do from Israel. Of course, that was probably someone's plan from the start. Politics in Boston was like a fast-food menu. Sure, things seemed to change frequently, but the truth was it was all the same crap, just packaged in a different way to see if people would buy it.

There was a break in the traffic and Sann and McKenna had already stepped off the sidewalk. Morris turned to join them. "Watch your neck," Morris shouted to Bruce, and he ran to catch the two ahead of him.

As they crossed Dartmouth Street and stepped onto the red-brick walk, Goldilocks again caught a heel. She looked quickly at Morris. "Not a fuckin' word."

Pat McKenna turned around quickly, and Sann just smiled back as if to say everything was fine.

"I ain't goin' to give you shit, Goldi," Morris said. "I think we've got bigger problems on our hands."

"No kidding," said Goldilocks. "Everyone is freaking out that the homeless had something to do with Bob Sosa's death. Last night they started rousting people from around North Station."

"Who?" asked Morris.

"I don't know," said Sann. "It wasn't us, and BPD said they had no one down there."

"That doesn't sound right," said Morris.

"I heard from Tin Man," said Sann. "The homeless are getting agitated. You and I know both know that isn't good. You have a lot of desperate people who might do some desperate things."

The three followed the walking path that provided South End pedestrians a respite from the hazards of Boston traffic.

"Have you heard of the Archangels?" Morris asked Goldilocks.

"Yeah, kind of like the Guardian Angels of the homeless?"

"You got it," said Morris. "Started a few years back. Basically the homeless figured they had to start protecting themselves. One of the orchestrators of the thing was a kid named Ferret."

Sann stopped and stared at her fellow T-cop.

"Yeah, that's him," said Morris. "If the Archangels get involved, they aren't going to take shit from anybody. Then it becomes time to break out the riot gear."

"Ferret's dead though," said Sann.

"Maybe, but it doesn't matter," said Morris. "Plenty of people willing to take up the banner in his place. Like you said, a lot of desperate people."

Morris then stopped and gave a short whistle to Patrick McKenna who was twenty feet ahead of the two T-cops and their destination. "We're here, Pat."

Boston's South End featured all the manifestations of a trendy neighborhood – brownstone townhouses, tree-lined streets, walking paths, and an industrial ventilation shaft hidden in plain sight.

The structure had the appearance of a neighborhood brownstone in height, scale, materials, and color, but the only people who used it as a domicile were the homeless who could access from it within the subway system. The T relied on the massive ventilation shaft to exhaust fumes from Back Bay station. Previously, the air-quality had become so poor at the transit hub that people with lung conditions had been advised to avoid going there.

McKenna removed the forcible-entry tool that he had slung over his shoulder, but before he could demolish the side-door entrance, Morris reached into his pocket and retrieved one of the MBTA's "P" keys, which provided entry to most of the maintenance areas in the system.

Morris inserted the key, turned the knob, and opened the door, allowing McKenna to walk in first. He thought he saw a slight expression of disappointment on the firefighter's face. As Sann followed, Morris said, in a barely audible voice, "I sure hope he didn't bring his big tool along for nothing."

Sann sneered, but her expression quickly changed upon entering the confined area. Many of the city's most destitute called the ventilation shaft home, and the evidence of it was right inside the door, with mattresses and bedding turned upside down and tattered clothes dumped in a corner of the shaft

Goldilocks turned to Morris. "What the fuck?"

"Huh?" asked Patrick McKenna turning around.

"Sorry," she said, gathering herself. "Someone has been here. This is the way the city deals the with homeless. They're not going to arrest them or physically throw them out. They destroy where they're living, making it a pain in the ass for them." She shook her head. "I mean come on, it's not like they don't have it hard enough, but now they have people messing with their shit."

Morris stayed quiet. Boston Police weren't known to enter T property like this ventilation shaft. Then again, it wasn't like T-cops frequented it either, but he had to concur with Goldi's assessment. Someone was messing with the homeless.

The three looked around, but there was no sign of Beetlejuice or anyone else for that matter.

"Next?" Morris queried, looking at Sann.

"Maybe we walk on down near Copley. It's starting to get cold, and the grates by the library turn out to be a major gathering spot. Plenty of places to look."

A thought struck Morris. "I was talking with Joanne Manning earlier. There's a crazy rumor that the Lost Boys might be mixed up in this somehow."

Goldilocks shrugged. "I guess we could swing down by Boylston, too. I don't know about them, though. They kind of stick to themselves."

"Well, here's the thing," said Morris. "I think Beetlejuice was trying to say 'the deuce did it.'"

"The deuce?" responded Goldilocks.

"Yeah, number two," said Morris.

"Oh yeah, deuce, two," said McKenna nodding along.

"Oh, the survey!" Goldilocks said. "Well, what about the nine of spades?"

"No fucking clue," answered Morris.

"What's this?" asked McKenna, looking at some spray paint along the walls.

"Graffiti," said Morris. "Just not very good," he added upon further inspection. What caught his attention wasn't the amateurish nature of it, however. It was the fact that twice in less than twenty-four hours he had seen a piss-poor rendition of the anarchy A, but Morris decided not to share that detail with Sann and McKenna. "Come on," he said after a moment. "Let's head over to Copley."

Copley Square was only a couple of blocks away, and this time, Morris took the lead, giving Sann and McKenna an opportunity to chat. He felt like a chaperone at a junior high dance but with no flask to spike his own punch. They talked a lot without saying much. McKenna seemed more the quiet type, but it might have been that with Goldi, once she got started, it could be an endless stream of chatter with an occasional profanity thrown in. Morris could tell she was trying to constrain her vocabulary, but when a Prius nearly took her out crossing Huntington Ave. she let out an F-bomb followed by the C-word that even Morris avoided. McKenna took it in stride, and that seemed like a good sign.

Suddenly a loud horn rang as they walked in front of the Prudential Center. Morris turned, expecting to see a truck and instead was facing a boat – Beantown Bettie as a matter of fact.

Boston's Duck Tours were a fleet of authentic WWII amphibious landing vehicles that traveled on land and water, cruising by all the places that make Boston the birthplace of freedom and a city of firsts.

"Quack, Quack, Morris!" shouted one of the captains.

"Nicky, how the hell are you?" responded Morris as he recognized an old T-worker, who was now stepping down from the vehicle.

Nicky gave Morris a firm handshake. "Shit, I heard you retired."

"Not 'til they pack me in ice buddy," replied Morris. "What the fuck are you doing here?" He then turned to Sann and McKenna. "Nicky here used to be a commuter rail conductor."

"I still am a conDUCKtor," he quipped with proper emphasis.

Morris laughed.

"Seriously, it wasn't that hard to get my captain's license. It's a good gig and has some perks."

"Oh really?"

"Yep, picked up my third wife here about a year ago."

"You don't say?" responded Morris.

Nicky proceeded to pull out his cellphone to show Morris a picture of a young Filipino woman. "She was visiting Boston with friends, took a tour, and the rest is history."

"Jesus, Nicky, looks like you're robbing the cradle," said Morris.

"And she's robbing the grave," he shot back.

“OK, Nick, good to see you but we gotta –”

“That’s why I stopped you,” the boat captain interrupted. “See something, say something, right?”

Morris shrugged.

“I was giving these two tourists a ride this morning, and they tell me they blew out the tire on their rental car last night going over an open manhole. Sure enough, I drive by where it is, and the cover is a little off.”

“So?” asked Morris, feeling a little lost.

“So it says MBTA,” countered Nicky. “I didn’t know the T had any manholes. Plenty of assholes, but I didn’t know of any manholes.”

Morris laughed. “OK, where was it, we’ll have someone check it out.”

“It’s right around the corner,” said Nicky, pointing.

“Sure, Nick. You know, thanks for saying something.”

“No problem,” he replied. But Morris detected a tone in his old friend’s voice.

“What is it Nicky?”

“Listen, my wife’s parents are in the Pru right now, and I’m trying to show them a little local color. I was wondering if you could help me out?”

The two spoke a little further, and Morris was happy to oblige Nicky’s interest in showing his new in-laws some authentic Boston culture. He then exchanged goodbyes with his friend and gathered with McKenna and Sann on the sidewalk.

“What’s going on?” Goldilocks asked her fellow T-cop.

“Come on,” said Morris, leading the trio around the corner. “I just have to do one thing here.”

About a minute later, Morris heard the distinct horn of Beantown Bettie as it was about to turn the corner. That was his cue to step off the sidewalk.

With another sudden blast of the horn from Nicky, now right in front of Morris, the T-cop turned, and shouted toward the duck boat, spotting an older Filipino couple, “Watch wheah ya fuggin’ goin ya turkey! Use ya fuggin’ blinkah next time!”

With that, Nicky gave a shorter toot on the horn as he edged around Morris.

“Hey, there’s a cah fuggin pahkd right heah! Ah, go back to Wustah, you fuggin’ bastahd!” the T-cop shouted as Nicky gave him a wink, and the Filipino couple held out their cellphones, apparently attempting to capture a Bostonian in his natural habitat.

Morris stepped back onto the sidewalk and just raised his eyebrows at his two compatriots.

“Go back to Worcester?” Sann offered.

“Sorry, I was improvising,” replied Morris.

“Where to now?” asked McKenna.

Morris looked at Sann. She didn’t say anything, but he knew what she was thinking.

“Well, it should be right around here,” he said as Sann nodded in the affirmative.

The three ventured a short way down the block and instantly spotted a manhole cover slightly askew. Patrick McKenna stepped out into traffic, holding up a hand and waving traffic around. Morris and Goldilocks looked down at the cover. They both looked at each other but didn’t say anything. It probably was a coincidence.

“Hey Patrick,” Morris said. “Do you think you can use that weapon of yours there to pull this cover back into place?”

McKenna nodded, grabbed the forcible-entry tool and used one end of it to push the cover flat.

“Where’s that go?” Goldi asked as the three made their way back to the sidewalk, not without McKenna and a motorist exchanging the one-finger salute so common to Boston traffic. Maybe he and Goldi were made for each other.

“I’m not sure,” said Morris. “Probably down to the old Boston and Albany platform.”

“What are you thinking?” asked Sann.

“I’m thinking the only other way to get there is to walk the tracks from Back Bay,” said Morris. What he didn’t say was that if someone wanted to get in or out of the MBTA system without being seen, these manholes were one way to do it. He did the math in his head; it had to be a quarter mile from Back Bay, which was probably only a half mile from Tufts Medical Center. No way. It had to be just a coincidence.

"I say we go then," said McKenna.

Morris and Goldilocks both looked at the firefighter.

"What?" he said. "This is fun. And I'm enjoying the company, too."

With that, a smile broke across Goldilocks' face. A dozen comments raced through Morris' mind, but he decided to let the two have their flirtatious moment in peace.

As the three turned to head to Back Bay Station, Morris suggested that Goldilocks should call dispatch to alert them they were going to be on the tracks.

"If we do that, we are going to have to get clearance and wear protective vests," she said. "Didn't you learn anything in right of way school?"

"I missed that day," Morris said sheepishly. "I think I was in court, probably busting Beetlejuice."

"You old timers got away with everything," she cracked.

"Yeah, well remind me to make it up some time."

Chapter 11

As they walked about a quarter mile down the cold, dark and dingy tracks, Morris cautioned Goldilocks and McKenna to be careful of the broken wine and beer bottles.

“I’m more worried about the hundreds of needles lying around here,” said Sann.

Morris nodded in the darkness. The three of them were making their way through the devil’s trash heap, every utensil of escape discarded onto the right of way.

“The bottles and needles are nothing compared to the rats the size of rabbits,” Morris said looking back at McKenna. “Imagine getting woken up by one of those gnawing at your feet.”

If the firefighter was shaken by the comment, he didn’t show it. “So you think someone came through here yesterday?” asked McKenna.

"I don't know," said Morris. "Kind of hard to tell. The guy we're looking for, though, he knows these tunnels as well as anyone."

"Beetlejuice," interjected McKenna.

"We'll make a T-cop out of you, yet," responded Morris. "Of course Goldi might have something to say about the T's policy on fraternization."

He couldn't quite see where it came from, but Morris felt a distinct and pointy elbow thrust into his side at the comment. Before he could muster a verbal retort, McKenna spoke.

"Whoa, check that out."

Goldilocks shined her flashlight on the abandoned platform ahead of them, and about thirty feet farther down Morris could make out a metal grate, about the size of a fireplace.

"How often have you been down here?" Goldilocks asked him.

The truth was Morris hadn't been this far down the tunnel in a long time. He was a vintage member of the transit police. Unlike most of the younger cops, who preferred the comfort a cruiser to a walk down some deserted tunnel, he wasn't afraid of going where the crime was on the subway. However, even he had his limits, and this tunnel was one of dirtiest and creepiest in the entire system.

He just wasn't going to let Goldi and McKenna know that.

"Honestly," he answered Sann, "not too often. I can't even tell you when this platform was built. Maybe the '20s. That's 1920s," he added turning to the young couple next to him.

On the other side of the grate was a metal tube, which at one time likely served as a ventilation or an access shaft. Morris observed the debris that had been pushed aside. "Yeah, someone's been through here recently."

The trio knelt down as Sann shined the light through the tube. "Tears of Allah?" she said.

Morris nodded in the darkness. "Yeah, I think you may be right."

"Tears of what?" asked McKenna.

"Tears of Allah," said Goldilocks. "Homeless talk about it. To get there you have to crawl through some kind of shaft. It's a hideout kind of."

"More like a drug den," said Morris. "That's how it got its name." From the ensuing silence, he figured his associates may have been confused. "Years back, Osama bin Laden claimed he had made some new kind of heroin, and he was going to unleash it on the West. Kill the infidels with drugs or whatever."

"I first heard about it a few months ago," said Sann.

"So you think that might be it?' said McKenna.

"Well, I've never been there," said Morris. "And this is one of the few places in the system that I haven't been, so ...."

McKenna crouched down and peered through the grate as Sann continued to shine the flashlight. "You know, I could call over to Ladder 15, get rappelling equipment, lights."

"I like the sound of that," said Morris.

McKenna fumbled with a hand-held radio and tried to reach Boston Fire dispatch.

"It ain't going to work," said Morris. "Our radios don't work in the tunnels either."

McKenna then reached for his cellphone.

"And you can forget about cell service here. You might a get a signal closer to Back Bay, but we're too far away from where they strung the cell antennas."

"OK, I'll head down toward the station," said McKenna. "Are you sure you're OK here?"

Morris was certain the inquiry was directed at Goldilocks and waited for her to respond.

"Yes," she said "we'll be fine. You be careful going back there. Stay on Track 2. The commuter rail should be coming in on Track 3 sometime soon."

McKenna headed back toward the station while Morris and Goldilocks continued to poke around the abandoned platform. A thought struck Morris.

"Hey Goldi, shine that light over here."

Sann turned and cast her light near Morris.

"Try to get a little lower, just above the platform," he said.

Initially, he doubted his idea might work, but then he caught a slight glimpse as Sann moved the light.

"What?" she asked.

"Just hold the light there for a moment."

As Sann steadied her flashlight, Morris pulled out his phone and began to snap pictures.

"I don't get it," Sann said, still holding the light.

"Footprints," said Morris. "But I don't think there's anything useful here."

"What are you?" asked Sann, "A cobbler?"

Morris laughed. "Hey, I figured it was worth a shot." As he finished the words, his eye caught a glint of gold. "Shine the light over there, toward the grate."

Morris removed a pen from his coat pocket and used it to start picking through trash and dirt on the ground. At first, he thought his eyes had played tricks on him, but then he saw it again. A gold-looking necklace. He pulled it slightly, and it came free from some discarded rubbish. Holding it up into the beam of the flashlight, Morris could see the Irish Claddagh pendant on the end.

"Looks cheap," said Goldilocks.

Morris didn't disagree. He looked more closely and then gazed at the grate next to it.

"What's the deal?" she asked.

"I think my cousin Cathy had a necklace like this."

"Oh," Sann said.

Morris stood up and started opening the grate. "I'm going to go take a look down there. Your boyfriend should be back here with the other Jakes soon."

"Fuck you," Sann said. "You're not leaving me here in this creepy place. And he's not my boyfriend."

"Whatever," said Morris as he crouched down to go through the tube.

"And what the fuck is a Jake?" added Goldi.

"Jesus, Goldi," he said as he started to move down the tunnel. "I gotta teach you everything."

"And I gotta keep your ass out of trouble," he heard from behind him as the beam of her flashlight danced ahead of him.

"Jake," Morris said. "It's what we in the Boston area call firefighters."

"No shit?"

"No shit," he replied as he reached the end of the tube. "You see years ago, to get in the fireboxes they used what was called a 'J' key. Get it?"

He then stood up and reached his hand back into the tube to help Goldilocks.

"So they had a J key. How the fuck do you get Jake out of a J key?"

Morris held his laughter. As Sann heard her own voice, she apparently saw the connection.

"OK, I get it. I may have blond hair but I'm not a blond," she said.

"Watch it. You're stereotyping, Goldi."

She seemed like she was about to say something, but her flashlight caught the full expanse of the structure they had climbed into.

They were standing on a metal platform, in a giant cavern of a room. Water dripping from the ceiling had formed stalactites and strange orange-colored formations on the walls. To the side was a rickety ladder, leading down, and they moved toward it.

"I've got a bad feeling about this," she said. "There's a lot of ways I'd rather die than being scared to death."

"Can you shine the light down there?" Morris asked.

Goldilocks obliged.

"What's that?" Morris asked, spying what he thought might be a body.

The pair began to descend the ladder, and almost immediately they felt a temperature change and were hit with a blast of steam from a broken pipe.

"Tears of Allah," said Goldilocks.

It perhaps had once been a beautiful room, built in a bygone era when even the most utilitarian of spaces was built with craftsmanship and style. Now, it was a drug den with glorious arched brick walls, covered in graffiti. The floor was littered with hypodermic needles, broken bottles, and sewage. It was home to the most desperate of lowlifes in the homeless community.

"Welcome to Wonderland, Alice," Morris said as he reached the floor, eyeing a corner where it looked like a skin-and-bones frame was slumped against the wall. He took one step, but then the odor hit him.

"What's that smell?" shouted Goldi, putting a hand over her nose and mouth. "I'm goin' to fuckin' puke."

It was like rotten eggs. He took a step toward the body but lost his balance. "Oh shit," he said as he became woozie.

Morris' next conscious thought was the recognition of a pair of hands under his arms, pulling him up the ladder and through the metal tube and grate. His mind and vision cleared enough to process that he was on the abandoned platform again, now brightly lit.

"Anyone ever tell you you're a shit magnet?"

Morris looked up to see Deputy Chief Jay McKenna. He raised his eyebrows. The answer was yes, but he didn't want to spoil Jay's humor. "How about Miss Shit Magnet? How's she doing?"

"They're carrying her back to the station. She'll be alright."

"Not for long if she has to breathe all the diesel fumes there," Morris cracked.

"You're probably right," said McKenna. "That shit you were breathing probably is better for you than what the T recirculates."

"What was it?" asked Morris.

"Shit," implored McKenna. "Literally. Sewer gas. Hydrogen sulfide. You're a lucky leprechaun, Fitzgerald. No one in their right mind would go in that hell hole without a hazmat suit."

Morris tried to clear his throat. "Where's Patrick?" he said weakly.

"Lucky for you I didn't raise an idiot. He called the cavalry, and we were able to get you out of there in the nick of time. He's escorting your partner to the station and then probably the hospital I think."

"You might want to keep an eye on those two," Morris said in between coughs.

"Come on, you're going there too. Hydrogen sulfide is colorless, heavier than air. That's how come it hit you so strong on the bottom."

Morris tried to wave him off as they walked toward Back Bay. "Body," he finally got out. "There's a body there."

"I know" said McKenna. "We're recovering it."

"Who?" said Morris.

"No idea," said McKenna, who seemed to recognize a personal tone to Morris inquiry. "A woman, though, 50s, maybe 60s. Probably an OD."

Morris nodded as his personal guilt incapacitated him more than the sewer gas.

"Come on," said McKenna, pulling the T-cop along. "EMS is goin' to check you out and then take you to the hospital. You don't want to mess with this shit. It's deadly. You get it in the sewers and subways. You can even get it from mixing household chemicals. They call it detergent suicide in some places."

As they approached Back Bay, Morris could see a flood of state agencies setting up on the platform. It was a familiar scene. He could imagine what would come next. All branches of state law enforcement would vie for top dog at the scene. The Feds might even want a piece of the action. Jay and the firefighters would try to contain the hot zone, which meant Back Bay would be shut down. When that happens, the shit would really hit the fan at the MBTA.

"OK, Sherlock of the Subways," McKenna said as he turned to Morris. "The EMT's are here, and they need to strip you of all your clothes, including your gun belt and phone. Then off to Boston Medical for evaluation."

Morris continued to cough. "You forget, I've been through this before."

"That was fentanyl," McKenna said, referencing the gassing at the Broadway T stop eighteen months ago. "That's like chugging two bottles of Jägermeister. You start puking and go delusional. This stuff is like guzzling a bad batch of moonshine. It'll kill you."

The two eventually made their way upstairs and to the ambulance. Morris could see that a panic had returned to the city as word spread of another chemical attack. Except in this case, it wasn't an attack, just a lot of shit gas, but forget trying to put that genie back in the bottle in the age of social media.

As much as Morris had started feeling better, he began to feel motion sickness in the back of the ambulance as the driver cranked the siren and began weaving through traffic. Within minutes, however, they had safely arrived at Boston Medical Center, which appeared to be gearing up for a mass casualty event.

Above the din of an episode of "Wheel of Fortune" being shown on a wall-mounted TV, Morris heard a "Code Orange," meaning an incident involving hazardous chemicals. He also heard the names of Poole, Kildare, Chandler, and Craig being paged to the emergency room. He laughed as a young medical worker checked his vitals.

"What's that?" Morris asked the man. "Some kind of code?"

The worker, who couldn't have been more than 25, gave him a blank stare. Morris reconsidered any further conversation. Better to let the kid think he was delusional than to explain they were the names of doctors on various television shows.

The next thing he heard was the booming voice of Dr. Herman Poole. "Goddam my cousin Elijah. I never should have cleared you to return to work in that electric sewer in the first place."

Morris turned. "Doc, how the hell are you?"

"A load better than you, that's for sure."

Morris was happy to see Herman Poole smiling. It meant that he probably wasn't in too bad of shape.

Poole gave Morris a quick look while the kid continued taking vitals and hooked up some kind of monitor to Morris' finger. The doctor then stepped away with the kid. After about a minute, he came back in.

"Well, it's serious, Morris. It looks like you have an acute case of shitheadosis. We'll have to amputate."

Morris laughed and Poole joined in.

"You're fine," he said. "We'll release you in a bit. Your partner, we're probably going to end up keeping her overnight – strictly precautionary," he added, apparently recognizing the concern on Morris' face.

"She's not my partner by the way."

"I feel relieved for her then," Poole quipped.

Morris then inquired about the body recovered from the scene, but Poole had no information. Likely, the corpse would end up with the medical examiner, but the doctor theorized that it might take a while because, first, they would want to make sure the hydrogen sulfide had dissipated.

"Yeah, you don't want to be transporting that stuff anywhere, even to a morgue," said Poole.

Morris nodded and then pulled out his phone to call Elijah to see if he could round up Happy. He was pretty sure the body was his cousin Cathy, and Happy would be the next of kin to make the ID once the medical examiner got the body. Morris left a message and then tried to pull himself out of his melancholy.

"Hey, so what's that Kildare, Chandler, Craig code you've got going there?" he asked Poole.

"What do you mean?" replied the doctor.

"Those are all made-up names, from TV shows, right?"

Poole shook his head. "Well, I guess, delirium is one of the symptoms of exposure to hydrogen sulfide." Before Morris could object, the doctor continued. "We do have a Kildare, Chandler, and Craig, and I am sure a dozen other names they use on TV, so many goddamn hospital shows."

"And I am sure all of them are about as accurate as cop shows," said Morris.

The two men chuckled, and Poole said, "Well, you can't trust everything you see on TV." At that point "Wheel of Fortune" was interrupted for breaking news from one of the local stations.

The anchor quickly gave way to a live shot in front of the Back Bay station, and Morris instantly felt dread upon seeing the face and figure of Dyani Swan on the TV. Morris then heard a yelp from two bays down, shrouded by the curtains separating them.

"What the fuck is that bitch doing?"

"Settle down Goldi," Morris shouted back.

But he had to admit, the same thought went through his head. You don't calm hysteria by having a press conference in the middle of chaos. Swan went on to say that an incident had occurred on an old abandoned platform, and a chemical spill had been contained. She said two transit cops had been hospitalized in the incident as they were searching for a homeless suspect in connection with the death of deputy director Bob Sosa.

"You might as well just sprayed Viagra on this cluster fuck," mumbled Morris.

From past the curtain, he heard two "fuck-yous" followed by a "you better not." In a moment Goldi was standing in front of him.

"Can you believe this shit?" she said to Morris. "It's going to be like 'purge of the homeless.'"

"We don't even know if Bob was murdered," said Morris.

"Well, apparently Dyani Boobs has made up her mind!"

With that, Patrick McKenna joined a nurse in trying to get Susan Sann back to her bed in the emergency room. They were eventually successful, but Morris kept playing Goldi's outburst in his head. The question wasn't whether the T's new director of security believed Bob Sosa was murdered. It was why.

Chapter 12

Morris was growing antsy. He sat up on the edge of the emergency room gurney and looked around for a pair of scrubs or anything he could wear so he wouldn't look like an escaped mental patient when he left the hospital.

There was a cabinet near the head of the bed, and he bent over as he opened the door to see what might be in it.

As he was in the awkward position, he heard a familiar voice exclaim, "Oh Jesus, I've been blinded!"

Morris turned around to see his friend and fellow T-cop, Elijah. "Oh come on, it's not the first ass you have ever seen," he said turning around.

"Shit, and I thought your ass looked bad," said Elijah looking at Morris face-to-face. "Man, you look like you've been bleached."

"You got something against white?"

"Just as long as it doesn't have something against me first," answered Elijah.

"I don't suppose you brought anything for me to wear."

"Well, I did the best I could on short notice," Elijah said. "I forgot I had Bonita's car today, and well ...." With that, Elijah tossed a couple of items onto the gurney.

The hot pink sweatpants were a tough call, but the gray T-shirt seemed simple enough. Morris started to change.

"Whoa, buddy, what are you doing there?" Elijah interrupted.

"What?" asked Morris.

"Those are my wife's sweatpants. You can't go commando."

"You got something else for me?"

Elijah seemed to ponder the possibilities but then rolled his eyes. "Shoot, she'd probably want me to burn them anyway."

Morris pulled on the sweats. They were tight at the waist and a little short for his legs, but they would do the job for getting him out of the hospital. Then, he grabbed the T-shirt, and pulled it over his head. It was V neck and a fairly tight fit. Morris looked down and contemplated some joke about cleavage but then noticed lettering on the shirt. He tilted his head and made sense out of the words.

"Black by popular demand?" he said quoting the shirt he was now wearing.

Elijah started laughing. "It looks good on you, though."

"Lovely, just lovely," said Morris.

"Here," Elijah said tossing a pair of firefighter boots at the base of the gurney. "Jay gave me these."

Morris stepped into the boots. "I won't forget this," he said.

Elijah gave Morris a thorough look. "Yeah, but I wish I could!" he replied.

"What's the word on Goldi?"

"Herm says they're going to admit her overnight. She's been nauseous, puking her guts out. Apparently, your 'more significant' body weight, resulted in the gas having less of an impact on you," he added, using air quotes to distinguish the reference to Morris' girth.

"Come on," pleaded Morris. "I'm the same weight I was when we left the Marines."

"I'm just the messenger, buddy," said Elijah. "But seriously, Herm says Goldi should be alright. They'll probably release her in the morning."

Morris then went through the discharge process. Five minutes later he and Elijah were ready to exit to the street.

"Did you get in touch with Happy?" Morris asked.

"Yeah, he's already at the morgue. I found him at an AA meeting, down at St. Anthony's."

Morris nodded. Happy had fallen from that wagon plenty over the years, but at least he was trying. "Since I'm here, I should probably head over to the medical examiner's office. See if I can talk to him."

"Sure," said Elijah, who then paused. Morris sensed what might be coming next. "How about William?" he said.

"What about him?" replied Morris.

"It's his mom, right?"

"Mhmm," was all Morris could muster.

"Hey, it's not my place," said Elijah. "But I get it. There's two sides of the tracks in my family too. You were just trying to do the right thing." With that, Elijah pushed open the door, and the two stepped onto the sidewalk, feeling the brisk November night air.

Morris reflected on what Elijah said. "You know, the fucked up thing was I think Happy held it against Mary Ellen and me more than Cathy ever did. She knew she couldn't take care of him. So we adopted him."

"When was the last time you saw him?"

"Fifteen years ago, his seventeenth birthday," Morris said flatly. "We had a cake. Happy was there. Cathy, she said was going to be there, but she never showed. Then, he hands us his papers for the Marine Corps."

As the two prepared to cross the street, they both gave a gaze toward the adjacent parking garage.

"Vultures?" Morris asked.

"I don't see any," answered Elijah.

In April 2013, the nondescript parking garage across the way found itself as a media favorite. It was from that vantage point that news stations were able to stake out the rear of the city's morgue and get pictures of the Boston Marathon bomber Tamerlan

Tsarnaev's body when it was brought there after Tsarnaev's brother ran him over during a gunfight in Watertown.

"What? You're afraid Eyewitness News is going to catch a pic of you dressed like that?" chided Elijah.

Morris heard him, but he was too busy checking the latest in a non-stop barrage of texts and voice messages being left for him. "You know I think I've even managed to shock myself with the number of people I have pissed off in twenty-four hours."

"A new personal best?"

"Maybe," replied Morris, looking at his phone. "And I am talking quality on top of quantity."

"Well, maybe they wouldn't be so pissed if you actually texted back every now and then?" Elijah added as the two darted across the street to the rear entrance.

"Why?" said Morris. "So I can have three different women tell me to perform a sex act that is anatomically impossible?"

Elijah laughed as he pulled open the door. "That would be an impressive trifecta, even for you."

"What do I get if I hit it?" Morris asked he stepped in.

"Nothing," said Elijah. "I'd be a fool to bet against your ability to infuriate womankind."

The two T-cops entered the building where there was a small waiting room with a guard who checked their IDs and buzzed them into the restricted area. With a little inquiry, they found that Happy was in one of the examination rooms. He had positively identified his sister, and the medical examiner had given him a few moments by himself while she went to attend to another case.

"This place creeps me out," acknowledged Elijah as the two walked down one of the hallways.

"Oh come on," answered Morris. "People are just dying to get in here."

"That joke sucked the first time you said it, and sucks the thousandth time."

Morris couldn't argue with Elijah's assessment. The truth was he was trying to distract himself from his own nervousness. It had nothing to do with the morbid nature of the medical examiner's office and everything to do with having to look family in the face.

Cathy was still a toddler when her dad was killed by a landmine in Vietnam. Happy, being the big brother, always watched out for her. But to Morris, they were his little cousins. Once he got to a certain age, hanging out with them became more like babysitting. Then, when their mom re-married to an asshole, things really fell apart.

Looking back now, the pieces all fit, but when you are a kid, you don't see it. Happy and Cathy were just the ones with the dirty clothes and bad attitudes. You tried to avoid them, and if you couldn't, you joined with others in making fun of them. By the time Cathy reached high school, Morris was already in the Marines. Much of her story he never knew. By the time he came home, she had a newborn and was an alcoholic before she even reached the legal drinking age.

The two T-cops poked their heads into one of the rooms. There Morris could see Happy standing over the body of his sister, laid out on a stainless steel table.

Morris felt sick at the sight. He had seen plenty of dead bodies, but Cathy was skin and bones, clearly a sign of drug use and its consequent malnutrition. He stepped closer to the table, and Happy began to speak without turning around.

"She's at peace now," he said.

"Listen, Hap, I don't know what to say," Morris said. "I should have been there. I should have found her sooner."

Happy seemed unnaturally calm. Maybe it was shock. Morris had expected some sort of tirade. After all, just two days ago, he had to implore Morris to go looking for her.

"No," he finally said. "We all should have been there for her – years ago." He turned around, tears in eyes, but a clenched mouth and fists. "Goddamn it. No one believed her then. We turned our backs on her, Morris. We turned our backs on her!" He then collapsed to the floor and put his face in his hands.

Morris raised his eyebrows and looked toward Elijah, who gave a little nod, as if to say, go to him. Morris took a couple of steps and got down on one knee.

"Hey Hap, shit happens. She fell in with a bad crowd."

"No!" Happy said raising his head. "She was raped and mom made her have the kid. Goddam Irish Catholic fuckin' bullshit!"

Morris was taken aback. He walked through some things in his head. He was away. What did he know? All his mother ever said was that his cousin was mugged, and by the time he was home and saw Cathy, William was already probably a year old. Had he been that distant from his cousins that he never put it all together?

"Hap, what are you saying?"

Happy composed himself and looked as though he wanted to say something, but then finally let out a "Forget it." He stood up, and Morris rose with him. "It doesn't matter now," Happy said. "She was never the same." He looked at her lifeless body and repeated, "She was never the same."

"Does William know?" asked Morris.

"Yeah, I called him. Told him she was dead."

"No, I mean does he know?"

"Know what?" Happy said evenly.

Morris looked for words to say, but as he opened his mouth, Happy cut him off.

"And he ain't going to know."

Morris agreed and nodded along. "I'm sorry, Happy. I never knew."

He smiled back at his cousin. "How could you, Morris?"

Happy didn't say it. He might not even have implied it, but Morris couldn't escape the meaning of his words. He couldn't have known because he wasn't around. They were the side of the family that the rest of the family disowned. Oh sure, they exchanged Christmas cards. Happy and Cathy were invited to his wedding, but quietly Morris had hoped they wouldn't come. That was the truth. He was so self-centered back then. He still was. How many times over the years had he the chance to reach out to Cathy, and he never did. He always assumed that her quest for popularity led her to the wrong places, the wrong boyfriends, the wrong choices.

He couldn't imagine the scar inflicted upon her by some cretin, and then to only have it reinforced by her own mother. A thought struck Morris.

"Did she ever say who it was?"

"No," Happy said turning from the table. "It happened –" he stopped mid-sentence, finally having a good look at his cousin's attire.

"I'll explain this later," said Morris.

Happy blinked his eyes like he had just been dazed by a punch, and then returned to what he was saying. "It happened when I was in the corps. I didn't know for the longest time. It just came out one time when she was drinking, and she laid into mom about it."

Morris put his arm around Happy as the two stood looking at Cathy. It was as close as he felt to either of his cousins in decades, and he felt ashamed that it took her death to do it. "Whatever you need, just let me know."

Elijah stood quietly, apparently yielding to the moment between the two men.

After a minute or two, Morris finally spoke, "Hey, what do you say we get out of here? Maybe a nice dinner at Amrheins?"

Happy smiled. "Thanks, Morris, but I have to make some calls."

"I can help you with that," Morris responded.

"Nah, it's something I gotta do," said Happy. "Don't worry. I'll be alright."

With that Morris and Elijah escorted Happy to the reception area and eventually put him in a cab.

"I just hope he stays away from the sauce," Morris said as he and Elijah stepped back inside.

"Come on," Elijah said. "Let's find the doc."

Morris nodded and the two walked back to the exam room where the body of Morris' dead cousin lay. They entered the empty room, but the silence was quickly disturbed by the monotone voice of Dr. Katherine Crowley, the state's chief medical examiner.

"Good evening, gentlemen," she said.

"Good evening, doc," Elijah said, but before he could say anything more, Bruce Donohue came through the door.

"What are you doing here?" asked Bruce.

"What are you doing here?" responded Elijah in kind, as Morris turned around.

"I'm following up –" Bruce then noticed Morris' outfit. "What the?"

"We'll explain that later," Elijah said waving his hand.

"Yeah, well I was following up on that body they pulled out of the Muddy River. Apparently, it was some sort of gay bashing down in the Fens."

At that moment there was a commotion in the hallway, and a large a man lunged through the doorway toward Bruce, shouting, "I told you my brother was not a fag!"

Elijah spun around to tackle the man while two uniformed officers rushed into the room as well. Bruce hit the ground in self-defense, tripping Morris, who had moved toward the door. The two tangled T-cops on the floor inadvertently took out the large angry man at the knees, and with him, Elijah, who clung to him with a bear hug. As the pile collapsed, the two uniforms, who had been reaching to assist Elijah, fell forward landing on top of the four men beneath them.

Amidst the commotion, from his viewing angle at the bottom of the scrum, Morris saw a familiar pair of woman's shoes.

"Oh damn," he mumbled with someone's knee against his cheek.

"What the fuck is this shit show!" shouted Sergeant Joanne Manning, launching into a verbal hurricane. The officers managed to get to their feet and cuff the large man, and the pile-up began to disintegrate while the homicide sergeant continued to lambaste the men. As Morris stood, he noticed Manning was holding a small cardboard box. She was still in the midst of her tirade but turned dumbstruck at the sight of him.

"You know, this get-up might have a use after all," he whispered to Elijah.

During the melee, Dr. Crowley never looked up, continuing to move through an orderly identification and examination of Cathy Fitzgerald's body, but as some order came to the room, she said, "I'd prefer if all visitors, including law enforcement, could exit. I find people very distracting."

Bruce looked at Elijah and Morris and shrugged. "Dr. Death."

Morris couldn't disagree with the moniker Bruce had assigned Crowley years earlier. Whether it was in her DNA or something acquired from working with the non-living for so long, Crowley seemed constantly uncomfortable with human interaction, but she was a meticulous medical examiner.

The group exited the exam room, gathering in the hallway outside. Manning had already moved several feet away and was on her phone.

Morris heard an exasperated voice call his name and turned to see the large man, still being partially restrained by the two officers.

"Holy shit, Tom?" Morris said, knowing the answer. "What are you doing here?" He then turned to his partner and then back. "You remember Elijah?"

As the two exchanged nods, Bruce asked his fellow T-cops, "You know this guy?" Then he paused. "Fuck that, you two know everybody."

Tom Cashman began to say something, but Bruce cut him off.

"His brother was the guy they pulled out of the river. Looks like he got his head smashed in."

Morris looked at Cashman. "Quisp?"

Cashman nodded. Tom and his brother Cliff played for the Dorchester Eagles in Boston's park league football program. They regularly battled the South Boston Chippewas, which featured Morris, Elijah and the Mantis, Bob Sosa. Tom was the prototypical brick shithouse, earning the name Quake for his thunderous inside play. His younger, more nimble, brother was nicknamed Quisp, giving the pair the title of two of the most popular breakfast cereals in the 1960s and '70s

"Jesus, Tom, my condolences," Morris said.

Cashman seemed to calm down a bit as Manning returned to the group, carrying the box of items.

"Tell this bitch my brother was not a fag," Cashman said looking at Morris and Elijah.

"His brother was not gay," Elijah said to Manning.

"Not that anything is wrong with that," added Morris.

Manning glared at Morris and then surveyed the group. "Maybe he wasn't gay, but he was definitely murdered." She gave a quick glance to Cashman. "Yes, my condolences." Then turning back to the T-cops. "We found him near a known cruising spot in the Fens, and the last time I checked there wasn't a subway stop in the Muddy River. So what the fuck do I care what any of you think?"

Cashman started to shout something, but Morris intervened. "Hold on, hold on. Wait, wasn't Cliff working at the MWRA these days?"

"Yeah, that's what I was trying to tell her. He was working. He wasn't no fag."

At that moment, Manning's phone rang. She shifted the box she was holding into her other arm and answered the call as she turned and stepped away. The group stood silent, only being interrupted by the occasional buzzing of Morris' phone.

The Massachusetts Water Resources Authority, like the MBTA, was a quasi-public state agency. Few people today realized how much of a role water played in the region's geography. When the Puritans first arrived, Boston proper was nearly an island. Over the centuries, so much land had been filled in, the original outline of the city had been swallowed up. Throughout all this growth and modernization, the region's sewer system always trailed. Especially during the heavy rains of the unpredictable New England weather, the combined sewers would overflow, dumping raw sewage into the Boston Harbor and other waterways. The state legislature ignored the issue, and finally, the federal government sued the state, forcing a massive cleanup and reorganization of the region's resources, giving birth to the MWRA.

For a brief period, the Boston Harbor Cleanup was the state's most notorious boondoggle, but then the Big Dig came along, which dwarfed the project in terms of expense and infamy. Steadily, the harbor and its waterways, like the Charles and Muddy rivers were cleansed, and sewers and water run-off were better managed, but being a densely populated area, at essentially sea level, water remained one of the city's most valuable assets and constant threats.

Manning hung up her phone and turned back to the group. She glanced over at Cashman, shook her head, and spoke. "Are you going to behave?"

Cashman nodded. "All I want is to get out of here and go to Murphy's funeral home. I gotta make arrangements for my brother."

"Alright, take the cuffs off him," she said. She then handed him the box. "Here, these are the personal items we found on him. We don't have any need for them, except we're holding onto this." And she raised a plastic evidence bag containing about an 8-inch long cylindrical object.

Cashman flipped out. "Fuck you. You planted that. I told you he's not –"

"Shut up you moron!" shouted Manning, shoving the plastic bag in his face. "It's a refractometer!"

Cashman fell silent. Confounded by the term. He turned toward Morris, who shrugged, and turned back toward Manning.

"It's a scientific instrument," she said, then turning toward Cashman. "It was in your brother's coat pocket."

"See, he was probably working, doing just engineer stuff," Morris said looking at both Manning and Cashman. He could tell Manning wanted to say more, but he hoped that she read his expression accurately.

After a moment, Cashman relented, grabbed the box, and pushed his way past the cops, uttering a profanity as he went down the hallway.

Once he was out of earshot, Manning turned to the three T-cops. "So what the fuck are you doing here?"

Elijah started to speak, but then caught himself. "You know what? It's too long of a story."

Manning nodded. Her eye caught Morris, and she started laughing. "You're a fuckin' piece of work, you know that?"

"He's an acquired taste," said Elijah.

"Yeah, well, how do I un-acquire you?" Manning said, glancing toward Cashman as he exited the hallway.

Morris was at a loss for words.

Then Manning spoke again. "Listen I checked with his brother's boss at the MWRA. Clifford Cashman was a problem child. He had just been bounced from one job and was getting placed on another. Now we find him with his pants around his ankles, and his skull bashed along the banks of Muddy River? And by the way, refractometers are also used in meth labs."

"I know," said Morris, "but I didn't want to get into that with Tom."

"His brother don't know him like he thinks he does," said Manning.

Morris put up his hands. "Joanne, I don't give a shit. All I know is Tom Cashman is a fuckin' ox and would have crushed my head like a grape if I had agreed his brother was gay."

"Not that there's anything wrong with that," inserted Elijah with a straight face.

"You homophobic Micks," Manning said as Elijah looked incredulously. "Just stay out of this case, and do your job chasing those perverted mole men who killed Bob Sosa." Manning then nodded to the two uniformed officers, and the three began to exit the morgue.

Morris thought of saying something, but he was a bit confused himself. Within one day, three people he knew – Sosa, Cathy, and Cliff Cashman – had passed through this morgue. Maybe he was just bad luck, or maybe there was a connection he wasn't seeing.

As Manning approached a door at the end of the hallway, she shouted back, "And get me that video!"

After she left, Bruce remarked, "Geez, she's a little high strung."

Morris and Elijah laughed.

"Hey what video was she talking about?" Bruce asked.

"She wants the Medical Center video from when Bob Sosa got killed," said Morris.

"Oh," said Bruce, pulling out his phone. "You mean this one?" And he started thumbing the screen.

Morris and Elijah looked over Bruce's shoulder as he scrolled through hundreds of links to video feeds.

"How'd you get that?" said Elijah.

"I don't know. It's an app or something," said Bruce. "I was over at MassDOT a few months ago, investigating someone smashing lights in the stations. They just set me up with this. I think they got tired of me always asking for video, so they just gave me access to everything."

"Jesus Christ, you do have everything on this," Morris said.

"Pain in the ass really. It takes forever to find anything. Do you know every bus has like three cameras on it?"

"Where's the video from the station?" countered Morris.

"Yeah, it's like Swani said. Here, you see Bob climb onto the tracks. No idea why, and then the next thing you see is the train clip him."

Morris looked closely at Bruce's phone as the video played. It was disturbing to see Sosa get corkscrewed. Morris looked closely as Bruce rewound the video. Maybe his eyes were playing tricks on him. It was right at the edge of the tunnel, in the darkness, but it seemed like a hand was holding Sosa. Did someone grab him only to throw him into the train?

"Hey, can you rewind it more?" he asked Morris.

Bruce rewound farther, but no one seemed to go into the tunnel ahead of Sosa. Neither did anyone seem to come out of after. Maybe Morris was seeing things. Bruce replayed the video again, and then Morris caught it.

"Go back," he shouted.

Bruce obliged as Elijah moved in to see what his partner had picked up on.

"You see it?" Morris asked Elijah, who had a grin on his face.

"That's how come he didn't have a cellphone," Elijah said, nodding along.

"What?" asked Bruce.

"Rewind one more time," said Morris.

Bruce replayed the video and slowed it down. To the untrained eye, the tall homeless man, who most called Beetlejuice, may have looked clumsy, but to a T-cop accustomed to scanning the subway for criminals, the slight bump and then reach into Bob Sosa's coat was the unmistakable technique of a highly skilled pickpocket.

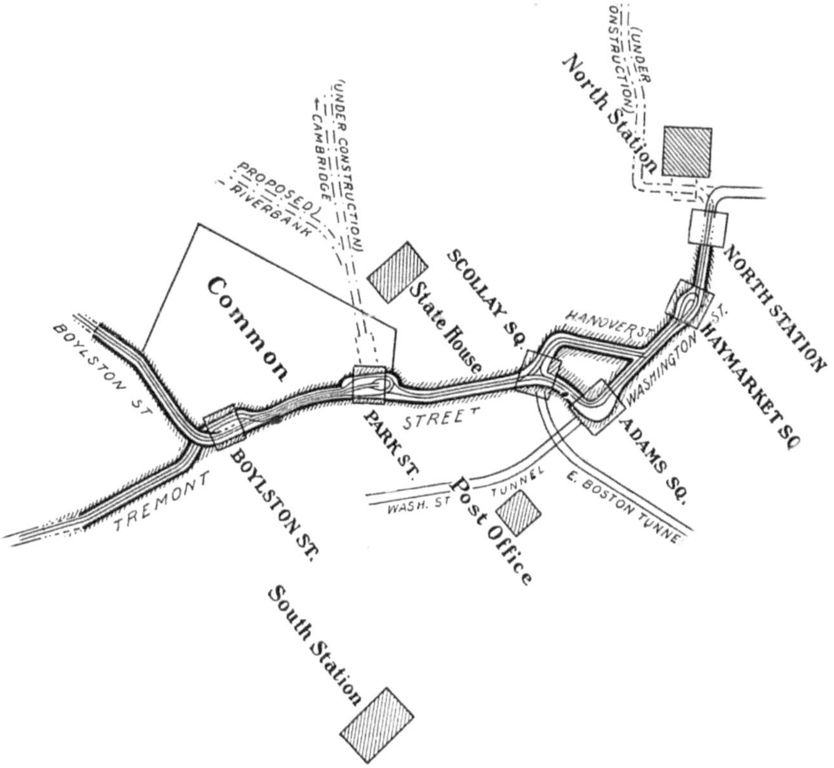

Chapter 13

Morris took the Tremont Street stairs out of the Park Street Station. Still dressed in the awkward attire he had indirectly borrowed from Bonita Poole, he looked up at the Park Street Church clock in front of him. Just past 8 o'clock, and there was a November chill in the air. Supposedly, warmer temps were coming in tomorrow, but tonight was a different story. At least Elijah had loaned him his sportcoat. Of course, Elijah filled it out much better than Morris could.

He walked one block up and then darted across the heavy Tremont Street traffic to find himself at the entrance of one of Suffolk Law School's buildings.

He pushed through the door and began to scan the lobby for a directory.

"Excuse me," he said to a twenty-something woman who looked to be hurrying out the door. "I'm looking for the legal clinic."

The woman said something, but her gaze stayed forward and the words seemed nonsensical to Morris. Just as he was about to repeat his query, he noticed the earphones. She must have been on some sort of headset, speaking to someone other than Morris. "All these kids on social media so they can be anti-social," Morris mumbled to himself.

"Do you need some help?"

The voice startled Morris. He spun around and saw another twenty-something woman. This one was looking at him, and no headphones were noticeable.

"Yes," he said. "I'm looking for the legal clinic."

"Oh yes, let me help you," said the woman very sympathetically. As she escorted Morris up a set of stairs, he caught his reflection in one of the glass windows. Wearing hot pink sweatpants, firefighter boots, and an oversize sportcoat, he discerned the woman's tone to be maybe more pity than anything else. So be it, he thought. He actually was beginning to like the color of the sweatpants anyway.

She brought him to a reception area and left him with a smile.

"Yeah?" said a young man sitting at the desk.

"I'm looking for Robert," he said.

He offered no verbal response but stood up and walked somewhere. This was the state of higher education and the future of American society thought Morris – decent-looking, bright, college kid who had no clue how to interact with other people. This was the cost of every human transaction being replaced by a few swipes of a thumb.

Morris had probably first met Ferret seven or eight years ago, he was a bi-racial orphaned graffiti artist who rose to lead one of the city's more violent subway gangs. He was a brilliant kid, plucked from foster homes by Father Michael McGovern and given a chance to attend one of the area's elite prep schools. His life reflected his DNA, with one foot planted on the shore of the city's upper class and another foot rotting with the homeless in the subway.

"You were looking for Robert, right?"

"Yes," said Morris.

"OK," and the young man walked away again.

When Ferret crossed paths with a charismatic skinhead who had assumed leadership of his former gang, he recognized him for what he was, another prep-school kid trying to escape a maniacal father and a legacy of wealth and privilege. This new leader was verifiably insane, however, first gassing the innocent at the Broadway T stop on St. Patrick's Day and then devising a plan to ram a bus of the city's politicians into one of his father's chemical plants.

The plan was foiled to some degree by Morris, but Ferret had been the real hero. The official word was his body, like that of everyone else, had never been recovered from the bottom of the Charles River. Today, Morris was one of only two people in the city who knew Ferret's genuine fate and identity. To everyone else, he was Robert Andrews, a law school student hovering just above the poverty line.

As he spied a rail-thin young man coming his way, he noticed the beard Ferret had grown, perhaps to hide his old persona along with a nasty scar he once received from a bottle smashed across his face. The button-down shirt and jeans were a sharp departure from what the drug-addict graf wore in his days in the subways.

"Can I help you, sir?" Ferret asked.

"Yes," Morris said. "I need to find a mutual friend of ours."

"Bullshit," Ferret said flatly. "Everyone knows you have no friends."

Morris smiled and could see the stoic Ferret grin slightly.

"Why don't you follow me," Ferret said to Morris, and the two moved from the reception area to an open desk, removed from others.

As the two sat, Morris could see Ferret catch a glimpse of his T-shirt.

"I'd ask you why you are wearing that Mo the Fist, but honestly, it doesn't surprise me as much as it should."

"I've had a shit day."

"Best I can tell, you've had a shit life."

Morris nodded. "Listen, I need to find Beetlejuice."

"I have no idea where he is."

"No way of getting in touch with him?"

Ferret laughed. "Fist, I'm an addict. The only chance I've got of staying clean, doing anything productive, is to never go near that world again."

"He may be in trouble," said Morris. "He lifted something from a guy who ended up dead."

"From what I hear a lot of the homeless are in trouble," said Ferret. "The cops have been hassling them bad."

Morris quietly nodded.

"They're calling a meeting of the Archangels," said Ferret.

"That might only make things worse."

"I'm not sure they can get much worse," said Ferret. "You've looked everywhere?"

"Yeah, all the usual places, even Tears of Allah."

"I saw that," said Ferret. "I should've known that was you." After a pause, he added, "I can't help you, man. That ain't me anymore."

The two then ticked down a number of places and some of Beetlejuice's accomplices. They were working off the same game plan, but coming up empty on new ideas.

Morris struggled with a few thoughts. He had hoped Ferret had some lead, but at the same time, it was good to see the kid had left his life in the tunnels.

"Well, I am glad it ain't you anymore, I guess," Morris said. "Although I have to say, they sure as hell could use you. No one can paint for shit anymore."

Ferret laughed. "Hey, I'd be lying if I said there weren't times I didn't miss some of it, but a lot of it? I'm leaving that in my rearview mirror. I'm going to finish law school and then go about setting the world right. I already got my domain name: SueRichWhiteFolks.com."

Morris laughed. "God help the establishment."

The two stood up, and Ferret extended his hand. "Fist you always were one of the good ones even though you could be a bastard at times."

"Thanks," Morris said, shaking Ferret's hand. "I think that's a compliment."

Ferret stepped around the table and began to escort Morris out of the clinic. Part way, he leaned toward Morris. "Hey what are they doing down by the old Boylston tunnels?"

"What do you mean?" asked Morris.

"There's been people down there. They've been surveying or something."

"I thought you couldn't go back there?" responded Morris.

"I gotta ride the T, don't I?" Ferret said as the two descended the stairs. "We picked up a pro bono case around there anyway. The city wants to move the Emancipation Statue in Lincoln Square. It's got something to do with the expansion of the parking garage or some re-development bullshit."

"You don't say?" Morris said.

"Personally, I wouldn't mind blowing the thing up, black man kneeling in front of a white man."

"You got something against the Great Emancipator?"

"Yeah, I got something against the fact that black people should be 'thankful' or celebrate someone for ending institutionalized oppression, and white folk think it's mighty white of them to have given us such 'opportunity.' That's like telling a parish of Catholics to be thankful that the cardinal shipped a child molester off to some other place."

Ferret always was quick on his feet. He would make a hell of a lawyer as long as didn't threaten a judge or club opposing counsel.

"Whether you use pity or you use chains, you're still enslaving me. You're still thinking I'm less than you. You're still thinking you're giving me something. So, sorry if I don't get on my knees and praise some bearded white man. Now, if Lincoln had decided to give the plantations to the slaves, or enslave the owners?" Ferret paused at the building entrance to contemplate his own question. "Shit, it still wouldn't make it right, but at least it might be closer to even."

"Eye for an eye?" responded Morris.

"Yeah," said Ferret.

"Listen, where my ancestors came from, they've been living like that for a couple hundred years. It don't solve much."

"That's easy for you to say," shot back Ferret. "You haven't had to live through this crap."

"Hey, we all have crap," said Morris. "Granted it's not the same for everybody, but we all got it wrong. It ain't rich. It ain't poor. It ain't black, and it ain't white. It's the shitters and the shit upon. Too many fuckin' people in this world who need to feel they are better than everyone else."

"Amen brother Fist," Ferret said pointing at Morris' T-shirt.

"I'm black, and I'm proud," Morris said, putting on an Irish brogue.

"What the?"

"You ever see *The Commitments*? It's a movie about an Irish band?" asked Morris.

"Why the fuck would I go see a movie about an Irish band?" responded Ferret. "I swear, Fist, for a smart guy, you can be an idiot."

Morris started to speak but realized he had been caught on cross-examination. Case closed.

Ferret opened the door to the street. As Morris stepped through it, he turned back. "Hey, good luck," he said with sincerity. "I don't ever want to see your tag in the subways again."

Ferret nodded but remained quiet as Morris exited and headed back toward the Tremont Street entrance to the Green Line.

Up ahead he could see the Park Street Church. It was now nearing 9 o'clock. If the Red Line was running without delay, he'd be home and in bed by 10. He needed it. However, on his next step, he nearly stumbled, sensing something at his feet. He looked just in time to see a black cat dart in front of him and scurry into the Granary Burying Ground adjacent to the sidewalk.

"Tsk, Tsk, Nightmare."

Morris spun around and saw the pale face of Ginger, framed by an oversized black hooded sweatshirt, which covered nearly all of her red hair. "You know, I thought I recognized that cat," Morris said.

Ginger didn't say anything. She looked Morris up and down, and he couldn't tell whether she was sizing him up for a conversation or a maybe a cannibal's main course.

"What brings you up here?" he asked.

"Maybe I am just stalking you," she said, sending a nervous tingle up his spine. "I'm just looking for someone," she continued.

"Does Gary know?"

She gave Morris a death stare that only increased his anxiety. "It's not that sort of someone. A man I thought I recognized from long ago." She glanced at the firefighter boots Morris was wearing. "Did we give you the wrong size?"

"This is my third pair of footwear in two days."

Ginger smiled. "I understand you're looking for Beetlejuice."

"Yes," he said plainly.

"He hangs around with that kiddie fiddler they call Kenny the Clown."

Morris nodded, he couldn't tell whether it was a statement or a question, but Kenny was well-known to the T-cops.

"I've never been a fan of that type," Ginger said off-handedly, turning to face the burial ground while giving a whistle toward her feline companion. "As you might be able to surmise, I've had to confront a few matters of my own. I am not one to judge anyone. We all have our paths to take, but we should find that path when it's the time of our choosing, not someone else's."

Morris felt a little unease, standing in front of a cemetery and speaking to Ginger, but he fought it off and focused on Beetlejuice.

"So do you know where he is?"

Morris wasn't sure she had heard him. She kept staring at the cemetery, watching Nightmare frolic among the tombstones. Just when he was about to repeat the question, she spoke.

"It's hard to believe that in Belgium they used to throw black cats from a tower as some sort of celebration. People enjoyed the brutality, justifying it with tales of witchcraft and sorcery. Loathed and feared, misunderstood, no one wants the black cat, but see how gorgeous and sleek she is in the night."

Morris felt somewhere between lost and frightened. This Ginger was as creepy as they come. There was nothing physically imposing about her, but her voice was even, showing no sign of pretense or worry. Morris had learned long ago that on the street it wasn't about size or strength. It was conviction. The insane were always the most dedicated to a cause, and if that cause was survival, heaven help the soul who crossed them.

She then turned toward Morris. "I will help you find Beetlejuice. Consider it a debt paid."

Morris was confused. "What do you mean?"

Ginger smiled. "Do you believe in fate, sergeant?"

He thought about an answer but finally settled on a truth. "Ginger, I don't know. I think what I believe is that what I believe doesn't make a shit's worth of difference. I used to think it did."

"I believe in fate," Ginger responded. "I think it's obvious, actually. We don't control how we are born or certainly to whom we are born. It's decided for us. For me, it was decided that I would be born to a brutal drunk of a father. Friday nights he would give me a shoe shine kit and send me into the bars along Dorchester Ave. Some men wanted me to shine their shoes. Others, they wanted ... or they took ... other things. Either way, if I didn't return home with enough money to make my father happy, he would beat me senseless. He could be a very greedy man."

Ginger shook her head and broke into a smile. "My dear mother, her answer was prayer, sending me to a young parish priest every Wednesday afternoon. I would beg and plead not to go, and when I finally explained my protest, it was the leather strap again. This time for making up such stories about Father Charles, that spawn of Satan."

The empathy must have shown on Morris' face.

"Oh sergeant I'm sure you've heard plenty of stories like this before. In proper circles, no one talks of such things, but you and I, sergeant, we don't travel in proper circles, do we?"

She was right on both counts.

"Anyway," she continued. "One night after shining shoes at Aces High – I recall I had done pretty well that night – I was jumped by three thugs at Andrew Station. They stole my cash and were putting the boots to me. One even had a bat, and he ...." Her voice trailed off as she looked toward the ground, but then she gathered herself. "They would have killed me, but then a cop showed up. One of the thugs instantly bolted. The two that remained, the cop sent them to the hospital, using nothing but his own fists."

Morris had a sudden moment of recall. Travis McCarthy, the shoeshine kid. It was in the late 1980s. Fortunately, Morris' role in the incident, including the allegation by one of the thugs that he was handcuffed at the time the T-cop broke his jaw, was overshadowed by the rest of Travis' story.

According to the court-appointed psychologist, Travis could recall nothing past being jumped by the thugs. When police arrived at the McCarthy's apartment to find the kitchen on fire, his mother stabbed to death, and his father in a pool of blood, it was clearly a homicide, but the details were awkward. Murder-suicide? Whatever happened, the boy had witnessed it all. Yet, he seemed traumatized to the point of detachment. Without evidence to the contrary, the case never moved forward. Travis found himself civilly committed to a state mental institution, but what quietly circulated among law enforcement, however, was that the father had bled to death, not from some accident or blunt trauma, but from bite marks.

"I always wondered what happened to you, Travis," Morris said.

"Please," said Ginger. "That was a past life, one that you helped me shed."

Morris felt uneasy, and Ginger must have recognized it. "No worries, sergeant. You were just an instrument of fate. You showed me that I didn't need a boot, a leather strap, or even a bat to fight back. All I needed was the will, and I had plenty of that."

"And so where did Ginger come from?" asked Morris.

She smiled in a patronizing way. "I was always Ginger. As a ward of the state, I was dumped alongside other troubled youth and adults at the Gaebler Psychiatric Unit."

"The Gaebler Gulag?" Morris interjected, referring to the title that had been placed on the facility when a series of atrocities came to light.

"Yes, I lived in a cage smaller than a parking space. The only sounds I heard the first night was the hum of a dim fluorescent light that never went off and the screams of other children echoing through the building. Of course, you could bang and scream all you want. The staff didn't care. That is unless they found you drinking your own urine."

"Screams and urine, no wonder the subway doesn't faze you," said Morris.

"Hardly," said Ginger. "The smells and sounds of the subway are nothing compared to the literal excrement of institutionalization. Fingerpainting by feces was not an uncommon pastime for some residents, but it wasn't the residents you watched for. It was the counselors."

She looked back for Nightmare, still roaming among the tombstones. "But I wouldn't trade any of the hell I had to go through because it all helped me evolve from the trapped soul I once was, and it started with you."

"So how much of this does Gary know?"

"I keep my past life in the past," said Ginger. "He's never asked. I think he understands my journey has been painful at times. After the Gaebler, I ended up in other state facilities, but they all kept closing, budget cuts and all. Eventually, someone decided I was 'cured' and I found myself on a bus heading as far away as possible from this decrepit city. Over time, though, I worked my way back here. I found Gary, and while our relationship began pragmatically, if not profitably, we've found a love that needs no explanation."

She paused and looked back toward Nightmare as she spoke. "You know that Red Line train they have parked outside South Station?"

Morris nodded, it was a prototype the General Manager had installed along Atlantic Avenue to generate some positive publicity, which the T was always desperate for.

"The Juice and Kenny have been using it. They lifted the keys from one of the workers when they put it there. They take a bus up to Manchester every now and then."

Morris nodded. The state of New Hampshire had just dumped $2 million into opioid court and treatment programs. With the New England winter fast approaching, a court-ordered stay in a treatment facility would get them out of the cold, and Beetlejuice hadn't been looking so good lately. The panhandler was probably onto his third generation of judges in Suffolk County. There was a diplomatic art to committing a crime that could land you in jail until your court date but be trivial enough to convince a judge to let you go with time served, ideally just as the good weather returned to the area. Beetlejuice was smart to seek a change of venue.

"Thanks Ginger," Morris said.

She smiled. "A debt paid." Then she gave a whistle, and Nightmare ran from the cemetery, hopping through the wrought-iron fence. As he turned back to see Ginger, she was already across Tremont Street disappearing into the shadows of an alley.

Morris could pick up the Red Line at Park Street. South Station was just two stops away. Still, he decided to call ahead to the transit police substation in the terminal. He needed to make sure Beetlejuice and Kenny weren't getting on a bus before he could get there.

As he rushed down the stairs and ventured past the Green Line platform of the station to get to the Red Line, he continued to talk to the officer at the substation. "Yes, he's the one we're looking for from the Medical Center incident yesterday. Just make sure he doesn't get on a bus if you see him."

Given it was 9:30 on a Wednesday night, Park Street was relatively calm. There were a few young professionals, heading home from either working late or having hit a bar for a few post-work drinks. Some college-age kids were on the platform too, looking dolled up for some of the city's nightclubs.

Morris pondered that if he found Beetlejuice, he could arrest him as the video showed him stealing Bob Sosa's cellphone, but he wanted Beetlejuice talking. Morris needed to know what he saw when Sosa got corkscrewed.

As the Red Line train pulled up, Morris felt anxious. Beetlejuice had become a suspect in Sosa's death, but he chalked that up to Dyani Swan rushing to judgment. Then again, maybe it was all some calculation?

The train journeyed its short distance to the next stop, Downtown Crossing, and it now jerked forward and began its roll toward South Station. Morris closed his eyes and tried to collect his thoughts. Happy had dropped a bombshell on him about Cathy. It made sense. Guilt pangs returned. Happy and Cathy were always his shunned cousins. They had given Morris plenty of reasons over the years. Any time either ran into trouble, no matter the jurisdiction, his phone rang, but Cathy was especially prone to drop the name of her T-cop relative. She had become a pain in Morris' ass, and now it seemed so much of her personal demons may have been inflicted and not self-imposed.

He shook his head. One problem at a time. He needed Beetlejuice.

South Station is a three-block transportation complex. At the northern end is the train station with the Red Line running underneath it. The southern portion of the complex is "Terminal Illness," the nickname every T-cop gave to the massive four-story bus terminal into which visitors from all corners of the globe arrived and where the poorest of Bostonians ventured to escape the city.

As best Morris could, he ran up the stairs of South Station. Hindered by the firefighter boots and occasionally catching the glances of passersby, his anticipation grew. Beetlejuice would have some answers. Whatever they may be, they would also raise questions. Most relevant for Morris was why was the new deputy director so rash with judgment as to how Bob Sosa died. Was it a matter of incompetence or was there some ulterior agenda at work? Over the years, Morris had learned that MBTA was equal parts both.

He ran out of the train station section of the complex onto Atlantic Avenue. Staring him in the face sat the prototype that Ginger had mentioned. The windows of the motorman's cab were blacked out, but the others appeared to be only slightly tinted. Beetlejuice and Kenny were adept at inconspicuousness despite their outrageous appearance. Morris recalled the time he got a call from the campus police of Boston College. Apparently, the two homeless men had been living in a room off the basement of one of the dorms for two months. The freeloaders were discovered only when one of the resident assistants grew concerned that they weren't attending the dorm social events.

Beetlejuice and Kenny knew a good thing when they had it. Still, as Morris peered through the windows, he saw little sign of life. He stepped back, trying to figure out how to proceed when he heard a loud thud and the screech of brakes from behind him, past the entrance to the bus terminal.

He turned to see two women running toward him on the sidewalk. As he moved forward, he could see the oxymoronic combination of people running from a location and people also gathering around it. Morris ran, and as he pushed past one or two others fleeing, he saw the focal point.

A sapling planted in the sidewalk out front of the terminal had been cleaved in half and lying on the pavement next to it were the shattered bodies of two men. While they were not immediately discernible, Morris could tell from the black and white checked pants and purple sportcoat, one was Beetlejuice. Just from the round shape of the other, he could tell it was Kenny the Clown.

Instinctively, Morris looked up and caught a dark outline peering over the ramp that ran from the interstate overpass up to the parking lot on the top floor of the terminal. Morris pressed closer around a small ring of people who had already taken out their cellphones to record the scene. Vultures, thought Morris.

"Step back," he shouted. "I'm a cop."

While initially some of the crowd stirred, others seemed unmoved by his announcement. The awkward manner of the fall – or possibly push – of both men was head first. Blood was still gurgling from what had been Beetlejuice's skull. His body was nearly upside-down, with his waist wedged in between remnants of the sapling's trunk. Kenny's body was face down, flat, about a foot away from where Beetlejuice's brains splattered on the sidewalk. Already, Kenny's remains were being engulfed by his own blood seeping out from various bodily fissures.

Morris stepped forward and began to examine Beetlejuice, wondering if Sosa's phone might be on him, but no such luck. While there was a small roll of bills and some cellophane bags, presumably containing crystal meth, nothing else was on the homeless pauper.

Just as he was was about to turn around and make a second, more forceful announcement for the crowd to step back, his eye caught sight of a sparkle off the light of one of the cellphones. It was a key ring, laying on the ground, a few feet away from Beetlejuice's upside down body. Morris stepped closer. The crowd remained focused on the macabre scene to his left as he reached down with his right hand and picked up the key ring.

Staring him in the face might have been the literal key to solving what happened to Bob Sosa. As he turned and looked back at what was left of Beetlejuice and Kenny, he wondered how the new deputy director might distort this incident. He decided the best course might be to leave the scene with the keys and pursue this lead on his own. In this case, the right decision would be to do the wrong thing.

Chapter 14

As the crowd continued to gawk at the horrific scene behind him, Morris ventured down the sidewalk of Atlantic Avenue toward the prototype subway train. In his right hand, he held Beetlejuice's keychain. It had remarkable heft to it considering that its owner had no real residence or place of employment. There must have been at least thirty keys on it, and Morris began to differentiate them based on feel alone.

His eyes remained forward, seeing some curiosity on the faces coming toward him. Most of all, however, he saw a continued effort to make no eye contact. Then he remembered his current garb. He must have looked like one of the city's panhandling homeless. That explained why no one was looking at him. It also explained why Beetlejuice and Kenny the Clown may have been able to come and go from the train without consequence. *See Something, Say Something* only works if you're comfortable enough to look around.

Most Bostonians, despite their outward liberal lean, turned remarkably isolationist when it was just them and not some government program interacting with the downtrodden.

At that moment, his fingers hit on a key that was much different from the others. It was more like a cylinder with a squared-off end. It resembled some of those currently used by conductors.

As Morris approached the prototype, he timed his pacing so that he would be able to find a break in the groups of passersby. While it was now moving past 10 p.m., the only thing in this section of the city was South Station. While there were bars and clubs to both the west and east – across the Fort Point Channel – the transportation complex had limited pedestrian traffic right now.

He spied the access panel, lifted it, and inserted the key. With a quick turn right, Morris expected the doors to slide open. However, all he heard was a click. A moment of panic was replaced by the recognition that the train had no power source. He reached to the doors, and while they were still shut, he found he could easily part them. He removed the keys from the panel, stashing them in the pocket of his borrowed coat, and slid himself between the doors. Once inside, he immediately pushed them shut.

While the train featured a row of windows, they weren't as large as traditional trains. This was mostly due to needing to incorporate all the additional electronics for the flat panel displays, which were designed to replace the static maps and advertising. Through a combination of crouching and taking advantage of the limited fenestration, Morris was able to hide from outside view while he moved through the train.

He reached into Elijah's coat and removed his cellphone. Using just the light of the screen, he was able to see his way around. It looked as though Beetlejuice and Kenny had been relatively clean tenants. It fit with something Morris had observed about the homeless for years. Those with few possessions treated what they had with the utmost care.

Up ahead, toward one end of the train car, he could see some items stacked. He crawled on the floor toward them. As he slid his hand forward, it caught something rubbery.

"Aw shit," he said aloud, catching himself from speaking at full volume. He shined the light forward. It was a condom, presumably used. He must have been in the nest of Kenny the Clown. He scanned ahead and saw boxes of generic prophylactics – only in Massachusetts, where politicians made sure condoms were free and plentiful from every high school to every homeless shelter. He recalled the counsel of the late Sonny Barret. "As long as people are screwing, they don't realize they are getting fucked."

Morris wiped his hand on Bonita Poole's sweatpants and spun around to move in the other direction. He crossed midway of the car, in front of the doors he originally entered. His knees began to ache against the hard rubber floor, but at least it was the cleanest smelling subway car he had ever been in.

The light from his cellphone caught sight of items stacked in a row of seats. He looked closer – watches, neatly organized, ready to sell on the street or at a pawn shop. Beetlejuice was a talent. He turned to the adjacent row and saw several laptops, tablets, three canes and a prosthetic arm. "Talented, but devious," Morris said to himself.

He pushed ahead past some backpacks. He had entertained maybe looking through them but decided, instead, to continue his tour of ill-gotten goods. Then he hit the mother load. A row of seats with cellphones stacked at least ten high. There had had to be more than a hundred of them. Again, they were well organized, but Morris had no idea which phone may have been Bob Sosa's. He flipped himself around and sat down on the floor. At that moment, he saw blue lights flash by on Atlantic Avenue. It was either another cruiser or maybe a wagon to take Beetlejuice and Kenny to the morgue. He imagined the news vultures would be on the scene soon too.

He entertained calling Elijah, but it was getting late. Plus it was bad enough that one T-cop had gone slightly rogue. As it was, if Morris found Sosa's cellphone, he needed to concoct a good story for how it came into his possession. It wouldn't be too hard to do. He could have found it anywhere. The real trick was how would he lose the cellphone permanently if it showed Bob was mixed up in something unsavory. Those were the rock-and-a-hard-place cases.

The reality was most good people were only one bad choice removed from a perp walk. It was just too easy for them to get caught. Crime was no different from acting. Those who had been doing it all their lives were just a natural at it, but for the amateurs lured onto the stage of deceit, they'd blunder like a second-grader reciting the Gettysburg Address.

As Morris sat on the floor and exhaled. He glanced at the clock on his phone. If there were a hundred cellphones, and he spent two minutes looking at each, he could be sleeping before 1 a.m. Time to get to work.

Morris could hear the traffic outside. It was louder than normal. His daughter must not have closed one of the windows tightly. He rolled over, reaching for his pillow but his hand hit hard plastic, and he suddenly felt a crick in his neck. Opening his eyes, he had a moment of disorientation before his brain caught up to the scene around him.

He had fallen asleep in the prototype subway car. It was getting light out but not quite morning rush hour. Next to him were three cellphones, the candidates from the stack around him that he saw as possibly belonging to Bob Sosa. Each was locked with a code. He slid them into the pocket of Elijah's sportcoat and then got to his knees.

Scurrying to the doors, he peered out the window. The sidewalk appeared clear, and he pushed the doors open just enough to wedge himself out. About fifty yards down the sidewalk, he saw a news crew near the entrance of the bus terminal. He thought for a moment and reached for the key to the lock the train. It was better to leave everything as it was than to have the possibility of people rummaging through it.

As Morris slipped the keys back into his pocket and began to walk toward the South Station train terminal, his head remained trained in the opposite direction, on the news crew behind him. They didn't seem to notice as he continued to walk, somewhat blindly, toward the train station entrance. Then suddenly, he heard a voice in front of him.

"Hey!" it shouted as he spun his head around to meet the bright light of a TV camera he had nearly walked into.

"Great! We've got a homeless guy here!" he heard a woman's voice say excitedly.

Morris raised his hands to block the light and then turned and ran in the other direction. He looked back and saw a reporter and crew follow him. Turning his eyes forward, he could see the crew that originally had his attention down by the bus terminal. When they saw Morris coming with the other news station following, they turned and began heading toward him.

"Hey that's our homeless guy!" he heard someone shout from behind.

"Yeah, but he's coming our way!" the crew in front of him yelled.

As he continued toward the bus terminal entrance, and the distance between the two crews narrowed, he heard a barrage of expletives. In his mind, he determined his next move, taken right out of his park league football playbook. A jab step to his right, and then a spin to the left would freeze the crew in front of him and give him clear access to the bus terminal stairs and up through the doors.

As he clomped along awkwardly in the firefighter boots, it was like he was 25 again. The Mantis, Bob Sosa, would be the outside receiver, taking the defense wide. Morris, with his quick feet and balance, would do the jab and then cut underneath for an easy completion. Morris could sense a smile crossing his face, and then, suddenly, that face was on the sidewalk.

The combination of the boots and Morris being more than twice the age he was when Mantis and he were part of the championship park league team had caused his jab-cut-and-spin to become more like a stumble-dive-tuck-and-roll.

But as he looked up, he saw the two cameramen who had been chasing him collide. In turn, they stumbled into the reporters. While not nearly as he had drawn it up, he now had unfettered access to the bus terminal entrance. Picking himself up, he gingerly jogged up the steps and through the doors.

As he took a stride onto the escalators, he could see the collection of reporters still getting to their feet, and it was at that moment that the adrenaline began to subside, and he realized how tired and aching he was. Looking at his right knee, he saw the tear in Bonita's sweatpants. It was now Thursday morning. His Monday morning visit to his wife's grave seemed so long ago.

He exited the escalator and walked the circular concourse toward the police substation at the bus terminal. As he was about to enter the door, Detective Homer Moy came through it, going in the other direction.

"Oh geez, sorry" he said not recognizing Morris.

"Don't worry about it," Morris said stopping his fellow T-cop.

"Holy crap, Morris?" Moy responded, who then stepped back and took a look at his attire.

"Don't ask, and I won't tell," Morris said.

Moy then grabbed him. "You don't want to go in there. They're all freakin' out over the latest homeless killing."

"Huh?"

"Come on, let's get to headquarters," said the Flyin' Hawaiian.

"Actually, how about you give me a ride to Southie? I need to change."

Moy laughed. "You sure do," he said as he led Morris around the concourse and toward the parking area reserved for the transit police. "Have you considered black tactical. It's apparently really in this fall."

"Huh?"

"Swani's got her gestapo crew running the show," said Moy. "They're all getting decked out in their SWAT stuff. They're planning on rousting all the homeless from the subways, looking for this guy."

Moy then held up his cellphone. It was a grainy security photo taken from the top floor of the bus terminal. It showed a disheveled, balding man in a sportcoat, sweatpants, and firefighter boots bending over the bodies of Beetlejuice and Kenny the Clown. Morris looked at Moy and didn't say a word.

"Yeah, they think this guy may be the one going around bashing in the skulls of homeless. Apparently, he got an MWRA worker over by the Muddy River the other day, too."

"You don't say," said Morris.

"Hey," Moy said shifting tone. "One of these guys was Beetlejuice. You think there might be a connection with Sosa?"

"Geez, I don't know," he answered as they reached Moy's cruiser. "What does Dyani Swan think?"

"No idea. I've been here since last night, but get this. She's been talking about the Smiley Killer."

"Urban legend," responded Morris.

"Just like Mo the Fist," shot back Moy with a wink.

The two T-cops climbed inside the car, and Moy exited the bus terminal. The Smiley Killer was a myth that cropped up in cities like Boston and New York in the wake of unsolved homicides and disappearances. Generally, the pattern involved young men fished out of some body of water near an urban environment, and somewhere nearby there was a smiley face painted or drawn.

The part of the pattern that never made the public eye, at least with the same notoriety as the Internet-fueled theories, was that typically all these bodies of water were near bars and nightclubs. Cops had long ago figured it was far more likely that the young men got themselves so drunk that they stumbled into a river and drowned than it was that some multi-city serial killer was working the eastern seaboard.

As they made the short drive over the Broadway Street Bridge and the Fort Point Channel, into South Boston, the Flyin' Hawaiian explained that Swan had formed her own special operations unit a few weeks ago, but no one was really clear on what they were doing.

"Where did that picture you showed me come from?" he asked.

"Oh that crazy-looking homeless guy?" responded Moy. "She texts them out on some alert group or something. Apparently, it's what they used to do at 'Homeland.'"

Morris laughed. "Hey, who's the best at getting into a locked cellphone?"

"Oh talk to Bruce about that," said Moy. "He's got all the James Bond stuff. I bet he can get in."

"Or blow it up," added Morris

The Flyin' Hawaiian nodded as he turned right onto G Street. Bruce Donohue could be a hit-or-miss resource.

Morris peered out the windshield, looking toward clouds rolling in over the Boston Harbor. "They said more rain today."

"They say rain every day," shot back Moy as he weaved between sets of double-parked cars.

Morris nodded as the cruiser stopped at the corner with 8th Street, and he prepared to get out. "Thanks for the lift."

"No problem. Southie is the only part of this city where the roads make sense. Too bad all you Micks here can't park for shit."

Morris looked over the open door of the cruiser and saw a SmartCar double parked next to a Prius. "Times they are a-changin,' Homer."

He slammed the cruiser door shut and quickly ran up the stairs of his triple-decker, his mind focused on whether he wanted to shower first or just hit his couch and grab some genuine sleep.

However, as he opened his door, he felt his phone vibrate. Recognizing the number, he pushed answer.

"What's up, buddy?"

"Based on the picture I'm looking at, it would seem like you were busy last night," Elijah Poole said.

"Shit, I didn't think I was that recognizable."

"No," said Elijah, "But I know my own sportcoat."

"Yeah, about that, I'll get it dry cleaned," said Morris.

"Better if you just burn it, along with my wife's sweatpants at this stage."

Morris continued to speak as he went upstairs to his kitchen, explaining his meeting with Ginger and his discovery of Bob Sosa's phone.

"Did you hear about the meeting today?" asked Elijah.

"What do you mean?" responded Morris.

"Community meeting with Secretary of Transportation and the GM," said Elijah. "McGovern and Lake are going to be there. Rumor is the Archangels are going to crash it."

"No kidding, does Goldi know?" asked Morris.

"I don't know," said Elijah. "They should be releasing her from the hospital this morning. All I know is they moved the whole thing to the meeting room at the Transportation Building. Swan's prepping for a war. Fortunately, I'm bowing out. I've got to be back at Police Command School."

"I forgot all about that," said Morris. "How's that going?"

"Like a root canal," quipped Elijah.

Morris laughed, and he and Elijah exchanged their goodbyes. After hanging up he looked at his texts and noticed he had just one from Sergeant Manning over the night. The truth was Morris liked Manning as a cop. She was tough, persistent, and focused on getting the job done without concern for ruffling feathers. However, as a detective working for the DA's office, she was also a political appointment. She knew how to play the game. He could see her running for office someday.

As Morris looked at the text, the phone began to vibrate with an incoming call. He didn't recognize the number, but at 8 a.m. in the morning, it couldn't be good. Maybe it was one of his daughters.

"Hello," he said.

"Morris, have you heard this shit about the Archangels?"

"Hey Goldi," he responded, smiling to himself over Sann's unique conversational style. She was a teddy bear with the vocabulary of a Quentin Tarantino movie. "Yeah, I heard they're meeting at the Transportation Building today. I was thinking of giving Father Michael a call. He'd know about it."

"Morris, the homeless are pissed right now, and the police are panicking. Someone with a cool head needs to be there or it's going to get outta control."

He couldn't agree more. Goldilocks then went on a rant, but midway through, her tone lightened. It was like Quentin Tarantino decided to do a remake of *The Sound of Music*. Then he caught a voice in the background.

"Goldi, who's there with you?"

She then paused. "Oh well, there's the doctors," she said. "A nurse was by earlier. Oh, and firefighter McKenna came by to check in."

"Goldi's got a boyfriend, Goldi's got a boyfriend," Morris started to sing-song. In response, he could hear a forced laugh. He imagined Patrick McKenna was in the room and Sann was fighting the urge to unleash a profanity-laden rebuttal on Morris.

Partly out of fear of what might eventually come his way when Goldilocks didn't feel the need to exercise such restraint, Morris decided to shift the subject back to the Archangels meeting. "Listen, I have an idea. I can make some calls."

"You know what it's like," she said. "You're dealing with a population that already has their back up against the wall. A slight push, and the only place they have to go is to push back, hard."

"I know."

"And have you seen that fuckin' photo that Dyani Double Ds sent out on the alert?"

"No," answered Morris, presuming Patrick McKenna was no longer in earshot. "How come I'm not on these things?"

"Consider yourself lucky. The woman can't spell for shit either. She spells operations with three Os"

"Oh yes, I heard about her special ops crew," said Morris. "Steph Tam is going to be bullshit when she gets back."

"It might be too late by then. She's got her bootstompers running through the subway looking for this guy, and you know what, I think it's all bullshit."

"Why do you say that?" asked Morris.

"I've never seen the guy. I bet it's just someone she hired to give her a reason to go after the homeless."

Morris caught sight of himself in a hallway mirror. "So the guy doesn't look homeless to you?"

"The photo is a piece of crap. I mean the guy has the look, all deranged, and shit like that," explained Sann, as Morris turned in the mirror. "But the big problem is he is too fuckin' old. Homeless don't live to be that long."

Morris was at a loss for words. In the bigger picture, Goldi was right. The guy in that photo wasn't homeless. As a matter of fact, he was standing in his own home right now, but for some reason, Dyani Swan was using him to stir a pot of panic.

"I mean what's her deal?" continued Sann. "What do the homeless have? Nothing. Why is she going after them?"

"They're an easy target I guess," said Morris.

"Yeah, but she is not a fuckin' ditz or something," said Goldi. "Why wake a bunch of sleeping dogs."

It was a good question. Morris thought of telling Goldi that he may have found Bob Sosa's phone, but the more this week went on, the more Morris was convinced to hold his cards close to his vest.

"So what's up with you?" he said finally.

"I'm out of here, as soon as the doctor comes back."

"Well, you seem to be back to your old self," Morris said.

There was a slight laugh followed by "Oh thank you, Morris." Patrick McKenna must have been back in the room.

"So what's up this afternoon? I might have some more information by then and maybe we can check out the Archangels rally or whatever."

"Oh, I think that might be possible," still in her Julie Andrews tone. "I am going to go with firefighter McKenna, and get some of my things from yesterday."

"Oh, going to the firehouse?"

"Yes," said Sann.

"Alright, how about I meet you there around 11?"

"Yes, I think we should be there by then."

"Great," said Morris. "I'm sure you're looking forward to playing on the fire pole."

Goldi let out her loudest and most forced laugh yet, and Morris laughed along. He then heard a knocking at his door, and turned and went down his stairs while still talking to Goldi.

"I'm just giving you shit," he told her.

"Oh I know, Morris. I'll be sure to return the favor."

He laughed as he opened the door.

Sann continued to speak, but Morris didn't hear her as he looked at the man standing on his steps.

"Goldi, I've got to go," he said, instantly hanging up the phone.

While the two men hadn't stood face to face in fifteen years, the blue-gray eyes instantly gave away his identity even though a beard hid much of his face.

"Sorry," the man said. "I hope I didn't wake you, but I got to town earlier than I expected."

"No worries, William," Morris said. "Like I told you before. Once your home, always your home."

Chapter 15

Morris sat at his kitchen table, looking at the man across from him, whom he hadn't laid eyes on since he was a teenager. William was still a quiet, introspective type. Even in the years when Morris and his late-wife were his legal guardians and he was in their house full time, he never found much trouble.

There were a few incidents here and there, and William clearly had the Fitzgerald blood in him. When he was 13, he sent a larger 15-year-old classmate to the hospital with a broken nose and a cracked rib. Morris couldn't remember the details, but he remembered picking up William from school. He was sitting in the vice-principal's office, calm, quiet, and appearing to just daydream out the window.

The last time William was in this house was his 17th birthday when he asked Morris and his wife to sign his enrollment papers for the Marines. He had stayed in touch, and when his adoptive mother, Morris' wife, passed away five years ago, the two had about as close to a heart-to-heart chat as they ever did, but other than knowing William was a lance corporal based at Camp Lejeune in North Carolina, Morris had little idea what he had been up to. Even now, conversation came sparingly.

"You want more coffee?" Morris asked his adopted son.

William shook his head. "No thanks. This is great as is."

He had always been austere with both his words and his lifestyle. Even in his name. It was always William. Never Bill, Billy, or any sort of nickname.

"You know, Morris," he said. "She had a lot of struggles."

"But she loved you."

Morris didn't fully believe the words, but they seemed the right thing to say.

William smiled. "I remember her coming to my Southie Little League games," he said after a moment. "Especially if I was pitching. She didn't want me to know she was there. I think she thought it would make me nervous."

"I remember," Morris said.

"And then, it would be around like the second inning, and the ump would call a ball, and you'd hear from behind the stands 'ref that was a fuckin' strike!'"

Morris burst into laughter recalling the scene, and William laughed along too.

"Yeah, she had a real stage whisper, too," said Morris. "She was a hot ticket."

"It must have been tough," William said staring at the table. Morris couldn't be sure if there was a specific reference in the comment or just a general assertion that Cathy had lived a difficult life. He decided to shift the topic.

"So what are you doing with the corps now?"

"Same thing. Force Recon," he said casually.

Morris nodded. "Overseas?"

"Yeah, a few trips to Afghanistan. Actually, I'm due on another one in April."

There was no additional comment.

"You know if you are ever looking to get out, I can always see about getting you a date for an exam somewhere," said Morris. "It doesn't have to be transit police. Staties, BPD, you name it. Personally, I'd take the fire exam. People love firefighters. They hate cops. They hate the T, and they especially hate T-cops."

William laughed. "Maybe," was all he said as he regained his composure. Something seemed to be weighing on him, but Morris couldn't place it.

"And the cigarettes," William said with no prompting and showing a reflective smile.

Morris cracked a grin. "Pall Mall unfiltereds, right?"

William nodded. "I always thought they were going to get her. I should've seen the drugs coming."

Morris changed his expression quickly. "We don't know that for sure, yet," he said.

"But you found her in some kind of drug den, with a needle in her arm, right?"

"Yeah, that's what one of the firefighters said."

William stayed quiet for a moment. "So here's the thing," he said, leaning forward. "If that place was some sort of toxic sewer, how did she live long enough to shoot up?"

Morris had his mouth open for a response, but nothing came. William had a point, one that had escaped Morris. "Well, we don't know about timing," he stammered. "Or even what actually killed her, yet. The medical examiner should be letting us know."

William nodded, but the rest of his body said the same thing Morris was contemplating. Something wasn't adding up. Then a thought struck Morris.

"Umm, listen, about Happy," he began.

"Don't worry. I'm not going to trouble him with any conspiracy theories," William said, getting up from the table and bringing his mug to the sink.

"Probably best," Morris said. "He's doing better, you know."

"Yeah, we talked a bit on the phone last night," he said rinsing the mug and drying his hands. "I told him I would swing by this morning, help him with the service."

"Service?"

"St. Anthony's downtown. He's having a little memorial service or something this afternoon."

Morris felt stunned. Happy didn't say anything about it to him.

"He probably was going to call you," William said, apparently sensing Morris' feelings. "I think he said it's at three. You should come by."

"I don't know," said Morris. "I'll talk to Happy."

William nodded assuringly. "Just remember he's got a lot on his mind."

Morris smiled. If William only knew all that was on his mind. He continued to dwell on the idea that maybe foul play had been involved in Cathy's death. He then remembered the three cellphones he had found overnight.

"Listen," he said. "I've got a work meeting in a bit, but you're welcome to stay as long as you want. Don't feel like you have to run off or anything."

"Thanks," said William. "But I figured it might be best if I check in on Happy. No offense to him, but there was a reason I lived with you."

He always was a perceptive kid. "Like I said, he's doing better now," said Morris.

"Well, let's hope it stays that way," said William.

Morris then escorted his adopted son downstairs, where he picked up his olive drab duffel bag and slung it over his shoulder. Morris offered to give him a ride, but William insisted on walking to Happy's apartment in the Old Colony housing project, just on the other side of Carson Beach. It was probably best, Morris hadn't gotten the Ghetto Glider to turn over in at least a month.

Closing the door behind him, Morris spied a clock in his front hall. It was 10:30 in the morning. He had only a half hour before he was supposed to meet Goldilocks, and he still hadn't showered. He turned and caught sight of himself in the mirror. Tilting his head left and right, a Who lyric came to mind. "I know that I've been wearing crazy clothes, and I look pretty crappy, sometimes."

Morris had time to fix only one of those conditions. He ran upstairs, changed into a pair of jeans, a T-shirt, and grabbed a navy blue windbreaker. He also made sure to grab the three cellphones as he was planning on tracking down Bruce Donohue after meeting up with Goldilocks.

As he ran out the door to head to the Broadway T stop, he noticed the clouds forming over the harbor. While the outside temperature wasn't as cold as he anticipated, it did look like rain was on its way. "I might get that shower after all."

Morris hopped on the Red Line and then picked up the Green Line at Park Street, venturing a few stops west to get off just a block from the firehouse.

As he crossed the street, a light rain began to fall and he pulled out his phone to call Goldilocks and let her know he was there. While he had his phone out, he noticed three text messages from BPD Sergeant Joanne Manning. He saw only two expletives. Progress.

As the phone was ringing, he looked up and could see Sann running out the front door of the firehouse. Her attire was leaning more toward her lobsterman side today as she was back in her Sperry boots, a pair of Boston Fire sweatpants and a matching sweatshirt.

"What the fuck? You're ten minutes late!" she shouted.

It was nice to see Goldilocks was feeling herself again. "Sorry," he said, hanging up the call and putting his phone away. "I got hung up with someone."

"Yeah, yeah," said Sann sarcastically. "Come on I'll grab my things. Hope you brought an umbrella. It's going to pour today."

"This is nothing," said Morris, looking at the sky and walking toward the firehouse door that Sann was holding open. As he stepped in the small station, he nearly bumped into Patrick McKenna.

"Sorry about that, sergeant," said the firefighter carrying some sort of electronics.

"No worries," said Morris stepping out of the way as McKenna continued into an adjoining room. The T-cop then poked his head in and saw what looked to be a console of radio equipment and computers partially assembled. "What's all that?"

McKenna spun around. "Oh this, it's just a new E-911 system."

"You guys install these yourselves?"

"Hey, if you want to have a job done right...." quipped McKenna.

Morris thought to himself and then nodded. "You know much about cellphones?"

"What do you mean?"

"I got three cellphones here, and I need to get into them."

"Like get around passwords and stuff?" asked McKenna as he crouched under the console.

"Yeah."

"I don't know," the firefighter said. "What are you looking for on them?"

"I don't know," said Morris. "I mean, don't I need to get into know what's there?"

"Not necessarily," said McKenna, pulling on a cable. "I mean let's say there's a memory card in there. You can pop that out and read it."

"No shit, you know how to do that?"

McKenna shrugged as Morris sensed someone come up behind him.

"Do what?" said Sann, as she nudged her head around Morris to look into the room.

McKenna peeked out from the console and gave a smile toward Goldi. "The sergeant here is trying to get into some cellphones."

"I may have found Bob Sosa's cellphone," said Morris turning to Sann.

"Nice," said Goldi.

Morris reached into his jacket and pulled out the three cellphones. "The problem is I don't know which of these it is, and they're all locked."

With that McKenna stood up and walked over to Morris and Sann. Morris handed him the three devices. The two T-cops watched as the firefighter looked at them, and then began to rummage through a drawer of cables.

"Geez, he sure seems handy," Morris said quietly to Goldilocks.

Sann shot him a look.

"What?" he replied, feigning innocence. "I am just saying he seems to be very good with his hands."

With that, Morris felt a subtle kick to his left shin. As he grimaced, he spotted the clock on the wall. "Crap, we have to get going!" he said to Sann.

"Sorry, I lost track of the time," she said glancing toward Patrick.

"Here," McKenna said handing some keys to Sann, "take the pick-up. I'll take a look at these phones while you're gone."

Morris and Sann looked at each other and nodded. It seemed like a good idea. Plus, the weather outside seemed to be turning. By the time the meeting was over, it could be a downpour.

Sann grabbed the keys, and the two T-cops made their way to an old fire-engine-red truck that perhaps had been a command vehicle a decade or two earlier.

Sann drove toward the Transportation Building, parking on Tremont Street in front of a round brick building, which was the former home of the Church of all Nations. At one point it had served as a refuge for the poor and the downtrodden of the city. However, Morris noticed one of BoBo Powers' signs plastered over the door. The sanctuary apparently had been given last rites to be reborn as one of the city's latest parking complexes.

He shook his head and started singing "*pave paradise, put up a parking lot*," as the two made the short walk to the Transportation Building at Ten Park Plaza. However, even if he were on key, Sann likely wouldn't have been able to discern his melody. The sounds of the city were being dominated by some sort of cheer or chanting. As they passed the Milner Hotel, the words became clearer.

"No justice. No peace. Fuck the T-Police."

When they came around the corner, they observed a group of more than one hundred protesters, carrying signs and picketing in front of Ten Park Plaza. Morris' quick scan of the crowd revealed the common phenomenon he had seen over the years. Predominantly, the shouters shared a similar demographic, young college kids. While there may have been some ethnic diversity, if they had been holding Starbuck's coffees and lattes, visually it very well could have been a group attending some weekend jazz festival. Audibly, of course, there was a difference, but truthfully Morris preferred the profane shouting to jazz.

As the pair pushed through the crowd, Morris marveled at the assortment of dress. "Designer dishevelment," he called it. People spending the equivalent of his first paycheck on a pair of jeans, already ripped and faded. It made about as much sense to him as ordering a hamburger that someone else had already bit into.

But this is Boston, home to dozens of colleges and the intellectually challenged men, women, and everyone in between that chose to work and study there.

One sign read "Save Are Subways." Morris just shook his head at the gaff. Of course, at any of these events, there'd be the evangelists. The days of "Jesus Saves!" had apparently ceded to the more direct message of "You're All Going to Hell." At least the Jesus freaks get their spelling and punctuation right.

Another sign read "Money for whores but not the poor." He couldn't tell whether it was an accusation or a suggestion. An older woman held up "Transit Apartheid." Kids these days all went to "fascist" or "Nazi" as their political insult. It was nice to see the throwback.

Then a young man in Birkenstocks and a knit hat was yelling some sort of insult as he was waving a poster board that read "End oil dependency. Ride the T." Morris was on the verge of trying to explain to the young scholar that the buses, trains, subways, and boats of public transit didn't run on unicorn farts, but then he spotted the contingent of Boston Police and T-cops on bicycles up ahead.

Recognizing the on-site commander as Captain Jack Denzell of the BPD, Morris turned to pull Goldi along, but she was in the middle of a shouting match with some pink-hatted protester. The only word Morris could make out on the sign was "vagina," and he figured it best if he just pushed through the crowd and let Goldi find him.

When he came up to Denzell, the Boston cop was grinning from ear to ear. "This is great. In the past year, I've been spit at, had bottles thrown at me, you name it, but this group loves the Boston Police. They hate you guys."

"Lovely," Morris said surveying the scene.

At that moment Goldilocks pushed through, still yelling but at no one in particular. "That fuckin bitch spills her fuckin mocha latte choca whatever all over me, and she's like 'oh, hee, hee ....'"

"Goldi, Goldi," Morris said, bringing his fellow T-cop out of her tirade and initiating an introduction. "This is Jack Denzell, Boston Police. Jack, this is Susan Sann."

As he shook her hand, recognition came across his face. "Three bears, right? You're Goldilocks."

Sann sheepishly nodded.

"Well, from what I understand, they may be three bears but only five balls now," added Denzell.

They all laughed, and then Goldi turned to Denzell. "What the fuck did we do to make the mob mad at us?"

Pulling a crumpled flier out of his jacket pocket, he handed them the paper. "This sums it all up pretty good."

Morris grabbed it and read, "A man is banished by the State Police for a great crime, by the Boston Police for a small crime, and by the MBTA Police for no crime at all!"

Morris shook his head. "Next stop, body cams."

"You can bet on that," said Denzell. "And if you think they're angry, wait until you go upstairs to the meeting room."

Goldilocks looked toward the transit police bicycle unit. "They seem more pissed than the protesters."

Morris listened to an exchange between the T's bike patrol and the crowd and started to laugh. "No wonder. They're calling them 4-0."

Sann looked confused.

"Most cops are considered 5-0," he explained. "We're just 4-0. Get it?"

Denzell let out a laugh.

"Oh thanks for understanding, buddy," Morris said sarcastically. "We're the Rodney Dangerfield of police. We can't get no respect."

"Yeah, well you bring it on yourself," said Denzell. "Five minutes ago they were calling you guys 'Panda Police.'"

"What does that mean?"

The Boston Police captain just raised a hand and pointed toward a pair of transit police cruisers parked in front of the New

England School of Law across the street. As opposed to the old, more traditional coloring of blue and white, the new cruisers had large black and white panels.

Sann burst out laughing. Morris couldn't blame her. Then he turned to her. "Hey, we better get inside." He then stuck out a hand that Denzell met with his own. "Good luck out here."

Out of the corner of Morris' eye, he noticed a young man, probably a college kid in the area, coming their way and looking fairly intoxicated. "Hey Jack," Morris said, "You may want to keep an eye out for that vomit bomber."

"What?"

"Vomit bomber," Morris repeated pointing over Denzell's shoulder.

The captain shook his head, apparently confused by the T-cop lexicon. Morris and Goldilocks turned to go in the building, but as they did, they heard the distinct sound of a nauseated exhale followed by Captain Jack. "Fuck! All over my shoes."

"You warned him," Sann said as the two pushed through the crowd to the lobby inside. They took the escalator to the second floor. Immediately outside a packed meeting hall, Morris saw several police officers dressed in full black tactical uniforms. Initially, he couldn't place their affiliation until he saw Axe and Smash among them.

"Dear God," was all he said as he and Goldi entered the meeting hall. Axe and Smash weren't bad guys, but somewhere in the psychological exam to become a T-cop, they cheated. Both men had that make-up that viewed a badge as a license to be an asshole. Now they were running around looking like overweight Navy SEALs.

"Check it out," Goldi said giving a nod to the front of the room, and Morris recognized the Secretary of Transportation. She seemed comfortable sitting behind a nameplate, surrounded by three uniformed State Police officers.

Turning ahead, Morris spotted two fellow transit police officers, one a tall well-built officer whose name was Paul Flynn. The other was a short rotund officer named Roscoe Carroll.

He turned to Goldilocks and pointed ahead toward them.

"They make a perfect ten," she said.

Morris had barely contained his laughter by the time he had reached the two. "You two have your hands full today."

Carroll shook his head. "No. We've been ordered to stand down. The Black Legion is handling event security."

Morris showed his confusion.

"It's the name we've given to Swan's new special ops unit," explained Flynn. "Personally, I liked 'costumed crusaders.'"

"I think we should have stuck with 'Men in Black'" added Carroll.

"But that would have been sexist," said Flynn.

"Nothing wrong with sexy," Carroll said.

"OK, OK," said Morris, laughing at the exchange as in walked the T's security director and acting chief.

"Holy shit," said Sann. "It's Double D Dyani."

Carroll and Flynn looked at each other as if to say "why didn't we think of that one."

Swan had chosen attire identical to her special ops crew, which followed in behind her, providing a human tunnel through which the T's General Manager walked to his chair on the platform next to the Secretary of Transportation.

"God save the T," whispered Morris, not immediately noticing that Swan had started coming his way. By the time he spotted her, it was too late to find an exit, and going anywhere else in the room would have made it obvious that he was trying to avoid her.

"Well, hello sergeant," said Swan in a seemingly pleasant voice. "I'm glad to see you are out of the hospital."

Morris smiled and nodded.

"Please introduce me to your fellow officers," she said.

"Sure thing," said Morris. "Director Dyani Swan it is a pleasure to introduce you to Paulie, Roscoe, and Goldilocks."

Swan gave Morris a double take, but Sann saved him.

"Officers Paul Flynn, Roscoe Carroll," she said, pointing to her fellow T-cops. "I'm Susan Sann. We've met."

"Oh yes," said Swan. "Sorry, I didn't notice you. And you're doing better as well?"

"Oh, I'm doing great," shot back Sann.

Even though Goldi was giving up at least two inches and probably twenty pounds to Swan, Morris' money was on her in a fair fight. In an unfair one, he'd double down on the blond scrapper.

"Love the entourage you got there," Morris said nodding to the special ops group.

Swan looked behind her and then back. "Oh, you mean the Special Security Operations Unit?"

"Yes, the SS or whatever you call them," Morris said, nonchalantly slipping in the Nazi reference. "You know in Southie we call them leg breakers, but whatever."

"What's that sergeant?" Swan responded with a scowl.

Morris was ready to launch into the deputy director but was suddenly tugged to the side.

"Oh that sewer gas," said Goldi shaking her head. "Bad stuff. He's been mumbling all day."

Swan didn't seem to buy the defense, but she turned and walked off with two of her stormtroopers to take up a post about thirty feet away in front of one of the exit doors.

"Goldi, I can handle myself," said Morris.

"Yeah, how does that work for you normally?"

OK, she had him on that point, but he had been playing a few choice comments in his mind ever since the prior night when he realized that Swan was trying to stir trouble with the homeless.

"Somebody needs to put her in her place," Morris said.

"Yeah, you do that, and you get yourself bounced for a month," said Goldi, shaking her head. "Then who am I going to have work with? Axe and Smash?"

"It's going to end up happening anyway," he replied as the two moved their way toward the back. "I'm a white male. I'm like O-positive, the universal donor for everyone else's shit. Perpetually open for vilification, with no grounds upon which to reply."

"Wouldn't that make you the universal recipient?"

"Whatever, you know what I mean," he said. "The point is I'm sure my mere presence offends her. So if I am on thin ice, I might as well jump up and down and get something out it."

"Uh, I don't think that's what you're supposed to do on thin ice, Morris."

Before he could offer a retort, a familiar voice came over the speakers. It was Father Michael McGovern calling the group to order. Morris looked up and could see the priest joined by the Reverend Eugene Lake on the rostrum.

As Father Michael spoke, however, Swan's Black Legion began to line the perimeter of the room. At one point, the old Irish priest interrupted himself, breaking into a verse of "*Come out you black and tan and fight me like a man.*"

"What the fuck is that?" whispered Goldi.

"Black and tans?" said Morris. "How much Irish you got in you?"

"Just whatever I drink on St. Paddy's Day," she said. "I'm like Norwegian and Dutch."

Morris rolled his eyes. "Pat McKenna will make a decent woman out of you yet. Black and tan, those were the colors of the British occupying force in Ireland, thugs."

Goldilocks nodded, understanding McGovern's reference. The priest, however, then continued with the tale of the Molly Maguires. Morris could see where he was going even though it may have been lost on the audience. Unlike the crowd gathered out front, the one inside the building occupied the extremes of the city's culture. There were a few city councilors in attendance, but Boston's power class appeared to be represented mostly by the man and woman with a police escort up front and by aides to the other elected and appointed. Elsewhere in the room were the genuine residents of the city, not the college interlopers or the suburbanites who merely hopped on a train or bus every morning, but the men, women, and a couple of kids for whom the transit system was their lifeblood and, in a few cases, their home.

As McGovern told the tale, the Maguires were an underground fraternity in Ireland, a band of Robin Hoods in a way, offering protection to the poor from the predatory landowners. In the late 1800s, after many Irish had immigrated to the U.S., they appeared in Pennsylvania after the governor there gave railroad barons the right to raise a fully deputized and armed police force in the form of the Pinkertons.

Morris did a quick scan of the crowd. No Tin Man or any of the other usual suspects. As the priest spoke, Morris recalled that the first incident involving the Archangels may have been two decades ago, not too long after Father Michael had been banished to his role of overseeing a homeless shelter after supposedly beating a pedophile clergyman to within an inch of his life.

Much like the Molly Maguires, the Archangels were somewhere between legend and a secret society. For a group of homeless avengers, they could appear remarkably well organized, and yet despite their vengeful lean, in Morris' experience, no true Archangel ever crossed a legal line, at least not one Morris wouldn't cross on his own.

Hearing McGovern speak, he realized for the first time who may have been the founder of the movement. He returned from his thoughts to catch just the end of McGovern's speech.

"... and that Justice would lie bleeding in the subways when the jack-booted thugs, dressed in black, smashed the poor and the downtrodden in the belly of the beast in the city of Boston."

Morris thought maybe it was time he tried to make it to Father Michael's Sunday sermons. Then he glanced over at Dyani Swan, who seemed more uncomfortable than agitated. Morris grinned. Even in his 70s, Father Michael needed nothing more than a microphone and his steely-eyed resolve to put someone out of their comfort zone.

Reverend Eugene Lake, who had been labeled the "Prince of Provocation" by the local media, began by quoting Dr. Martin Luther King. "Injustice anywhere is a threat to justice everywhere," he said in his deep baritone. "And we will take our noble cause to the streets, from Ferguson, Missouri, to the subway stop at Fields Corner in the city of Boston."

The two men were like holy versions of Axe and Smash. Different style, equally effective.

"There's more fruit in a rich man's cocktail than a poor man's plate." Morris almost wanted to write that one down. The good reverend had outdone himself. "Let us recall Proverbs, 14:31, 'He who oppresses the poor shows contempt for their maker, but whoever is kind to the needy honors God.'"

Morris saw the faces of the audience filling with inspiration. Lake then turned to the Secretary of Transportation and the MBTA General Manager, and in his best preacher's voice exclaimed, "How can you worship a homeless man on Sunday, and ignore him on Monday!"

With that, the crowd erupted into an ovation.

Morris turned to Sann and whispered, "Careful, I think he just told this crowd that the T's managed to piss off everyone, including God."

Lake then proceeded to read a list of demands issued to the MBTA and the Secretary of Transportation.

They ranged from the sensible, such as getting rid of the Black Legion, to the plausible, such as retrofitting a few MBTA buses to be mobile showers and toilets, to the ain't-going-to-happen, such as handing out free transit passes to the homeless and removing the "racist" depiction of an Algonquian on the state and T police insignias.

What happened next, however, Morris found particularly interesting. As the General Manager began to speak, Dyani Swan intervened.

"We'll take your demands under advisement," she said, cutting off further talk.

"Advisement?" responded Father Michael. "We're not hear to advise you."

With that, some agitation began to show around the crowd, and Swan made a signal to her special ops group. "We appreciate your comments, but in the interest of public safety, it is time to disband this meeting."

Lake began to speak, but Swan cut him off. "Reverend, you've had quite enough time to talk. Now, we are out of time."

The crowd started to stir, but Morris watched McGovern and Lake. They seemed calm, and Morris thought he detected a subtle nod by the Irish priest. Some shouting erupted between some homeless and one of the Black Legion, and Morris grew nervous that a riot might break out.

At that moment the doors of the meeting room were opened, and several men and women in wheelchairs, being assisted by others wearing red berets and red jackets, entered.

"Who the hell are they?" Morris heard from an audience member.

Morris and Goldi turned to each other and whispered at the same time "Archangels."

Swan turned, pushed through a row of people and over to where Morris and Sann were. "What do they have planned?" she growled.

"I think they're on a mission from God," Morris deadpanned.

Swan started to lay into Morris with a verbal assault, but his attention turned elsewhere when he saw a skinny, but not as skinny as he once was, twenty-something, bi-racial man step into the room behind the other Archangels. He was dressed in black jeans, but instead of the red that the other Archangels were wearing, he had opted for a familiar-looking jean jacket that Morris assumed had ended up at the bottom of the Charles River.

As Morris remain fixated, he felt Goldilocks nudge him. He turned and saw her inquisitive expression.

"Ferret," was all he said.

Swan had been on a rant, but as Morris ignored her, she became insistent to know why. "What did you say? Who is that?"

Morris nodded. "For you? Probably you're worst nightmare." With that Swan, moved off toward where the GM and Secretary of Transportation were sitting while speaking into her radio affixed to one of the epaulets on her tactical uniform.

No one in the city had knowingly seen Ferret in eighteen months. Even then, he was more known by name and graf tag than by face. Rendered an orphan by a freak car accident, Ryan Baxter had bounced among foster homes for a few years, before turning to the subway as an escape from a drug-infested home.

There he learned to ply his skill as a graffiti artist, rising to fame in the city's subculture, but like his own lineage, Ryan was a walking conflict. With the help of Father Michael McGovern, the naturally intelligent ward of the state had earned a prep-school scholarship. By day he walked among the elite. At night, however, he joined the denizens of the homeless, making his life in the subways where he rose to the leadership of one of the city's notorious gangs.

Still, Morris was surprised to see Ferret. He had seemed so resolute against getting involved in the fray only a night ago, but then Morris remembered it was Beetlejuice who had taken Ferret under his wing in the subway, even giving him his nickname for the frenetic way the young tagger painted.

On a few occasions, drugs and violence nearly did Ferret in, but somewhere in the morass of illogic that was his life, he always pulled himself to the safety of Father Michael's shelter. To Morris, that was the most remarkable thing about the kid. Many brilliant people live with some curse or cross, but rarely do you find someone capable of saving themselves.

Even though it had become a buried story, Morris wondered if the truth would ever spread that it was Ferret, not the cops, who had saved the city from a lunatic terrorist. For his part, Ferret seemed happy to let his legend sleep. With the help of a handful of authorities, themselves interested in hiding the actual events, he assumed the new persona of Robert Andrews, law school student.

Amongst the commotion, Reverend Lake began to speak again. "We must end the criminalization of poverty and the violations of the poor and disabled citizens of the city," he said. "Since the transit police refuses to do its duty and protect the most marginalized, this group of Archangels," and he moved his hand in a semi-circle in front of him, "will be patrolling the subways and bus stops, protecting them from harm."

With that Swan, grabbed the microphone that had been set up in front of the General Manager. "You'll do nothing of the sort," she said. "The greatest danger to the city's homeless is themselves. As we speak, the transit police is working diligently on the spate of recent homicides that not only seem to point to homeless attacking homeless but innocent people being caught in the crossfire as well."

A murmur arose among the crowd. It was hard to tell whether there was agreement or not. Morris didn't trust Swan, but even dressed in special ops gear, she could speak persuasively. Even though many in the crowd were among those Swan seemed to hold in disdain, they couldn't know that. People at the lower end of the socio-economic spectrum are drawn to law and order. It's the thing that's supposed to protect them from all the forces hell-bent on keeping them where they are. What they fail to see is the courts and even the cops are run by the power class – the appointed, the elected, and, most important, the wealthy wizards behind the curtain who fuel their campaigns and whisper in their ears.

"We are the answer," said Swan, "not some vigilante group that has no authority!"

There was even a smattering of applause. Reverend Lake appeared ready to respond, but Morris noticed Father McGovern had put his hand over his fellow clergyman's microphone and nodded toward the back of the room. Morris traced the stares of the two gentlemen and saw Ferret stepping toward the center.

Swan turned, and Morris noticed her dropping her right hand over the holstered 9 millimeter at her side.

While at first, the crowd seemed unaware of the pause or shift in attention, after a few seconds all eyes turned toward Ferret who had now stopped in the middle of the room. He was a natural leader. Morris had to admit his admiration for the kid, but he also recalled their conversation the night before. He could be so much more than being another subway anarchist. By his own admission, the underground was unhealthy for him, and yet, he seemed to relish toying with his own self-destruction if it meant proving a point to some asshole in power. He was a man after Morris' own heart.

Morris could see the Secretary of Transportation pull her microphone toward her, asking the speaker to identify himself. However, the sound system had been turned off. Swan tried the microphone in her hand, too, but it was to no avail. Nonetheless, Ferret obliged the question, at least partially.

"Who I am is not important," he said, his voice filling the room. "I represent those without representation. I defend those who have not been defended, and I am here to empower all who feel powerless."

Reverend Lake ought to be taking notes, thought Morris.

"As to our authority," Ferret continued. "'That whenever any form of government becomes destructive of these ends, it is the right of the people to alter or abolish it.'"

God love the kid, quoting the Declaration of Independence to a bunch of bureaucrats.

"OK, enough," Swan shouted back toward Ferret. "The transit police are well equipped to protect the patrons."

"Maybe," answered Ferret, "But it's the homeless that need protecting from the T-cops!"

With that, the room erupted in applause, but not everyone shared in their support of the Archangels. Morris looked at his fellow T-cops. They all seemed to glare back at him. Then he noticed Swan had become agitated. She said something into her radio and then stepped toward Ferret.

"OK, time for everyone to leave!" she shouted, and the Black Legion moved in starting to usher people toward the exit. "In the interest of public safety, we are asking all of you to disperse immediately!" Swan shouted. "Any who resist will be arrested."

Ferret and the other Archangels stood their ground. Morris watched as Father Michael rose from his seat, and began to shake his head, as though he were advising Ferret and the others to exercise discretion.

As members of the unit closed toward Ferret, Morris realized the situation wasn't going to end well. "Come on Goldi, I think we have to go be the voice of reason here."

"Lord help us then," said Sann, as the two moved toward Ferret.

As Morris made his way to the middle of the room, he could see Axe standing inches from Ferret's face. "You want to get mouthy with me, boy!"

Ferret stood his ground. "This is a public building. Why you asking me to leave, Barney?"

Morris almost laughed. Axe was probably in his thirties. He'd never seen an episode of Andy Griffith with his bumbling deputy Barney Fife. Then again, neither had Ferrett. It's just everyone knew that if you wanted to insult a cop, you called him Barney.

While some of the other Archangels had retreated, they all kept their eyes on Ferret.

"I'm not asking!" yelled Axe. "I'm telling. I'm more than happy to haul you off, you wise ass."

"Sure, I'm leaving," said Ferret, taking a tiny step back. "See, I'm moving."

But Axe wasn't easing off. Then Swan came into the scene. "Arrest him!"

Axe reached for Ferret's collar, but in one lightning-quick move, Ferret retrieved a kuboton baton from inside his jean jacket and smashed Axe across the ribs, under his left arm. While the

Kevlar vest of his tactical outfit likely prevented any serious damage, it knocked the T-cop off his feet.

With that, a swarm of three other members of the Black Legion dove toward Ferret, but from behind him leaped the Tin Man, taking out all three with one well-timed block.

Chaos erupted, and Morris saw Swan reach for her sidearm. With that he rushed forward, pushing her to the ground.

"Get the fuck out of here," he shouted toward Ferret, who had his kuboton wound up ready to strike. Morris then jumped in between a T-cop and the Tin Man. "Just get the fuck out."

Tin Man and Ferret looked at each other and then bolted as Swan got to her feet with her 9 millimeter drawn.

"You're through!" she shouted at Morris. "I want him arrested!" she shouted turning to another T-cop. The commotion caused the police in the room to stop, allowing the remaining Archangels to escape.

"Hold on," said Sann coming in with hands raised. "He just saved your job. What the fuck were you thinking lady, pulling a gun in a crowd like this?"

Swan looked around. The General Manager and the Secretary of Transportation were in the room. She grew flustered. Morris helped Axe, whose expression seemed to recognize that Swan had pushed things to the edge of control.

She looked like she wanted to explode. "You and your foolish friends will soon learn that I was the best hope they had to survive," she blurted out at Morris. "No one gives a shit about the homeless. They live stupid and die young. It's for their own good. They can't be living in the subway, stinkin' it up."

"Hey, fuck you bitch," Goldi interrupted. "You think they want to be there? They're just trying to survive."

"Well, I'd wish they'd stop," shot back Swan. "Better if they just jumped in front of a train."

The words struck Morris like someone had loosed the restraint on a catapult. "Hold on there madame fuhrer, in this Commonwealth, it is not against the law to smell funky. Sure they might not be the most upstanding citizens, but I'll take any of them over a bureaucrat with a stick shoved up her ass!"

“Oh real clever sergeant,” she shot back. “I have a job to do, and it’s all because you and your police department are incompetent. The Lieutenant Governor has appointed my team as special State Police officers, we have full jurisdiction to restore order on the MBTA. I don’t give a shit if they’re homeless. Our job is to clean the subway of the vermin who live beneath the streets of Boston. The homeless are like a fungus that weakens society. They are the homo genus without the sapien. They are bastards, prostitutes, drug addicts and criminals.”

She then stormed out of the room, followed by members of the Black Legion.

Goldilocks looked at Morris. “What crawled up her ass. It sounds like she’s going to start a war on the homeless.”

“Well, if she is, she already has the uniforms,” quipped Morris. “The T’s board of directors will love hearing about the Black Legion.”

“Obviously she has some juice somewhere,” said Goldi. “She’s got the Lieutenant Governor in her corner.”

Morris stayed quiet. What worried him about the Lieutenant Governor signing off on the special ops unit was that it meant something more than just politics was at play in this. Politically, the easy thing to do was to ignore a problem but spin it like you solved it. But the bureaucracy all seemed to be aligning on this. The Secretary of Transportation, the General Manager, the Lieutenant Governor, no one would risk the political fallout unless there were deep pockets involved.

“She’s right about a few things, though,” said Morris.

“What do you mean?” asked Sann.

Morris cleared his throat. “People hate the homeless. Their lives don’t matter. People hate the police. People hate the T.”

“So we’re screwed then?”

“Goldi, didn’t anyone ever tell you what MBTA really stands for?”

She shook her head.

“More Bad Times Ahead.”

Chapter 16

Morris and Sann exited the Transportation Building. In the forty minutes they had been inside, the wind had freshened quite a bit bringing with it more rain but moderate temperatures for the first week of November. The crowd of protesters had dissipated.

"Jack, what happened?" Morris shouted toward Captain Denzell as he strode past the entrance. "Did you pepper spray everyone?"

Denzell laughed. "Fair weather fans, just like Occupy Boston."

Morris saw Sann roll her eyes as the two scurried across the street. "What?" he asked.

"Hey at least they were doing something," said Goldilocks. "Someone needs to stand up for the homeless and poor."

"You think that's what this was about?" Morris asked rhetorically as the two headed toward their borrowed pickup truck. "I see all this crap as more using the homeless and poor than helping them."

"I know, I know," said Sann raising a hand. "You're going to tell me it's all politicians pulling the strings. I get that, but it's better than sitting on your ass and doing nothing."

"Like Jack said," responded Morris. "Occupy Boston, half of them were suburbanites, living in nice houses, hopping on the commuter rail each day showing up at some tent they had their servants pitch for them. Politics Goldi. Once a little weather came in, they all gave up."

"Oh, come on," countered Sann.

"Remember, I grew up in a neighborhood filled with people ready to go to war with people who lived less than two miles away from them because that's what they were told to do," said Morris. "It's just a political flash mob, Goldi. All it takes is one pied piper, and the next thing you know you have a few thousand people at a rally to nuke the gay whales for Christ or whatever. Around here, we've done everything from burning witches to stoning buses. It never changes."

"Jesus, Morris, you are jaded," said Sann.

"Maybe," he acknowledged. "But I've been around the block a few times. Never underestimate the willingness of people to follow the crowd. People just want to be popular."

"You obviously don't have that problem," quipped Sann, as she opened the door to the pickup truck.

Morris had no retort. As he pulled the door handle, his eye caught a pair of black Cadillac Escalades in the parking garage across the street. He could see members of Swan's special ops unit standing around. They wouldn't be there without BoBo Powers' permission. Morris was surprised he hadn't gotten a call from his old friend.

He suddenly realized that Sann was speaking to him. "Sorry, Goldi. I missed that. My brain was somewhere else."

"You want me to give you a suggestion as to where it was?"

Morris smiled. "You were saying?"

"I was saying, I think you're an asshole sometimes. You're an endearing one, but what's so wrong with people doing the right thing even if it is for the wrong reasons?"

With that, Sann put the pickup in drive and pulled a U-turn from the parking spot, simultaneously steering and flipping her middle finger to a taxi who had honked. She had skills, no doubt about it.

"I just don't like seeing people used," Morris said as he fastened his seatbelt.

"Well, we agree on that," said Sann.

"Good," said Morris. "We'll start there. I'll try to be less of an asshole, and you try to be less of a fairy princess."

"Fuck you, Morris."

"See, you're already making progress."

Goldilocks drove the short distance to the firehouse through Boston's Back Bay while Morris contemplated the events of the day. He couldn't help but feel everything he had witnessed had been some unintentional distraction. The Archangels, Swan's goon squad, it was all on the periphery. The real issue was something else, but Morris couldn't see it.

Sann pulled the pickup into the driveway of the firehouse, and then quickly executed a three-point turn, backing the truck into its former spot.

As she threw the transmission into park, she exhaled. "Here's the real problem, Morris. What are we going to do?"

He could see the genuine concern on her face even though he wasn't sure what she meant.

"Are we just going to go to work for Dyani the fem-Nazi?" she continued. "I'm just not feeling it anymore. I just don't know if I can do this job."

Morris nodded. He had been down this road plenty of times before. "Don't let her get to you, Goldi."

"Kind of hard considering she's my boss right now."

"I know," he answered. "Whatever this is, it's temporary. It's like that cold you get in the middle of winter. When you got it, you feel like shit. You think you're dying. Then after a couple of days, you wake up and you feel good."

"Until the next cold hits," Sann said. "Is that what you're telling me?"

Morris shrugged, and Sann opened her door. As Morris did the same, he searched for the right thing to say. Goldilocks was a good cop, trying to do something right for the segment of the city's population that most needed a break. "Listen, Goldi," he said as he rounded the front of the pickup and the two crossed the bay of firetrucks. "You have to take the good with the bad in this job. Whatever Swan has going on here, it's not going to change what we do. Our job is to keep people safe. Don't lose track of that."

"You don't see it, do you?" Sann said, stopping to look Morris in the face. "Maybe you've built up an immunity to bullshit, but how are we supposed to keep people safe when the biggest threat to them are the people we work for?"

"Come on," pleaded Morris. "Chief Steph Tam will be back soon, and ...."

"So what?" interrupted Sann. "She doesn't matter shit. If she did, none of this would be going on right now."

"Hey, take it easy on Steph," shot back Morris.

"You're all the same," she said hotly, and then calming a bit. "It's not your fault. You've seen a lot. I just don't want to end up like you. That's what worries me most."

The words stung Morris a bit. He didn't have a comeback to them. Maybe his life had been a matter of redefining reality to fit his comfort zone, but his thoughts were quickly interrupted by the door to the firehouse swinging open.

"Hey there, Sue," Patrick McKenna said, surveying the two T-cops. "How'd everything go?"

Sann gave a look at Morris, and he could see the concern on her face morph into a smile, albeit an insincere one. She turned and said, "It went fine. No big deal."

McKenna looked at the two. Morris could tell he doubted Sann's words, but he seemed smart enough to know not to press for more. "So sergeant, I think I found that cellphone."

The words shook Morris from whatever mood he was experiencing. "Were you able to get into it?"

"No, like I said, I was just able to read the memory card he had."

"Whatever that means, I like the sound of it," said Morris.

McKenna laughed. "Come on, I'll show you."

The three entered the firehouse and walked into a small office next to the dispatch room. As they did, Morris tapped Sann on the shoulder. "See, just work the job, never mind the bullshit."

She smiled, but he could tell she was still struggling.

"So this guy was like the T's realtor or something, right?" McKenna said, angling a flat-screen monitor toward Morris and Sann.

"Yeah," answered Morris, pushing past an opportunity to correct him with Bob Sosa's actual title. The truth was the firefighter's description was probably more accurate than the T's org chart anyway.

"OK, so I think this is it," he said holding up a black cellphone. "He's got a little more than a thousand photos on it, and ...."

"Any porn on there?" asked Morris.

McKenna and Sann looked at each other and then at Morris.

"Listen," Morris explained, "rumor was he was mixed up with the Lost Boys somehow."

McKenna appeared totally confused.

"I'll explain later," Sann said to her boyfriend.

McKenna shook his head. "Anyway, no porn. Opposite of it really." He then pointed to the screen. "It's just a bunch of photos of the T. It's trains and tunnels." He paused. "There isn't some sort of transit fetish or something?" he asked with sincerity.

Morris rolled his eyes. "No, no," he said. "Actually in this job, who the fuck knows," he added looking at Goldi. "But no, we're talking normal porn." The words caught Morris as they exited his mouth. As a T-cop, it was a regular occurrence to utter odd phrases, but that may have been the most-odd yet.

McKenna nodded. "Anyway, you can click through it all, but I think this is your guy."

Morris watched the screen as McKenna scrolled. It was all images of the T. There was definitely enough that, if they had to, he and Bruce Donohue could get a warrant to get into the phone. It had to be Bob Sosa's.

His eye then caught a few images of the Fenway station, a light-rail stop on the MBTA's D Branch of the Green Line. "Hold it there," he said.

There was a grouping of photos. The first few showed the Fenway portal where the trolleys made their descent into the bowels of the Green Line tunnel. The next showed a series of buildings and a parking lot adjacent to the Fenway stop. They weren't on T property at all.

"Can you sort these by when they were taken?" asked Morris.

"That's the order they're in right now," said McKenna.

Morris looked closely. "These are when they were taken?" he asked pointing to a column that showed creation dates.

"Yeah, it's an exact duplicate of what was on the card," said the firefighter.

Morris looked at the dates and times. "Scroll some more."

McKenna paged down.

Morris shook his head. He couldn't make sense out of the images, and there was nothing from the Tufts Medical Center platform. He had hoped there might some clue as to how Bob ended up on the tracks.

"Hey, but look at the times," said McKenna.

Morris scanned the dates and times. Sure enough, most of them were all in the same window.

"Holy shit," Morris said. "He was doing this on his lunch hour."

Morris leaned back against the wall. Sann leaned in toward the monitor and then spun around. "You think that means something?"

"Let's put it this way, Bob was an honest public servant, but he was a public servant." He looked at the firefighter and the T-cop in the room with him. He could see they understood what he was getting at. "Bob wasn't the type to skip lunch to get caught up on paperwork."

"So what are you getting at?" asked McKenna.

"This all was something he was doing on his own," Morris said pointing toward the monitor.

"Something not T-related," summarized Sann.

"Or maybe something he didn't want his bosses to get wind of," added Morris.

At that moment Goldi's cellphone beeped, and she grabbed it. "Interesting," she said looking at the screen.

"What's up?" asked Morris.

"I got a text from Reverend Lake. They have a lead on the Lost Boys." Sann's phone beeped again. "But it looks like so does Swani." Sann then walked out of the room as she dialed a number.

"So what else is on that thing?" Morris asked McKenna.

The two scrolled through more images, but Morris couldn't make sense of them. While many were T properties, others involved a bridge that went over the Muddy River and a series showing the Charles River, Museum of Science, and Leonard Zakim Bridge.

Then Morris spotted a large brick facility that he recognized. "Holy shit," he gasped.

"What?" asked McKenna.

"I was there two days ago. That's the Gridley Dam."

"What was this guy working on?" pondered McKenna. "A coffee table book of Mass. infrastructure?"

Morris laughed as Goldilocks re-entered the room. "Father Michael's going to go look for the Lost Boys," she said. "I'm going to go with them."

"You just got out of the hospital," McKenna pleaded.

"Pat, I'm fine," said Sann. "I've got a job to do," she added turning toward her fellow T-cop.

"Yeah, the question is what do you do when the stormtroopers show up," said Morris. "Are you going to join them in shoving the homeless out or are you going to find yourself on the side of the Archangels?"

"I'd like to think if I do my job right, I won't have to choose one or the other."

With that, her phone rang again, and she answered it, turning her back on the two men in the room.

Morris could see McKenna looking to him for help in convincing Sann not to go hunting through the T's tunnels. The only response he could offer was a shrug. Goldi could handle herself. Plus, he learned from a life of being around strong women that the more you pushed against the female will, the more determined it became.

Morris' phone buzzed, and he looked at it. It was another text from Sergeant Manning. The truth was he didn't have much new to report. Sure, he had found Sosa's cellphone. How he had found it wasn't exactly according to protocol, but the larger reason why he was allowing Manning's calls to go straight to voicemail was that he was growing increasingly frugal with his trust. Manning was a good cop. He had figured that much out. But this was the city of Boston, and here in the Athens of America, any piece of information became leverage. He knew that as well as anyone.

Already Acting Chief Dyani Swan had managed to leverage bits and pieces of the truth into a larger fabrication, but why? What did the homeless have? Nothing.

"OK," Sann said, "I'm going to meet Father Michael at three-thirty. He's got some service at St. Anthony's he has to do first."

With that Morris' mind snapped to attention. He glanced at his phone. It was getting close to three. "I have to be at that service," he said to Sann and McKenna.

The two responded with puzzled expressions. "My cousin, Cathy, it's a service for her."

"Oh right," said Goldilocks. "Sorry."

Morris surveyed his attire. "Hey Patrick, you got a sportcoat lying around here or something?"

"Have you got two of them?" chimed in Sann, who looked at Morris. "I figure I'll go with you."

The three went to the upstairs of the firehouse and raided the open lockers where some of the firefighters kept their formal dress. Removing the badge and nameplate, the single-breasted navy jacket would do the job. He also borrowed a white shirt and clip-on tie from Patrick McKenna. Sann was a trickier fit. The two female firefighters who worked out of that station were both close to six feet tall, not much help for the 5' 4" Goldilocks. However, McKenna managed to size her to an apparently diminutive male firefighter named Rodriguez.

As the two T-cops adjusted their dress and hair in front of a mirror, it dawned on Morris that he was short on both showering and sleep. He glanced at Sann and whispered. "So are you nervous at all that your boyfriend was able to eyeball your dimensions to a fellow Jake."

Goldilocks smirked. "Remember what I told you about being an endearing asshole?"

Morris smiled.

"I take back the endearing part."

The two ventured downstairs to where Patrick McKenna was waiting in the pickup truck to drive them across the congested streets of Boston to 100 Arch Street. Yielding to young romance, Morris decided to climb into the cramped back seat, allowing Sann to sit next to her Mr. February. The entire drive, the two exchanged playful banter. At least some good came out of Bob Sosa's death.

As they pulled up in front of 100 Arch Street, McKenna handed an umbrella to Sann. "Here," he said. "It's starting to pour out there."

Sann opened the door and pushed open the umbrella while Morris awkwardly climbed out. "Hey, we needed the rain, right?" Morris said.

"Not right now," said McKenna as the rain thundered on the umbrella. "King Tides."

Morris slammed the door shut, and looked at Goldilocks. "You two are made for each other."

The Lazarus Ministry at Saint Anthony's Shrine was an oasis of peace in the city. It provided Christian burials for the poor souls who otherwise would be placed in paupers' graves. The ministry paid for opening and closing the graves, a modest grave marker, and clothes for the deceased as well as the continued prayers of the community.

As Morris pulled open the door to the shrine, he noticed a familiar Cadillac across the street. The window was open slightly , and he could see puffs of cigarette smoke exiting. A fiber of rage built in him, but reason told him the best thing was not to make a commotion or it might set off Happy.

Upon entering, Goldilocks closed the umbrella and left it in a corner. She awkwardly stepped aside for Morris to lead. "I'm a Protestant," she whispered.

"I'm a Sagittarius," he shot back.

The two stepped cautiously, not knowing what might be around the corner in the chapel. Morris could hear the familiar Catholic verbiage from the voice of Father Michael. He had never been sure of all the words, but it was rote enough for him to be able to say "pray for us" at the right times as he and his fellow T-cop slipped into one of the small pews.

Even though the stained-glass art didn't look like much from the outside, it illuminated the inside with a kaleidoscope of color. Morris could see Happy up ahead, just standing at the front. His face was ashen and his pants were only half zipped. William was standing next to him, towering over his uncle. He had an arm around Happy. To most, it might have seemed an embrace of some sort, but Morris knew better. Happy was drunk.

Morris scanned the room, and his eye quickly fell on a shock of red hair, belonging to a tall figure sitting next to a much shorter individual. Ginger and Gary made it. There was a bag lady behind them, and Morris also thought he recognized a couple of Happy's Marine buddies.

He then turned to the adjacent pew and spotted BoBo Powers. The Cadillac and its driver across the street were the giveaways, but he wondered what his old Southie buddy was doing here. Powers knew Happy and Cathy, but it's not like they were tight.

When BoBo noticed Morris, he got up and slid into the pew behind him. As he did so, Morris caught sight of the parking king's dark blue suit, which matched perfectly with his brightly patterned silk tie and a handkerchief poking out of his jacket pocket. He couldn't see them, but Morris was sure BoBo was wearing a pair of well-styled shoes that cost more than his last car.

Father McGovern then gave a nod, and the Arch Street Band, a six-piece ensemble, began playing *Amazing Grace*. It was a beautiful rendition by the group whose members came from all walks of life, the commonality among them was that at some time, their footsteps had led to St. Anthony's.

"I'd go to Mass more if the singers had bodies like that one," BoBo whispered.

Morris grinned. He turned slightly. "Oh, I can introduce you if you want."

"No kidding?" said BoBo.

"Sure," said Morris. "But I don't think Haley is your type. He's got a great voice and all, but he's always tied up weekends with his shows at the Jacques."

He turned to see BoBo's eyes widen at the mention the Boston nightclub best known for its drag queen review.

"She's a he?" Powers said.

"Biologically, I think it's more like he's a she."

As the service progressed, Father Michael offered his reflections, often referencing words such as "struggle" and "sin." Morris kept his eyes on Happy, who seemed fairly unaware of the service.

To his credit, Father Michael never broke stride. He paused toward the end. "Is there anything the family would like to add?" Happy began to move, but William gave him a nudge while he shook his head "no" toward the priest.

As Father Michael continued on, Happy finally forced himself to his feet, nearly falling the moment he stood. "It's not fair!" he simultaneously shouted and slurred. He seemed to want to turn to say something but tripped and fell to his left, away from William.

There was a loud thud on the pew, and Morris instantly ran to the front, joining Father Michael, members of the Arch Street Band, and William in trying to help Happy.

As Morris neared the pew, he could see his cousin had a pretty serious gash on his left forehead. William had already removed his tie and was using it as a sort of compress to contain the bleeding.

Morris reached for his cellphone and called Boston EMS while looking at Father Michael.

"He's going to need stitches," the priest said succinctly.

"He needs more than that," said Morris.

The group assisting Happy propped him up on the bench, all the while the old drunk kept protesting. William had fashioned quite a passable bandage out of the necktie. True to his character, he hadn't said much during the entire episode even though Happy rambled in his cantankerous stupor. Even though most of the words were inaudible, Morris did hear "rape" and "guilt" at certain points.

"Hey, how about we move him outside?" Morris said, trying to prevent his cousin from uttering anything more profane or revealing.

"It's pouring out," countered BoBo Powers, who had come up to the front. "I've got a car. We can drive him over to the hospital."

Something in Morris' mind resented BoBo's offer. Maybe it was the way he said it, or maybe it was just his disdain for BoBo's driver. "No, no," he responded. "EMS is on the way. We should just get him some air."

"I think we just keep him where he is," said Father Michael assuringly.

Morris was about to say something – he wasn't quite sure what – but William spoke. "The priest is right."

There was a calm finality in his voice, nothing ambivalent, nothing forceful, just a statement of immovable fact. That's what a career in the Marines will do for you, thought Morris, but he also noticed that William seemed fairly unfazed by any of Happy's ramblings.

For the next few minutes, his mind focused on hoping Happy would find enough discretion in his inebriated state to keep his mouth shut regarding certain family topics. However, as Boston EMS finally arrived, it dawned on him that his cousin and William had spent at least a couple of hours together this morning. Did Happy tell him?

"I'll go with him," William said as the EMTs rolled him on a stretcher toward the ambulance. Undoubtedly, the destination would be an emergency room. The question was which would be treated first, the laceration on his forehead or the acute alcohol poisoning.

Morris felt a pang of guilt. It's not like he didn't occasionally struggle with having one or several drinks too many.

"Is everything going to be OK?"

Morris turned to see Goldilocks. "Yeah, where were you in all this?"

"I don't know. I thought it was some Catholic thing," she said.

"You don't know how right you may be," said Morris. Then his eye caught one of the Arch Street Band. "Hey Goldi, isn't that Sandy the spoon lady?"

"Spoon?"

Morris and Goldilocks turned to see BoBo Powers apparently confused by what he overheard.

“Oh BoBo, wait till you hear Sandy play music. It bubbles like water from a leak from the Big Dig. Morris then nodded over to the band. “Hey, Sandy!”

With that Boston’s most talented player of spoons raised her head and broke into a wide smile that was framed by her curly gray hair. As she rushed toward Morris, he could sense Powers take a step back.

Sandy, who probably stood no more than 5’ 2”, then greeted Morris with a big hug.

“Oh, and officer Susan,” she said giving Goldilocks a similar embrace. Immediately behind Sandy came a woman with matted black hair. She and Sandy could have been the same age, which is to say anywhere between 35 and 75. Living on the streets had a way of aging people in inconsistent ways. “You all remember Mary,” Sandy added, stepping aside so the two T-cops could see the woman.

“Of course, Mary,” said Sann. “How are you?”

“Not good,” she said, shaking her head nervously. “Radio waves. They’re all over. Need to be safe.”

“Oh, we’ll help you with that,” Sann assured.

“Yes, Mary. Don’t worry about it,” added Morris.

In the meantime, BoBo Powers kept his distance as Morris and Goldilocks spoke with the two women. Once their brief conversation finished, the women returned with the band.

“A couple of characters there, huh?” said BoBo, who then turned to Goldilocks. “By the way, I don’t think we’ve met, Robert Powers.” BoBo may have offered his hand, but the way his eyes looked at Sann, his intentions may not have been entirely gentlemanly.

Goldilocks shook his hand. She could handle herself.

“So how do you know those white trash refugees?” he asked the two T-cops.

Morris intervened more on behalf of Powers than anything. He could see the anger in Sann’s eyes. “Sandy’s actually a former concert pianist with the Boston Symphony Orchestra,” he explained. “Years ago, her husband was killed in a vicious mugging at Symphony Station. She was never the same since.”

“No kidding?” said BoBo.

"Here's the worst of it. She was actually in your income bracket for a while before Senator Sonny Barrett got his hooks into her. Got her to put every penny she had into some real estate deal that went belly up."

"The other lady is Mary," said Goldilocks. "Everyone just calls her Microwave Mary. She washed out of MIT after she lost it working around their nuclear power plant."

"Yeah, she's a tinfoil-hat type now," added Morris. "Constantly worrying about radio waves and all that."

Just then they heard a commotion out front. Morris and Sann joined the others and ran to the exit of St. Anthony's to see Happy off the stretcher and on the pavement. About thirty feet away, in the street, in the middle of the downpour, William had his left hand grasping the Squid's shirt and suitcoat, just below the neck. In his right hand, he was holding a bat, presumably taken from J.J. McHugh moments earlier.

The EMTs were in a clamor. William, despite the predicament, appeared relatively calm, glaring at the Squid, but not saying a word. The typical Fitzgerald physique leaned toward the stocky side, like Morris and Happy, but William stood tall with long arms that appeared to give him a phenomenal reach. Staring at the scene, a thought rushed through Morris' mind, but before it could take root, he heard one of the EMTs in front of him, waving his hands and shouting.

"Whoa, hold on there pal," said Morris. "Slow down. What's going on here?"

"The old guy on the stretcher, he just flipped out," the EMT said.

"What?" Morris replied as the rain pelted down.

"We came out here, and he sees the other guy over there with the curly hair sitting in the Caddy, and he just fuckin' loses it. So that guy gets out with a bat. If it wasn't for your buddy, there," the EMT said nodding toward William, "it would have gotten real ugly."

The others who had been at Cathy's service had stepped onto the sidewalk. The Fitzgeralds in all their glory were on display. Morris could see Gary and Ginger hurry along the sidewalk pausing to look at William and the Squid.

"Jesus Christ!" BoBo Powers surveyed the scene. "What the hell is going on here?"

"Hey, William!" Morris shouted. "Don't waste your time with that piece of shit. Come on. Happy needs you."

"Fist I am going to fuck up you and your family!" McHugh screamed while being held by his neck.

"Some bodyguard you got there BoBo," Morris said to Powers. "Tell him to shut the fuck up or I'll do it for him, permanently."

BoBo raised a hand and nodded as he stepped into the street while the rain poured down, but before he reached the two combatants, William, in one smooth motion gave the Squid a shove, throwing him to the ground while letting him go. He then walked toward Morris but didn't say a word as the EMTs gathered Happy back onto the stretcher.

Morris saw an unexpected resolve in William's eyes, and he wondered just what Happy may have said to him earlier in the day. As the EMTs loaded Happy into the back of the ambulance, William climbed in, still carrying the Louisville Slugger.

Meanwhile, the Squid and BoBo were still yelling at each other.

Morris then heard a voice behind him. "What did I miss?"

He turned to see Goldilocks.

"You're kidding, right?"

"No," she said. "I was inside talking to Father Michael. They think they have a good lead on the Lost Boys. He's going to try to get them into a shelter. With it being a war on the homeless, someone has to do something."

"Where do they think they are?" asked Morris.

"Tremont Street tunnels," Goldilocks answered.

"Be careful there," he said.

Sann smiled, and the two exchanged goodbyes so that Goldilocks could join up with Father Michael.

As she went back inside St. Anthony's, Morris heard a familiar voice.

"Where's she going?" asked BoBo Powers.

"Spelunking," quipped Morris.

"Hey, what's with the attitude?"

"What's with you bringing a shithead to my cousin's service?"

"Come on, Morris. I told him to wait in the car."

"Fuck you BoBo. I told you he is no good."

"Hey, hey, let's not ruin any friendships, here," Powers said.

"You know, BoBo, just because we grew up together, it doesn't mean we're friends. You screwed over anyone you could just to get out of Southie."

"You're crossing the line there, Fitz."

"Oh yeah, and what lines have you crossed?"

Powers grew frustrated and looked around, as though he was searching for a physical exit as much as verbal one. Finally, Morris saw Powers' eyes lock in on something above him. "Just remember," he said, pointing to the cross over the entrance of St. Anthony's, "the guy they nailed to that thing was betrayed by a friend for thirty pieces of silver. I'm a great friend, Morris, but give me a reason, and I'll be your worst enemy."

At that moment a Boston Police cruiser rolled down Arch Street, and Powers apparently assumed it was a good time to leave. He didn't say another word, just turned his back and began walking toward his Cadillac across the street.

"Thanks for the theology lesson, BoBo," Morris shouted angrily.

In response, Powers merely raised his left hand and extended his middle finger as he opened the door to the SUV.

Standing in the rain in front of the shrine, Morris came to a realization, one that had been building since childhood. Powers had always been a self-centered opportunist. He had his moments of generosity and gregariousness, but they were all fake, part of some narcissistic calculation as to how he could get what he wanted. If there had been any good to Powers, it faded long ago. He was now a walking advertisement for the seven deadly sins. Their friendship was destined to end badly.

Chapter 17

Morris walked the two blocks from St. Anthony's to the Downtown Crossing T stop. The transit police had a substation there, and he figured he might be able to dry off before heading home to South Boston.

As trooper Paulie had noted earlier in the week, it was a warm front that had come in over night. That was New England weather; a twenty-degree swing in temperature from one day to the next was nothing, and for a few moments, Morris felt refreshed by the downpour. People everywhere were scurrying to avoid the deluge, but there he was, just walking through the middle of it.

The gridlock enveloping the city's streets was worse than typical rush-hour – if that was even possible. Morris figured it was only a matter of time before some sub-compact would stall out in one of the impromptu lakes that formed on Boston's ancient roadways.

Pedestrians were darting between buildings as they worked their way toward the subway. He could see others sprinting to waiting cars double-parked on the narrow streets, only adding to the traffic jam.

Yet, he simply kept walking through the mess, undeterred by the heavy but warm precipitation. Maybe it was a meteorological metaphor for his life. Perhaps it symbolized that he embraced many things that most other people shunned. Then again, maybe all it meant was that he was a fool getting soaked in the rain.

Morris entered the substation and immediately spotted his fellow T-cop, Bill Feltrup, who he had run into on Monday on the way to his wife's grave. "Hey Bulldog," he said as he tried to brush the rain off his borrowed firefighter sportcoat.

Feltrup had to do a double-take before recognizing Morris. "You look like a drowned rat," he said.

"No kidding," said Morris. "It's not letting up out there either."

"You ought to see Park Street," Bulldog said. "It's like the friggin' apocalypse. Everyone is trying to get out of the city."

"I don't suppose there are any sweats lying around or maybe a towel?" Morris asked.

Feltrup laughed.

No such luck apparently. It was fine. Morris had already planned to walk the pedestrian tunnel that linked Downtown Crossing and Park Street Station. From Park Street, he could take the Green Line down Boylston Street and make the short walk to the fire station where he had borrowed his current attire. There, he'd change back into his old dry clothes.

As Morris exited the substation and made his way toward Park Street, the original terminus of the Tremont Street Subway, he could feel the humidity in the underground. As the T's patrons rushed about, covered in raincoats, several holding umbrellas, there was an uncomfortable stickiness in the cavern that formed the country's oldest public subway station.

Cramming into the Green Line train didn't help matters at all. The windows were fogged up, dripping with moisture. Each car was filled past capacity with the rush-hour commuters trying to flee the city. Remarkably, however, despite the fact that most of the patrons were wearing at least one outer layer, the stench of body odor wafted throughout the cattle car.

He was sure there was some branch of science that could explain it, but it struck the T-cop as baffling that when it rained, people smelled more. If anything, one would expect the impervious nature of rain gear, trench coats, and the like to impede such human pungence, but the moisture seemed to reanimate a century and a quarter's worth aromas that had been buried in the subway along with those of a more current vintage on its patrons.

The car jerked forward and began to roll toward Boylston Station. Immediately above, ran Tremont Street. It was below where Tremont intersected Boylston Street that the Boylston Station lay. There, the Green Line would take a sharp turn west and follow Boylston Street to the outskirts of downtown Boston.

Up until the middle of the last century, there was an additional fork to the line that continued under Tremont Street, forming the original Tremont Street Subway, which opened in 1897. The long-abandoned tunnel was full of nooks and crannies, which had become refuge for many homeless, including the Lost Boys.

As Morris thought of Goldilocks and Father Michael searching the tunnel before Dyani Swan and her stormtroopers invaded, he returned to wondering about Bob Sosa.

At that moment, the train halted, having reached Boylston, and the driver announced that it would now be an express to Kenmore, essentially leapfrogging over all the downtown stops. While groans went up from several commuters, who now had to face the prospect of waiting for another train, Morris felt relieved to get out of the claustrophobic environment.

A thought then struck him. He was only a block away from the Transportation Building. Somebody might still be around who could let him into Bob's office there. Maybe he could figure out what Sosa had been working on.

Still wearing his makeshift funeral attire, Morris made his way toward the rear entrance of Ten Park Plaza. On his way, he pulled out his cellphone and called MBTA dispatch, looking for the duty officer for the evening. After a few moments, Lieutenant Billy Fredette came on the line.

“Morris, unless you’re calling to fill a shift, I don’t want to hear from you,” Fredette joked.

“Sorry, I’m not on until Monday,” Morris responded. “But I was just on a Green Line that went express to Kenmore. How crazy is it out there?”

“Normal crazy for now. One of the cars ahead of you broke down. Trust me, it’s express to nowhere right now. Everyone is just trying to get out of the city,” said Fredette. “By the way, I talked to your friend, Sann, about an hour ago. She’s leading some expedition into the old tunnels.”

“I know,” said Morris. “Hey Billy, do you know anyone in the T’s real estate office by any chance?” Morris asked.

“Not really, but they’re all gone for the day. Non-essential personnel were sent home early. The General Manager himself made the call.”

Morris was now standing in the brick-lined alley that led to the rear entrance of the Transportation Building. On the ground, he saw a discarded sign from the protest that had been hours earlier. “The End is Near,” it read. It wasn’t quite a black cat, but he took it as an inauspicious omen.

He said goodbye to Fredette, walked into the lobby, and made his way toward the bank of elevators, where he pressed the up arrow. As he stepped into the elevator, he resigned himself to the fact that he probably wouldn’t be able to get into Sosa’s office, but given that the Transportation Building was dry, he figured there was no harm in postponing the walk down Boylston Street.

The door opened on the sixth floor, and he walked the short hallway leading to a single door with the MBTA circle-T insignia on it. He approached the doorknob and tried to turn it, but it seemed locked. Everyone must have left for the day.

For the next five minutes, he searched for alternate ways into the office. Eventually, he concluded to make the best of the situation. He’d go to the fire station, get out of his wet clothes, head home, and get a good night sleep. Tomorrow, maybe he would come back.

“Hey.”

Morris was startled and turned to see a security guard coming his way. Morris smiled and was about offer an hello when the guard spoke again.

"Another inspection?" he asked.

Initially confused, Morris then remembered the firefighter's coat he was wearing.

"Yeah," he said. "Office manager was supposed to meet me here."

The guard laughed. "It's the T. You think anything runs on time with them?"

"No kidding," Morris said. He then paused for a moment, sizing up the guard. He was short but stocky. The uniform didn't quite fit, and he definitely looked young. He probably was a student at one of the nearby colleges, just picking up extra cash and quiet study time. "Well anyway, I guess this was a waste. Pain in the ass, I tell you."

"Yeah, you sure they're not coming?"

"It's a monsoon out there," said Morris. "I don't really need them here. I just need someone to open up the office."

"Oh, well I can do that for you," said the guard, falling into Morris' hint. The security guard grabbed a softball-size keyring from his right hip and fumbled through a few keys before finally finding one that managed to fit the keyhole and work. Turning the knob, the guard gave Morris a smile that showed a feeling of accomplishment. Poor kid, it was probably the most excitement he'd see all night.

"Great," said Morris. "I just close this when I leave?"

"Yeah, that should be fine. I'll check it on my next walk-through anyway."

With that, Morris scampered inside and began looking for Bob Sosa's office. As he walked through a hallway, he could hear the rain slamming against the side of the building.

Past the row of offices, all with windows looking out onto the city, there was one tucked off by itself, featuring only a view of a copy machine. Morris came up to the door. There was no nameplate on it, but a plastic holder was screwed to the outside of the door so that people could leave envelopes or paperwork there. The label affixed to it read "R. Sosa."

Morris entered the office. It looked functional. Still, he found no laptop, and the file cabinet under the desk seemed oddly empty. He rifled through the draws quickly, but they were sparse, just some pens, a ruler, a gray pen case or something like that. Over in the corner, there was a small table with what appeared to be architectural drawings. Morris stepped toward them with the anticipation that they'd be detailed drawings of some piece of infrastructure that would somehow explain his death.

No such luck. They appeared to be just the layout of different buildings. Some seemed like offices. Others were retail space. There even seemed to be a theater in there. Of course, there were also plenty of drawings of the MBTA stations. This must have been the type of stuff Bob had to stare at all day. Morris was glad he never had to work behind a desk. Next to the table, leaning against a small bookcase, there were some long cardboard tubes. More drawings no doubt.

He went back to the desk and sat down. Maybe Bob just fell on the tracks. Whatever the cause, the answer didn't seem to be here. He decided to go through the drawers for a second time. Nothing, just office supplies. Maybe Bob stuck something in the pen case, and he pulled it out and put it on the desk.

It was a hard plastic case, a little smaller than the size of a brick, with a clasp on the front. He popped it open and felt an adrenaline rush upon seeing a lone item inside. Yet, he no idea what it meant. He reached into the case and held up the instrument. He had seen a nearly identical one only twenty-four hours earlier, in the plastic evidence bag that Sergeant Manning thrust in front of Tom Cashman's face.

Morris sat back. The first thought that came to him was why did Bob and Cliff Cashman both have a refractometer. The second thought was why didn't he pay more attention in high school chemistry. He wasn't even sure what the device did. It looked simple enough, like a mini telescope or rangefinder, slanted at one end. As Manning had noted, these days the device was most frequently found around homemade drug labs. They were a way of measuring potency, but he couldn't see Bob or Cliff pulling a *Breaking Bad*.

Then again, both were bright enough, and money did make people do a lot of things that their morals might otherwise block. It's not like he had really kept in touch with either of them. Maybe they had fallen on hard times.

Then his mind stepped through the hypothesis. If that was the case, then there should be more evidence of some lab. It didn't fit. Morris was missing something. He got up and walked over to the table again. Maybe Bob discovered some meth lab in the tunnels. Maybe that's what it was all about. Morris scanned through the pages of the drawings, but nothing struck him.

He exhaled. He felt his mind going around in circles. Sleep was a good idea. He now had a connection between two dead friends. What it meant, he had no idea.

He put the papers back, closed the drawers, and slowly retraced his steps to leave the office. Morris opened the door to the hallway. No one was around. He stepped forward, pulling the door behind him. As it clicked closed, he suddenly realized that he was still holding the refractometer. His brain was shot. It was like one of those moments where you look for your keys for five minutes only to realize you were holding them the whole time.

"Hello, sergeant!"

Morris turned suddenly. His panic gave way to relief.

"Doc, you just scared the shit out of me."

"I did, didn't I?" Herman Poole said with a hint of surprise.

The doctor stood at the sixth-floor elevator, briefcase in hand, and pressed the down arrow.

"Sorry, I just wasn't expecting anyone. You're working late tonight, huh?"

"Yes, I had a late appointment. Another T-cop, Piacenza. He says he was hurt in the ruckus earlier today in the meeting room."

"Stevie Piacenza?" Morris said using the proper name for Axe. "How bad is he?"

"Not bad at all," said Dr. Poole as the elevator doors opened. "But he does have an acute case of full-of-shititis."

Morris looked at the doctor.

"I think he's hoping for a disability pension."

Morris shook his head.

“Wine making?” the doctor asked making a nod toward Morris.

“What’s that, doc?” Morris said, unsure he heard correctly.

“Are you making some wine? Oh, maybe you’re a homebrewer?” Dr. Poole responded, but the confusion was apparent on Morris’ face. “The refractometer you have there,” he said pointing toward the instrument in the T-cop’s hand.

“Oh,” said Morris as the elevator doors opened. “No, no, just something I found. Hold on, you know about these things?”

“Refractometers?” Poole asked rhetorically. “I guess. I know people use them a lot for making wine or beer. It replaces a hydrometer.”

“You’re going to have to help me with that one, too, doc.”

He laughed. “Sorry sergeant. They measure specific gravity, how dense a liquid is compared to water. Brewers use them to tell when something like sugar converts to alcohol.”

“Interesting,” said Morris as a few thoughts raced through his mind. “I just know we find them in meth labs.”

The doctor nodded as the two crossed the lobby. “That makes sense. Anything you have in solution, it can measure. Sugar in fermenting wine, proteins in blood, salinity in water, anything.”

Morris heard the words. His brain was distracted by understanding the device had several innocuous uses, but somewhere, the recesses of mind heard a word, seized it, and was now trying to pull it toward his frontal lobe. “Wait a second doc. What was that last one you said?”

“Last what?”

“How you can use these things.”

“Oh, proteins in blood, salinity of water.”

“Yeah, water quality,” Morris said.

“Not quality so much, but I guess you might say thickness. Salt water is more dense. That’s how come it’s easier to float in it, but light doesn’t go through it as easily. That’s what that device measures.” he said pointing toward the refractometer.

The two stopped as Herman Poole looked out the door to the alley behind the Transportation Building. A discarded sign from the protest earlier was blocking one of the drains, forming a puddle nearly the width of the brick-lined alley and probably a foot deep.

Dr. Poole groaned, but Morris' mind remained focused on trying to figure out what Sosa and Cashman may have been up to. He exhaled a sigh. Whatever the answer was, it would come easier after a hot shower and dry clothes.

"Come on doc," Morris said as he pushed on the door.

The doctor was shaking his head, looking at the clogged drain. "It just goes to show you, when everything relies on one thing, and if that thing breaks –"

"We're all screwed," Morris said finishing the sentence with the words trooper Paulie used the previous day. He let go the door, allowing the wind to push it shut. "That's it!" he shouted.

Dr. Poole gave Morris a confused look.

"Doc, come with me," Morris said as he turned to go back to the elevators.

After a second delay, Herman Poole appeared to give into curiosity and turned to join the T-cop. Morris was looking back at him while he repeatedly pressed the up arrow.

The doctor sprinted up to him, his briefcase swaying with each stride. "You know, you only have to press that once," he said as he caught up with Morris. "What are we doing?"

"Breaking into the MBTA real estate office," Morris said excitedly as the doors opened.

"Oh good, I thought you might be dragging me into something ridiculous," the doctor joked as they stepped into the elevator.

Morris pressed the up button three quick times. He turned to his companion. "I know, I only have to do it once."

On the ride up, Morris pulled out his cellphone and called into the MBTA dispatch trying to get a message to Rico Paulie at the State Police marine unit.

As he hung up, he looked at Herman Poole who had a serious look on his face. "What's going on here, sergeant?"

"I'm not sure, doc, but the city might be up the creek, literally."

As the elevator doors opened, Morris hurried around the corner to the office that he had left minutes earlier. Morris tried the doorknob, but it was locked. He then, stepped back and laid into it with his right shoulder, grunting as he did so. No luck despite feeling a pop in his shoulder.

Stepping back, Morris raised his leg and tried to kick the door just above the doorknob, but he slipped and landed on his back. Surprisingly, the fall did not hurt as much as the T-cop thought it would. He credited adrenaline and noted that he would be feeling the pain in the morning.

"Doc, maybe if we try this together," Morris said getting to his feet.

Herman Poole shook his head. "Southie knuckleheads." He then looked Morris square in the eye. "This is on the up and up?"

Morris nodded in the affirmative.

"Fine," said the doctor, who then raised his briefcase, turned his head away, and smashed a narrow, floor-to-ceiling glass panel next to the door.

Knocking out the rest of the glass, he reached in and opened the door from the other side. "Work smarter, not harder, sergeant."

Morris smiled as he pulled the door fully open and walked into the office. Dr. Poole followed behind as the T-cop made his way to Sosa's nondescript office.

Entering, Morris turned on the lights. "Doc, any chance you can give your cousin a call? This could be all hands on deck." He then went to the table with the architectural drawings.

The doctor nodded as he pulled out his cellphone. "Should I tell him to bring bail money?"

As Morris flipped through the pages of the drawings and scanned the cardboard tubes nearby, he could hear Dr. Poole leaving a message for Elijah. "Have you got any idea how to read these things?" Morris asked as the doctor ended the call.

"I don't know. What are you looking for."

"Anything that might involve the Charles River."

Morris felt his phone vibrate and answered it as he raised it to his ear.

"What the hell's this message about?" the voice said.

"Rico!"

"Yeah, it's your friendly Uber driver."

"Rico, listen, I think you were right. Someone's been screwing with the locks, or the dam, or both. I mean, if someone was checking for salt water in the river, what would it mean?"

There was silence on the other end.

"Rico?"

"Yeah, I heard you. Salt water in the river would mean things were working backwards."

"Right!" exclaimed Morris.

Then there was more silence. The T-cop couldn't tell if the trooper was preparing to discount Morris' conclusion or whether he was playing through some scenario on his own.

"I need to check with someone at DCR," Paulie said finally. "The water's pretty high already, and it's not even high tide. If the dam's not working right...."

The trooper's voice then trailed off. The repercussions could be significant given the storm and high tides.

Dr. Poole then thrust one of the drawings in front of Morris, who pulled away his phone to look at it. "No, no," he said, "that's over by Fenway. Look for something about Science Park or maybe the Mass. General stop on the Red Line."

The doctor grew more emphatic, pointing toward an inset diagram that showed the Muddy River, a tributary of the Charles River, that met it at a right angle in Boston's Back Bay. From there it winds through parts of Olmsted's Emerald Necklace.

"Holy shit!" Morris exclaimed as he saw Bob Sosa's handwritten notes all over the drawing. "Rico, you gotta handle the dam. I have to go."

Morris lowered the phone and looked at the blueprint of the Fenway Portal, where the Green Line trains journeyed from above ground down into the bowels of the city. Sosa had circled the elevation numbers. That's what he had been looking at. But even without the numbers, anyone who was in Boston in October of 1996 would know the danger.

A little more than ten inches of rain fell in one day, pushing the Muddy River over its banks and flooding the adjacent Fenway portal. From there, the water poured into the underground Kenmore station, filling it nearly from platform to ceiling.

Morris couldn't make exact sense of what Bob's notes said, but, clearly, he was looking at the potential for another flood. If something wasn't working right with the dam, it would cause the Charles River to back up, and that in turn could send a torrent of water toward the Fenway portal.

Morris called MBTA dispatch again. "Get me Billy Fredette."

"Hey, how about a please," chided the dispatcher.

"Now!" shouted Morris, who then pulled away the phone and looked at Dr. Poole. "Call your cousin again. Tell him Kenmore is going to flood." He then heard a voice on the phone.

"Billy, it's Morris. Are you getting any flooding?"

"Just the usual," Fredette said. "The Harvard bus way is flooded out. Wollaston's got some water, and Quincy's an open toilet, but it always is when it rains."

"I mean at Fenway. The Muddy River."

"Calm down," said Fredette. "We're watching it. Nothing has tripped on the monitoring station. Last I heard, they're going to shut down Kenmore within the hour, and a crew will start sandbagging the portal then. Standard procedure."

Morris took a deep breath to gather himself. "OK, OK," he said agreeably. "What are they saying at the control center?"

"No idea," said Fredette. "Budget cuts made us pull a sergeant from there. Everything goes through chief's office, now. Like I said, last I heard they were going to shut down Kenmore within the hour."

With that information, Morris' mind leaped to a suspicion. "Give the control center a call. You need to know what's happening with the river. "

Fredette seemed quiet, offering no objection. At the same time, Morris heard Herman Poole answer his phone.

"OK, I'll give a call down to the control center," Fredette finally answered. "But if any shit comes out of this, you need to have my back."

"No worries, blame it on me if I'm wrong," said Morris as he ended the call and looked over to the doctor, who was nodding on the phone.

"Hold on," Dr. Poole said as he pulled the phone away and handed it to Morris. "It's Elijah."

"Hey buddy," he said. "I think we might be in for a flood tonight."

"They fixed all that years ago," Elijah said.

"No, I think Sosa and Cashman figured something out. The Charles is backing up."

"Sosa and Cashman?" responded Elijah. "Where are you going with this?"

"Sosa was worried that the Muddy would overflow again into the Fenway portal."

"And that would flood Kenmore," added Elijah matter-of-factly. He then paused for a moment, apparently evaluating whether to trust his friend, who was still recovering from a brain injury. "Alright," he said after the delay. "I'll head over to Fenway. I want to hear more about this Sosa-Cashman thing later."

Morris hung up and went back to looking at the drawings with Dr. Poole. They shuffled through more papers and found tide charts and floodplain maps. More and more, the pieces of what Sosa had been chasing fell into place.

In the back of Morris' mind, however, he considered the political complement to the scenario that Sosa had discovered. Having the control center notifications go through the chief's office would inadvertently put Steph Tam on the hot seat even though she was out of the country. It was a setup so perfect that it couldn't be accidental, thought Morris. He looked across the table and saw Herman Poole fixated on a diagram of the city.

"This is insane," he said. "Not only might the Green Line be looking at another flood, but look at how much of the city is at or near sea level. The damage could be in the billions! How could someone make a mistake like this?"

"Maybe it's no mistake," said Morris.

"What? You think terrorism?"

The T-cop shook his head. Rightful concerns about security had given way to a boogeyman mentality where the public could be cajoled, if not frightened, into giving up everything from their privacy to their shampoo bottles. Morris grinned as his mind rolled back a few hours to the meeting at the Transportation Building. This time around, the boogeyman wasn't wearing a beard and carrying the Quran. No, the monster that had been pushed in front of the public wore tattered clothes, hunted through trash barrels, and slept on benches.

"Doc, I've been blown up, gassed, stabbed three times, and once had a T patron try to choke me with a necktie. But you know what I fear the most? A politician with a shallow soul and deep list of favors owed."

Herman Poole pulled back from the table. "What are you saying? What possible gain is there to causing this much damage?"

"The one thing in this city that is better than cash is land," said Morris. "In the space of twenty-four hours, you could turn property values upside down, wash the slate clean."

The doctor let out a whistle just as Morris' phone rang.

"That dumb mother fucker," began an exasperated Billy Fredette. "Apparently, the control center is non-essential personnel! The General Manager sent nearly everyone home!"

"What's going on, Billy?"

"An hour ago, a monitor on the Muddy went off, and no one noticed!"

"What?" said Morris.

"The Muddy River's been at flood stage for an hour," rephrased Fredette. "It could be eight, ten feet above its average. We've got water pouring onto the Green Line at the portal."

"Shit!" said Morris.

"We're evacuating Kenmore, and I'm ordering the D Line shut down," said Fredette. "But with this much water coming in, we might flood all the way down to Park Street."

"Isn't there supposed to be a crew of laborers on standby at Fenway any time there's a chance of flooding?"

"I know, I know," said Fredette. "Those guys and the truck carrying sandbags already went to Boylston for some reason."

"Why the fuck did they do that?"

"I don't know. I'm trying to get them over to Fenway now."

"It may be too late," said Morris. "We haven't even hit high tide yet. We have to worry about the rest of the line going into the city."

"I know," responded Fredette. "Those stations will be buried under twenty feet of water. If it reaches Park Street, we'll lose the whole line."

"Yeah, Park Street...." Morris' mind stopped his mouth. Father Michael and Goldilocks were in the Tremont Street tunnels, just off the Boylston Station, one stop before Park Street. "Billy, where's Goldi?"

"Sann, you mean?"

"Yeah, has she checked in?"

"No, she...."

Fredette's voice trailed off. The same thought must have struck him as it did Morris. If the waters reached Park Street, Boylston and the Tremont Street tunnels would surely flood.

"I'm on it," Fredette said, hanging up the call.

Morris pulled his phone away and looked over at Dr. Poole.

"What's wrong?" asked the doctor.

Morris paused. "I think I need to call Boston Fire and tell a guy that his girlfriend is marooned on the Titanic right now."

Chapter 18

Morris and Dr. Poole, leaped off the sidewalk, barely clearing a steady stream of water that was rushing through the gutter of Stuart Street.

"What's this about a hatch?" shouted Dr. Poole as they ran through the downpour to the protection of a building across the street.

"There used to be an entrance," Morris said, bent over, trying to catch his breath. He straightened up and pointed toward Boston's theater district. "Right over there, but they got rid of it in the '50s or '60s when they abandoned the line. They left a hatch in the sidewalk as an emergency exit. Quickest way down into those tunnels."

It was hard to perceive the risk facing Sann, Father Michael, and the others in the tunnels, which had comprised the Tremont Street Subway when it opened in 1897. They were in absolute darkness, loaded with dirt, dust, debris, and any number of things that in a rushing stream – especially one you couldn't see – could kill you.

Morris and the doctor then ran down the sidewalk to the intersection with Tremont Street, taking shelter at the entrance of a high-rise. As they did so, Morris' phone rang. It was Elijah. He had driven over to the Fenway portal, stopping his cruiser on the Park Drive overpass, which gave him an ample view of the station below.

"My God, Morris! The water level's above the Red Sox mural on the outbound wall. It's a river pouring into the portal."

"You see anyone there trying to sandbag the entrance?"

"Not yet," said Elijah. "It might be too late at this point. The water has to be waist high already, and it's moving."

At that point, Morris heard sirens coming down Stuart Street. "Alright, see you down here in a few."

Morris hung up and stepped toward the roadway as three fire trucks came down the road. A wave of water was pushed up, spraying both Morris and Herman Poole as the vehicle pulled over.

"Geez sergeant, you look like a mess," Patrick McKenna said as he stepped out of the truck. "So where's this entrance you're talking about?"

"It should be right up here. It's a hatch," Morris said, starting to walk toward the Wang Theatre. "Where's your dad setting up?"

"Incident command?" said McKenna. "I have no idea. The entire city is an incident right now."

One of the other firefighters then shouted, and Morris and McKenna ran up to the spot. "That's it," said Morris noting the insignia of the Metropolitan Transit Authority, the precursor to the MBTA. "No idea how we open it though."

McKenna laughed. "Don't worry about that," he said as two other firefighters walked up with a portable generator and hydraulic tools.

"I forgot, you Jakes just love breaking shit." Morris smiled, but he could see concern on McKenna's face even though he was joking along. No one had heard from Goldilocks since she left the Boylston Station for the old tunnels. They were abandoned decades ago. Every now and then you could get cell signal depending on where you were, but they were a part of the city that time and civilization forgot. That's how come they were a refuge for the homeless and the most marginalized of society.

As the firefighters cut at the hatch, Morris called Fredette again.

"I know," he said before Morris even had a chance to say hello. "We're trying to get a crew to the portal, but the water is moving too fast. We need heavy equipment there."

Morris could sense the panic in Fredette's voice. "What are you seeing at Kenmore?" he asked.

"It's already under water. Thank God that car broke down. Everyone was already leaving the station, but from what I'm hearing at the portal, we might have a tsunami heading toward Hynes."

In the October 1996 flood, the Kenmore station ended up completely submerged with an estimated 14 million gallons of water. The station immediately downstream, Hynes Convention Center, saw much less damage. The saving grace in the T's design is that upon leaving Kenmore and heading downtown, the tunnel has to make a dip in order to fit under the base of the Muddy River. This creates a U-shaped depression that acted like a trap between Kenmore and the Hynes Convention Center Station.

However, once the water gets past that obstacle, it's a downhill shot, right through to the Hynes, Copley, Arlington, and Boylston stops. Any flood waters reaching Boylston would overflow into the abandoned Tremont Street tunnels.

"How long do you think it is until we start seeing water past Kenmore?" asked Morris.

"Any minute now. I've already evacuated everything between Kenmore and Park Street," said Fredette.

"Have you heard from –"

"No," said Fredette.

The two T-cops were silent for a moment.

"Depending on where they are," said the duty officer, "they might be OK. Isn't there a platform down there?"

"Yeah, but if they are in the narrow part of the tunnel, there's nowhere for them to go." At that moment, the firefighters snapped open the hatch. "Billy, there's a crew from Boston Fire about to head down there."

"Great," Fredette responded with sarcasm. "Jimmy Clark and Tommy Palardy just went down there too." Clark and Palardy were a pair of young transit detectives. Most of the young T-cops didn't care for the tunnels, but when one of your own was in trouble, you pushed aside whatever fears or bias you had.

At that moment, Morris heard a strange sound above the rain coming down. It seemed to be coming from the hatch. "What the?"

Suddenly several dozen rats leaped from the opening. One of McKenna's firefighters swung an axe at a larger rodent that was the size of a small dog.

"Holy shit!" exclaimed the firefighter, but McKenna appeared to pay little heed to the beasts.

"Hey Pat," Morris yelled while pulling his phone away. "You see any water, you get out of there in a hurry."

McKenna nodded, but Morris sensed the firefighter didn't need to be reminded of the delicate equation that can shift from being rescuer to someone in need of rescue.

"How much time you think we've got?" Morris said into the phone while watching McKenna and three others descend down the hatch, each linked to the other by a rope.

"I'm guessing five, maybe ten, minutes at tops," answered Fredette. "This is fucked up. Any day of the year, no one is in those tunnels."

"Other than the Lost Boys," interjected Morris.

"Come on," pleaded Fredette. "They're a bunch of sex offenders and drug addicts. When they aren't robbing tourists, they're swapping sex for cash."

"Yeah, well Goldi believes homeless lives matter," Morris said plainly.

"It's going to get her killed."

With that Morris saw the blue lights of a transit police cruiser coming down Stuart Street.

"Hey, doc!" Morris yelled over to Herman Poole. "Our ride's here." He then turned back to the phone call. "Billy, give me a heads up once that water starts hitting Boylston."

"It just started coming into Hynes," said Fredette. "I'd get Boston Fire out of there now."

Morris hung up as Elijah pulled the cruiser into the waterlogged gutter.

The doctor and Morris hopped in the cruiser, barely waiting for it to come to a stop.

"Any word from DCR?" Morris asked.

"No idea. I texted you. I couldn't get in touch with that Paulie guy either."

"Text!" Morris said as a thought struck him. Quickly he texted out a message to Sann: "Flood. Pat at Boylston Street exit."

"She's smart," said Elijah, and Morris knew by his tone that he was talking about Sann. "She'll figure it out."

Morris shook his head. "Come on, let's find Rico Paulie."

With that, Elijah made the drive down to the marine unit on the edge of the Charles River. There was at least a foot of water on the city's streets as the catch basins were overwhelmed with a combination of water and debris.

As they neared the facility, they could see all sorts of commotion. Morris could make out two ambulances in the lot along with two trucks from DCR as well as half a dozen State Police cruisers. Elijah pulled over to the side, and the three men got out.

"Where's Rico Paulie?" Morris asked a trooper, who pointed toward the ambulance.

Running up to it, Morris saw EMTs hovering over a bloodied man on a stretcher.

Dr. Poole pushed past Morris. "Here, I'm a doctor," he said to the EMTs. "How can I help?"

Paulie was covered in blood with his right arm mangled.

"Rico! What happened?" Morris asked as the rain pelted down.

The trooper mumbled something.

"Hey!" shouted an older state trooper coming toward the ambulance.

"Hold up," said Elijah raising his transit police badge.

"They're good," Paulie managed to get out.

Morris and Elijah introduced themselves, but the statie didn't offer his name, such was the second-class treatment T-cops usually got from other law enforcement.

“The fuckin’ idiot,” said the trooper. “He dove into the water trying to fix the locks.”

Morris looked at his friend, who rolled his eyes.

“He’s got a pretty serious injury to his arm,” Dr. Poole noted. “He needs surgery. I’ll ride with him.”

Over the next few minutes, the EMTs loaded Rico Paulie into the ambulance. Dr. Poole climbed in back with them. Once out of the lot, the older trooper pulled Morris and Elijah aside. “So were you the one that told Rico about the dam?”

“Yeah,” said Morris. “It was broken.”

“Still is,” said the trooper. “We’ve got a few guys from DCR trying to fix it right now while we try to get a straight answer out of these two.” And he pointed at a pair of young men, who looked like they may have just been out of high school. “They were the crew on duty tonight.”

“Major Walsh! You’ve got a phone call.”

The T-cops turned to see where the voice came from as the trooper shouted back, “Take a message!”

Morris now presumed the statie was Rico’s infamous boss.

“It’s the Lieutenant Governor!”

With that, Walsh gave a heavy exhale and turned to take the call.

Morris nodded to Elijah, and the two went over to where the young men were sitting on the curb.

“So what’s the story on you two?” Morris asked.

“Seriously, we have no idea what’s going on,” said the taller one. “Tell them that.”

“Guys, we have a disaster on our hands here, and it all started with the thing you’re in charge of.”

“Fuck that,” said the other one. “I’ve been working here a month. All I’m supposed to do is push a button.”

Morris and Elijah continued to press the two, but the more they did so, the more it became clear that the pair likely couldn’t even get into McDonald’s U.

“You gotta believe us, we don’t know nothing,” said the more talkative of the two.

"Gentlemen, I'd say you've made that perfectly clear," said Morris, who nodded to Elijah. The two then turned away from the pair of imbeciles.

"Corruption through incompetence?" Elijah offered.

Morris smiled in agreement. It was something they had seen plenty as T-cops. If in the structure of politics you wanted to get around some check meant to balance your power, you simply hired – or had someone else hire – an idiot to do the job. Problem solved.

The question was who had something to gain by dumping the Boston Harbor into the Charles River. Morris stared out at the locks. A suspicion entered his mind, but it just didn't make sense to him. "Sometimes incompetence is just incompetence," he said.

At that moment, Elijah's phone rang, and he took the call. At the same time, Morris saw Major Walsh coming back his way.

"So what are you two T-cops doing here?" he said.

"I was down here the other day with Rico. He wanted me to take a look at the graffiti on the locks."

Walsh seemed lost.

"He thought one of the subway gangs may have been behind it," Morris explained.

"Oh," said Walsh. "I'm still trying to figure out if we have a crime scene. Two of the three locks had been jammed open. No one seemed to notice it as they don't get a lot of use this time of year. Of course, it didn't help that Abbott and Costello over there," he said throwing a thumb toward the pair sitting on the curb, "fucked everything up."

"Well, what happened to Rico?" asked Morris.

"He was in the lock, trying to force it closed somehow. Knucklehead."

"Hey, I'd cut him some slack," responded Morris.

"Yeah, I'd mind my own business," shot back Walsh.

"Gentlemen," Elijah interjected having just got off his phone. "I got some good news. Boston Water and Sewer managed to get the Brookline Ave. gate open. That's going to help with the overflow of the Muddy."

"Yeah, and the Lieutenant Governor just told me that the DCR managed to close the old lock next to the Science Museum, and they got the pumps at the dam working the right way again. We still have the two locks here that are jammed opened."

Elijah turned to Morris. "Boylston has to be under water right now."

"Any word on Goldi?"

Elijah shook his head.

"Fucking T," said Walsh. "You get a little rain, and the whole thing goes to shit."

Morris weighed several responses, most of which were highly ill-advised, but Elijah grabbed and pulled him away before his lack of judgment met up with his lack of patience.

Walsh shouted something at the two T-cops, but Elijah remained focused on moving away from the scene.

"That guy's an asshole," Morris said as the two neared the transit police cruiser.

"Takes one to know one," responded Elijah as he opened the driver's side door.

Once in the car, the pair decided to head to Boylston Station to see how bad the situation was. Along the way, Morris checked in with Fredette, who was reserved in his assessment of things. No word from Sann and her crew. The Aquarium Station on the Blue Line, probably the most below-sea-level section of the entire transit system was flooding. From Kenmore to Park Street on the Green Line was completely underwater, too. The other low-lying stations had seen some water, but the flooding wasn't too bad. Cutting through the city, some of the streets had a foot or more of water while others had no standing water at all, reflecting Boston's temperamental geography.

Oddly, during this entire episode of chaos, Acting Chief Dyani Swan had yet to be heard from.

Elijah drove down Tremont Street, passing Boston Common on the right. As they neared the intersection with Boylston Street, with the Green Line entrance on the corner, Elijah pulled the cruiser over, hopping the curb and driving up onto the wide sidewalk.

Right in front of them were two MBTA trucks, full of sandbags and wooden planks, with several T laborers engaged in some animated conversation. Morris recognized one of them as Mark

McLoughlin, a young kid from the Brighton neighborhood of the city.

"Hey Mark!" he shouted over the rainfall.

McLoughlin, dressed in overalls and a hard hat, turned, his arms still waving. "What the, oh, it's you."

"What's going on here, buddy?"

"This place is all screwed up. This afternoon I was out at Fenway to make sure we had everything to dam up the place in case the Muddy overflowed. Next thing I know we get called off that to go put sandbags around this place near the Transportation Building. Then they call us back to Fenway, and it's already too late there. So then they bring us back here, but now Boylston's underwater."

"OK, OK, just take a breath," Morris implored. "Listen, nothing you guys could have done. The Charles River Dam was broken. That's how come everything overflowed."

Elijah started to ask McLoughlin about the location near the Transportation Building, which was only a block away, but suddenly Morris' eyes caught a glimpse of headlights coming his way. Before he could process what they were, his ears were overwhelmed by the thunderous horn blast of a fire engine.

McLoughlin and Morris jumped to one side, Elijah to the other, as the engine came up over the curb and halted next to the station entrance.

Morris recognized the man getting out of the passenger side as Deputy Chief Robbie Lenehan. Before he could say hello, Lenehan, pointed a finger at Morris.

"I'd watch out for Jay McKenna if I were you," he said.

"What's up?" replied Morris.

"Jay's bullshit at you. He's more bullshit at his kid. He went in there looking for your friend there. The blond."

"Did he find her?" Morris asked.

"No. He unhooked from the rest of the crew to go after them. It took the other three to drag him back. We almost lost all four them."

"Oh shit," said Elijah who had come around from the other side of the engine.

Morris felt sick. He should have known better than to let Patrick go in after Goldilocks.

Lenehan started directing the crew, but he must have recognized the concern on Morris' face. "Don't beat yourself up about it."

"How bad is it down there?"

"Word is we have twenty feet of water in Kenmore."

Elijah let go a whistle of shock.

"Exactly. The good news is we caught this thing when we did," Lenehan said, giving a glance toward Morris. "Who knows how much of the city could have ended up underwater. We've got plenty of flooding in the low parts as it is, but we're getting ahead of it. This," he said pointing downward, "is ground zero right now. Best we can tell, everything between here and Fenway is submerged. All power's been cut – video, monitors, everything. We're in the dark."

He then yelled a couple of orders. Turning back to Elijah, Morris, and McLoughlin, Lenehan lifted his deputy chief's helmet slightly. "Right now we have every pump in the city trying to get ahead of this water." He then grabbed his radio and walked toward the station entrance.

"Damn it!" yelled McLoughlin, as Lenehan walked away.

"What's wrong Mark?" asked Morris.

"It's just we had everything in place. Whenever there's heavy rain forecast, we're ready for it because of the '96 flood. It's like how everyone gets milk and bread whenever they say it's going to snow because we're all scared of the Blizzard of '78."

"Hey, so where did they have you go instead of Fenway?" asked Elijah.

"Oh, right down there," McLoughlin said pointing across Boylston Street toward the Transportation Building.

"Show us," Morris said, looking at Elijah.

With that McLoughlin led the two T-cops around the corner and then a block down Boylston Street.

"Right there," he said pointing across the street to an old building.

Elijah looked at Morris. "The T doesn't own that."

"That's the old Steinway Building," said Morris.

"All I know is the new maintenance director tells us to go over here, and some guy will tell us what to do," explained McLoughlin.

"Who was the guy?" asked Elijah.

"Some creepy dude with a shitty haircut and a bad attitude," said McLoughlin.

Morris and Elijah looked at each other. Then they looked at McLoughlin. "Come on," Elijah said as the two T-cops ran across the street with the foreman in tow.

The building sat on the corner of the flooded alley that Morris and Dr. Herman Poole had looked out on earlier from the back of Ten Park Plaza. For all purposes, it had been abandoned, but years ago it had served as a popular piano store.

Morris scanned the facade. "Mark, there's no sandbags here. What gives?"

"That's the fucked up thing," said McLoughlin. "He had us go inside to this basement theater place. We put sandbags around one of the exits. That's it. It was like real Phantom of the Opera shit."

Morris recalled that among the architectural drawings he looked at in Bob Sosa's office, there had been the layout of what appeared to be a concert hall. The three walked around to the front of the building. Morris spotted the gold lettering on a red background: "Steinert Hall."

"Of course," he half said to himself.

"What are you thinking?" asked Elijah.

"You ever hear of Steinert Hall?" Morris asked as he rummaged around the entrance for something. He then looked at McLoughlin and grabbed the foreman's hard hat from his head. Stepping toward the entrance, Morris continued the story of Steinert Hall. "It was built around the same time as the Tremont Street Subway," he said, "and four stories down. It was an underground concert hall."

"Oh yeah," said Elijah. "I remember reading about this."

"Yeah," said Morris. "So let's go see what's so important about the place." With that he threw the hard hat at the door, spidering the glass but not breaking it. Morris contemplated how to continue, but Elijah stepped forward, holding his right arm out to block Morris. With his left hand, he reached for the handle of the door and pulled. It opened freely. Elijah turned to Morris. "Work smarter, not harder, buddy."

With that, Elijah, Morris, and McLoughlin entered the building.

"Come on, it's this way," said McLoughlin taking the lead.

"Tell me, Mark," said Morris. "Anything more about the guy who was here?"

"I don't know," he said. "He was old, maybe not as old as you. Probably taller than you."

"Thanks," said Morris as they came up to a partially open door with a dim light behind it. McLoughlin pulled it open, revealing a circular staircase leading downward.

Elijah pulled out his cellphone and turned on its light to guide the group. As the three descended the stairs, they were hit by the musty smell. On one side of them was a plaster wall, peeling but still intact. The other side of the staircase was open, but in the dim light it was hard to discern the expanse of the area they were entering. Across from them, Morris could detect a parallel staircase that met theirs at a platform, now immediately in front of them.

Morris turned to the left, and he could see through a pair of doors, a majestic but dilapidated former concert hall. He let go a whistle of amazement.

"Like I told you, Phantom of the Opera," McLoughlin said.

Morris laughed, but he couldn't disagree. They continued down few steps.

"Wow," remarked Elijah with sincere awe.

In front of them was a deserted cavernous hall that prior to the 1940s served as a theater for live performances. Like the nearby Tremont Street Subway, it was a relic that most of Boston had forgotten. Every now and then some developer would have plans to renovate the building, but the cost of bringing the structure up to code always proved far more than what it was worth.

"So what happened to this place?" asked McLoughlin.

"Cocoanut Grove," answered Morris succinctly.

"Huh?" McLoughlin was lost, and Morris realized the foreman was bit younger than himself. For anyone of Morris' generation growing up in Boston, the words "Cocoanut Grove" were always uttered in a tone of horror, most likely by parents and grandparents who were alive in the 1940s.

"The Cocoanut Grove was a nightclub," began Elijah, picking up on Morris' reference. "In 1942, there was fire there, no sprinklers, not enough exits. Nearly five hundred people died."

"Oh my God," said McLoughlin.

"After that, everything changed in the city," added Morris. "Forget underground concert halls, at least ones with only one real entrance and exit."

"Yeah, I'm not even sure I could remember how to get out of here," said Elijah, spinning around and casting the cellphone light toward the staircase. It hit on some lettering. "To Carver Street," he read aloud. "Carver?" he repeated, looking at his fellow T-cop.

"It's gone," answered Morris. "Another victim of urban renewal, but it used be right by the alley that backs up to the Transportation Building."

"OK," said Elijah. "If the street is that way, then the Common should be over there, and that means over there is ...."

Elijah and Morris turned together, and both stopped at the same spot. They looked at each other, and reached an identical conclusion. "The subway!" they said in unison.

McLoughlin was confused. "I'm not following along guys."

"That's the Green Line," said Elijah.

"Well, not exactly," said Morris. "We're probably a good ten to twenty feet below the subway."

"Yeah, it's still bone dry in here," said McLoughlin. "They sent us here for no reason."

"Yeah," said Elijah. "But the thing is someone was worried this was going to flood."

"Which means," added Morris. "They had to know that the tunnel was going to flood." A thought then struck him. "Where did they have you put the sandbags?"

"I think it's up one floor," said McLoughlin. "It was right off the staircase."

Led by Elijah with his cellphone light, the three then made their way up the parallel staircase, past lettering that read "To Boylston Street," to a second-floor balcony.

"This must have really been something," remarked Elijah. Morris was about to concur, but before he could speak, he felt a vibration from his phone. He grabbed it.

"You get signal down here?" Elijah asked holding his phone up and looking at his screen.

"I don't know," Morris said as he read an incoming text message. Initially, he couldn't make sense of the words, but then, he noticed the sender.

"Holy shit! They're alive," he exclaimed.

"Who?" asked Elijah and McLoughlin.

"Goldilocks!" said Morris. He then held up his phone, showing the text message which read. "WTF!! We're in old fallout shelter. Fr. Mike needs help."

Morris then began to text back.

Elijah looked at his phone. "Buddy, I've got zero signal down here."

Morris continued to work his fingers. "LTE Direct, two cellphones near each other can talk directly."

"I never heard of that," said McLoughlin.

"Time to get an upgrade," joked Morris. However, he tempered his exuberance. Maybe the message had been sent a while ago, before the tunnels flooded. He finished his reply and pressed send. He wasn't sure where the shelter was.

After a minute, Morris' heart sank. No reply. Maybe it was an old message. Then he felt the phone vibrate and saw Goldilocks' reply. "OK for now. Fr. Mike needs med attention. Send help."

"They're alive," Morris repeated as Elijah and McLoughlin both stared at the phone. "They're near here. It only works within about quarter mile."

"We need to let Lenehan and McKenna know," said Elijah.

"Go ahead," said Morris excitedly. "I'm going to text her back. Let her know to sit tight. We'll get her out."

Elijah and McLoughlin sprinted from the balcony to the stairway as Morris tapped on his phone. They weren't out of the woods yet. The tunnel was under water, but it sounded like they were dry wherever they were.

He let Sann know he was going to get help, and he wouldn't be able to respond. Waiting a minute to make sure the message sent, he put away his cellphone and rushed up the stairway.

Chapter 19

Morris could feel himself drifting toward sleep. The bench inside the MBTA command vehicle wasn't the best of beds, but it was doing its job, along with the set of transit police sweats he was now wearing. Just a quick nap was all he needed.

"BWAAAAAAAAAAHHH!"

Morris shot straight up at the sound. His eyes wide open. He turned and saw Deputy Chief Jay McKenna smiling at him with an air horn in his right hand. "So sorry, did I wake you?"

Morris managed a smile. "I deserved that."

"Not really," said McKenna. "Patrick's more the one to blame. He should know better than to pull a stunt like he did."

"He wouldn't have ended up there if I hadn't told him about the emergency entrance."

"Listen, as far as I can tell, Morris, you have this odd combination of shit luck and nine lives," McKenna said. "Keep that in mind the next time you are talking to one of my firefighters."

Morris smiled and nodded.

"Come on," said McKenna. "We think we've figured a way to get them out of there."

He got up off the bench and followed the deputy fire chief out the command vehicle that had parked on the corner of Boylston and Tremont streets. The rain seemed to have lessened. As the designated emergency management commander McKenna had set up his post in a portable tent next to the Boylston entrance.

Morris took a quick look around and spotted Elijah and Bruce Donohue over to one side with coffee cups in their hands, and he made his way toward his fellow T-cops.

"You got an extra one of those?" he asked, nodding toward the coffee.

"Hey Morris, how are you?" asked Bruce.

"Good, I think I nearly got some sleep in there," he said as he went about fixing himself a coffee. "What time have we got?" he asked his fellow T-cops.

"A little after midnight," said Elijah.

"Our fearless leader, Dyani doesn't work late night?" asked Morris.

"Jay booted her," said Bruce. "She was pissed, said she was going to call the Lieutenant Governor."

"So what's the latest on Goldi?"

"We've managed to figure out where they're holed up," said Elijah. "Jay had to dig out an old civil defense map from the '60s, but apparently they converted part of the tunnel into a fallout shelter at one point. Boston Fire managed to drop a couple of repeaters down in there to boost her signal."

"That's good news," said Morris.

"Yeah, but the bad news," said Bruce, "is that the tunnel is flooded. We can't even get in from the emergency hatches."

As the words sunk in, Deputy Chief Robbie Lenehan gathered everyone around a table.

"OK everyone, we're on the clock here," Lenehan began, "We have eleven people trapped in a tunnel. One of them, a 75-year-old male, has sustained a serious injury."

Morris turned to Elijah as the deputy chief continued the briefing. "Any word on Clark and Palardy?"

"Palardy got out. We think Clark's with Goldi."

Back at the table, Lenehan nodded to Jay McKenna.

"So to follow on what Robbie was saying, based on the fact that the water level reached the roof of the affected stations, our estimates are that it could take a week to pump the contaminated water out of the abandoned underground tunnels. That obviously won't do.

"So we've been talking to Boston Water and Sewer, and we think we've come up with an idea. Granted all this is based on maps that are older than anyone here."

McKenna then rolled out a drawing of the Boylston Station. He circled a series of emergency exits and passageways and then pulled out a much older map of the Tremont Street Subway. "So what you can see here is these all align with another below-grade section of the tunnel, which runs from the corner of Boylston and Tremont and along the southerly side of the Common. It pretty much parallels Boylston all the way down to the public gardens."

Of course, thought Morris. The original portal that brought streetcars into and out of the Tremont Street Subway was located inside the public gardens. It wasn't until 1914 that the line was moved slightly to the south, running directly under Boylston Street, where a new portal was built in what's now a brick-lined median. The old portal was closed up and filled over.

"I don't get it," said a young man who looked like he had stepped out of an LL Bean catalog. "How's that going to help the water in the station?"

Morris nudged Elijah. "Who's that?"

Elijah shrugged. "Some pinhead from the Lieutenant Governor's office."

Morris nodded while McKenna explained. "The plan here isn't about draining the tunnels completely, but if we can drop the water by six feet or so, that gives us room to mount a rescue operation. Now, the key to this is we've got to get a dive team in there and open up those passageways, basically turn them into drains."

"And also pray that the Boston Common doesn't collapse," added an older gentleman that Morris didn't recognize.

"Oh yeah, I forgot that part," said McKenna. "Tom Kilgariff of Boston Water and Sewer, everyone, and as Tom was saying, there's also a pretty good chance we might just turn the Common into a giant sinkhole."

"To explain," said Kilgariff, "the soil around the Common is like Jello, and it's already saturated from the rain. It's also the site of the central burying ground."

"The what?" asked Bruce Donohue.

"The central burying ground," continued Kilgariff. "It's a mass grave of hundreds of British soldiers who perished during the siege of Boston. Then also in the old days, the Common provided a convenient burial spot for the city's lower classes and any number of undesirables, murderers, thieves, witches."

"City councilors?" Morris interjected hoping for some comic relief.

The gathering broke into laughter. That was, everyone but LL Bean.

"Yeah, so to summarize," said McKenna returning the focus. "We're relying on 60-year-old drawings to tell us how to dump several million gallons of water into 120-year-old tunnels that basically run through a pudding-filled cemetery."

"Are you crazy?" asked LL Bean.

"We'd be crazy not to try," Lenehan shot back.

"That's right," Morris added. "Those tunnels will hold. We have to try it. Otherwise, they won't last in that fall-out shelter."

LL Bean didn't seem impressed. "Well, I'm not sure how the Lieutenant Governor –"

"We're not asking for permission here," said McKenna. "We're telling you what the plan is. We're assembling a volunteer joint operation, involving dive teams from Boston Fire, Mass. State Police, and Boston Police. They should be in the water in about twenty minutes. We should know within the hour whether this plan is working."

With that, McKenna broke the meeting. Morris moved to speak with him, but LL Bean had already cornered the deputy chief.

"When I tell the Lieutenant Governor –"

"Listen, needledick," Morris interrupted. "You're not going to tell the Lieutenant Governor."

"Oh, I'm not?" LL Bean said, turning around to face Morris.

"Of course not," said Morris. "Because let's say this thing goes sideways, she can deny the whole thing. She never heard about it. Don't they teach you anything these days?"

LL Bean grew flustered. "You, you, just realize that if something goes wrong, it's all on you."

"It always is," said McKenna. "Just make sure they spell my name right."

With that, the young man rushed off.

"Listen, Jay, the transit police doesn't have a dive team, but I know the tunnels like the back of my hand," said Morris. "I've got to tell you that water is going to be a mess. Snakes, rats, insects, germs, fungus, needles, and God know what else. It will be like a mudslide that ran through the depths of hell. Good luck."

McKenna laughed. "The T is finally getting what everyone has been suggesting for years, a giant enema. After this, the whole underground will be wiped clean. They'll have to start from scratch."

Morris laughed along, but he couldn't help but wonder if that hadn't been someone's plan all along.

"If phase one here works," McKenna said, "we're going to need you leading phase two, getting to where that shelter is"

"You can count on me," said Morris.

He then sought out a cup of coffee and found Bruce and Elijah warming themselves next to a portable generator that was throwing off heat.

"What's up gentlemen?" he asked, seeing the two staring at the Boylston Station entrance.

"Nothing," said Elijah. "Bruce was just saying how it looks like a mausoleum."

"Yeah, you know, carve a name in there and add some death heads or gargoyles to make it look more gruesome," said Bruce.

"You know there's always been a stigma of death with this station," said Morris.

"I know," said Elijah "I saw the stone marker over there. The last expansion in 1985, they unearthed bodies and had to relocate them."

"Oh it goes back further than that," Morris said. "Just before the subway opened in 1897, a spark from a streetcar ignited some gas leaking from a pipe. It was a massive explosion, right here," Morris said pointing at the intersection of Tremont and Boylston streets on which they were standing. "Bloodied passengers, mangled remains of horses, glass flying everywhere from shattered windows in the buildings. Something like ten people died and more than fifty were badly injured."

"Tunnel of doom," said Elijah.

"Yeah," continued Morris. "Some folks say it was a curse, all the dead souls disinterred at the central burial ground to make way for man's latest invention."

"Jesus, Morris, you're giving me the creeps," said Bruce.

"Here's the kicker. A dozen decades later, and what do we got? A bunch of the city's undesirables trapped underground, screwed by the rich and powerful again."

"What do you mean?" asked Bruce.

Morris looked over at Elijah, who gave a confirming nod.

"Bruce, this doesn't seem like it was any natural disaster," he continued. "Someone tampered with the Charles River Dam."

"Why would anyone do that?" Bruce asked.

"Oldest reason there is," said Morris.

"Prostitution?"

"Reason, not profession," said Elijah.

"Money," completed Morris.

"I don't know guys," Bruce said looking around. "I don't really see anyone winning the lottery here."

"Listen, first thing in the morning, I need your help with something. I found Bob Sosa's phone," Morris said. "I already got a good idea what's on it, but we need everything. He knew something was going on."

He then proceeded to recount for his fellow T-cops how he had acquired Sosa's phone and what he had found in the T's real estate office.

Bruce exhaled a sigh. "Morris, I hate to tell you this, but depending on the judge, they can be real pains when it comes to evidence. Let's say we do find something, I'm not sure there's a DA who can make it stick."

"I know, Bruce. I'm not worried about a judge. I'm worried about getting played by an old friend."

Donohue nodded along.

"Speaking of old friends," Morris continued. "Did you ever get anything more on Cliff Cashman?"

"Who?"

"The dead guy they found in the Muddy River, the one whose brother flipped out."

"Oh the gay-bash guy?" said Bruce.

Morris and Elijah rolled their eyes. It was a good thing Tom Cashman was nowhere nearby.

"I don't think Dr. Death had anything other than what she found the other night."

"Blunt force trauma to the head, right?" confirmed Morris.

"Yeah, a bat or something, but he actually drowned. Shitty way to go. I mean the Fens are pretty and all, but – hey that reminds me," Bruce interrupted himself. "The doc said your cousin was in the Fens not too long ago, something about wildflower seeds on her pant leg."

"Makes sense," said Morris. "She loved it over there." A thought then struck him. "Any chance you can find out the flowers, or get the doc's report? It might be nice to plant what she liked, in memory of her, you know."

The truth was the mention of Cathy loaded another stress onto Morris' shoulders. He couldn't go there right now, and that only made him feel guilty for being a shitty cousin. To be a good cop sometimes meant being a lousy person. You didn't always make it to the birthday parties or graduations. Even your close friends, if you still had them after a decade or two on the job, you kept at a distance because sooner or later everyone needed a favor.

What started as a "no problem" of fixing a ticket or getting a parking spot for someone could quickly become a "no way" of stalling an investigation into someone's daughter, son, or cousin. The next thing you knew your pension was gone, and you were fighting to keep yourself out of jail. There's nothing judges love more than making an example of a dirty cop.

So the best defense against letting friends or family suck you into their personal hells was to lock yourself into your own purgatory, keeping yourself on neutral ground even if it meant eternal penance for being an asshole to everyone around you.

"They're in the station now."

The voice startled Morris from his thoughts, and he and his fellow T-cops turned to see Tom Kilgariff standing next to them.

"They've been in there maybe ten minutes," he said looking at his watch.

"How soon will it be until we know whether this is working?" asked Elijah.

"Oh, well, if it is working, we should start to see the water levels go down quickly. My guess is by daybreak, we'd be able to get a rescue crew down there."

"That sounds pretty good," said Bruce.

"Of course, if it doesn't work, we'll know a lot sooner than that," Kilgariff countered with a laugh. "The entire south side of the Common will cave in, and who knows what will get churned up in the process. It might look like the zombie apocalypse."

"You're not afraid of the *Globe* running the headline 'Boston Water and Sewer Desecrate Burial Ground?'" Morris joked.

Kilgariff smiled. "Of course not."

Morris looked at his fellow T-cops. They all seemed buoyed by the man's confidence.

Then he spoke again. "We all know the *Globe* will blame the transit police first."

Chapter 20

The next morning, Morris was awakened from a nap, again curled up in the transit police command bus, by Deputy Chief Lenehan. “Rise and shine gentlemen!” he bellowed.

Morris looked across the bus to Elijah, who seemed to be just coming out of his slumber as well. “Best sleep I’ve had in a couple of nights,” he said.

Elijah gave a wide yawn. “Yeah, it wasn’t too bad.”

The two then looked at Bruce, who was snoring.

“Should we wake him?” asked Elijah.

“Nah,” said Morris as he stood and stretched his back.

The two men stepped out of the bus into a crisp, cloudy but dry morning and made their way over to the command tent.

“Good news,” Jay McKenna said to the T-cops with some others gathered around the table. “The tunnels held up, and the water level has dropped several feet. We should have a shot at this."

"That's great," said Morris. "When do we go in?"

"We're pretty much staged up and ready to go. We cut away the grates blocking the old tunnel so we should be able to get the rafts in and out no problem. Boston EMS should be here any minute now," said McKenna.

"We've got one issue," said Lenehan. "We haven't heard from her since about four this morning."

Jay McKenna put up a hand as if to say don't worry. "She told us she was getting low on battery. Maybe it ran out, or she shut down to save it."

"One of her last texts said Father Mike wasn't doing so great," said Lenehan, who then joined with his fellow deputy chief in gathering the teams that would be involved in the operation. Morris spotted Patrick McKenna and walked over and nudged him on the shoulder.

"Glad to see you're OK," he said to the young firefighter.

Patrick turned and extended his hand to shake the T-cop's, and Morris could see the worry on his face.

"OK everyone, settle down," the elder McKenna said to start the briefing. "As best as we can tell, we have seven to eight homeless in the shelter along with the priest, transit police Sergeant Susan Sann and a detective, James Clark, also of the transit police."

For the next three minutes, the two deputies detailed the presumed location and layout of the shelter that Morris had helped them identify the night before. They also stressed that since the tunnels were draining, there may be a subtle current.

"The trickiest part of this whole thing is we don't know the water level at the shelter," explained Lenehan. "We think it is at the far end of the tunnel, where it starts going up again. The water level should be pretty low, but we gotta go through the deep end to get there. Still, there could be several feet of water outside the door."

"Shouldn't we wait then?" said a woman Morris recognized from Boston Police dive team.

Lenehan and McKenna looked at each other. "We haven't had contact with the group for going on two hours now," explained Lenehan. "In speaking with Mr. Kilgariff, the assessment from an engineering standpoint is that it might be safer to mount an operation now, while there is still water in the tunnel, than later."

Kilgariff interrupted. "We're dealing with cut-and-cover excavation that's more than a century old. The water right now is providing some support to the walls, but as it drains, not only does that support go away, but we'll likely see a greater possibility of structural damage."

"That," continued Lenehan, "and we've got a known injury with uncertainty about the condition of the other occupants. We want this to be a rescue, and not a recovery, operation."

The suggestion of fatalities brought a somber feeling across the group. Morris saw Jay McKenna's eyes scan the faces in front of him. "Basically, Robbie and I figured we're here, we've got the resources," said the deputy chief. "If we wait another hour, people above our pay grade start calling each other, and it turns into a clusterfuck. So I say let's go get 'em."

With that, a small cheer erupted from around the table. McKenna and Lenehan handed out assignments. Morris was to be in the first boat alongside Patrick. In all, six rafts were going in. Morris' raft would be pulling a rope that would go from the relative safety of the Boylston Station to the shelter. A diver would be on each raft as well as two firefighters. Morris' job would be to guide the flotilla.

It was a good plan, as was pretty much everything Jay McKenna touched. At the end of the briefing, the deputy chief stepped toward Elijah and Morris. "Rogers and Hammerstein, walk with me for a minute."

The two followed McKenna to the Boston Fire command vehicle, which was essentially a converted Winnebago. He pulled open the door and stepped inside. As Morris and Elijah entered, McKenna turned around with a significant change in his demeanor. "So who the fuck is this Dana Swan you got over there?"

"Dyani," Morris said.

“Whatever,” McKenna said as he removed his jacket and helmet.

“Hey, don’t ask me,” Morris said leaning toward Elijah. “Talk to him. He’s management now.”

“So I heard,” McKenna said squeezing past the two T-cops and going to the other end of the vehicle.

“Thanks, buddy,” Elijah began with some sarcasm. “Yeah, she was hired as part of some federal grant, and when Chief Tam had to go on this Israel trip, she was put in charge.”

“Oh there’s some political bullshit,” McKenna said opening a narrow door and closing it behind him.

Morris was initially confused, but it soon became apparent that the deputy chief had gone into the vehicle’s bathroom. It didn’t stop him from talking, however.

“She’s telling the Lieutenant Governor that she ought to have incident command down here. Did she work for Homeland or something?”

“Well....” said Elijah.

“Well, I don’t give a fuck,” said McKenna from behind the door. “And I told her that!”

Elijah shot a look at his fellow T-cop. Jay wasn’t the type to suffer fools, especially bureaucratic ones. They heard a flush and some commotion. Then the door opened.

“Fuckin’ city councilors give me a hard time. ‘Oh why do you need an RV?’ I should tell them to try going to work without a bathroom or a table.”

Jay was probably going on twenty-four hours of no sleep with at least half of them being under constant stress.

“You know what ruins this job,” McKenna continued on his rant. “Two words for you, T fuckin’ V.”

Morris and Elijah looked at each other. They seemingly agreed it was either two letters or three words, but neither chose to interrupt.

“Yeah, that’s it. We’re *Backdraft*, every day here,” McKenna continued, putting on his jacket and helmet. “That’s what I want you to put on my tombstone, ‘He did it like *Backdraft*.’”

“Actually, maybe you should say *Chicago Fire*. That’s what all the kids are watching these days,” Morris finally quipped.

McKenna did a double take and broke into a laugh. “OK, I guess I got a little carried away,” he said recapturing his normal demeanor.

“Yeah, I can only imagine how your conversation with Dyani Swan went,” said Elijah.

“About that,” said McKenna. “I have a feeling I’ll be taking some heat for that.” He then squeezed past the two T-cops and stepped down toward the door. Looking back, he said, “But right now, I’m more worried about how we get six boats down a subterranean mudslide without getting anyone killed.”

Upon exiting the command vehicle, McKenna was back in control, working in tandem with Lenehan to coordinate the rescue effort. Boston Fire lent Morris a pair of overalls and fire boots. They weren’t going to keep him completely dry, but they would be a fair attempt.

As dawn broke over the city, more people began to take notice of the activity on the corner of the Common. At least two news crews had set up across the street, and another local station had a helicopter overhead.

Morris stepped down into the Boylston entrance along with a dozen firefighters. The six dive team members were already in the station, assembling the small armada intended to bring back Goldilocks, Clark, Father Michael, and the Lost Boys.

About two-thirds down the stairs, he could see the rafts set up among ripples of floating debris. The closer he got, the more he noticed the carcasses of dead rats, discarded needles, and a range of 21st Century waste.

But what he could see was no match for what he could smell. As much as he had grown accustomed to the range of odors in the subway – significantly influenced by the predominant aromas of urine and brake dust – this scent was something distinct. The floods had stirred up more than 120 years of human and technological refuse, and it was anyone’s guess as to what the long-term ill-effects might be.

While the firefighters were all equipped with their breathing apparatus, they had opted for the particulate masks you find in the hardware store. Not only did it save the air in their tanks, but visibility and hearing could be much better with the disposable respirators.

"Here," Patrick McKenna said handing Morris a couple of the masks. "The stench down here is awful."

Morris grabbed them and put one over his mouth and nose, only to pull it down again to speak. "What have we got for radios down here?"

"We're all on the same channel, but we're trying to stay off them," said Patrick. "Who knows who's listening these days."

"They're not going to be much good once we get into the old tunnels, but at least we can stay in touch with each other," said Morris stepping into the waist-deep water. He could feel cold water seep into his boots, and it sent a shiver through his body.

"Just like wading in at L Street on New Years Day," he joked with Patrick. He then climbed onto the first raft and began to survey his resources. There was a large coil of rope and two banks of portable LED lights up front.

Patrick and another firefighter placed a set of pry bars and paddles into the raft as they climbed in as well. "Here," Morris said handing a paddle to Patrick. "You paddle, I'll navigate."

"I wouldn't have it any other way, sergeant."

Morris laughed. As the LED lights came on, he got a good view of the river upon which they were going to travel. "My God," he said surveying the scene. It almost could have been mistaken for Willie Wonka's chocolate river given its color, but the distinct odor and the range of trash floating on the surface proved the analogy false.

Suddenly, he heard a diver twenty feet away call out. Morris moved the light and could see a body floating face down. He could tell just by looking at the clothes and unkempt hair, it wasn't one of the daily visitors of the subway. No, it was one of the T's more entrenched patrons, possibly one of the regulars who relied on the Boylston platform as shelter.

"That's the third one we've found," Patrick said.

One of the firefighters handed a rope to the diver who then secured the corpse. Patrick then radioed upstairs that another unidentified body had been located.

As unknown in death as they were in life, thought Morris.

As Lenehan had noted, it felt like there was a slight current, but it was impossible to know the specific direction.

Morris got his bearings and began to use a paddle to push forward while a member of the improvised dive team gave additional propulsion.

"If I look at the GPS, we should be heading just about due south," the diver started saying.

"This is a subway," Morris responded. "We've only got two directions, inbound and outbound." Then Morris rethought his statement as he headed past what used be a grate blocking access to the old tunnel, where it broke off ninety degrees from the main line, essentially creating two outbound lines. "Well I guess in true Bostonian fashion, when given two options, we created a third," he corrected himself.

Upon entering the ancient tunnel, there may have been as much as six feet of headspace above the urban swamp they were floating on, but Morris remained nervous. The tunnel travels on a slight decline for about two hundred yards or so meaning, they would have less and less head space going forward. After its low point, under Stuart Street, the tunnel starts traveling upward again moving toward what was known as the Pleasant Street incline because it was right near the junction of Pleasant and Tremont streets that the subway would emerge from its portal. Like the Tremont Street Subway, however, Pleasant Street disappeared from Boston maps, a casualty of urban renewal in the 1960s. The portal had long been sealed with a park built over it.

"I don't like the looks of this," Patrick McKenna whispered, his mask still pulled down, as the head space began to shrink.

"Just duck if you have to!" Morris shouted to the flotilla. "This whole tunnel is only about a quarter-mile long. We'll be alright."

As they proceeded slowly through what felt like a concrete dungeon, Patrick kept swatting aside dead rats.

"You don't like 'em, do you Pat?" Morris observed.

"As long as they're dead, I don't care."

Morris looked up ahead and could see the tunnel widen slightly. "I think we're getting close," he said. "I haven't been down here in years, but there should be an opening up here."

Morris moved the light along the rounded brick and concrete walls. In the claustrophobic surroundings, he was wondering if he had lost his bearings, but then the light made a shadow, indicating a gap in the wall.

He tapped Patrick on the arm, and instantly the firefighter started yelling "Susan!"

"Hold on a second," Morris said, but before he could finish, they heard shouting. Then he turned to the rest of the rafts. "We're here!" he yelled.

A muffled sound continued to come from the other side. It definitely sounded like Sann.

Morris looked at Patrick. "I can't make out a word she's saying," he said to the young firefighter.

With that Patrick, jumped into the water. The mud and debris came up to his chest, and he started trying to communicate with Goldilocks. In addition to needing to warn her of the nearly five feet of muck and water in the tunnel, he also had to figure out how to open the door.

Two other firefighters jumped into the sordid flood waters and joined Patrick at the door with pry bars and a hydraulic wedging device hooked up to a generator on their raft. Meanwhile, the remaining rescuers tried to get closer to get more light on the area. As was emphasized during the briefing, if someone slipped and went under in this the muck, they might never be found.

"Listen, I think this is going to be like one of those ripping off the Band-Aid things," said Morris. "We just gotta do it, and do it quick."

The firefighters nodded, and they gathered around the door, which was secured by a latching device that could be worked from the inside and the outside. Patrick pounded on the steel and then placed his hands under water while shouting "1 – 2 – 3" and putting what weight and strength he could into moving the latch.

From the other side, Morris could hear Goldilocks let go a couple of profanities.

"I could make out the words that time," Morris said.

Patrick returned to the latch and began to lean in the opposite direction this time. With that, the two other firefighters worked the pry bars and tried to insert the wedge mechanism. The force of five feet of water turned the old steel door into a potential guillotine. It would be easy to lose fingers or even a hand with a single mis-step. One of the firefighters shouted to turn on the generator. With it, the eerie silence of the pitch black tunnel was shaken.

As thundering as the generator was, Morris welcomed it as it somehow gave a sense of normalcy to the otherwise ominous environment. However, then he noticed splashes in the water. Initially, a wave of panic struck him, believing the tunnel was collapsing, but it soon became evident that the precipitation wasn't the structure, but rodents, dropping from the roof of the tunnel, and these ones were alive. Apparently, the water hadn't completely filled all the way up the incline and the rats had taken refuge among the pipes lining the top of the tunnel.

Morris swatted away a few as the firefighters continued to work the door. Eventually, enough space opened so that two other firefighters and a diver could enter the room. Morris jumped in to help, and the muck came up almost to his neck. Making his way to the door he started to help the others pushing it open, allowing the flood water to rush in. Turning to his right, he could see the frame of detective Jimmy Clark pressing on the door from the inside. He gave a slight nod, and as he did, he caught a glimpse of blond hair next to the detective.

"Funny meeting you here," Morris tried to shout while putting pressure on the door.

He could see Sann smile, but then her eyes caught Patrick, and she sloshed through oncoming and rising water to throw her arms around him. With that, the firefighter let go, and for a moment, Morris and Clark were the primary ones holding open the door.

"Hey, a little help here," Morris grunted.

Patrick and Goldilocks then helped regain control of the door. The remaining members of the rescue group quickly entered the small room to protect the inhabitants from being overwhelmed by the incoming water. Steadily, as the room filled with about five feet of water, pressure equalized and those inside the room climbed up on rotted bunk beds and shelving that at one time housed food and water meant to outlast a nuclear winter.

"How's Father Michael?" Morris asked Goldilocks, but she just shook her head with tears in her eyes.

First into the rafts went the group of young Somali teens known as the Lost Boys. They had come to Boston a few years ago, seeking a chance in the supposed land of opportunity, but they were cornered by a combination of circumstances and criminals.

Given few other options for survival in one of the most expensive cities in the world, they turned to being pickpockets and prostitutes. In the equations being run somewhere above ground, no doubt some well-suited advisor, attorney or politician was pointing out the incongruity of the risk taken to save such seemingly worthless creatures, but as Morris looked at the lifeless body of Father Michael, now being carried out of the shelter, he felt a hint of some grander balance.

He even felt an envy for people like the old priest and Sann. Their judgment of someone's worth wasn't clouded by the trees of what someone had done or failed to do. No, they saw the forest of humanity. Maybe that's how come the seemingly worthless were in fact so special to them. Those who had either stumbled or had been pushed to the bottom of society's ladder stood without any accouterment of wealth or power. Even in this muck, filled with the debris of society, these homeless had an ironic purity. They were humanity without any decoration, and for a moment, Morris' mind drifted to thoughts of his late cousin. Too often, he couldn't even pick up a phone to say hello, and here was Father Mike, who gave his life to save a group of criminals he barely knew.

"Rebar."

Morris turned, shaken from this thoughts, to see Goldilocks staring at him from the raft.

"We got separated. He ended up down at the incline, and we were deep in the other tunnel, right where it goes under the station. We heard him call-out. He must have just run into rebar, and tripped and fell or something," explained Sann. "It actually probably saved our lives. Otherwise, we would have been in the lowest part of the tunnel when the water hit."

He nodded as one of the Lost Boys was shouting something that sounded like "nee boo."

Goldilocks shook her head. "He's been saying that all night. I think he is just losing his mind. It's been pretty damn claustrophobic," she said.

Morris' mind focused. They still needed to get out of this muddy hell, and it would be only a matter of time until other delusions and panic set in.

As the rescued climbed inside the rafts, they were given foil blankets to help control their hypothermia. Patrick McKenna climbed into the raft where Goldilocks was now curled up, trying to get warm. As he reached an arm down to pull Morris up from the water, he paused.

"Did you hear that?"

Morris shook his head, but then he heard it, too. It sounded like a muffled moan, and it was coming from farther down the tunnel. He nodded to Patrick, who pulled him onto the raft while shining the light toward the Pleasant Street incline. They heard the moan again and, with the help of the diver, moved their boat toward the far end of the tunnel while the other five boats started heading in the opposite direction, back to the Boylston Station.

As they continued along the incline, they heard the voice again. Morris finally was able to figure its origin. He spun and looked up just as the body of a middle-aged portly white male fell, knocking Morris into the cesspool with him.

Under the water, Morris struggled to keep his eyes and mouth closed. He could feel an arm around his neck, almost pulling him down. He felt completely disoriented. He couldn't tell which direction was up. Just as panic was about to set in, he felt the bottom of the tunnel and was able to get his feet under him. From there, he stood himself up. The murky water came up to his chest, but he was able to shout, "Here, over here!" He could see the lights of the raft fifteen feet away and was shocked that in the brief moment, he had traveled so far.

The man who had dive-bombed Morris from the ceiling of the tunnel had already been pulled into the raft by the time the diver guided the vessel toward Morris and helped him get back in. Rolling over, Morris spotted the greased pig of a man that had fallen on him.

“Thank you. Oh God bless you. Thank you,” the man was saying emphatically. Even though his graying comb-over was out of place, and thick white mustache was shivering, Morris recognized the man as Charles Shanley, the former priest turned power broker and lobbyist.

“What were you doing down here, Charlie,” Morris asked, already resolving not to trust the man’s answer.

“Oh, I was concerned about some of the homeless,” mumbled the former priest. “Thank the Lord you came by.”

Exhausted, few words were spoken by anyone in the raft as they caught up to the others and continued on their creepy journey through the ancient flooded tunnel. As they neared the station platform that they had left only a half hour earlier, Morris could see a crew of Boston EMS waiting on the stairs, just above the water line.

As the flotilla neared, Morris could see Jay McKenna and Robbie Lenehan run down, stepping into the murky water.

“Thank God,” Lenehan said as he counted all the rescuers. His fellow deputy chief elbowed him and pointed toward the lifeless body of Father Michael McGovern, and his expression grew more disconsolate.

Behind the gathering on the stairs, Morris recognized a familiar pair of black army boots. The trademark black jean jacket only confirmed the identity, which quickly drew the attention of the emergency personnel on the stairs, who moved to get rid of the intruder.

“No, no guys. He’s good!” Morris shouted as he noticed other members of the Archangels and homeless gathering behind Ferret. “They’re all good!” Morris shouted.

Father Michael had served in many capacities, including being fire department chaplain, but in this mournful circumstance, Morris grasped that Father Michael would most appreciate the homeless of the city acting as his impromptu pallbearers.

Sann jumped out of the raft and waded to the stairs as Ferret, Tin Man, and Ginger joined a group of firefighters taking hold of the priest’s body.

"Hold on," she said, making a sign of the cross. Then she nodded to the group, who then reverently lifted the priest and relayed his body up the stairs to others who had gathered.

As Father Michael rose from the depths of the station, Sann stood next to Ferret whispering a prayer. Noticing the look on his face, she asked, "Aren't you a believer?"

"I believed in Father Mike," he said somberly. "I'll call Jesus when I need a carpenter."

As most of those in the station were focused on the dead priest, a live one, or former one to be exact, scurried up the stairs. Morris grimaced as he didn't get a chance to get a straight answer out of Shanley, but then he noticed Ginger had spotted the man as well.

Outside the station entrance, a throng of emergency response workers, media and gawkers had gathered. The sunlight shined directly into Morris' eyes, causing a painful throbbing in his head. For a moment he wondered if he might prefer the darkness of the tunnel.

He skipped the opportunity to be examined by Boston EMS, deciding, instead, to see if he could still find some coffee at the command tent, where he bumped into fellow T-cop, Elvis Norton.

"What's good today, Elvis?"

"You tell me, sergeant."

"I'm afraid I'm not the one to be asking this morning. Bad is all I'm seeing."

"Hey Fitzgerald," Deputy Chief Lenehan said as he walked into the tent. "Come on, you need to get checked out. EMS is waiting to give you a ride down to the hospital."

"I don't need a doctor to tell me that I stink and need sleep. Why don't you just tell Elvis here that you don't need him. He can give me a ride home, and I can get a hot shower and be in bed before the nightmares start."

Lenehan looked at Morris and sniffed. "Jesus Christ, you do stink." Then he turned to Norton. "Alright get him out of here. He earned his rest."

Chapter 21

Morris tried to climb into the passenger seat of officer Norton's cruiser, but the mobile computer and the T-cop's gear bag took up all the space.

"Geez Elvis, are you going to make me ride in back?"

"Honest sarge," he replied. "You kinda stink like rotten cheese. Would you mind?"

Morris wasn't in the mood to debate. He climbed in back and laid down across the seat. "Elvis, my head is throbbing, I smell, and I'm having trouble remembering all the words to the Our Father."

"Looking for some divine intervention," Norton said as he put the cruiser in drive.

"No, just praying for the repose of Boston's last good soul."

With that, Morris closed his eyes, and the frost heaves and potholes that lined the city's streets rocked him to sleep.

As his subconscious took control, the events of the past week replayed in his mind. It was only then that he started doing a body count. He had started with his late wife's grave, and then came the deaths of his cousin, Bob Sosa, Cliff Cashman, and now Father Michael. He almost forgot about Beetlejuice and Kenny the Clown. Then again, didn't everyone else forget about them? That was the fate of the homeless.

Morris told his mind to be quiet. He just wanted sleep.

In what seemed to be a moment later, Morris could feel Elvis Norton shaking him. While at first, he resisted the notion of sitting up – the rear seat felt too comfortable – he realized his own bed might offer him a more restful sleep. He rolled himself into an upright position and then grabbed the door jamb to pull himself out the rear of the cruiser.

"Thanks, Elvis," Morris said, stretching his back.

"No worries. Anything else you need?"

"Nothing that a little self-delusion won't address," quipped Morris.

"Sarge, I don't know what the hell is going on, but if you want some advice, be guided by the words of the King: 'Truth is like the sun. You can shut it out for a time, but it ain't going away.'"

Morris smiled, and Elvis then climbed back in the driver's seat. "Thanks again, buddy," he said into Norton's open window. "And tell everyone that's been talking shit about me that they can all go to hell."

"Oh sarge, no one talks shit about you – as far as you know," Elvis said as he pulled into the street and drove away.

Morris started to climb the stairs of his triple-decker, but his neighbor poked his head out the door.

"Oh, hello, sergeant!"

"Hello, Fillmore," Morris yelled over.

"The weather seems to have improved," the neighbor responded cheerfully.

"It's November in Boston, Fillmore. The weather is supposed to suck. As a matter of fact, it will suck for another six months. Then sometime in May, we'll have a week and a half of good weather. Then after that, we'll complain it's too hot. You see, that's what Bostonians do."

With that, Morris opened his door and stepped inside and pondered a simple question. "Shower or bed?" he asked quietly of himself. His mind began to process the question in a way so logical that it affirmed his sleep deprivation. As awful as he smelled, Morris concluded that to step into the shower without having rested would risk a slip and fall. He could knock himself out or break his neck. The idea of a debilitating injury or even death didn't frighten him as much as being found naked.

"Sleep," he said aloud as he pulled himself up the next flight of stairs to his bedroom, where he kicked off the firefighter boots, undid the Grundens overalls, and then removed the borrowed sweatpants and sweatshirt that were now soaked through.

At some point during his sleep, he heard loud knocking on his front door. He ignored it, assuming that after a minute or two, whoever it might be would leave. However the pounding at his door continued, except for now, it was accompanied by yelling. After a moment, he thought he placed the voice. He sprang up, grabbed a bathrobe, and hobbled down the stairs.

As he did so, he noted the time on his mantle clock. It was just getting to noon. Peeking out the front window, he nodded to himself as he saw the person still knocking on the door.

"Nevertheless, she persisted," Morris said as he opened the door to greet Boston Homicide Sergeant Joanne Manning.

"What?" she said.

"Never mind, Joanne. What's up?"

"I'll tell you what's up. I get into work today, and I get a call from some damn reporter asking me to confirm that Bob Sosa was killed by some subway vandals who were responsible for breaking the Grimley locks."

"Gridley," said Morris.

"Whatever!" said Manning as she stepped into the entry way.

"Please, why don't you come in," Morris said sarcastically, turning to talk to the sergeant already in his living room.

"What's that?"

Morris noticed Manning was looking at his bathrobe, which read "Marriot Courtyard."

"Free hand-out during National Police Week in Washington," Morris quipped.

"Yeah, right."

"It was a verbal understanding."

"Please," chided Manning. "I'm familiar with how you T-cops conduct yourselves during police week, trashing hotels, bathing in fountains, being too drunk to make it to the candlelight vigil."

"A few rotten apples," replied Morris.

"More like a rotten orchard, and speaking of rotten, what smells in here?"

"Funny, my wife used to tell me my best attribute was that my feet didn't stink."

Manning rolled her eyes, and Morris gave her the same expression back. "Come on Joanne, I've had a shit night. What do you want?"

"I don't want anything from you," said Manning. "I can't figure you out. You're either the most incompetent T-cop there is – and that's saying a lot – or everyone else involved in this case is getting it wrong."

Morris was exhausted, and truthfully, he wasn't sure what he had right and what he had wrong about Bob Sosa's death and the river flooding.

"Come on, grab a coat," Manning continued. "Dr. Crowley is about to do the autopsy on your priest friend."

"I don't know Joanne. I prefer to remember Father Mike as six foot two with an imposing frame and an Irish-rebel smile – not lying on some morgue gurney, getting sliced open with a steel saw."

"Splash some water on your face and get dressed," said Manning. "And if I were you, I wouldn't check your Twitter feed."

"I don't Tweet," said Morris.

"I knew you weren't a complete idiot," she said.

After a little more imploring, Morris realized that, if nothing else, he should be there for Father Michael. He ran upstairs. Washed his face, threw on an extra coating of deodorant, dressed and went down the stairs.

Manning took a quick look at him in the hallway. "Do you own a washing machine?"

"What?" Morris said, looking over himself, only to notice he was wearing the same sweatshirt he had worn two days earlier when he met the sergeant for hot dogs at Castle Island. He brushed the mustard stain, but it seemed fairly permanent at this stage. Scanning the hallway, an idea struck him.

Stepping past Manning, he reached up and grabbed Elijah's sportcoat that he had borrowed earlier in the week. "There," he said. "Do you feel like you can be seen with me now?"

Manning just shook her head as she opened the door, and the pair went to her cruiser that was double parked on G Street.

On the ride over to the Chief Medical Examiner's Office, Morris tried to grab a nap. Leaning against the passenger window, he felt something shift in his left pocket. He reached in and touched the key to the prototype train. At some point next week, he needed to return to the train and process all the stolen items. At least, a lot of commuters were about to have their stolen property returned to them.

Invariably, during the drive, the Twitter topic returned. Morris' curiosity got the best of him.

"So just what is it that I am not supposed to see?"

Manning groaned as her eyes darted at the city traffic. "The Lieutenant Governor basically wants to canonize your Dyani Swan."

"What?"

"She's getting credit for the rescue, and rumor is Jay McKenna's head is on the chopping block for giving her shit."

Manning then pulled out her phone and started tapping while she also offered a few choice words for a driver in front of her.

"You know distracted driving is dangerous driving," chided Morris.

"Yeah, well I could have my head in a paper bag and still drive better than this asshole," she said as she handed the phone to Morris.

Morris scrolled through the Tweets. One featured a headshot of Swan. The next one showed her helping Charles Shanley up the stairs at Boylston.

"Shit, I didn't even see her there," said Morris.

"Of course not," said Manning. "Look at where the sun is in that picture. That was like an hour after the actual rescue."

Morris' anger momentarily gave way to a twisted admiration. "She's shrewd if nothing else," he said.

"She's got juice," added Manning. "A lot more than I do. That's for sure."

Yes, Swan seemed to have connections, but more important, she had the guts to use them. She and BoBo Powers were cut from the same cloth.

After a few more minutes, Manning pulled her cruiser up to the the medical examiner's building and walked inside with Morris. They eventually made their way down the hallway where both had stood two nights earlier, trying to calm Tom Cashman, and turned left into the primary exam room.

There was Dr. Crowley, already in the middle of the initial examination of the Father Michael's body.

As disturbing as it was to see the priest's body on the table, to Morris, it only vaguely resembled the man. He had seen enough corpses over the years to realize they were, at best, echoes of the living. It was proof to him that God made people to live. Of course, that also raised the great paradox of why did God insist on taking away life, too.

"Upon initial examination," Crowley said, without offering any greeting to the officers, "it seems that he was struck by a piece of rebar in the left chest. This, in turn, led to two broken ribs, one of which punctured his lung, causing internal bleeding," Crowley summarized.

"He drowned in his own blood," said Manning shaking her head. "That water must have come into the tunnel with such force that it threw everything up ahead."

"No," said Morris. "It was before the tunnel flooded. He just ran into it. It's pitch black in there."

Crowley nodded. "But he must have fallen with some force and on multiple pieces of rebar, as there are multiple areas of injury." She then lifted the priest's left arm. "You can see here, at the base of the palm, clear indentations matching rebar."

"So he fell, and used his hand to brace himself," said Manning.

"No," interrupted Morris. "The way that mark is, he had his hand balled into a fist in front of him, like any good boxer."

"What are you saying?" asked Manning.

"What if someone swung the rebar at him?" he suggested.

"How about you wrap up one homicide investigation before you open another?" she chided.

Morris was exhausted. Maybe his mind was playing tricks on him. "Did you talk to any of the Somalis?" he asked, referring to the Lost Boys.

"Not really," said Manning. "Most of them can't speak English, and one of them just keeps saying 'need Booran' or something like that."

"Oh 'nin buuran,'" offered Crowley. "Fat man."

The two cops stared at the medical examiner.

"I was in Somalia with Doctors Without Borders, and one of my associates was rather rotund," she explained.

"Well what the hell does that mean?" asked the Boston homicide sergeant.

A distinct person came into Morris' mind, but he didn't want to say. Charles Shanley certainly met the description of "fat man." Moreover, there had been plenty of rumors over the years that the man had quite a sexual appetite. Only Congress rivaled him in terms of sexual harassment settlements.

Crowley then brought out the saw, preparing to open the priest.

"OK, that's the cue for this T-cop to leave," Morris said.

He offered his goodbyes to the medical examiner and Manning and walked out the exam room, through the hallway, and up the stairs of the building. The sky had cleared, and he could feel a fall crispness in the air as the shadows began to grow with the afternoon sun.

Morris decided to walk the six blocks to the Orange Line's Massachusetts Ave. Station. From there, he'd pick up the Red Line at Downtown Crossing and ride the T outbound to Andrew Square, leaving him about a quarter-mile walk to the transit police headquarters.

The ride gave him the opportunity to dwell on the events of the past twenty-four hours. The flooding and destruction had a deliberate nature to them. Maybe that's what Bob Sosa and Cliff Cashman had sensed, or perhaps it was all just bureaucratic incompetence. Maybe it was some sort of undetected accidental damage combined with untrained and unsupervised DCR employees?

It wouldn't be the first time the fate of the city hinged on the superficial. Anyone familiar with the backstory of the executive leadership of MassPort, the state agency in charge of Logan Airport, would agree. While Logan was thrust into the global spotlight when a bunch of terrorists slipped past security and hijacked two planes from there on September 11, 2001, it was two years earlier that the airport and a bare-breasted passenger on a booze cruise saw plenty of local attention.

The passenger was a guest on a junket hosted by the then executive director, a former Congressman. During the six-hour tour of Boston Harbor, someone tipped off the local newspaper, which sent a photographer to the dock. For some inexplicable reason, as the boat pulled in, the young lady decided to lift her tank top. Coincidences of coincidences, the passenger, who happened to have been a Hollywood stunt woman, decided to leave her bra at home that morning, too.

The director resigned the next day in disgrace and was replaced by someone whose qualifications to head an international airport were grounded in her work as a political campaign manager and press secretary.

Over the years, there had been plenty to suggest the incident was a setup, but that was Boston; incompetence and patronage were givens in politics, but a scandal, even a PG-13-rated one, would get you bounced in a hurry. It's not that MassPort, like the MBTA, hadn't always been a dumping ground of political favoritism, but as liberal-leaning as Boston may be, it still had its Puritan roots. Nipples were a no-no.

As Morris transferred to the Red Line at Downtown Crossing, he was surprised it wasn't more chaotic. The T operations had brought in a fleet of buses to compensate for the Green Line being shut down from Boylston to Kenmore. Still, there was no making up for losing a key artery of the system.

However, it was a Friday. It appeared as though commuter traffic seized whatever excuse they could to work from home, as was the custom with these millennials. Having spent thirty years in a profession where he and most others tried desperately to leave their work at the office – even if that office covered an entire legal jurisdiction – Morris wanted to warn these progeny of yuppies of the hazard of inviting professional stress into their domicile. But these Tweeters and texters were a different breed. They had been raised to think multi-tasking was not only possible but a necessary attribute.

Morris had long ago realized that no matter how mentally agile you think you are, the brain really only does one thing at a time. For anyone who doubts that, they should step into a ring sometime and see how well they do absent a full focus on their combatant.

As the Red Line made its way toward Andrew Square, he tried to heed his own advice and not let his mind wander through too many events of the past week – his cousin's death, Bob Sosa's possible murder, the flooding of the city. Manning was right. He needed to address one thing at a time.

As the automated voice announcing the Andrew Square stop floated above the sounds of the subway car, Morris got up from his seat and moved to a gap among the commuters crowding near the doors. For a moment he felt the presence of Father Michael as the words of the Prayer of St. Francis came to him:

Lord, grant me the courage to change the things I can,
The patience to accept the things I cannot,
And the wisdom to know the difference.

And then he stepped in a pool of vomit with his right foot. At least it was mostly dried at this point. He looked left and saw a woman with a scarf pulled up around her nose spin away. To his right was a young man laughing quietly, holding his cellphone, making a video of Morris' foot hitting the regurgitation. The best-educated generation America had ever seen – thank goodness D-Day happened in 1944. Today, they all would have hit the beach and posed for a selfie.

"Patience," Morris said quietly as he came up out of the subway and turned right onto Southampton Street.

Mentally, he deliberately moved Cathy to the rear of his mind. That was personal, but even in doing so, he felt the guilt of abandoning family.

Who, if anyone, had something to gain by flooding the city?

He walked into 240 Southampton Street and immediately recognized a malignant energy in the building. Morris spotted Officer Shannon Frost, a T-cop he helped train nearly two years earlier.

"Frosty, what's going on?" he asked.

"You didn't hear? The Lieutenant Governor is asking the legislature to merge us with the State Police."

Morris laughed a bit. He heard it all before. Every now and then someone gets an idea about the efficiency of merging the transit police with someone else. The reality always proved that no one else wanted the job, and the proposal never went anywhere. Still, it didn't take away from the anxiety.

"Did you hear about Goldi?" Frost added.

"What?"

"She handed in her papers. She's quitting," she said. "She's upstairs right now, clearing stuff off her desk."

With that, Morris broke into a run and immediately remembered how tired and ailing he was. Pulling himself up the stairs, leaning heavily on the railing, he could feel pain in each knee and decided to pace himself slightly.

Upon reaching the second floor, he scanned right and could see three officers gathered around a desk, but in between them, he caught sight of a worn Red Sox hat with a blond ponytail coming out the back. Understandably, Goldilocks was having a bad hair day.

"Hey," Morris said, approaching her desk. "What's this I hear about you quitting?"

Sann turned toward him and broke into a smile although it had been clear there had been some tears at some point.

"I'm done," she said simply. "I can't do this anymore."

"I know some days this job sucks, but you can't give up," he said.

"I'm not giving up," she responded. "But I just can't keep banging my head against a wall. I'm not you."

Morris was unsure what to say. "Did you tell Swani?"

"I told her two weeks," said Goldilocks. "She said, 'Fine, why not make it today?'" She smiled, but her eyes showed the pain. The one thing that kept any decent cop coming back day after day was the sense that you mattered. Swan obviously didn't understand that. Likely because she wasn't really a cop. She was just a bureaucrat with a badge.

"Tell her 'No,' and stay until at least Steph gets back from Israel," said Morris.

"That's not going to change anything, and let's face it, do you think Stephanie Tam is going to have her job long?"

The words hit him. Not that it hadn't been on his mind. He stepped back and sat down as Goldilocks turned around and picked up a box on her desk.

"Morris, I'll call you," she said. "We'll have drinks, but right now I just need to get out of here."

He nodded, understanding that Sann was resolved in her decision but still feeling a sense of shock.

Morris sat staring at the floor a few minutes. Maybe he should finally put in his papers, too. BoBo Powers had offered him a job, but he couldn't see himself working for the hustler. He couldn't trust him. Plus given their last exchange, Morris was sure Powers understood that their old friendship had soured.

"Jesus, what stinks in here?"

Morris lifted his head and saw Bruce Donohue looking at him. "Smells like someone puked," Bruce added.

Morris moved his right foot backward slightly. "It's been a long day," he said.

"Been a long week, am I right?" responded Bruce.

Morris smiled and nodded in agreement.

"Good thing you're here," Bruce said opening up a folder in his hand and removing a piece of paper. "Here's that report on your cousin, the one about the flowers and stuff."

Morris held out his hand and took the paper. "Thanks," he said.

For the next few minutes, his mind focused on his future as a T-cop. He had weathered several different regimes, but he wasn't sure he could handle Dyani Swan on a full-time basis. With Susan Sann gone, who was going to stand up for the homeless in the city? Then again, with the flood and Swan's goon squad, were there any homeless left in the subway?

He exhaled and decided to distract himself with his cousin. He had long wanted to plant something at his family plot and figured whatever pleased Cathy was as good a place as any to start.

He lifted the paper and started reading it. He had seen these reports enough to understand their format and language. It was a bit like reading the box score for a baseball game. There was an antiseptic nature to such a thing. As much as they were accurate accounts, they did not fully capture the drama and occasional brutality of what transpired.

The technical cause of death was stated as "opioid toxicity," perhaps a bit kinder than the more plain "heroin overdose." There was a noted degree of "adulterants," an awkward term for any number of impurities or additional substances that are found in street-grade drugs. The one thing the report couldn't summarize was the degree to which it may have all been accidental. Morris wondered whether Cathy intentionally overdosed. He wasn't sure which option gave him more comfort – that his cousin erred in injecting a drug she was addicted to or that somewhere in her desperate life, she had reasoned a way to escape it.

He kept reading, but eventually paused on one line. He re-read it twice. An anger swelled in him, but it gave way to a form of reason.

He looked at his watch and realized he may still have time to pay a visit to his old South Boston friend. Morris walked down the stairs and checked out a transit police cruiser.

It was a short drive over to the South Station area. Morris double parked in front of SideCar Lounge adjacent to the train terminal. He walked into the lounge and spotted someone who looked like a manager. He moved toward him, but before he could pose a query to the man, he heard a loud, unmistakable laugh.

He turned and saw BoBo Powers leaning with his elbows up against the bar. Next to him, facing the bar, was the buxom MBTA director of security who had been acting as chief for the past week.

Morris walked up to the bar and observed how Powers' expression shifted when he saw him.

"Funny meeting you two here," Morris said.

Powers grunted, "What the fuck are you doing here?"

Swan spun around and saw Morris and then turned toward the parking king next to her.

"You invited me, remember, BoBo?" Morris said.

"Yeah, I remember," he said as a large man moved next to Powers.

"I'm just wondering if that job is still open," said the T-cop.

Powers was straight-faced for several seconds, and his entourage reflected his seriousness. Then Morris' old Southie friend broke into a wide smile. "Look who's become a capitalist!" With that, Swan, the large man, and others gathered broke into laughter. "Here," Powers said, reaching an arm out to Morris, motioning for him to come closer, "meet James Jordan. I call him 'Shaft.'"

Morris stuck out his hand, and it was enveloped by a large hand.

"Jimmy here used to be the police chief in Oak Bluffs on the Vineyard," Powers said.

Morris nodded, recalling Dr. Poole's tale of being kneecapped in high school.

"Robert, I didn't know you were hiring broken drunks," Swan interjected into the greetings.

"Dee, come on," said BoBo. "Morris has skills. He was tight with Sonny Barrett, and rumor's been he's got dirt on the former governor."

"Who told you that?" asked Swan.

"The former governor," laughed Powers.

Morris shook his head at the joke. "So where's the Squid?"

BoBo rolled his eyes. "Jesus, you and your Irish Alzheimer's. You really want to bury JJ, don't you?"

"I just realized that the place didn't smell like shit, so obviously he had to be missing."

"He's not here," said Jordan plainly.

"Yeah, but he's supposed to be here," Powers said, sounding a bit perturbed.

For the next forty-five minutes, Morris eased himself into BoBo's cabal. Jordan appeared every bit the asshole of his reputation. What he lacked in personality he compensated for in abrasiveness.

"You were a Boston cop before you went to the Vineyard, right?" Morris asked, trying to make small talk.

Jordan had an empty look on his face. "Yeah," he said, grabbing his beer off the bar and turning his back, but in the motion Morris spotted the answer to a riddle. The hot solder that had scarred Jordan's hand, apparently had hit the old cop in a fairly symmetric way. Some might say the pattern formed an "H" on Jordan's hand, but perhaps to a recently deceased homeless meth addict, the scar left by the drops of molten metal looked like something else.

"The nine of spades," Morris said quietly, breaking into a smile.

As opposed to Jordan, Dyani Swan, seemed to soften with conversation, or more likely, alcohol. Morris had seen this over the years. Everyone dealt with the stress of policing differently, and for Swan, it seemed as though her response was to create this hard exterior that, once cracked, revealed a gooey interior.

"You know, I'm not really the bitch everyone thinks I am," she slurred to Morris. "I just have a job to do, and no one else wants to do it. That's what it is. Someone has to clean up these fuckin' homeless."

"I don't know," Morris said. "I mean it's not like they ever did something to you."

"Oh really?" she shot back. "You know people see me, and they see this professional." Morris fought the urge to object, pointing out that most people see something very different. "But I will let you know a secret," she continued with glassy eyes. "I started as trailer trash. My mom was dirt poor, and she used to hang around with other homeless trash. It made me sick."

Morris nodded his head. He wasn't feeling sympathy, but it was more an understanding as to the acting chief's motivations.

"Yeah, think about what it was like to be a 13-year-old girl whose mom kept having these despicable men over, how they leered at me, oh and when they touched me ...." she said with a fire in her eyes. "Anyway, they're scum. All of them."

"Hey, look at you two," Powers burst in, putting a hand on each of their shoulders and pulling them into a group hug. "Good to see you getting along." Morris looked at Swan and both seemed to have reached the same conclusion: This was a forced amiability.

"Anyway Dee, we should get going soon," Powers said, turning toward Morris. "We're flying out to Vegas tonight."

"Geez, BoBo what does Debbie think about that?" Morris said, referencing the parking king's wife.

He laughed. "She thinks it's a convention."

Swan laughed along, "Maybe we'll join the mile-high club on the way out."

Morris smiled. "Mile high? You ever try the mile-long club?"

"Mile-long?" Swan said, rubbing up against Powers. "What's that?"

"Oh come on," he said, "and you call yourself a transit professional. It's never occurred to you that a subway car, with the overhead bars, poles, seatbacks, wouldn't make a great sexual jungle gym?"

"I like where you're going with this, Morris," Powers said, giving Swan a squeeze toward him.

"Oh cut it out, Robert," she responded playfully.

"I gotta go take a piss anyway," Powers said leaving the bar area.

Swan looked disappointed but then moved toward Morris. "What's your game here?" she said with a smile. "I don't trust you."

He laughed along. "Oh come on, you know how things are in this town, you have to pick the right wagon to hitch yourself to."

"Robert Powers is a pretty good wagon to choose," she said.

"Yes, he is," answered Morris as he fished around in his sportcoat pocket. "You're seriously thinking about the mile-long club, aren't you?"

Swan laughed, her head tilting uncontrollably. "You forget, I know where the cameras are."

"I've got a solution to that," Morris said, taking the key out of his pocket. "The GM's prototype train, right in front of South Station. No one will ever see you. Here, you go out there, and I'll bring BoBo when he comes back."

She laughed. "Oh, and will you be joining us, sergeant?"

"Well, that's quite an offer. I say we let BoBo decide that."

She giggled. "You're serious."

"Only if you are."

Swan laughed, as if to say it was a ridiculous idea, but then she swiped the key off the bar, saying, "See you soon."

Morris then pulled out his phone and began to send a text.

"Where did Dee go?" Powers said as he returned to the bar.

"She's waiting for you in the subway car out in front of South Station."

"What the fuck is she doing that for?" said Powers.

"BoBo, you're not too smart sometimes. She wants to join the mile-long club."

"More like the foot-long club," he responded elbowing Morris. "Seriously, she does this thing with her –"

"I don't want to know BoBo," Morris cut him off. "Come on, from what I understand, it don't take you long. You go do what you have to, and we can talk later about the job."

With that BoBo nodded to the bartender and threw several hundred-dollar bills down. The two old friends walked out the bar and toward the South Station train terminal.

"Listen, BoBo, I have to ask you one thing," Morris said as the two approached the prototype car. "Do you have any idea what happened to my cousin Cathy? It's eating me up that she'd just OD like that."

"You know buddy, these things are hard to figure out. You look for a reason, and there just isn't one. I know she's family and all, but you have to let it go."

Morris reached the door and started to push them apart. "Thanks, BoBo, thanks for having my back."

"No worries," said the jocular parking king, stepping into the car. "You ought to come in here, too. We could tag team."

Morris laughed. "Call me old-fashioned, but I consider three a crowd."

BoBo said something, but Morris was already closing the door. Soon after, he was walking back toward the bus terminal while leaving Powers and Swan inside the subway car to have their fun.

As he strolled down the sidewalk, he saw the van come by with the familiar logo. He could hear it stop, and the crew of people get out. He smiled, knowing that at this point the fate of Powers and Swan were sealed. Somewhere inside him was an anger, but whether due to his exhaustion or some subliminal wisdom, he didn't give into it. Instead, he heeded the counsel of Boston's most beloved mayor, James Michael Curley. He didn't get mad. He got even.

Out of the corner of his eye, he could see the bright light of a news camera reflect off a building to his right, no doubt the consequence of a station following up on an anonymous tip about the parking king of Boston and a high-ranking T official having sex on MBTA property.

As he kept walking, Morris wondered if anyone noticed Dr. Crowley's report that he had left on someone's desk at MBTA police headquarters. The FBI's Forensic Automotive Carpet Identification Database is a fascinating investigative tool, especially in the hands of thorough professional such as Dr. Katherine Crowley.

As she identified three separate wildflower varieties on the pants leg of Cathy Fitzgerald, she also managed to detect maroon fibers matching a FACID entry only found as an option in late-model Cadillac Escalades.

Chapter 22

Morris was having such a good sleep that he actually became aware of it. Of course, given that his conscious and subconscious states were now cognizant of each other, it raised the question as to what had disturbed his restful slumber. Suddenly, he heard the pounding at his door.

He took a deep breath and rose slowly out of his bed, noticing his blood-stained pillow. It was then that the pain of his broken nose fully brought him back to reality. As he ventured downstairs, he could feel the crackled and dried blood along his nostrils.

The thumping at the door hadn't subsided, not that he suspected it would. As he entered he hallway, the sound was interrupted by "Open up the fuckin' door, Boston Police!" confirming an assumption he had formed moments earlier when he first registered this morning's disturbance.

Without getting the door even fully opened, Sergeant Joanne Manning stormed in with a detective in tow. Both had their guns drawn.

"Where are your weapons secured?" barked the detective.

Morris shot her a look. "My weapons are all in my locker at the police station, except for my Sig Sauer 229, which is next to my pillow upstairs."

The detective ran upstairs, while Manning holstered her gun. She didn't say a word as she looked at Morris. Clearly, she was angry, but Morris had grown accustomed to that expression as he seemed to elicit it quite a bit. There was something else in her face, shock mostly, but maybe a hint of admiration. Disappointment would be soon to follow, thought Morris.

He turned to walk into his kitchen.

"Where the fuck do you think you're going?" said Manning.

"My kitchen, to get a towel. In case you hadn't noticed, I've got a bloody nose."

Morris walked while hearing the footsteps coming down the stairs. He grabbed a towel and sat in one of his kitchen chairs while leaning his head back, trying to stop the blood flowing from his nose.

He spotted the detective and Manning coming into the room. "While the two of you are here, do you mind getting a mop and cleaning up the mess you're making on my linoleum?"

"Shut up funny man," snarled the detective.

Morris shot a look toward Manning, who responded, "Detective Martha Hamilton, meet Morris Fitzgerald, the T-cop whose shitheadedry knows no bounds."

However, Manning's introduction didn't seem to tame Hamilton. "What happened to your nose Fitz? Somebody slam a bedroom window on it."

"Nope, your girlfriend got excited, and crossed her legs a little too quick," Morris snapped back.

Hamilton moved toward him, but Manning held up an arm to block her. "I told you he had the charm of a centipede crawling around the inside of a toilet," she said.

Hamilton was about to say something, but Morris' patience had worn. "Can you tell me what's so important that you had to bust into my house this morning and ruin the first decent sleep I had in a week?"

Manning started to laugh, but then she eyed Morris more closely. She shook her head. "Maybe you are as stupid as you look."

Morris pondered an objection, but Manning continued. "They found John Joseph McHugh floating in the harbor this morning, just at the end of G Street here, but I suppose you don't know anything about that, do you?"

"Jesus, a piece of shit like him? He could set the Boston Harbor clean-up back thirty years."

"Come on, Fitz," said Hamilton. "You know how this goes. What was it? Self-defense?"

"Serious," Morris said. "I'll waive my Miranda Rights right here and tell you I wanted that fucker dead."

"Well, you got your wish," said Manning. "Seems like someone worked him over pretty good with a bat first, broke his arms, his legs, his jaw. Best we can tell, it seems like whoever did this, basically beat him to the point of incapacitation and then left him on the shore to be drowned by the tide."

"Yeah," said Hamilton, "it looks real fuckin' personal."

"Hah, go figure, a Squid can't swim," Morris said laughing, hoping his expression didn't reveal his recollection that the last he had seen William he was holding one of the Squid's Louisville Sluggers.

Manning then went over to the sink and wet a towel. She handed it to Morris, saying, "Wipe your face. We're going to secure the rest of your place as a potential crime scene."

"More like a hazmat scene," added Hamilton.

"Go ahead," said Morris. "But you're wasting your time." He paused for a moment, cleaning some blood from around his nose. "There isn't a single person I know that didn't want the Squid dead for some reason."

"OK, where were you last night?" Manning asked calmly.

"I went over to the SideCar to meet up with my old friend BoBo Powers," Morris answered. "Plenty of people there, and I'm sure they've got video."

Manning and Hamilton looked at each other and laughed a little. "Oh, there's video all right," said Hamilton.

"Whatever do you mean?" Morris said with just a hint of sarcasm.

Manning gave him a long look, shifted expression, and then pointed at his nose. "How did you get that?"

"Well, as I left the SideCar, I started walking down Atlantic Ave., but I saw all this commotion, so I turned around," Morris said. "You can imagine my shock when I saw a news crew and several onlookers gawking at this naked couple engaged in some love-making in that subway car they put out in front of South Station."

"Right," said Manning, doubting Morris' sincerity.

"Yes, fortunately, someone must have alerted the MBTA because K-9 officer Nancy Steiger was already on scene with her German Shepherd, Kaiser. She managed to enter the car, where, as you can imagine, the couple was quite distressed to learn their private rendezvous had turned public. And can you imagine my personal shock when I discovered the participants were none other than my good, dear, friend Robert Powers and my acting chief, Dyani Swan, who I hold in the utmost professional regard?"

Manning and Hamilton glanced at each other while Morris continued. "In any case, in the process of trying to remove the pair, apparently some words were exchanged or something, and Ms. Swan ended up stumbling out of the car. I immediately went to assist, hoping to give her my sportcoat so that she might have a degree of discretion, but as I bent over to give it to her, she kicked me in the nose. I can only assume she failed to recognize me."

"Enough!" shouted Hamilton. "You're full of shit."

Morris remained calm. "In any regard, had I anything to do with JJ McHugh's untimely demise, you would have found my blood all over the crime scene."

Hamilton looked at Manning with frustration. Manning shrugged back. Apparently, they agreed with his point.

"If you ask me," Morris inserted. "I'd start with the Squid's most recent employer, Robert Powers, or perhaps one of his associates, Jim Jordan. He's an old cop from the Vineyard."

Over the next three weeks, Manning wasn't able to link Jordan to the Squid's murder. However, thanks to obtaining all the video from the Tufts Medical Center incident, it became clear that Swan had been selective in what she had released to the public and fellow law enforcement. Manning threatened the former deputy director with obstruction of justice, and it was enough to get Dyani Swan to roll over on BoBo Powers, acknowledging he was the master manipulator behind the entire scheme.

She identified Jordan as the one who lured Sosa onto the tracks and then pushed him into the train. She also claimed that Jordan and the Squid threw Beetlejuice and Kenny the Clown off the roof of the South Station bus terminal.

Still, it was an uphill battle for Manning to build a case. Like Sammy Albany, she encountered the challenge of trying to find evidence against Jordan.

However, the matter may have resolved itself when Jordan was found dead near the old Harvard T station, electrocuted by the third rail. No one knew how or why the former Oak Bluffs police chief came to be in such a place. What was never reported is that on the wall above the old platform was a fantastic piece of graffiti of a style that hadn't been seen in the subway in almost two years. It depicted an open manhole, a desperate young man, and a grotesque large figure, wearing a badge, and carrying two solder pots.

His entire life Jordan had gotten away with being a malicious bully, but he seemed to have underestimated the resourcefulness among the homeless. The murder of Beetlejuice had to be avenged.

Given her significant and public fall from grace, Swan immediately resigned her role. The Lieutenant Governor went into damage control and fired half of DCR and vowed to cleanup the department. As a result, her popularity achieved a new high as she embraced the role of reformer. However, a small obstacle appeared in the way to her rise to political success.

Shortly after the flood, she received an envelope with no return address. All it contained was a printout of an email from the MBTA's deputy director of real estate to the Lieutenant Governor. In it, he detailed his concerns about a proposal for a massive casino development involving the T's abandoned tunnels.

As innocuous as the document might seem, the Lieutenant Governor and General Manager notably became more hands off with the transit police, allowing Chief Stephanie Tam the leeway to police the country's oldest transit system in a manner she saw fit.

The Lieutenant Governor also made public note of the contributions Robert Sosa had made to the MBTA and the downtrodden of the city. There never had been any nefarious motivation for the deputy director's involvement with the homeless. As Morris learned during a casual but pleasant lunch with Barbara Sosa at Sullivan's on Castle Island, Bob held a secret that few knew. Prior to moving in with relatives in South Boston, he and his mother had been homeless. He never forgot where he came from, apparently even to the point of stepping onto the tracks at the Tufts Medical Center because he thought he heard some wayward soul asking for help.

Whatever development deal may have been in place disintegrated the moment Robert Powers was recorded in the midst of infidelity. His wife immediately sued for divorce and exercised their prenuptial agreement. In all likelihood, BoBo would be penniless by the time the proceedings were finalized.

But that was the least of his worries. Chinatown's underworld boss, Henry Chin, wouldn't take too kindly to discovering BoBo had a role in submerging half his neighborhood. In a more private matter, Powers had recently sold Chin, at full market value, two Back Bay properties that would have been wiped out had the flood achieved its full potential.

Still, the greatest offense to Dragonhead may have been that he had been cut out of the casino deal by Powers.

One person apparently included in the deal, however, was the former priest Charles Shanley. Like Powers, Shanley had made some key real estate investments over the years. He had recently reached an agreement over the purchase of Steinert Hall, but to what extent he and Powers were working together would remain unknown. Shanley had gone missing. In a case that stumped investigators, Shanley had vanished from within his own locked hotel room. The only clue was that among his belongings was an extra suitcase, entirely empty even though the bellhop felt it weighed quite a bit when delivered.

A black-and-white video also showed an unknown chambermaid working on Shanley's floor. Morris was certain a color version would have revealed a glint of red hair, but he opted not to intervene in the investigation.

In truth, Shanley's disappearance was probably best for the former priest. Once police found a Somali translator, they discovered that the "fat man" was also known as Charlie Tuna among the Lost Boys. It was a moniker assigned on the basis of his being known as "white meat" to the homeless youth who peddled in illicit sexual encounters.

Given the information, Morris helped orchestrate "Operation Wonderland," a raid on multiple properties owned by Shanley. In doing so, authorities discovered an underground brothel that also doubled as a porn studio. Aiding the effort in obtaining the necessary warrants was an affidavit from an unnamed source, William Fitzgerald. Prior to Morris and his wife, adopting him, William spent nearly a month with a foster family in Dorchester along with two other wards of the state. On a weekly basis, the three boys would have counseling sessions with Shanley. While William had managed to escape the predator, his friends did not. Still, the tales of Father Charles' perversions were well known among certain youth in the city. Unfortunately, adults had turned a deaf ear to them over the decades.

With the help of a local foundation that assists special forces who want to transition to civilian life, William chose to leave the Marines and began pursuing an undergraduate degree in criminal justice while also volunteering as an investigator with the Suffolk University legal clinic. His supervisor there was a tall, thin young man with a nasty scar hidden by a beard. While he went by the name Robert, William felt as though the man was hiding some portion of his identity. People trying to distance themselves from a past life can recognize such things in each other.

The legal clinic also received a significant financial contribution from the former Mrs. Debbie Powers. With such backing, it was able to hire a new homeless liaison, Susan Sann. However, in no time, her associates learned to call her Goldilocks.

While most didn't understand exactly why, the name seemed to fit her even though her vocabulary often seemed a bit inappropriate for a children's fairy tale.

Her firefighter boyfriend, Patrick, didn't seem to care, however. According to Morris' sources on the matter, Patrick was under consideration to make lieutenant, perhaps on his way to following in the footsteps of his father.

Jay McKenna, for that matter, remained unchanged. Dyani Swan held very little sway in the city after the video of her and Powers went viral, certainly not enough to damage the armor of Boston's best firefighter.

For Morris Fitzgerald, he returned to full duty as a detective sergeant with the MBTA police, but every Wednesday evening, he volunteered with the Boston Police Stress Unit. Its director, Sergeant Brian Gregg, suggested that Morris, with his more than thirty years policing, would be a valuable asset to the program. However, privately, Morris believed the offer was just pretense from Gregg and his K-9 officer cousin, Nancy Steiger, who worried that the old T-cop had reached burnout. If that were true, he was still happy and thankful to go along with the ploy. The more he worked with the stress unit, the more the migraines began to fade and so too did his drinking.

On Saturday evenings, Morris wouldn't touch a drop of alcohol because those were nights he spent with Happy. Occasionally his daughters and William would join, too. For some reason, they always ended up bowling. As certain as he was that no one with Fitzgerald blood ever liked the activity, they all seemed to tolerate it for the value of spending time with family.

Despite their thoroughness, Manning and District Attorney Anne Marie Melia had yet to produce any indictments related to Sosa's death or the flooding. Suspects had gone missing or turned up dead. While Swan was cooperating, Powers had been quite adept at hiding any trail that could lead to him. Still, Morris was sure the parking king would get what he deserved. It just might not be in a courtroom.

After all, this was Boston, a city known not just for dirty water but also dirty politics. Morality might rise and fall like a tide, but it always remained tethered to a vengeful shoreline. Maybe Ginger was right. Perhaps there was some grander force at work that somehow sought equilibrium. Then again, maybe it was something more primal. In this city, it didn't matter if you were a politician who ignored a neighborhood, a Sox player who went to the Yankees, or a gangster who screwed over his own backyard; Boston neither forgave nor forgot.

Whether it was called fate or retribution was a matter of perspective, but for his part, Morris was fine with being an instrument of either as long as his pension stayed in place and there was at least one decent coffee shop in town.

While it did take some time, Bruce Donahue managed to unlock Bob Sosa's phone, gaining access to all the texts and call history. While Sosa may have had concerns about the use of T property in some large-scale development, it was Cashman who first came across a hint that something was wrong with the Charles and Muddy rivers. While the first contact between Sosa and Cashman appeared to have been a phone call about two months earlier, shortly after that, Cashman texted a video with the note "This is what made me think of calling someone at the T."

Bruce finally got around to sharing the video with Morris to see what he could make of it. It was shot down by the Fens. Cashman was trying to illustrate that the water level of the Muddy River hadn't dropped even though the region was seeing drought conditions. Off the screen there was a woman's voice, one Morris instantly recognized.

"Hey, whatcha doing?" she said as Cashman panned to reveal a middle-aged woman in tattered jeans and a soiled tank top. "Are you here about the plants? They're all dying, you know. The problem is there's too much salt in the water. Taste it. It's bad water. I keep telling the cops and the park people, but no one cares. I know you think I'm a nobody, but I got a cousin who's a big wig at the T. He's a fuckin' hero, that's what he is, but he don't want me using his name anymore. He's the best cousin in the world, though. He took care of my kid. He took care of me. I wanna get better to thank him, but I can't. He's the best, though. He's the best."